Praise for the Ben Candidi Mystery Series

Amazon Gold (2003)
(advance notices)

A Rainbow
Murder Mystery

"*Amazon Gold* is a masterful combination of adventure, state-of-the-art drug discovery, science and fictitious corporate treachery."
— Georgina Nemececk, Ph.D.
Pharmaceutical Company Project Manager
in Drug Discovery and Development

"*Amazon Gold* is the long awaited fourth installment of the Ben Candidi science mystery series. Once again, Dirk Wyle gets the science right and even specialists will appreciate Ben's clever insights and perspectives on the use of protein biochips for drug discovery. In these days of scientific nonsense (witness movies of travels to the earth's 'Core'), *Amazon Gold* is a refreshing and exciting dose of intellectual endorphinism. Highly recommended."
— Arno F. Spatola, Ph.D.
Director, Institute for Molecular Diversity and Drug Design
(www.imd3.org) and Professor of Chemistry and Biochemistry,
University of Louisville

"Weaving contemporary social issues with the thread of science, this adventure mystery tickles the intellect."
— Robert C. Speth, Ph.D.
Professor of Pharmacology, Washington State University

Medical School Is Murder (2001)

"Wyle creates Ben as the playful idealized man: Mensa member; looks like Frankie Avalon; can fight like a pit bull; has a steady relationship with the beautiful Rebecca while tossing off adversaries with stumbling panache and outwitting the evil administration."
— Shelley Glodowski, *Midwest Review*

"Dirk Wyle has an extraordinary medical background . . . a fascinating story . . . keeps the reader continually immersed . . . entertaining . . . educational . . . fascinating."
— Lou Mobilia, *Murder on Miami Beach Bookstore* (review)

Biotechnology Is Murder (2000)

"Nifty, light-hearted and deadly."
— Edna Buchanan, *Garden of Evil*

". . . a potent mix of science, business and crime."
— *Publishers Weekly*

"Dirk Wyle . . . is a sure winner. His character Ben Candidi is just finishing his Ph.D., but Ben packs more punch per square inch than most veteran detectives . . . a timely plot with larger than life characters with which the reader has an immediate affinity. Ben Candidi is the young Jack Ryan of the biotechnological world."
— Shelley Glodowski, *Midwest Review*

"Dirk Wyle seems to know more about science and bio-tech thrillers than Robin Cook or Michael Palmer . . . a winner."
— Norman Bogner, *Honor Thy Wife*

". . . a very well written and clever second addition to the Ben Candidi series. Dirk Wyle is able to paint a vivid picture of Ben Candidi's world. . . . Halfway through this book, I reached the point where I happily lost track of time and had to remind myself to breathe. Wyle followed through with a stunning ending that felt realistic and complete."
—Andrea Collare, *Charlotte Austin Review*

". . . a combination of white collar crime medical thriller hard-boiled mystery. . . . Ben Candidi doesn't carry a gun or have a PI license. He's witty, complex and a very different sleuth."
— Lane Wright, *Mystery Books Review at About.com*

"Against the backdrop of this intriguing mystery, the author takes us on a tour through the Byzantine world of high finance and bio-technology."
— *Charles Ouimet in the H.M.S. Beagle*

"Science and exotic murders combine with America's favorite Gen-X detective to offer a perfect read for the educated mystery lover curious about the biotech industry. Highly recommended. Another movie script prospect." — Arno F. Spatola, Ph.D.,
Pres. & CEO, Peptides International, Louisville, KY

"Dirk Wyle fuses Miami's cosmopolitan setting with academic intrigue, scientific discoveries, romance and murder to create a unique read. . . . this book delivers. . . . Wyle explains scientific jargon and theories in clear layman's terms, mixing investigations with in-depth character studies to explore all aspects of the crime."
— Devorah Stone, *The Quill*

". . . a good solid interesting mystery in the traditional style of literate storytelling. . . . very smooth and intelligent."
— Sharon Villines, Archives of Detective Fiction

". . . so easy to pick up and so hard to put down!"
— Reviewer's Bookwatch

". . . written for the intellectual who loves mysteries . . . characters well presented."
— Under the Covers Book Reviews

"Wyle demonstrates a breezy style, a flair for drawing vivid and memorable characters with just a few deft strokes. . . . I've found myself thinking about it and admiring it in retrospect over an over again."
— Joe Lofgreen's Detective Pages,
Judged **Best First Detective Novel** of 1998

". . . step into the scientific world, the Mensa Society, be led down a heady path of suspense, and witness in our main character an emergence of love and vulnerability."
— Linda Tharp, *The Snooper*, Snoop Sisters Bookstore

"The reader is amazed at the author's ability to create tension, introduce a little love-making along the way, and tell a good mystery story."
— Kathie Nuckols Lawson, BookBrowser

Titles in the Ben Candidi Mystery Series by Dirk Wyle
(www.Dirk-Wyle.com)

Pharmacology Is Murder (ISBN 1-56825-038-X)
Biotechnology Is Murder (ISBN 1-56825-045-2)
Medical School Is Murder (ISBN 1-56825-084-3)
Amazon Gold (ISBN 1-56825-095-9)

Dirk Wyle

AMAZON GOLD

A Ben Candidi Mystery

Dirk Wyle

Rainbow Books, Inc.
FLORIDA

Library of Congress Cataloging-In-Publication Data

Wyle, Dirk, 1945-
  Amazon gold : a Ben Candidi mystery / by Dirk Wyle.
    p. cm.
  ISBN 1-56825-095-9 (trade softcover : alk. paper)
  1. Candidi, Ben (Fictitious character)—Fiction 2. Gold mines and
mining—Fiction. 3. Amazon River Region—Fiction. 4. Pharmacologists—Fiction. 5. Miami (Fla.)—Fiction 6. Hostages—Fiction. I. Title.
  PS3573.Y4854A83 2003
  813'.54—dc21

                                                        2003009744

Amazon Gold
A Ben Candidi Mystery
Copyright © 2003 Dirk Wyle
www.Dirk-Wyle.com
ISBN 1-56825-095-9

Published by
Rainbow Books, Inc.
P. O. Box 430
Highland City, FL 33846-0430

Editorial Offices and Wholesale/Distributor Orders
Telephone: (863) 648-4420
Email: RBIbooks@aol.com

Individuals' Orders
Toll-free Telephone (800) 431-1579
www.BookCH.com

First Printing • Printed in the United States of America

Dedication

This novel is dedicated to the biomedical scientists, engineers and visionaries whose inventions have moved us forward in quantum leaps and bounds.

Author's Note

In common with legal- and CSI thrillers, courtroom dramas and other forms of detective fiction, this novel contains examples of authentic professional dialogue. Business, scientific and anthropological terms are limited to those found in *Webster's New Collegiate Dictionary* and are explained in the novel within their immediate context. Likewise, utterances in Portuguese and German are explained within their immediate context. Following the example of authors of recent books on the subject, I have opted for "Yanomama" (vs Yanomamö) as the easiest route to the correct pronunciation of "Yanomama Indians."

The "DNA biochip" technology described by Ben exists today. It has identified genes that are abnormally expressed in breast cancer and is showing promise for identifying new "targets" for cancer chemotherapy drugs.

Acknowledgments

I would like to thank Betty Wright, my publisher, for her unshakable belief in my work and for her suggestions on its fine-tuning. I am also deeply indebted to Betsy Lampé for imaginative cover design and for tenacious promotion of my work.

I also thank the many readers who have written and e-mailed their reactions to the first three novels in the Ben Candidi Series. And thanks to the thousands of scientists who have visited my booths at major biomedical science meetings over the last three years. I appreciate their feedback.

The present novel has benefitted from the early-stage critiques from Gisela, Douglas, Yvonne, Duane, Suzy and Gregg. Thanks to Susan for her comments. I also thank Mimi for a lesson in Portuguese, Fred for selecting the firearms used in this story, Dr. Ben B. for a consultation on emergency medicine, Dr. Ilse W. for insights into the Amazon ecosystem, and Ildomar, Wilson and Geraldo for a trek in the Amazon rain forest. And special thanks to Ellen for comments on the screenplay.

Santa Isabel Blues 1

It was in Santa Isabel, not Rio de Janeiro, that Rebecca and I spent our last evening together in Brazil. Deep in the Amazon basin, we had no sandy beach with inviting water, no promenade to stroll at sunset and no cool breeze rolling down from green hills. Instead, we trudged down a muddy red bank and waded into the *Rio Negro*. Yes, the humus-saturated water served to wash from our naked bodies the accumulated grime from our four days of westward travel on a river freighter out of Manaus. But the water's reddish-brown cast was foreboding. After we had waded to knee depth, our feet were barely visible. And at waist depth, they were lost in a realm of impenetrable black. Smelling the river water in my cupped hand, I was reminded of stale tea.

Thus we didn't splash, we didn't swim, and we didn't linger. We washed ourselves quickly, then struggled up the muddy bank to retrieve our damp clothes from the bushes. The sun was low, only a few diameters above that narrow band of tropical green along the distant bend of the broad black *Rio Negro*. When the sun sets along the equator, darkness comes quickly. Hastily, we blotted the tea residue from our skin and dressed. Quickly, we made our way between the stilt shacks and found the rain forest path leading to our lodging.

There was no room service dinner, no moonlight-drenched balcony, no diaphanous curtains waving in a breeze, and no oversized bed with white sheets. There was no breeze, just tropical swelter. We ate from cans by lantern light, then retreated of our tent where we shed some of our clothes and sat, facing each other, on the two stretched-canvas cots. Expedition leader David Thompson was snoring in a nearby tent and I was slipping into a foul mood.

But the tropical moon did its best to stir romance. It shown down on us through the mosquito screen, glistening Rebecca's black hair and drenching her narrow, delicate face in a stream of cool light.

Sitting there, stripped down to my underpants, feeling hot, grubby and worried, I lost myself in thought.

Well, Ben Candidi, this is the price you pay for melding souls with an idealistic physician with a passion for Third World medicine. Rebecca's jetliner didn't take you to Rio de Janeiro; it took you to Manaus, 800 miles up the Amazon. You boarded that rickety freighter willingly. Nobody said you had to ride up the *Rio Negro* with her for those 400 winding miles. And you knew that your destination was an umbrella tent behind a Brazilian Indian bureau station across the river from a shantytown called Santa Isabel.

No, of course, a rough-and-ready guy like you wouldn't be complaining about the heat and humidity. Could it be that you're irritated about having to say goodbye to her for a month? Hell, Ben, you knew weeks ago that there wouldn't be enough room in that dugout canoe for you *and* their medical supplies. But now you're worried that it's unsafe for her to go 100 miles north, up the narrow *Rio Marauiá* into Yanomama Indian territory and work for a month in the health shed at that Catholic mission? Do you think she needs you standing guard over her?

Face it, Ben, you're projecting your own problems on her. Admit it, Ben: If you don't get back to Miami and pick up work on that report, your biomedical consulting career will be over before it gets started.

Rebecca must have been reading my thoughts at that moment. "Don't worry, Ben. I'll be all right." Her voice was so beautiful — resonant, high-pitched but self-assured.

"Okay" I replied. "Just be careful on the trip. I keep worrying about you running into bad guys — like rubber tappers, gold prospectors and smugglers."

"Access to the river is controlled. David has made the trip five times already. Nothing happened."

"I still wonder about those Indians outside the Mission."

"Ben, you're going by descriptions that Napoleon Chagnon wrote decades ago. The newer anthropological studies say the Yanomama aren't so fierce anymore. Don't worry, David will take care of me."

"Right!" I said it with a touch of irony. That guy would take care of her, alright. He'd start laying his paws on her the first night out.

Rebecca laughed. "You're not worried that I won't be able to keep him in his place, are you?"

"No, I promise not to worry about *that*. But there are a few things I want to run down with you."

"Yes," she sighed.

"First off, when you're traveling in the Third World it's a mistake to be too nice to people — especially ones you don't know. Let them get too familiar and they start taking advantage."

"Okay."

"That applies doubly to indigenous people."

"Yes, Ben. If they get too close to our bags, I'll bark at them," she said sassily, "just like you did in Manaus."

"Right. And when you're alone, don't let anybody get too close to you. If they grab you, hit them where it hurts."

In my thirty-some years, I've had more than my share of tough situations. Growing up around Newark will toughen anyone up, especially if he's in the habit of carrying his schoolbooks home at night. I left those troubles behind when I went off to Swarthmore College but they caught up with me in Miami, ten years later. That was when I'd enrolled in a pharmacology Ph.D. program and agreed to do an undercover project on the side. A Ph.D. won't keep people from trying to murder you when you go around uncovering their scams. Muscle memory of Newark has saved my life three times already.

Rebecca sighed like a teenager resisting an elder's advice. "Yes, if they grab me I'll scratch their eyes out."

"And don't depend on Thompson to protect you. Sure, his skin's made of leather, but he doesn't have enough muscle to put up a good fight. And listen — never give in to a threat. Never let them increase their advantage over you."

Rebecca sighed again. "If someone holds a knife to David's throat and says he'll slit David's throat if I don't throw down my pack, I don't do it. I pull out my own knife."

"Right."

"Yes, 'right' — for the fifth time. You know, Ben, I *have* learned a few things from you in the years we've been together. Just trust me. Promise?"

"I promise."

Yes, Rebecca had learned a few things from me. And I'd learned a lot from her. Although she's five years my junior, she's the mature one when it comes to professional goals. At 14 she was already planning to be a doctor. And she'd never wasted a year. I had wasted six of them. After Swarthmore I had worked half-heartedly in the medical examiner's laboratory by day, had bummed around Miami's Little Havana by night, and had boat-bummed around Coconut Grove every weekend. Hell, if I hadn't met her, I might never have finished my Ph.D. Left to my own devices, I'd probably go back to dilettante life.

Rebecca was still looking at me, waiting for an answer.

"Yes, girl, I promise not to worry. Now let's talk about one more thing — communication."

"I'll e-mail you as soon as we get to the Mission and David unpacks the satellite dish. My e-mail will get to Miami faster than you will."

"And I'll e-mail you every day."

Rebecca smiled. I'd probably sounded like a fatuous hero in one of those Merchant-Ivory period films. Her smile was so charming in the moonlight.

"But don't be upset if you don't hear from me every day. Some days it might be raining too hard for David to put up the dish. Or something might happen to the equipment."

"If David can't put up the dish when you arrive, then you have the Mission get on their shortwave radio and report back to the Indian bureau station here."

"It's called a *Funai* office," Rebecca said with an ironic smile. "It stands for . . . . Now *you're* the one who's supposed to be the expert on Portuguese."

Rebecca smiled as I fumbled and failed to translate the acronym into Portuguese. For the last four days I'd been having mixed success with my efforts to convert my fluent Spanish into acceptable Portuguese.

I suggested more backup plans for communication.

"Ben, you're looking worried again. Stop it!"

I willed myself to relax. Rebecca sighed. I looked at her, sitting across from me in panties and unbuttoned khaki blouse. She wasn't sweating. That thin, angular body would serve her well as she glided through the jungle, buoyed by the optimistic belief that her health care work would make a difference. Yes, we'd let David Thompson — over there in the next tent, snoring like the 60-year-old that he was — we'd let him sweat the details. Let the old snorer pay for spoiling my last evening with my fiancée in Brazil. I fell silent, listening for forest sounds between the rasps of Thompson's saw blade.

In the distance I could make out the rhythm of a fast samba. It was probably from a battery-operated boom box. It was probably the night's entertainment for a *caboclo* couple in a nearby shack. There's no single translation for *caboclo*. Fishermen? Pioneers? Subsistence farmers? I've even heard "backwoodsmen." If you're into racial definitions, call them mestizos. The husband probably fished the river. His wife probably grew açaí, manioc and peach palms in a small garden. After four days and a dozen stops on this river, we'd seen so many *caboclo* couples that I had no trouble imagining this pair. He would have mixed Indian features and would be gritty and unshaven, probably wearing a hat, an undershirt and long pants — his Friday evening finest. He might even be wearing leather shoes. She would be in flip-flops or barefoot, but wearing a long dress. I imagined them dancing, moving their feet and shaking their hips to the beat of cowbells, whistles, bead shakers, seed gourds and rubbed drum-skins. About as sexy as a sponge bath with stale tea.

Rebecca slid over to my cot and kissed me on the cheek. I opened my eyes and looked up. She was on hands and knees, in a cat pose. She caught my glimpse of her open blouse and smiled. She stretched forward and kissed me on the mouth — deeply and hungrily. But I still felt gritty and annoyed.

Rebecca pushed me down on the cot and kissed me again. "Don't let him irritate you anymore," she whispered. "He's deep asleep. We have the whole world to ourselves, just like on the *Diogenes*." She got up and made a minor adjustment to the tent's entrance flap. She wiggled out of her panties, tugged at my underpants, cast off her blouse and took charge.

Balancing on knees and toes on the wooden rails of my cot, Rebecca showed me how much a 25-degree shift in latitude could change a woman. It seemed like the tropical rain forest had unleashed a new species of passion. This was not the delicate, languid, open-air love that we had made while anchored in the Florida Keys. This was fast samba love. Something had converted her 120 pounds into an untiring, vertically resonant love machine. She shook me to the roots. It seemed like the spirit of the torpid jungle permeated her brain stem. Or maybe it was the spirit of the mythological Amazons.

Seemingly immune to heat exhaustion, she performed a dance of gyrating hips, pumping abdomen and fluttering arms. Tropical moonlight poured in through the opened roof flap, illuminating her small, charming breasts as they jiggled in Brazilian carnival rhythm. How much longer could she continue like this? She sensed my question and answered it wordlessly. As we reached our precious seconds of shared ecstacy, the chirps and squawks of rain forest birds and reptiles grew louder. Perhaps they were augmented by sounds from our own throats.

Expended, my body dissolved into the stretched canvas. Exhausted, Rebecca took three deep breaths before reaching for the cot's rails and collapsing onto me. She buried her face in my neck. A bony shoulder rested on my matted chest hair. Sensing that her legs were cramping, I raised my hips to unburden them. Our legs intertwined and she molded her broad hips to mine. Her skin felt cool on the surface and her flesh felt so hot at our pressure points. Spent and clinging to each other like vines, we shared heartbeats, breaths and whispered endearments. We shared these for a long time, filling each other's reservoirs with what only the soul can offer, preparing for a four-week drought.

Rebecca's reservoirs filled more rapidly than mine. But she didn't let go of my hand when she rolled into the other cot. "Don't worry, Ben, everything will be okay."

We slept.

The next morning, I woke to find Rebecca smiling down on me. She was already dressed for the expedition: light khaki, multi-pocketed shirt and shorts with Oregon rafting sandals. I dressed quickly. Rebecca's near shoulder-length hair was drawn up into a ponytail which she'd pulled through the back of her blue ball-cap. It stuck up at a sassy angle and bounced with her steps as I followed, carrying her two bags down to the dock.

David Thompson was standing next to a couple of canvas bags and was frowning down on a soggy 16-foot dugout canoe that was nosed up at the bank and was floating between two poles. Thompson was arguing in broken Portuguese with Hashamo, the native guide, about where to place the satellite dish. With a three-foot diameter, it was wider than the canoe. Why the hell hadn't Thompson retired that geostationary contraption and bought a hand-held satellite phone that works off the lower orbiting system? Do you have to be old-fashioned to be an academic?

With white hair, a long nose, gaunt cheeks and wearing a rumpled safari suit, Thompson did have the disheveled look of a university professor on a field expedition. He also had a desk worker's slouch. But grudgingly, I had to admit that whatever this tall, large-boned specimen lacked in athleticism, he could probably make up with willingness to persist in the face of obstacles. All he needed was a little more common sense.

Hashamo ended the discussion by setting the satellite dish on end towards the rear of the boat and by jamming in a box of canned food to secure it. He turned his attention to Thompson's bags, hauling them from the bank and packing them a couple of feet away from the slosh that had accumulated in the center of the boat. Hashamo had lively, intelligent eyes. He looked about 19 years old, but it is difficult to judge the age of an Amazon Indian. His five-foot, six-inch frame was lean and his reddish skin was stretched tautly over his well-developed muscles. His stomach was flat. And his only clothing was a pair of red boxer shorts.

Now, Hashamo was looking up at me, trying to tell me something. Over the last several days, I had learned to overlook the major differences in Amazon Indian and European physiognomy — the prominent cheekbones, that certain prominence of the mouth and forward set of the upper jaw, and the broad nose with large nostrils. I had also gotten used to their hair and hairstyle: their straight dark-black hair that was always cut in soup bowl fashion, creating a bang over the forehead and an abrupt overhang in back. Hashamo gestured that he wanted Rebecca's bags placed in the front of the boat. I did his bidding.

Hashamo moved forward to help Thompson aboard. After the old professor was comfortably seated, it was time for Rebecca to take her place in the bow. Quickly, I hugged and kissed her before helping her in.

Hashamo was now turning his attention to the outboard motor.

It was probably a Johnson, although it was hard to tell with the housing so bashed, scraped and painted over. Probably 15 horsepower and as many years old. It's hard to judge the age of an Amazonian outboard.

"Take good care of her," I yelled down to Thompson. He answered with an impatient frown. "Be careful on the river," I added. Thompson shook his head like I was talking trash. He had assured me yesterday that Hashamo had been making this trip for years, supplying the Mission and delivering goods on a regular schedule.

Then Rebecca surprised me.

"Ben. One thing I forgot. In two weeks, there's going to be a tropical anthropology conference in Miami. I'm preregistered for it — too late to get a refund. Could you attend it for me?"

"Sure."

"The announcement is on my desk at home."

"Anything special you want me to do?"

"Dr. Edith Pratt is going to speak. Could you take notes on her presentation?"

"Sure. I'll take good notes and e-mail them to you. What does she do?"

"She's a tropical anthropologist, specialized in Amazon Indians."

"Which tribe?"

Thompson was fidgeting. Hashamo pulled the starter cord and the engine came alive.

"I don't know," Rebecca called back over the roar.

Hashamo was goosing the accelerator, trying to keep the motor alive and was making a lot of white smoke in the process.

"Do you know her, David?" I asked.

"No," he said with a grimace. Obviously the fields of tropical medicine and tropical anthropology had nothing to do with each other.

"Just thought maybe I could say hi to her for you, David."

Thompson answered with a signal that I was to cast them off. Hashamo threw the motor in gear. The propeller beat a lot of air into the reddish water and stirred up a lot of silt in the process. Rebecca blew me a kiss as the boat pulled away from the dock. And for the next half hour, I watched as the boat traversed that vast expanse of black looking water — the *Rio Negro*. The river was very broad — several miles at least — and the far bank was just a strip of green. But I didn't stop looking at the boat until it disappeared between the black and green horizons where I imagined a gap that would be the *Rio Marauiá*.

Then I remembered something I had forgotten to tell Rebecca: "Don't forget to take your mefloquine once a week." I didn't want her to catch malaria.

I didn't want her to leave me, either. But she had left me there to sing the *Santa Isabel Blues*.

The Pilot's Tale   2

It was a real nutty blues lyric that I cooked up while standing there, needlessly, in the morning sun:

Oh, riverboat come get me, come take me away!
Take me down to Manaus, you can get there in four days.

Blow your horn and I'll come running with my backpack shouldered high,
An' four days later Saint Varig's chariot will lift me in the sky,

To a blue heaven where the air is cool enough to think,
Where you can get a glass of water that's pure enough to drink.

Ol' riverboat, come get me, or my consulting job I'll lose,
Ol' riverboat please don't leave me here to sing the *Santa Isabel Blues*.

If I didn't get back to Miami quickly, my consulting project would go down the tubes. I thought long and hard about that three-foot stack of papers sitting on my desk in Miami.

But my thoughts were not productive. Standing in the morning sun like a lazy river boy, I began to wonder if I was more like Tom Sawyer or Huckleberry Finn. Physically, I'd make a better match with Huck Finn. You might describe my features, inherited from my second-generation Italian parents, as Mediterranean. I have lots of black hair on my head, and on my chest, too. At five-foot-eight, I'm a little on the short side. But a lot of girls have said that I have a winning smile, so maybe that's more like Tom Sawyer. I did admire the way Tom handled that fence painting assignment. And, come to think of it, our love interests have the same name: Becky is just short for Rebecca. It was Aunt Polly who'd cracked the whip over Tom, and it was Chief Medical Examiner Geoffrey A. Westley who'd administered the kick in the butt that got me into the Ph.D. program.

Of course, my river was bigger than Tom's. The Amazon is a heck of a lot longer than the Mississippi and it puts out 12 times as much water. Even the *Rio Negro*, its northern tributary on which I was standing, puts out more water than the Mississippi.

And the sun over the *Rio Negro* was a lot hotter. Maybe that's why so many of the Brazilian *caboclos* sat around chewing hallucinogenic ebene seeds like Huck Finn's Arkansas rednecks with their "chaws." How hopeless, when your only source of food is the fish you can pull from the river and the vegetables you can grow in your garden. How lucky I was to be born in the U.S. and to have a white collar job, even if it did require a lot of hard work and scheming.

Standing under the brain-deadening sun, I began to understand the mindless exploitation of the Amazon basin. It's not easy to find a high-value product. It's easier to tear down forests to make paper pulp and charcoal. It's easier to rent your body to the owners of the gold and diamond mines. And if you turn stream beds into stagnant ponds and mountainsides into ugly pits, so what? Natural beauty is nice, but it doesn't put much food on the table.

I waded into the water and soaked my head. I unbuttoned my khaki shirt and splashed my chest. That was much better, but the water was full of decay products from the rain forest floor: tannin and carboxylic acids. Jacques Cousteau reported that the pH gets as low as 3.2. Actually, the average value is about 5.2, which is low enough to kill mosquitoes. I wondered how fish could live in it.

Attempting to fight off stupor with purposeful physical action, I walked along the river's banks in the downstream direction, working my way around stilt-mounted *caboclo* shacks, beached boats and fishing nets. One-half of a mile downstream, I found something interesting: a seaplane tied to a floating dock that extended a dozen yards into the river.

I recognized it as a Lake Amphibian. It wasn't just a regular aircraft mounted on pontoons. This was a truly amphibious aircraft that sits in the water. Its underside had the hydrodynamic design of a high-speed boat. I walked up the dock and peered through the plane's large, rounded windshield. The cockpit was enormous. The pilot and copilot would have plenty of shoulder room. The high-winged plane would also afford good visibility through the large, rounded side windows. The aft portion of the fuselage tapered and rose. From just below the tail assembly protruded a tightly stowed grappling anchor. It looked like someone had stuck a multi-barbed fishhook up the plane's rear end. Oh, what innovations these bush pilots think up!

The engine was mounted on a pylon, high above the passenger compartment and protected against splashing water. Retractable wheels were tucked in above waterline on either side. Nice plane if you live on the water. I heard that Jimmy Buffet has one of them down in the Florida Keys.

Painted on the side of the aircraft was "Amazon Touristic." Funny suffix they used to end the word "tour." Certainly not Portuguese or English. What kind of tours did this plane take, anyway? Being 400 miles northwest of Manaus, our location was too remote for an "eco-lodge" catering to ecology-minded North American and European tourists. And the sport fishing boats didn't prefer the *Rio Negro* either. The river was dead compared to the main branch of the Amazon. And it seemed pretty expensive to use an airplane for a fishing boat.

Maybe Amazon Touristic was providing "tours" for illegal substances. What would they be? The plane wouldn't have enough range to fly cocaine to the Florida Keys. It would have to refuel at the Venezuelan coast. And this area wasn't good for growing coca, anyway — too wet and hot. The Andean growing regions were over 600 miles to the west and northwest. Maybe the plane was shuttling untaxed diamonds from the south. Or maybe it was

supporting an illegal gold mining operation in the Yanomama
Indian territory directly north of us.

Several dozen yards up the bank was a stack of fuel drums.
Farther inland was a sprawling shack with a tin roof. Of course, it
would have been ridiculous and possibly dangerous to knock on
the door and try to talk with someone about the plane.

I went back to my tent and ate a quick lunch of combat rations.
Afterwards, I knocked on the door of the *Funai* station. The
husband and wife team who were running it invited me in for a
cup of coffee. Marcello and Lucia Campos de Carvaloh weren't
much older than me. Marcello had the dark curly hair and olive
complexion that you might expect to see in Lisbon. Lucia had a
long, handsome face with nicely formed eyebrows and a robust
head of black hair that made charming curls around the collar of
her white blouse. Trade their shorts and sandals for a J.C. Penney
ensemble and neither would have looked out of place in the
downtown of Providence, Rhode Island.

They spoke little English, so we made do with Portuguese —
their Portuguese and my Spanish which I tried to bend in the
direction of Portuguese. The conversation was hard work, requiring
ingenuity of everyone's part. Most of the time, Marcello stood
back with crossed arms, letting Lucia do most of the talking and
supplying only an occasional nod. Lucia worked hard to answer
my questions, emphasizing certain words with a blink of the eye
and elaborating on others with a diverse repertoire of gestures of
her shapely forearms.

She said that I was welcome to stay another night in the tent
and not to worry — a southbound freighter was sure to come by
the next day. She explained that this was their first government
assignment. They were responsible for indigenous affairs for part
of the *Pico da Neblina* National Park in the southwestern portion
of Yanomama territory directly north of us, on the *Rio Marauiá*.
The whole territory is about the size and shape of Pennsylvania,
with the southern part belonging to Brazil and the northern part to
Venezuela. She explained that a low mountain range makes the
division. Access from the Brazilian side is via a half-dozen rivers
that flow into the *Rio Negro*.

Lucia said that I shouldn't worry about Rebecca's safety
because *Senhor Doutor* Thompson has made this trip every year

for five years with no trouble. Theirs was not the busiest or most troubled of the *Funai* posts responsible for the Yanomama Indians. Of course, the eastern section by Boa Vista had a lot of trouble with the *garimpeiros* — the gold miners — when they invaded the region, 15 years ago. But the *garimpeiros* were thrown out and the damage is healed.

I thanked my hosts for the explanation and asked how they could help Rebecca if she got into trouble.

Lucia said that they control access up the *Rio Marauiá* and that no one is allowed up the river without a permit. They had shortwave radio contact with the Mission and had a satellite phone to speak to Manaus in a rare emergency. Sometimes they had to ship a young man down the river for treatment when he breaks his arm in a fight. But the Indians who are in contact are more peaceful, now. Machetes are allowed up the river now, because they are used to construct *shabonos* — the tribes' communal huts. But handguns, rifles and shotguns are not allowed.

Lucia said one of their jobs was to coordinate public health programs. Once a year, an Army doctor goes upriver to give vaccinations. "It is nice that *Senhora Doutora* Levis is helping at the Mission and giving them better health care," she said with a sympathetic smile. "No, there is no chance that she will come into danger."

The conversation took nearly two hours. I thanked Lucia and Marcello for their hospitality and retired to my tent where I ate a dinner that was a lot like lunch — freeze-dried military rations.

When nightfall came, it came very quickly. Although intending to go to sleep early, I was distracted by music wafting in from the distance. I wondered if it was coming from the waterfront bar that Rebecca and I had seen by the landing where our freighter had put in. Encouraged by the thought that I'd done something that day to earn a cold beer, and that alcohol would help me to get to sleep, I grabbed a flashlight and followed the jeep trail to the *Rio Negro*.

The bar was a couple of hundred yards up the river. It was built on poles for protection against flooding. I walked up a wooden stairway along the woven reed wall, ascending to a planked platform that held a bar and two rough-hewn picnic tables, lighted by several bare bulbs hanging from the thatch ceiling. The music was coming from an oversized boom box, also hanging from the ceiling. I guessed the power was coming from the portable generator I'd heard while approaching the stairs. The edge of the platform was secured with a rope strung between the outside poles that held up the roof. The bar was little more than a high, eight-foot-long table with a woven reed skirt. Behind it was a barmaid, wearing a string bikini bottom and a shapeless, tight-fitting halter top that flattened her small breasts. Yes, this was probably the halfway station to a cathouse further up the river.

One of the tables was occupied by three *caboclos* who were engaged in serious conversation. The other table was empty, but it sat directly under the boom box which was turned up full blast. So I grabbed a wicker stool at the end of the bar. At the other end sat a blond, gringo-looking guy who must have been six-foot-three. He had heavy bones, solid muscles, brooding posture and a broad, solid face that was deeply furrowed. He was probably in his upper thirties but could easily pass for mid-forty. His left cheek bore a long scar and his forehead bore a short one. Were these the result of an on-the-job accident or a knife fight? Coarse, wavy blond hair hung well over his ears but not to the shoulder. I gave him a respectful nod before sitting down.

"*Una cervesa*," I said to the barmaid. She understood that a beer was ordered and ducked under the bar and rummaged in a tiny refrigerator, the type that runs off of 12 volt power in recreational vehicles.

Although I hadn't spoken those two words half as loud as the boom box, the guy at the end of the bar got into the act immediately. He started telling me, in heavily German-accented English, that I wasn't pronouncing the word for beer right in Portuguese.

"*Uma cerveja*," he corrected. He said it again and again, drawing out the *m* in *uma* and the *j* in *cerveja* like I was a dumb kid who was hard of hearing. He gave me no choice but to repeat it after him.

He finally let me off the hook. "*So ist's richtig, mein Ami Brüderlein.*" His deep, forceful bass voice sounded strangely familiar. It was those records that a Swarthmore prof had played for us back in German 101 — of a guy singing in German about sailing the high seas and visiting ports all over the world. "Freddy" or "Heino" was the singer's name.

And this drunken Nordic Goth had just called me "little brother."

The barmaid pulled out a bottle, uncapped it and set it in front
of me, then disappeared behind a rope curtain. Having the glass
bottle in my hand made me feel more secure — against the case
where verbal defenses failed.

By putting together my college German and some experiences
around Miami Beach, I had enough banter to stand up to this know-
it-all. I couldn't yield an inch or he'd browbeat me all evening.
"Sure, I'm small enough to be your *Brüderlein*, but how do you
know I'm your *bon ami*?"

Over the din, he yelled back that he wasn't speaking any lady's
French and that "*Ami*" means *Amerikaner*. He pronounced the word
as "AH-me," like "army" without the *r*. Then I remembered this
was a sort of derogatory expression, like us calling the Germans
"krauts."

I tried to make a joke of it, yelling back something about
Amerikanischer Freund, a German film I'd seen on video. It was
directed by Werner Herzhog and featured Dennis Hopper. My
German friend picked up his bottle and dragged his stool over to
me, muttering something about Dennis Hopper in *Easy Rider* and
opining, "*Deutsche Filme, alles Scheisse.*"

It was strange to hear a German tell me that German films
were a crock. It was also strange to be sitting face to face with a
guy who looked like the German actor Klaus Kinski. Which one
of those widely spaced blue eyes was dominant, anyway? They
weren't focusing well because he was soused. And he was
gesticulating wildly, forcing me to stay on guard against a slap on
the back or maybe a punch in the face. And I wasn't the only one
who was worried: A muscular *caboclo* dressed in shorts, a
Hawaiian print shirt and flip-flops came in through the rope curtain
and busied himself with wiping the counter in front of us.

Finally, the Kinski look-alike rested his eyes on the barkeeper.
He shouted, "*Naõ vou causar problemas.*" He would not cause
problems. He muttered in German, "*Kein Problem,*" then in
English, "I won't tear down your bar, this time." He turned back to
me and smiled like we were old friends. He raised his bottle and
said, "*Trink, amerikanisches Brüderlein.*"

I raised mine and said, "*Prost.*"

We drank.

"To beer," he said, "the only language. To the beer what you have in your hand. To the only two cold beers in this *Affen-Dschungl* between Manaus and Caracas."

I drank to that, then asked, "What is an *Affen-Dschungl*?"

"That is where the *Dschungl-Affen* are. The jungle monkeys. So tell me, *mein Freund*, what are you doing in this *Affen-Dschungl*?"

"I came this far with my *Frau*. She's going to do some medical work at a mission, one-hundred miles up the *Rio Marauiá*."

"And you are staying here?" he asked with a snort.

"I'm taking the next freighter back to Manaus. The *Funai* people are keeping track of her."

"*Qwatch*," he said. That translates into bullshit. "How do you think they can keep track of her sitting on their *Arsch* on the wrong side of the river?"

"You seem to know a lot about this place. What do you do here?"

His face clouded over. "Sometimes, I fly tourists in my plane."

"Oh. Are you the one who owns Amazon Touristic? That's a nice Lake Amphibian."

"You like the plane? Maybe, you want me to fly you out of this *Dreckloch*. Get you out fast." He shouted his sales pitch in metronomic rhythm.

"How much would it cost to Manaus?"

He eyed me for a couple of seconds and thought for a couple more before answering. "Four *hundert* dollars, American."

"That's too much for me." Scientific consulting wasn't bringing in enough money, yet.

He leaned into me with a big conspiratorial smile. "Maybe I will take you along half-price if I have to go to Manaus in a day or two."

"Thanks, but I think it's better to get the next boat out of here."

"*Ja, ja*! If it doesn't stick itself on a sandbar." This came out in a sarcastic monotone. With its sharply pronounced consonants and low vowel tones, his type of German accent can be damn intimidating, anyway.

He didn't say more. He lit a cigarette.

I wondered if he would bother Rebecca if he came across her. It would be better to have him as an ally. "I bet you get some good jobs around here. Pretty smart, getting an amphibious plane. You have a lot of landing places."

"*Ja.*"

"What kind of flying do you do?"

"All kinds." Then he yelled to the barkeeper in Portuguese and repeated it in English for my benefit: "Another beer. And another one for my *amerikanischen Freund*, here."

While the barkeeper got moving on the order, my German friend picked up his bottle, drank it empty in one chug, and then banged it down on the counter.

So he didn't want to talk about what kind of flying he did. I gazed at his face diffusely, like I was a live-and-let-live kind of guy who didn't think he was making sense at the moment.

He frowned, shook his head and dropped his eyes to the counter while the bartender set down two new bottles. "I take Texas *Öl* millionaires up the river where the fishing is."

I acted like I believed him, but I didn't, really. There was plenty of good fishing off of boats closer to Manaus. "Yes, I see how a guy could make a lot of money with that."

"You talk like a businessman."

"No, I'm just a scientist who has learned to think like a businessman."

"*Ja, Brüderlein,* you have . . . how do they say? . . . a nose for money. And maybe you know something about dealing with *Bürokraten.*" He picked up his bottle. I followed suit and we clinked bottoms to notion of bureaucrats as something to be dealt with. "*Prost,*" he said, and took a swig. He was really drunk, and getting drunker by the minute. He brooded silently for a long time, then let loose a tirade. "*Prost* to the Indian-counters who don't want to risk their precious *Hubschraubers* over the *Dschungel* to count their *Dschungel-Affen* villages. *Prost* to the *Bürokraten* who pay me to count them."

So he was an independent contractor doing aerial surveys of Indian villages for the Brazilian federal bureaucracy. Great! Then he wasn't a smuggler and wouldn't be dangerous except when drunk.

The samba music subsided and was replaced by a slower number sung in a sad, plaintive voice that might have been Tania Maria.

My German friend relaxed, and so did I. During the next several minutes he told me that *Hubschrauber* was the German word for helicopter and those machines weren't especially good around here because the tail rotors could be damaged by logs and bushes in the forest clearings. Yes, maybe the *Hubschrauber* was okay for delivering soldiers in the *Vietnam-Krieg*, but not here. And the *Brazilianer* didn't have enough good mechanics to keep them going.

"What this country needs," he said, "is for some German mechanics to come here and take care of their machines — and their women, too!"

So there he was — a free lancer, operating in an exotic foreign land, but still chauvinistic towards his *Vaterland*. I'd experienced enough of these guys at the bars around the south end of Miami Beach to be able to guess at this one's history: son of a hard-working tradesman, didn't make the cut for the college-preparatory *Gymnasium* at the age of ten, channeled into the non-academic *Volkschule* until the age of 16 when his next option was to pick a trade and begin an apprenticeship. But in some Germans, the Teutonic spirit is too strong to be beaten down by the pedagogues of the *Latein Schule*. This guy was too much of a free spirit to let anyone box him into a narrow social category. So here he was — individualist and one-man social phenomenon, busted out of the German welfare state and seeking adventure in the Brazilian Amazon among the *Dschungel-Affen*.

"What brought you here from Germany?" I asked, with genuine interest.

He smiled at me like I was an old friend. "I came here on a *Bums-Bomber* for vacation. For fun in the sun." He grinned and rubbed his fingers together like some people do to suggest money. But since *bumsen* is slang for banging male and female flesh together, I was sure his gesture pertained to that. "Then I hear they need pilots to fly to the *Mienen*," he said.

"The mines? Were you flying *garimpeiro* supplies out of Boa Vista."

"Ja! You know about that?" he asked with enthusiasm. "I was flying a DC-3, just like the *Berliner-Luft-Brücke. Ja, das waren noch Zeiten*," he said, relaxing into a nostalgic trance.

"Around 1990?"

"*Ja.*"

I relaxed into contemplation, letting the music — now a raucous samba — fill the hole in our conversation. Yes, he looked old enough to have been in his early twenties about 13 years ago. So here was a guy who had flown "Berlin airlift" for the Garimpeiro Invasion, flying in diesel-driven pumps to wash out stream beds and barrels of mercury to extract the gold and poison the land.

Yes, those were the days, my friend. I'd seen pictures of that Alaskan gold rush scene in magazines: Crates stacked twelve high at the Boa Vista airport, the town surrounded by thousands of shacks and saloons, with whorehouses springing up like mushrooms, and everything paid in gold until you went bust. Save your last forty dollars for a flight out on a DC3.

"Yeah, those were the days," I said with irony.

My conversation partner drew himself up. "*Ja*, but the *Scheiss-Politiker* decided those swines were making too much *Dreck* in the *Dschungel-Affen's* rivers. Especially the *Quecksilber.*"

"Yeah, quicksilver is poisonous, you know. Poisonous to everything except the bacteria. They're the only ones who know how to get rid of it. They methylate it to get it out of their cells and into someone else's."

But science and sarcasm were both lost on this guy.

"*Ja*, they make a *Quecksilber Schweinerei* and then the *Scheiss-Politiker* make the army come in and throw us out. And for many years, I make a living flying your Texas millionaires to their fish camps. And here I sit, now, in this *Scheissloch* waiting for orders from a pink *Schwein* so I can go hanging my tail in the jungle and hooking sausages." He said that with agitation that forced him off his bar stool.

I understood the first part but couldn't understand what he meant by taking orders from a pink swine and hooking sausages with his tail. And although he was already drunk, I ordered and paid for another round. Didn't want to owe him anything. And as we drank our last round, he rambled on for quite a while, calling the indigenous Brazilians "jungle apes," saying that the Dutch were loud-mouthed and stingy, that the Japanese might have "fine-mechanics" but all their men had small equipment, and although the Americans have a big country and their men have big equipment, they don't have any *Feinmechaniker* and can't build good cars like Mercedes and BMW.

I couldn't let that go unchallenged. "I bet that the Americans probably manufactured the *Bums-Bomber* that flew you over here to go *bumsen*."

He laughed and slapped his knee. *"Bumsen! Ja, das ist gut. Bumsen!* You want to go *bumsen* tonight? We go together to the house down the path. There are four of them there." He reached into his left pocket and pulled out a wad of money. "I give you one, and I take three!" He let loose a loud bass laugh. *"Komm, Freund.* We go *bumsen* together." His heavy hand came down on my shoulder.

"No. Sorry. I'm too tired, tonight. But thanks. My name's Ben Candidi." I extended my hand. "Really nice talking to you. What is your name?"

"Klaus-Dietrich. Klaus-Dietrich Grünhagen. From Nörten-Hardenberg. That is where they make the good *Schnaps*."

"Glad to meet you Klaus-Dietrich. Maybe I'll come see you if I can't get a freighter."

"Ja, maybe I see you tomorrow morning." He let me go.

I didn't see him the next morning. He apparently slept in. So did the *Funai* couple. But I didn't, and before nine in the morning I was aboard a Manaus-bound cargo boat.

3   Down the Lazy River, Up the Fast Jet Stream

It was a 80-foot, diesel-powered freighter with a wooden hull and three wooden decks and a wooden roof that followed the hull's contour, producing a long, narrow, top-heavy structure that you'd expect to lean like the Tower of Pisa in a 40-knot blow. But amidships, all decks were open to the side to ventilate the hammock-class passengers, and maybe I'd underestimated the stabilizing effects of the bags of manioc roots that filled the boat's holds and crowded its lower deck.

I climbed to the high pilothouse where I negotiated with the first mate until he took my money and gave me a private cabin. It was probably his own. It was snug but acceptable: a three-foot by six-foot by six-foot chamber carved out of the rear of the pilothouse. It had a small sink and running water that was pumped directly from the river. Once we were underway, I opened the spigot and let it run for a while before filling my canteen. I popped in a chlorine-generating tablet and shook vigorously. With my diving bag stowed safely in the oven-hot cabin, I put my combination lock on the door and glanced sternward just in time to see Santa Isabel fall out of sight.

I shared a spot on the rail with a couple of *caboclos* who weren't idling in their hammocks or playing dominoes. They were friendly enough and we talked a little. The boat headed towards the center of the river, then meandered with it. Although we were cutting through the water at around 10 knots, the only visual indication of this rate of movement was when overtaking a floating log or a *caboclo* fishing from his dugout canoe. The sun told me that we were traveling in a generally southeastern direction and the throb of the diesel engine made me sleepy. In places, the river was about 20 miles wide and the tree-lined shores were just a thin green band that separated our shiny table of black water from a cloud-strewn dome of blue sky. The morning's only events were the slow approach of green islands which we steered towards or around, seeking out the maximal current and dodging occasional sandbars.

My mind threatened to slip into low gear and that was bad. I couldn't waste the next four days looking at the scenery. I had to work on my consulting project. Maybe I should have paid the German pilot $400 to fly me to Manaus.

The project could be in trouble. I had been out of communication with my client for five days now. That would add up to nine days before I got back. Going down with Rebecca had been a last-minute decision. I had only left a message on my client's answering machine.

My client, Michael Malencik, had hired me to work up a report on drug discovery. Like his Balkan name — his Michael was pronounced meek-HAIL and Malencik rhymed with "My pen's sick" — he was an unusual guy. He was a combination head-hunter, technology-consultant and deal-maker. And he needed my report to hook an unspecified client company. Michael didn't tell me much about the company. In fact, he couldn't tell me how much the company knew about the subject already! Worse yet, Michael had a short attention span and never gave me a solid echo on half the things I told him.

I did have plenty of information for my report — a three-foot stack of it, actually. And I'd never before had trouble organizing stacks of information into a 150 page report. And I'm usually able to reduce a 150 page report into a three-page executive summary. And I'm usually good at explaining things to people when I know a little about them. But Michael had denied me access to the people at the client company. He wanted all the communication to be through him. For me this was like fishing in the black waters of the *Rio Negro*.

Michael had given me a $20,000 down payment. His letter promised me an additional $20,000 "when an acceptable report is completed." The letter said my report must "predict for company executives how new drugs will be discovered 10 years from now." What kinds of instruments would be used? Could I predict any new strategies for finding new drugs? Would there be a big drop in the cost of discovering a new drug?

Michael had said that if my report uncovered an important business opportunity and if the company decided to go for it, he and I might even head up a drug discovery project!

So the $40,000 report was just bait to hook the client company on a bigger project. What a shame, having to think of scientific work in terms of fishing analogies such as lures and hooks. Oh, how chaotic, the career of the free-lance scientist!

While sitting there, I realized that I had only four days to come up with a three-page executive summary. It had to be both vivid and compelling — and also foolproof against *any* possible misinterpretation by *anybody*.

The boat turned to starboard to avoid a sandbar and we entered a channel between two tree-lined islands.

Well, it wasn't like I didn't have any vivid examples for drug discovery. Hell, imagine yourself as a Portuguese explorer 400 years ago and imagine those banks were lined with Amazon Indians with drawn bows — with curare-tipped arrows. Now that's what you can call drug discovery!

Curare was pretty efficient at dropping a monkey from a tree and stopping Portuguese and Spanish soldiers. And as a drug, it is very useful in surgery to relax muscles. Michael had no trouble understanding the "magic bullet" analogy of drug action. He even said that drugs are more like "heat-seeking missiles" because they home in on specific targets in the body — nerves, the heart, or inflammatory cells that cause arthritis.

But to the pharmacologist, curare is a molecule that binds to the *acetylcyholine receptor* proteins in muscles and puts them out of commission. To a pharmacologist, drugs are small sturdy molecules that fit into "drug receptor targets" as precisely as a key fits into a lock.

To a pharmacologist interested in drug discovery, the Indians' discovery of curare was a "no-brainer." After all, they have been living in the Amazon rain forest for maybe 13,000 years — which is plenty of time to chop up a vine and notice that the paste is poisonous.

Actually, hundreds of thousands of potential drugs are still out there waiting to be discovered. Swimming in our oceans, growing on our forest floors, and even in here on the *Rio Negro*, were tens of thousands of plants and lower animals that were busy manufacturing hundreds of thousands of small, sturdy molecules that are just waiting to be discovered as drugs. Those small, sturdy molecules are the culmination of millions of years of biochemical warfare — plant against plant, plant against animal — to promote their own species and vanquish their enemies.

We pulled into the next stop, Xamataweteri and my two fellow travelers got off. They were going to visit the Salesian mission. A few minutes later, we were underway again. I selected a shady but airy spot under the wooden roof, sat down, pulled a pen and three sheets of paper out of my backpack, and I spent the rest of the afternoon writing my executive summary. Towards the end of the day, we stopped at Barcelos. We stayed tied up there for the night. I retired to my stateroom for my MRE — "Meal Ready to Eat." I slit open the dark brown vinyl plastic that was shriveled around the vacuum-packed, freeze-dried package. I poured in a few ounces of hot, chlorinated water from my canteen and let it stew in the still-sweltering heat. On this river, reconstituted Salisbury steak and mashed potatoes was a luxury. By three hours after sundown, my cabin cooled to a reasonable temperature. I slept with the door open. By three in the morning it was almost cool.

The next morning, I went back to the executive summary. I spent the next three days looking for strong, useful analogies to drive home the points I knew were important. One point was that the Human Genome Project has shown that we have about 35,000 genes. Thus, our bodies have at least 35,000 different drug targets — different enzymes or proteins. And we haven't discovered *even a fraction* of the possible drugs that can hit these targets in our bodies.

My next point was that we need more efficient test systems to discover new drugs. Sure, we have had a lot of success discovering new antibiotics. There, the test system is easy — killing bacteria in Petri dishes. But what about finding a drug that will cure arthritis? You can't send out a regiment of scientists to grind up plants, put them into syringes and inject a camp full of arthritic patients that you've brought along. And you can't wait six months for an "ethnobotanist" to bring back a shriveled-up plant specimen that might work against arthritis. That wouldn't be enough to test on even a couple of rats.

I had an idea that was simple enough to be clear to everybody: Rapid drug discovery will be possible when we increase the efficiency of the process called "screening" — testing plant extracts for drug activity. The way to increase screening efficiency was *to take the laboratory along on the expedition*! Miniaturize the laboratory. Take each of the body's 35,000 drug targets — different enzymes and proteins — and put each one of them on a separate spot on a drug testing chip. Shrink the drug discovery lab down and put it on a few silicon chips — *biochips*. Give the ethnobotanist a few biochips and a hand-held device to read them out. Then he or she will be able to test for maybe 10,000 different types of drug activity in a single drop of plant extract!

I was sure that a drug-testing biochip would be invented by someone in the next 10 years. That was my $40,000 worth of insight.

The idea wasn't far-fetched. Scientists have already done something similar. I had already talked to Michael about the *gene* biochips that contained 10,000 dots, each with a different type of DNA. Put one drop of biological fluid — say from squashed up breast cancer cells — onto this chip, and its dots will tell you which genes have been turned on and which ones were turned off. Those devices were on the verge of revolutionizing medical diagnosis. Now what we had to make was biochips where the dots were drug receptors.

Yes, *drug receptor* biochips were the way to go. They would give us more and more testing on a smaller surface. Just like the engineers at Silicon Valley have been working to miniaturize computer chips to deliver more and more computer power, the manufacturers of analytical instruments are working towards miniaturizing chemical testing. I could back this up with the information in my three-foot stack of papers. That would be the point of my report: Miniaturize the laboratory, put it on a chip and send the scientist out into the field to search for new drugs. Hell, I'd told that to Michael before, and I thought it had sunk in. Hell, I'd told it to my landlord and he didn't have any trouble understanding it.

For each of those three long days, I scribbled madly on moist sheets of paper, trying to reduce these ideas into a carefully crafted three-page executive summary. During those three days, I tore up and threw a lot of sheets of paper into the *Rio Negro*.

Towards the end to the final day and my 16th draft, I looked out over the port rail and saw the buildings of Manaus on the horizon. Soon, the captain was piloting the boat into the São Raimundo inlet, which serves as a landing for the boats operating upriver from Manaus. With admirable skill, he eased our freighter between disorganized clusters of similar vessels that seemed to block every foot of riverbank frontage.

After walking the springy gangplank and setting foot on the steep, muddy bank that late afternoon, I had a fight with myself. My free-spirited, culture-loving side wanted to get a cheap hotel room so I could spend the next day seeing the sights. Hop on one of those excursion boats that takes you 11 miles downriver to the "meeting of the waters" where the black Rio Negro meets the red, muddy Amazon and these vast waters flow side by side for miles and miles before they mix. Then, for the rest of the day, take in this city of faded glory and present-day hopes. "We may never come this way again," echoed the refrain of that old hippie song. Take in the colonial-style architecture. See that famous opera house built in the glory days when the whole world was beating a path to Manaus' door for Brazilian rubber. Witness what Manaus could have been if Sir Henry Wickham hadn't "smuggled" 70,000 rubber tree seeds out of Brazil and if the English hadn't started growing their own in Malaya, as it was called back then.

But my more cautious and practical side demanded that I get back to Miami right away and assure Michael that the project was organized. So I caught a taxi — and caught only a glimpse of the opera house's gold and blue dome through a rolled-down window as the taxi whisked me away, speeding by the west portion of the city's old Central District, then through a chaos of commercial real estate, until we reached the airport, a low-lying, poured-concrete structure on the edge of the rain forest. And there, luck was with me: Seats were available on Varig Flight 8804 to Miami leaving early that evening.

The gate area looked out through brown-tinted glass onto one ribbon of savanna grass and two ribbons of asphalt that were carved and graded through jungle hillocks. Most of the Brazilian passengers waiting in the gate area were elegantly dressed, like they were headed for an expensive Miami Beach hotel. In my sweated-through khaki shirt, cargo pants and high-top leather shoes, sitting next to my backpack and zippered diving bag, I must have looked like the most rugged of the passengers. One of the flight attendants working in the gate area was taking pictures of a bunch of sport fishermen from Alabama. I guessed she was doing them a favor, taking their final trophy shot. It was nice to hear English again. And it was nice to get away from the heat. When I looked again, she was pointing the camera in my direction.

After we boarded and the plane took off, I enjoyed a nice view of the setting sun through my port-side window. All day, the rain forest had been doing its job, sopping up the carbon dioxide and giving off oxygen. Now was time the for the forest to rest, and for me, too. It was also the right time to think about Rebecca because we were crossing her latitude. Soon, we were flying over the Guyanan Shield, the ridge of mountains between Brazil and Venezuela.

The airliner's cool interior cured my cerebral edema right away and soon I was polishing the 16th draft of my executive summary. The analogies were simple but correct, like the key and lock analogy:

The drug-receptor protein (or enzyme) is the lock; the drug is the key. The key must have the right shape and configuration of teeth to open the lock. Similarly, the drug must have the right shape to fit into its receptor protein. Give the medicinal chemists one useful key, a "lead compound" like curare, and they will tinker with it, seeing how much they can cut away and still have it work the lock. They will go on playing with the cut-down key, "sawing off" a methyl group here or "soldering on" an ethyl group there in a quest for the perfect muscle relaxant.

I estimated that there are at least 115,000 small, sturdy key-like molecules free in nature or captive in drug companies' chemical libraries. And with 35,000 drug-receptor proteins in the human body (courtesy of our 35,000 genes), I calculated that there are at least four billion drug/receptor (key/lock) combinations waiting to be tested. That is really good news.

It is good news because those four billion combinations will include keys for the cure of every disease known to Mankind.

But there is also bad news: With present-day techniques, it will take several million scientists a whole lifetime to test each one of those combinations.

And that's why someone will invent a 10,000 drug-testing biochip in the next 10 years. A tool like this will make the scientist one million times more efficient. Hell, with that type of chip, a couple of hundred scientists could do the whole drug discovery job in a few years!

I leaned back into my seat and rested my brain for a couple of minutes. I needed a break because the technical part of the report was a lot trickier. It was full of good news and bad news.

The good news was that a 10,000-spot *gene* or *DNA* chip had already been developed by the Analytica Corporation. It can tell you whether any of 10,000 genes in that tissue have been turned on or off in a piece of breast biopsy tissue. The test works by measuring the amount of "messenger RNA" that the breast cells are putting out. The test works because the messenger RNA, or its copy, is a long chain that can be made to glow by attaching a fluorescent "tag" molecule as an extra link. The test results are reported when the DNA spot starts to glow when the tagged messenger RNA molecules bind to it.

And, of course, the DNA biochip is good news for cancer

patients because physicians and scientists will find out exactly which of the patient's genes has gone astray. It will help them to decide which drug to inject to clobber the cancer cells.

And the DNA biochip is also good news for the drug-testing biochip that I envisioned. The same technology could be used to attach proteins to the chip to make the spots. And it shouldn't be too difficult to get 10,000 different drug receptor proteins using biotechnology and information from the Human Genome Project. Those 10,000 different drug receptor proteins can cover hundreds of diseases — arthritis, hardening of the arteries, nerve degeneration and so forth. And there is more good news: The microscope-mounted video camera and computer that read out the DNA biochip could also be used to read the glow of the 10,000 spots on the drug testing biochip.

But there is also serious bad news for the drug testing biochip: The spots probably wouldn't glow.

The trouble is that the candidate drugs are, indeed, "small, sturdy molecules." They are much smaller than messenger RNA. Many of them won't have points for attachment of the fluorescent tag. And when a "tagged" drug tries to bind to its receptor protein, the fluorescent part would probably get in the way. The fluorescent tag would be like a key holder that's so bulky that the key can't get close to the lock.

I sighed. It would take a clever invention to make the drug-receptor biochip work. Then I thought for a minute and relaxed back into my seat. Hell! I didn't have to invent the drug-discovery biochip. All this lazy river boy had to do was estimate how many years it would take for someone, somewhere to invent it. And I estimated it would take 10 years. *Basta!*

What the hell had I been worrying about these last several days? I was in good shape. I'd gone over most of the underlying science with Michael a dozen times on the phone. And he'd *said* he understood it, even if he really hadn't. And now, with everything all nicely worked up in my executive summary, it was time for a break.

I looked out the window at the setting sun. My tired brain cells deserved a small reward and the drink cart was making its way to me. I asked the dark-haired flight attendant for a gin and tonic. She had to be Brazilian. She was the same one I'd noticed in the gate area. After she moved on, I looked out the window trying to locate Venezuela's Mt. Roraima, the site of Arthur Conan Doyle's *Lost Worlds* dinosaur adventure. Couldn't find it. Well, to hell with dinosaur melodramas, anyway. I liked Doyle's Sherlock Holmes a lot better.

It was a five-hour flight. The airline dinner over the Caribbean Sea tasted great. After the trays were collected, the flight attendant came back and asked if she could get me anything more. With the flight less than half-full, I had figured on getting some extra attention, but not like this. She put a knee into the vacant aisle seat, leaned over the middle seat and asked if I would like another drink.

"No thanks. But that gin and tonic was great." She returned my smile, so I stretched it out a little. "What kind of gin was that, anyway?"

"Bombay Sapphire," she said, conspiratorially. I smiled back, incredulously until her hand went up to her mouth and she broke into a laugh that wrinkled her nose. "We have a saying. *Só prá ingles vê!*"

I interpreted, "Just for the English to see?"

She nodded. "It is a common expression in our country. Just something we put up for the English to see."

I laughed, too. I could imagine how the expression was used around Brazil. And I imagined it in the plane: a bottle Bombay Sapphire paraded around for show on the drink cart but secretly refilled with Gordons Gin in the galley. And I thought about the "smuggled-out" rubber trees and laughed more. Then I pictured my old mentor, the pompous expatriate Englishman Dr. Geoffrey A. Westley traveling in Brazil and getting fooled, as payback for his nation's dastardly deed.

And as I laughed with that woman, a new thought about Brazil crossed my mind — whether a special sort of Social Darwinism might have been at work down there over the last three centuries, selecting and combining the genes for good looks, athletic sexiness and olive skin. She was damn attractive.

A speculative look came over her face. "But you don't look English."

So early in the conversation, and we were already deep into each other's eyes! This was turning into full-blown flirtation. I knew it was wrong, but a little part of me delights in feminine attention. "I guess you'd say that I'm an Italian-American . . . living in Miami."

Her face was beautifully proportioned, with dark eyes, naturally long lashes, shapely brows a shade lighter than her long black hair, with a cute European nose and full mouth, and with soft cheeks and a broad forehead.

"Do you speak Portuguese?" she asked. "You understand it well."

"No, but I speak Spanish fluently. I could almost get by with it back there."

She looked down on me with such a warm smile. "Did you have a nice time in Brazil?" She punctuated her question with a sway of the arm and a back-stretch of her long, slender fingers.

"Yes." I broke eye contact for a minute. Well, actually my eyes slipped down to take in the rest of her. Full figure with a lot of curves. More than ample breasts pressing against her blouse and uniform jacket, narrow hips and a flat stomach, all holding well for an age of about thirty. And it would probably stay that way for another 15 years if she took care of herself.

I looked up to find that she had been scrutinizing me as well. "You look like you were on an *expedition*."

"Well I guess I can claim it as an expedition. We took a steamer up the Rio Negro. Then we got off at a village. That's where I said goodbye to my fiancée." It was time to let her know I was engaged. "She took a motorized dugout canoe up one of its tributaries into Yanomama territory for a medical expedition."

The woman's eyes widened for a moment. For a moment she looked a lot less Latin. "What kind of medical expedition?" she asked.

"Visiting a health clinic for Indians. Checking on their health problems."

Cosmetically shaded lids lowered over dark eyes. Fabric stretched as she took in a deep breath. She was quiet for a second. Then she looked up. "I am engaged to a doctor, too. His practice is in Manaus."

Great, I thought.

She added, "But because of my schedule, I rent an apartment in Miami. You say you live in Miami. What do you do?" An innocent, almost girlish, enthusiasm had returned.

"I'm a pharmacologist."

"You study drugs?"

"Yes, mechanism of drug action. And I'm a consultant to industry for drug discovery and development."

She scrutinized me for a minute, looking serious. "Were you looking for rare plants in Brazil?"

"No. I wasn't doing anything with drug discovery there. I was just following my fiancée as far as they would let me go."

Long dark eyelashes fluttered. Her light-hearted mood returned immediately. How mercurial! "So interesting, that you study drugs. You must know all about *propolis*!"

"I'm afraid not."

Her enthusiasm redoubled. "It's really good. I'd like to know how it works."

"I don't recognize the name." I paused and she waited patiently. "You see, there are about ten thousand compounds listed in the Merck Index, and I am familiar with maybe only a fifth of them. Is propolis a natural product? What is it used for?"

"It is from bees . . . in Brazil. And it is good to keep you from getting a cold. You can get it in . . . pharmacies . . . in Brazil."

"Interesting. Do you take it by mouth?"

"Yes, I put just a drop in a glass of water and . . . how do you say? . . . gargle with it." Although she spoke with a Latin rhythm, her pronunciation was nearly accent-free. I guessed she'd lived in the U.S. for a while. Of course, there are always some words like "gargle" that are hard to put your finger on in your second language.

"That's very interesting. How do you get it from bees?"

"It's something that the bees . . . secrete . . . around their hive to keep it clean." She made a two-handed gesture like she was clearing away cobwebs.

"I see. To kill bacteria. Interesting."

"Well it was very important for me. After I had this job for four months, I started getting sore throats and stuffy noses" — she wrinkled her nose — "and I had to take off so many days that I was afraid I'd have to give up the job. Then I learned about *propolis* and I don't get sick anymore."

"I would guess that it's a topical antiseptic that kills bacteria and viruses before they can take hold in your mucus membranes."

"Wait just a minute and I will show you."

As she went to the back of the plane, I made a mental note to add hundreds of viruses and bacteria to the lists of pharmacological targets. A minute later, she came back and placed a plastic cup and a can of Seagram's seltzer water on my tray table. "Maybe you would like to see for yourself."

She handed me a small tincture bottle with an apothecary label made out in Portuguese. It didn't say whether it could be taken internally. But, what the hell, maybe it would kill any exotic parasites that might have survived the chlorine water in my canteen and were now lurking in my throat. I poured myself a couple of fingers of soda water, added a drop of the unknown substance with great ceremony, swirled it and tasted. "Tastes bitter. It probably contains amines."

She didn't comment on my chemistry, but she did have a lot of questions about my work. I told her a little about my consulting practice but left out my current project. She asked if I had a card and I gave her one. She seemed really excited, especially about learning how *propolis* works. I told her I would look it up when I got back to Miami. "Give me a call, and I will tell you what I find out."

"I will. Would you like to keep the bottle?"

"No thanks. I can go on-line to the National Library of Medicine and find out all I need to know." I tried to maintain a relaxed smile, but it felt like the edge of a slippery slope. Were my eyes and ears reporting an innocent amateur's enthusiasm? Was she just overjoyed by this chance to talk to a specialist who could confirm with theory what she already knew empirically? Was this really enthusiasm for *propolis*? Or did it have something to do to me?

She was beaming down on me with such an open smile and was signaling approval with such a repertoire of facial expressions and gestures that the conversation felt like a lovely fairy tale. And every smile and wrinkle of the nose seemed to invite me closer than the 16 inches that separated our faces. Maybe there's something wrong with my hard-wiring, but when the eye contact remains steady at 24 inches and doesn't falter at 16 inches, I usually find myself kissing the girl. And somehow I got the feeling that was exactly what she wanted.

I handed back the bottle. With a light touch that encompassed my fingers holding the bottle, she pressed it back towards me. "No, I want you to keep it. You might discover something about it, and it would be good for North American scientists to know more about it. We have many wonderful things in Brazil." She had such a light touch. Her expression was earnest.

"Okay, I will self-experiment with it and let you know what I think if you call me." I consciously smiled, probably blushed, and may have frowned.

She glanced up the aisle like maybe it was time to return to her duties. I nodded that I understood.

"I'll see you later, Ben. My name's Nica." She said it with a wink. And before she was five steps away, she turned her head to wink at me again.

I tried to focus my attention on the in-flight magazine, skimming pages full of Brazilian beach life, the industry of São Paulo and the resurgent glory of Manaus, including its opera house. I probably would have gone to sleep if Nica hadn't kept coming back for half-minute chats. In the first one she asked where I'd gotten my Ph.D. degree. She told me that she'd studied in the U.S. but didn't say where. Then she wanted to know Rebecca's name and whether she was affiliated with Bryan Medical School in Miami.

On her next visit she said it was nice that I had my own consulting business. What kind of clients did I serve? Obviously, she had taken a second look at my card. I gave her a shorthand description of my practice and then segued into a description of how I enjoyed working in my office-at-home. She asked where I lived in Miami and I said it was the same address as on the card. I told her about the house Rebecca and I rented on the north bank of the Miami River. But not wanting to dangle any come-ons, I didn't say anything about sailing. But no come-ons were needed. Cheerfully, she told me about her apartment in Miami Springs, her predictable flight schedule between Manaus and her long stopovers in the Magic City. Then, gracefully, we backed away from this topic by talking about the weather.

Nica proved as skillful in managing her comings and goings as she did our conversation. On her next visit, which came one-half an hour later with no visual invitation from me, she asked what I did for recreation in Miami. I answered that I enjoyed riding a bicycle and didn't own a car. This didn't blow her off. In fact, it seemed to make her all the more interested. She said she had a small car in Miami and had a bicycle plus carrier.

One thing did make me curious, and I asked her about it: Why she had taken my picture at the gate back in Manaus? My question seemed to catch her off balance for a few seconds. She said that photography was her hobby — especially people's faces. When I raised an eyebrow, she went on to say that people had so many different faces and ways they dress, and that it's hard to visualize them later. I asked if she was an artist, and she said she was taking up painting as a hobby. She quickly steered the conversation to the ambience of Miami, saying that the city of Coral Gables was "so European." Then she moved on.

I discouraged another visit by dozing off. The next time I saw Nica was while stepping out of the plane. She smiled at me like I was an old friend that she was sure to see again.

4   This Old House

I slept through the honks of riverboats until the morning sun found a way to get through the slits and penetrate my eyelids. Half awake, I stared at the ceiling. Slowly, I realized that it was the three-quarter-century-old plaster of the second-floor bedroom of our rented house, and that the honks had been from tugboats on the Miami River. Tripping over my unpacked bag, I stumbled toward the window to raise the shade. The *Diogenes* was still bobbing safely at its dock. Last night's somnolent spot-check was verified.

Next, I stumbled down the oaken stairway to the living room that serves as my office. I flipped on the computer, went on-line and checked for an e-mail from Rebecca. Thank God she was safe at the Mission.

From: RLevis@tropmed.epi.bryanmed.edu
To: ben-candidi@netrus.net
Subj.: Love You

I am writing to you at night, typing by touch on David's laptop computer. The only light is from the screen. It reminds me of the nights we spent on the *Diogenes* when you were writing on your computer. I guess I'm sailing, kind of. I'm sailing into prehistory. The Indians aren't really living like prehistorics because they have steel machetes and even radios. But a lot of their culture survives.

I am learning a few words of their language. And I am treating the medical conditions that present. I try to show them how to live healthier lives. And I am learning about their understanding of health. It is like many peoples of the earth. They have the right feelings but they make a lot of mistakes.

Some people want to keep them in the "native state." Others say there is no way for them to go on living as they have for centuries. It is hard to know exactly what is right, but making contact with them has been spiritually moving. Maybe it is the influence of the rain forest.

David just came to tell me that my letters can't be too long, so I will have to break off. I think he is worried about draining the battery in his computer. We have electricity here only an hour or so every day. He will try to send the e-mails tomorrow morning when we have power. I have to break off.

I love you,
— Rebecca

Some people have criticized Rebecca's idealism, like she is some kind of goodie-goodie. But she's the girl I fell in love with, and nothing is going to change that. I hit the print button. This cherished letter would be reread so many times that I'd soon be able to recite it with my eyes closed.

I went upstairs, showered, and got into a comfortable pair of shorts and a fresh T-shirt. Went to the kitchen and fixed a breakfast of coffee, toast and jam, and a couple of scrambled, two-week old eggs. Ate it standing at the tiled counter while looking out the rear window at my fine 36-foot, two-masted, teak decked Cheoy Lee sailing vessel. After breakfast, I walked barefoot across the lumpy backyard to check it out. Below deck, there was little water in the bilge and the batteries were topped off. Above deck, there was no evidence that the pelicans and seagulls had been partying. And there were no scrapes on the side of the hull. With only 50 yards between the *Diogenes* and that rusty Haitian freighter tied up at the warehouse dock on the other side, the tugs didn't have much maneuvering room. Their captains always did a good job lining up the container ships for that straight shot between the raised halves of the N.W. 5th Street drawbridge that stood a couple hundred yards downriver. But I can't say as much for the pleasure boat captains who often got in the way.

I inspected the house from the side yard. I was proud of that two-storey stucco even if we didn't own it. Upstairs were three good bedrooms. Rebecca uses the second one for a study, and the third houses a simple laboratory that I've set up with some surplus equipment. Add to that a nice backyard and a hurricane-safe dock for the *Diogenes*, and all our needs are taken care of. And the location is great, with Little Havana directly across the River to the south, downtown Miami two miles to the southeast, and the medical center only six blocks to the north.

I walked to the front of the house where morning sunlight was filtering through the tall trees. The approach to our house takes a visitor through a narrow gate in a snake-plant overgrown chain-link fence, along a flagstone path, and up three steps to the small covered porch.

Our street, which goes by the curious name of "Northwest North River Drive," is broad but carries no through traffic. It is lined with century-old trees, a mix of live oaks, palms, black olives, poincianas, Australian pines and banyans that have uprooted the sidewalks and tower over everyone's front yard. The predominant landscaping style around here favors natural subtropical ground cover.

Across the street lives Gertrude, a retired librarian, in her one-storey, flat-roofed stucco house. We can just make out each other's front porches if we want to. Next to Gertrude, on a massive lot full of palms and live oaks and surrounded by a stockade-like aralia hedge, live Jack and Morris, a couple of middle-aged guys who keep to themselves. They have been together for as long as anyone can remember. My landlord, "Pops," lives adjacent to us, upriver. His house is a two-storey stucco similar to mine, except that his has Key West shutters and a tin roof.

My eyes kept wandering to the buzzer button by the front door. It was installed in the Thomas Edison era. Mounted under it are two brass plates: One says "Benjamin Candidi, Ph.D., Biomedical Consultant." The other says "Rebecca Levis, M.D."

I entered the living room and office, leaving the front door open. The mid-September weather would be cool enough to do without the noisy room air conditioners. I hooked the screen door against casual intruders. The living room and office looks professional enough for occasional client visits. My large mahogany-stained desk is a good match for the wood panels that go halfway up the wall. The desk sits in front of the rough coral rock fireplace. The computer monitor is off to the side. A floral-cushioned wicker couch and a couple of matching, high-armed chairs are nearby to seat our guests.

I went to the kitchen, around the corner behind the stairs, and fixed a second cup of coffee. Then I returned to my desk and checked my website. It was still working faithfully, heralding my expertise and general usefulness for lawyers, drug company executives and investors. But my check through the remainder of my e-mails didn't reveal any new business leads. While on-line, I did a MedLine search on *propolis*, Nica's miracle mouthwash and gargle. It was a mixture of several dozen chemical compounds. Its antibiotic activity seemed to be due to polyphenols, flavenoids and esters of caffeine. It was a mixed bag, but I had to appreciate the lady's enthusiasm for a natural product from her own country.

The light on my answering machine was blinking and it obviously contained a message from Michael. I went right to work, transcribing my executive summary. I would use it as a script when I returned his call. I was almost through with the project when I was jarred by the bleating of the Edison-era buzzer. The screen door was filled with the silhouette of my landlord, Theodore "Pops" Harvey. At six-foot-one and with hardly a gram of fat on his

muscular frame, he was the handsomest, healthiest 79-year-old
I've ever known.

"Welcome back, Ben."

I got up and moved towards the door. "Thanks, Pops. Good to
be back."

To his contemporaries he was "Ted," and to anyone under 50
he insists on being called "Pops." The expression fits him to a tee;
he's a real good-natured kind of guy.

"Called Gertrude and told her you're back. We've been keeping
a good eye on the house."

"Thanks again." I approached the door with a come-on-in
smile.

"Hope that this old fart's not bothering you." He spoke in the
deep register with a voice that was equal parts pre-WW-II Miami
where he grew up, Texas plains where they sent him to flight school,
and airliner cockpit where he'd spent a good part of his life.

"No bother, Pops. I'm on my second cup of coffee, getting
ready for my third. Thinking up excuses to stay away from a big
pile of papers on my desk." Actually, I was looking for an excuse
to forget about Michael. Why couldn't he be a good listener like
Pops? "Water's still hot. Let's fix you up with a mug of freeze-
dried." I flipped the hook off the screen door.

"The doc says that's the best kind for my old ticker," Pops
said, letting himself in and replacing the hook in the eyelet with a
landlord's concern for his tenant's property. "And while we're
talking about doctors, how was the send-off for Miss Rebecca?"

Pop dresses like he talks — faded blue jeans with a big bronze
belt buckle and long-sleeve shirts with large patterns. But he isn't
into western hats or cowboy boots. He usually wears jogging shoes.
He still has plenty of hair on the top of his head — blond faded to
gray — and most people would take him for a vigorous 60-year-
old. The only clues of an older age are a slight tremor when he
extends his hand and tendency to sway his head when looking at
you, as if his vision were obscured by "floaters."

"The send-off took place four hundred miles up the *Rio Negro*
near a town called Santa Isabel. Had a riverboat landing, maybe a
hundred fisherman's huts, one Indian Bureau office about as big
as this room and a riverbank bar and cathouse." I drew Pops into
the kitchen and turned the porcelain knob of the ancient gas stove

to reheat the open pan of water. "I just kissed her goodbye and she stepped into a dugout canoe and they motored off. They disappeared into a gap in the trees on the other side of the river. Her Mission is about one hundred miles upstream."

Pops dropped his lantern jaw in exaggerated disbelief, flattening out the two deepest vertical wrinkles in his loose jowls. "Sounds like the old movie but you got it backwards!"

We finished laughing as the water came to a boil.

"Yeah, I know, Pops. Girl leaves guy sitting on the dock. That's the way I felt, too. Here's cream and sugar. Help yourself."

Pops followed me back to my living room and office. We sat in the rattan chairs.

"I delivered a crop duster to central Mexico, once, but I've never been in the center of Brazil. I'll bet things are pretty primitive there."

I told him all about the town and the black river.

"And Rebecca can't talk Brazilian."

"She can't very much. I got by pretty well with Spanish."

"And there's nobody there that speaks English?"

"Just a loud-mouthed, German know-it-all who flies a Lake Amphibian."

"Good plane around the water, but kind of finicky at the controls 'cause the motor's so high. He's probably using it for smuggling."

"Well that's what I thought too, but he told me he was counting Indian settlements for the Brazilian government."

Pops frowned and shook his head, like he was as good a judge of human nature as he was of aircraft.

"Look, Pops, it's okay. I just got a satellite e-mail from her today. She's made it to the Mission. And anyway, she's got Professor David Thompson from the Bryan Medical School taking care of her. He's an old hand down there."

Pops raised the coffee mug and sipped from it, then turned his big head slowly, surveying the room with his widely spaced eyes. He was proud of his two houses. He was living in the house he'd grown up in, and he'd bought this one 19 years ago. He was glad to see me living and working in it. Pops was very proud of the neighborhood and its history. As a lifelong member of the Historical Society, the Sierra Club and an active foe of Miami developers, he had placed both houses on the Historical Register. As an individualist and old-time Floridian, he savored revenge on City Hall in the form of a lowered tax rate. And as a 79-year-old widower, he valued this house more than a big pile of money that he won't be able to take with him ten years from now anyway. He was just glad to have someone reasonable living in it, paying a rent that would cover taxes and maintenance.

"Talking about Bryan Medical School, are they still taking care of you?"

" — To the tune of forty thousand a year for two years. I'm serving them as a 'consultant' — with no duties."

That wasn't new information. It was exactly what I had written on the rental application. But it seemed that Pops needed to hear it again . . . more out of concern about justice than about money. So I ran through the story again, mentioning that I had put the old professor's data up on a website, that the Medical School had agreed to take care of Mildred, his career technician, and that after what I'd uncovered at the Medical School, there was no way I could have stayed on with them as a research assistant professor, anyway. And I reminded Pops that I'd given up a good job as a patent examiner in training to accept that position at the Medical School

Pops shook his head. "Yeah, and I know you don't like to talk about it. And I know that you can't wear your metals because of the kind of world we're living in. Yes, I guess things are more complicated now than they were when I was a young man."

"I agree with you. My generation owes a lot to your generation — to my grandfather's generation."

Pops shook his head and laughed. "Keep on talking like that and I'll start getting the big-head." Pops was a WW-II hero, but didn't talk about it much.

I started to feel guilty about chatting with Pops when I should be calling Michael. But Pops was so nice.

He looked over to the three-foot stack of papers on my desk. "So, how's the consulting business? Who's your client on this project?"

"The name's Michael Malencik. You saw him, about four weeks ago. He's the guy in the expensive suit that came in the BMW when you were thinning out the bushes."

"I didn't peg him for a drug company executive. Looks more like a guy who sets up deals for building high-rise hotels."

"You may not be too far off there, Pops. He told me he'd once run a hundred-million-dollar venture capital fund for a Swiss billionaire. Probably financed all kinds of stuff besides pharmaceutical companies."

"Does he know his way around science?"

"He's teachable." I crossed my fingers.

"You mean he can understand how you're going to put a whole lot of wet chemical tests on a little computer chip like you were telling me before you left."

"Yes . . . on a silicon chip that can be read out by a robot-driven microscope and computer." It was a minor correction. "I hope he will understand it well enough to talk to the client company. Right now, I don't have any idea who the company is. He's keeping me in the dark."

Pops wrinkled his brow. "Wants to keep control of the project, I bet. Probably's afraid you'll run away with it. How much is he paying you, anyway?"

I told him.

"Only forty thousand dollars to show him how to discover drugs on chips! He's taking you, Ben."

"I don't have to *show* him how to do it. I just have to catalogue the available methods and make a prediction about how long it will take for *someone* to invent the chip."

I made an analogy about consulting for the aeronautical industry which Pops knew well. He had begun flying for Eastern Airlines at the end of World War II and had retired about 20 years ago.

Pops turned a curious eye towards the stack of papers on my desk. It was clear that he was itching to have a look at them.

"Go ahead. Take a look," I said. "Just remember to not tell anybody about the silicon chip business. That's confidential."

Pops walked over to the stack of brochures.

"Go ahead and take a look at them," I said again.

After one more round of encouragement from me, Pops started browsing through the brochures, studying pictures and reading captions. Sometimes he asked me to translate the jargon — high-throughput screening, combinatorial chemistry, chemical libraries,

HPLC mass spectroscopy, and so forth. He was so interested that it was easy to give him full answers. In fact, this was good practice for discussing these things with Michael. Finally, Pops came across a page I had torn from *Science* magazine. "What's this? All these red, blue, green and white dots in a grid. Looks like beads on an Indian belt."

"That's a microscope picture of the dots on the DNA biochip. That's the chip that can read out the activity of 10,000 genes from a single drop of fluid from a piece of living tissue."

"Sheesh."

"Pretty amazing, isn't it? The brightness of the glow on those dots can tell you what genes are turned on and which ones are turned off."

"Can you use that to discover new drugs?"

"The DNA biochip can tell you if a known drug is turning genes on or off. But to discover new drugs, we really need a different type of biochip that hasn't been invented yet. We need to make a chip where the dots are the *proteins* that the drug actually *binds* to when it works in your body. And someone will have to find some way to make the dots glow when the drug binds."

"Wow, wouldn't that be something!"

"And that's what I want you to keep —"

"Keep secret. Sure, Ben. You can count on me."

Pops put the brochure back on the pile, then searched my face for a sign that it was time for him to go. I gestured that everything was fine and that he could sit back down. He smiled sheepishly.

"Well, I'm sure you can keep up with the best of them, Ben. Good luck dealing with the men in suits." Pops broke into a grin. "Say, talking about guys in suits, you really had a walk-in closet full of them over here a week before you left." He sat down beside me.

"Yeah, the City's attorneys swooped in for high-powered deposition of me. I was the plaintiff's expert witness in a wrongful death case. You probably read about it in the *Miami Standard*. Two police officers arrested a guy for making a disturbance at one of the housing projects in Liberty City. He had overdosed himself on cocaine — was in a cocaine delirium — and he resisted. The cops hogtied him and left him in the back seat of the patrol car for a full hour. And when they finally brought him to Dade County General Hospital, he was D.O.A."

"What did you tell the lawyers?"

"That the cops should have suspected cocaine overdose, especially since they found some on him. — That hog-tying him was one of the reasons he stopped breathing. His core temperature was only one hundred and four degrees Fahrenheit. I said they should have monitored his breathing. If they'd taken him right to the drug treatment center, he could have been saved using chilled IV fluids and hypothermic blankets. I located some published case reports showing that people have survived with higher cocaine levels in their blood. And I said that when law officers bring a man in on the Baker Act, they have an affirmative duty to care for him in transit and get him quickly to treatment. Hell, the hospital was only ten minutes away but they took an hour."

"That's a mouthful. Sounds like you gave them something to think about. They give you any guff about having to take your testimony in this old house?"

"One of the defense lawyers did. But I told them how your dad was a famous lawyer."

Pops took the compliment silently. His big chest rose and he seemed to hold his breath for several seconds.

"They settled the case out of court the day before we left. I guess I owe my ex-boss Chief Medical Examiner Westley for the referral on that one. But the word's starting to spread that I'm a good expert witness on drugs and toxins. I hope to get more consults."

Pops was silent for a couple of minutes. He was looking at my desk with a funny smile that I found hard to interpret. Finally, he looked up and asked, "That HPLC instrument we were just talking about in the brochures." His brow wrinkled. "You said it is good for identifying different molecules?"

"Yes?"

"Is that the instrument you are setting up upstairs?"

"Yes, essentially."

"Could you . . . use it for analyzing cocaine?"

"Cocaine in the blood? Sure."

Pops looked at my desk again and the funny smile reappeared on his face. It looked like he wanted to ask a question that might seem goofy. "And could it be used to measure the purity of street drugs?" He looked me in the eye and held my gaze. He was serious.

"You mean like someone wants my advice on whether a sample of cocaine or heroin he wants to buy is watered down or has some dangerous impurities?" I held his gaze, trying to figure out what he was getting at.

"Well, yes." He was still looking.

"My HPLC would do the job just fine. But I would never use it for that."

Pops relaxed immediately. He looked away for a second.

"Have any of those lawyers ever asked you to do something like that?"

"No, and if they did, I'd tell them where to go."

Pops fell silent for a minute. He was acting like he couldn't decide whether to get up or stay seated. "Well, good luck to you, Ben. It's good to see your boat tied up to the dock next to mine. And it's good to see the old house being put to good use. Which reminds me. We have had some suspicious activity out front."

"Winos?"

"No. And not homeboys either. Suspicious vans coming and going for the last several days."

"Shouldn't be looking for narcotics. The neighborhood's clean. Do you think it's cops or private?"

"Gertrude and I haven't been able to get license numbers to do a Crime Watch check. I just wanted you to know." For a second, a worried look crossed Pop's face. He shook his head and stared thoughtfully at his coffee cup. "And there's one more thing I've got to tell you, Ben."

"Okay."

"When you were away, I caught a guy walking around your side yard."

"Yes."

"And as you can guess, I came down on him pretty hard. Would have come down on him harder if he hadn't been wearing a suit. Said he was with the DEA and was looking for you . . . Flashed his badge to prove it. Henderson was his name."

I felt a lump in my throat. "What did he want?"

"He wouldn't tell. That's just it." The goofy smile returned, this time pointed a little more in my direction. "I told him you were gone and when you'd be back, and that kind of took care of him . . . Although I have to tell you, Ben, I didn't care for him very much at all."

"You said he was wearing a suit. Then he's some kind of bureaucrat. Probably some kind of paperwork. Don't worry."

Pops looked me in the eye long enough to be sure I meant what I said. Then he broke into a grin. "Yeah, what would we do without bureaucrats?"

We laughed. I didn't have time to think about it right now.

"So, Pops, what's new with you? Got anything planned?"

"Yes, actually. In a couple weeks I'm going to use the pass to get up to Toronto. There's an Elderhostel on the Scots in Canada. It might be just the thing."

My involuntary smile came on so strong that it was painful, stretching my lips and pulling my ears. Pops grinned back at me, then blushed. Every time Pops went off to one of those things he came back with a new lady friend — sometimes two. The last time he came back with two guys and five gals and they took off in his cabin cruiser to the Bahamas for a week.

"Anyway, Ben, I'd appreciate it if you could keep an eye on the *Alabama Tiger*."

It's an Egg Harbor cabin cruiser, about 36 feet in length and squat in design. But it's a classic piece of workmanship in high-maintenance, white-painted wood planking — both above and below the waterline. I don't know how Pops picked that name to display in gold letters against the shiny brown background of that lovingly polished mahogany transom, but I understand that it has something to do with continuous parties.

"Sure, I'd be glad to keep an eye on things out back. And thanks for watching my place and letting me give your phone number to my alarm company."

"Say nothing of it."

Pops looked at his empty coffee mug. "I'm going to leave so you can work on that pile of papers." Against my protestations that it wasn't necessary, he got up. He insisted on taking his mug back to the kitchen before leaving.

I mused for a couple of minutes before returning to work. No, Pops wasn't nosey. He cared about Rebecca and me. And he was open with us — like when he told me he had about two million dollars in stocks and was thinking about his will and wanted my advice about whether to tell his unmarried granddaughters they would inherit the bulk of it.

I finished off the executive summary and then lit into the six pounds of mail that the postman had shoved through the brass-lined and shuttered slot in the door. I pulled out two promising-looking letters — the type with glassine windows. The first was from a Boca Raton stockbroker. It bore a check for $350. That was my payment for a quick-and-dirty, Internet-based evaluation of four biotech companies. He was trying to decide whether to advise a group of clients to invest around $50 million in them.

The second letter bore a Brickell Avenue return address and a heftier check: $2,458. That was my final payment for the hog-tied-while-overdosed-on-cocaine case. If I could get a couple dozen cases like that every year, I'd survive. Well, that was what I thought until I hit the playback button on my answering machine and listened to the first message.

The voice reminded me of an argument I'd once had with a truck driver.

5   Michael Malencik

Actually, the voice on the answering machine reminded me of an argument I'd once had with a *Newark* truck driver.

"You think you're so smart, you little snotnosed punk playing Monday morning quarterback and second-guessing the guys who are out there every day, laying it on the line. Well, let's see who answers the call when someone smashes up your car or breaks your front window and you need a police report, you little snotnosed . . . " He called me all kinds of bad names before hanging up.

The time/date stamp said it was recorded a day after we'd left. Well, my front window wasn't broken. And I didn't have to worry about him smashing my car because I don't own one. I just rent them sometimes.

I thought long and hard about that message. It had to be one of the cops in the hogtying case. Or maybe one of their buddies doing it for them. The lawyer told me right after the City settled with the plaintiff that both guys would be demoted. The call was too old to check using Caller I.D. But I would save the tape in case I needed to identify the guy.

I played the rest of the tape. After a dozen more telemarketing announcements came a message from Mr. Michael Malencik.

"Dear Benjamin, if I had been aware that you would be unavailable for two weeks, I would have called you earlier. The client must be supplied with some important facts *very soon*. Please call me as soon as you get back."

The date/time stamp told me that Mr. Malencik had called over a week ago. Hell!

I fast-reversed and listened to the message again. He had spoken as usual: in clear, measured tones: accent-free and well-pronounced. He had spoken with a patient dignity, maintaining his voice within a narrow dynamic range that never betrayed a trace of emotion. What should I make of the slight downward inflection he gave to the word "earlier"? Was he pissed off? Was there a crisis? And why was my pulse racing?

After a couple of minutes of thinking about it, I identified the real problem: Michael wanted to be a man of mystery and he was succeeding. Michael Malencik was as much a mystery to me now as he was when I first met him at a scientific conference. He remained as smooth and impenetrable as a block of black marble. Nature had given him the smooth, dark-haired, killer looks of the guy they've used in the last several of James Bond movies. He played that part to the limit — always impeccably dressed, laconic, quietly confident and elegant. His hard-to-pronounce name may have come from the Balkan Peninsula, but the rest of him seemed the product of a Swiss boarding school. I never did find out where he had studied. Although he couldn't have been ten years older than me, his business savvy put him light-years ahead.

Michael could make money talk: On the last day of the scientific conference, he handed me check for $20,000 and a letter of intent, which he asked me to sign. He seemed to be a world expert in dealing with super-wealthy investors. He actually lived among that crowd, in a condominium on Fisher Island, a private island for the super-rich that is located across Government Cut from Miami Beach and is accessible only by car ferry and by owner invitation.

He cultivated an air of mystery: He never gave me an address on Fisher Island. All I had was a fax and phone number for what was supposed to be an office on Miami Beach. To talk to him in real time, I had to dial his cellphone. Around here, I had met with him only three times: twice at my house and once at the Café Place St. Michel in Coral Gables. He always traveled light, carrying neither a briefcase nor a laptop computer — just that cellphone. But he must have had a laptop computer because he once asked me to e-mail him a file when he was doing business in San Francisco. He was flying around all the time.

Was the man of mystery a skilled trader on the high-tech Silk Route of the 21st Century? Okay, I could buy that. His trade secrets — contacts with suppliers, buyers and financiers and the locations of their secret watering holes — might be worth millions of dollars.

Expert trader, yes — but scientist, no. Hell, the average college sophomore in premed knows more biomedical science than him. When it came to science, Michael couldn't talk the talk. That was probably the real reason he was playing mysterious.

Well, let him be mysterious. I was glad to have written an executive summary that could be read and understood by anyone — scientists and executives from drug companies, investment bankers, and even stock brokers.

Basta!

I took a deep breath and dialed Michael's number. I got only his answering machine. I apologized to his tape for being out of the country and said I would await his call.

I released the pause button to make my answering machine play the rest of the calls. One was from my old mentor — Geoffrey A Westley, M.D., Chief Medical Examiner of Miami-Dade County — the guy who'd delivered the kick in the butt that was responsible for me getting my Ph.D. degree. Strangely, his recorded voice sounded both distant and insecure: "Nothing important. I just want to know how you are keeping."

No use trying to keep the line open for Michael. I owed Dr. Westley a call. I dialed his office number and got Doris, his middle-aged secretary of many years. She put me right through.

"Well Ben! How nice of you to call." He sounded as cordial as you can expect from an old-school Englishman, but his stammers, grunts and whines were my warning that I would have to carry the ball.

"I'm back from the Amazon. Just saw Rebecca off on her first expedition."

This was enough to prime him, and soon we were bantering about his stuff versus Rebecca's stuff: archaeology versus anthropology, ancient Egyptians versus rain forest Indians, and dead versus live subject matter. When the talk was about abstract principles, Dr. Westley could always keep it lively. As the repartee started to wane, I asked him how things were going at the Office. Yes, everything was going "swimmingly." And the toxicological lab? Yes, Dr. Steve Burk was carrying on grandly, extending the frontiers of their detection limits.

It was now 100 percent clear that Dr. Westley didn't have a project for me, and that he hadn't called to pick my brain. Still in a jocular mood, I continued the banter. "I am glad that professional matters are going so smoothly. And I hope all is going just as well, privately . . . I mean personally."

He answered after a long pause. "I am managing."

That got my attention. That was as close as Dr. Westley would ever come to sending an SOS signal. His words and delivery had a familiar ring, like in an old war movie where the British officer is struggling against impossible odds to hold his outpost. When, during the lull in his arduousness and increasingly hopeless struggle, the war movie hero is queried on his status, he answers resignedly, "I am managing," swallowing all of his A's but none of his pride.

When a distress flare arcs through the sky you have to respond. For too many seconds I said nothing. Was the old man lonely? Was he getting the right things to eat? Was the antique furniture in his condominium accumulating dust faster than he could bring himself to wipe it off? Did every stroke of the dust pad awaken a new memory of dear old Margaret? Should I invite myself to his Faire Isle condominium to check it out?

"We really ought to get together," I said. It was a regrettable choice of words. Rebecca and I had invited him a month before she had to leave, but the visit didn't happened. Dates were tentatively selected, then changed, and then changed again until it was too late.

"Yes, quite," he said, filling the remaining aural space with a high-pitched clearing of throat. It filled the embarrassing moment as comfortably as a stage laugh.

"What about coming for dinner tonight?" I asked, trying to pump enthusiasm into every word. "I have a couple of pounds of fresh shrimp in the refrigerator and a couple of good bottles of Rhine-Hessen Riesling in the closet. We could put on some CDs."

"Well . . . ." He tapered the word so that it could have held for an infinity.

I adopted a coaxing tone. "Now, you don't have choir practice, or a Faire Isle Condominium Association meeting, do you?"

"Err . . . no . . . but . . ."

"Good! Then I will expect you here between five-thirty and six," I said, intoning it as a command to squelch another round of protest. "Have Doris give you my address and directions. It's very easy — essentially a straight shot down Northwest Tenth Avenue. And don't worry about your car. You can park it in my breezeway where it will be safe. I'll leave the gate open for you."

It was beginning to sound like role reversal. It used to be Dr. Westley inviting me for dinners which Margaret had cooked. — Dear old Margaret, who passed away shortly after I completed that clandestine assignment for Dr. Westley. Dear old Margaret, whose uncomplaining, just and resolute example had carried me through two lonely months when I had nobody to talk to, just her memory.

Dr. Westley was politely slow in answering my invitation. "Very well, but I wouldn't want to put you out."

I assured him it was no trouble, that I really wanted to see him, and that we could talk about the Amazon Indians that Rebecca was working with. I hung up before he could initiate another round self-effacing denial.

I was glad for the chance to lift Dr. Westley's spirits. We were almost friends. And, to be perfectly honest, I needed him as a resource. True, I was a Ph.D. pharmacologist and a certified expert on questions of how drugs or poisons are detected in the blood. Yes, I was worth the $250 an hour I was charging lawyers. But I didn't have Dr. Westley's vast experience with drugs and poisons as a cause of death. I needed him as a sounding board.

I hurried off on my bicycle, crossing Wagner Creek Canal via the arched concrete bridge and picking up the Northwest North River Drive again. Followed it for several blocks south to the Florida East Coast Fisheries where I bought a couple of pounds of shrimp. A bicycle is the ecologically sound way of doing errands within a two-mile radius. The temperature was mild; I generated no sweat on the trip, over and back.

Just as I was hauling my bike and a bag of shrimp up to the front porch, I heard the phone ringing inside. I hurried in, picked it up, and answered, "This is Dr. Candidi."

It was Michael.

"Benjamin." He never called me Ben, and he sounded especially formal, now. "I am calling about the status of the project." He spoke smoothly, as always.

"Yes, I just got your message and answered it . . . just fifteen minutes ago, actually. I had to take off . . . ten days to accompany my fiancée to the start her anthropological field trip. It's in Brazil, on the Amazon."

"I see," he said, neutrally.

"Actually, it is a *medical* anthropological field trip.

"Interesting." But nothing in his voice suggested any interest. "I was a little concerned . . . for the project. What I was calling for . . . is to let you know that the client now considers your report to be of highest priority." He emphasized the last two words.

"I won't have any trouble meeting the schedule. I'll deliver it on schedule — the interim report in eight weeks and the full report twelve weeks after that . . . just like we agreed."

"I am calling to say that the client would like the reports sooner." He told me they wanted the interim report in six weeks and the full report eight weeks after that.

I argued that I needed the full time to submit the final report with hypertext links. That was a gimmick, but everyone uses gimmicks in negotiations.

He agreed on a compromise date for the final report. "But right *now*," he said, "the client is anxious for some preliminary information."

"Fine," I said. "Tell me what information they want. And maybe you could give me an idea of how many company scientists will be reading the report. Maybe you can fill me in a little on their background."

Michael let me dangle for a long time. Finally, he said, "Please outline the major points of your interim report for me now. I will communicate your points informally to the client." He spoke in such carefully modulated tones.

"Tell you now? Over the phone?"

"Yes."

The plastic bag was dripping shrimp juice on the floor. I picked it up and set it inside the wastebasket beside my desk. My bicycle was still out on the porch where anyone could steal it. "Could you excuse me for a second?"

"Yes."

I retrieved my bike from the porch and shut the door behind me. I picked up my executive summary and tried to work myself up into an enthusiastic, salesman-like mood.

Michael must have heard my breathing. "Just give me the bottom line," he said.

"Okay. Here it is. When the right technologies are put together, there is going to be a big speed-up in the rate of drug discovery. You might call it a revolution. It will have the same type of impact that the DNA biochip is about to have on human genetics and clinical testing. It will require a new type of biochip — a drug-receptor biochip. And the impact will be much greater."

We had discussed all of the facts before, but this time he would get the super-organized version that I'd perfected on the riverboat.

I told Michael that the DNA biochip technology could be adapted to put 10,000 drug-receptor protein microdots on a silicon chip and that it would revolutionize drug discovery when someone found a way to make the microdots glow when a drug bound to them. I said this would make it possible to do ultra-fast screening for new drugs from a single drop of plant juice. I took him through the argument about Nature's plants and little animals having over 100,000 small sturdy molecules with drug activity waiting to be discovered. I said there are more than 35,000 different types of protein molecule in the human body. I talked about how this makes over four billion lock/key combinations, containing cures for every disease known to man. I raved about the advantages of shrinking the drug-testing laboratory and putting it on a chip so you could hunt for 10,000 types of drug activity at a time.

Michael agreed you would need this kind of efficiency if you were going to test for drugs in every type of plant, mold and pond scum in the world. Soon, I had Michael marching along through the forest of facts like Paul Bunyon. Great!

I stopped talking and waited for Michael's next question. All I heard from his end was some cars driving slowly by — sometimes their engines and sometimes their radios. And I heard nearby conversation and clicking of plates. He was probably in some damn outdoor restaurant in the south end of Miami Beach. I just waited for him to speak.

"You say this is a revolution, waiting to happen?" he asked.

"Yes. Companies will be able to search for drugs a thousand times faster and a thousand times more efficiently."

"And you're saying this revolution hasn't happened yet?"

"Correct. Someone will have to develop the detector arrays for the drugs — the dots that will go on the protein biochip. It will probably evolve from microtiter plate technology that —."

"No, Benjamin," Michael said with firmness, "that cannot be true. The biochip technology has been developed already."

Oh, hell! Paul Bunyon was suddenly shrunk to human size and had just tripped over a tree stump. It would be important to answer him just as firmly.

"Yes, we have a *DNA* biochip. No, we don't have a drug-receptor protein biochip technology that will screen for drug activity."

"It is well-known that the DNA chip is already a powerful tool for drug discovery," he said, smoothly. It sounded like he was reading aloud from somebody's brochure. "DNA biochips can read out changes in gene activity when you give a patient a drug."

For some reason, he got me flustered. "What? Give the drug to patients? A drug that you are searching for in coral and orchid stamens? Hell, you won't have enough of it to give to *one* rat. You need a *screening* method that will read out the pharmacological activity with *one* drop of juice."

He couldn't object to that. I kicked the argument at him from various directions until he finally started to agree. I drove my point home by reading from my executive summary: "The real increase in drug discovery efficiency will occur when a scientist can take his drug discovery laboratory into the field — on a drug discovery biochip."

I said nothing more. No use competing against myself. Anything more would just muddle the argument. I waited. I waited through a full minute of silence.

Michael's next words were in a soft voice, not addressed to me. "No, just some more Perrier, please." Then to me he said, "Excuse me."

"Quite alright. I was waiting for you to finish writing your notes." I said nothing more, and there was another long silence on the other end.

"Okay, Benjamin, I will take your argument about orchid stamens under advisement. Now, moving a step forward, is it also your opinion that the revolution in DNA and protein engineering will not be our greatest source of candidate drugs ten years from now."

I told him why proteins and polypeptides don't make ideal drugs. I told him that the ideal drug is a small, sturdy molecule that works when you take it by mouth. I said that these molecules were designed by plants and lower organisms and that bioprospecting would be the best way to find them. I was very emphatic. I oversimplified a great deal to drive my argument home.

"Then why are the DNA biochip people saying their products can be used for drug discovery?" Michael asked.

I told him that was because those people had invested heavily in their technology and wanted to find more reasons for people to buy their DNA chips.

"Okay. Could you summarize our conversation and fax it to me — you have the number — by the end of the day?"

"You've got it, Michael."

He answered with a click.

Whew! I had to take a walk around the house to calm down. Well, maybe that's what was needed: a European playboy to mediate between me and the company executives. I could imagine the guy reporting back to them over an expensive dinner. I could imagine him right now at South Beach. Probably paying the waiter and taking a fashion model up to a room at the Cleveland Hotel.

I revised my executive summary to foolproof it against the problems I'd had with Michael. I also typed up a couple of pages distinguishing the existing DNA biochip from the drug discovery biochip that I envisioned. Soon, the wastebasket was full of paper

from several cycles of printing out and editing. After three hours
of work the two documents were almost ready for faxing.

Now was the time to start preparing dinner for Dr. Westley. I
went to the kitchen and got the pasta steaming. Then, I went into a
state of panic, looking for the shrimp. Finally, I remembered that
the shrimp were in the wastebasket under my discarded notes. Soon,
I had three burners going, with lids rattling over pots of boiling
shrimp and steaming pasta water. Added to that was the aroma of
the sauce I had whipped up. I went back to the computer screen to
see if the report needed any finishing touches. Feeling debonair
and not wishing to be burdened with hard copies at the moment, I
decided to go paperless, sending Michael his fax directly from my
desktop computer. But first, I had to return to the kitchen.

And while completing preparations in the kitchen, I glanced
at my watch. Hell! How the time flies. I rushed out to open the
gate for Dr. Westley.

An Evening with Dr. Westley   6

I wasn't a minute too early. Dr. Westley's white Rolls Royce Silver
Cloud was rounding the bend in the tree-lined street. Even from
one block's distance, I could make out his face, framed in the
windscreen — one must use the right terminology — his bushy
white eyebrows set low in apparent concentration required for
navigating his British Museum relic through this unfamiliar and
questionable neighborhood. I waved to him and he waved back at
me.

Dr. Westley's approach to the driveway was less than perfect,
but as good as can be expected of a 70-ish driver. No white paint
was transferred to the posts of my chain-link fence when he drove
the car into the driveway. Sometimes he can be such a fuddy-duddy.

I said admiring words about his car and he reciprocated with a
short architectural assessment of my house: "Nice two-storey
stucco affair. Exposed eves, yes quite typical. Kept the original

style of shingle. Windows, too. Nice, light and airy. Carport roof integral to the house, but quite narrow, as we have just noticed. Ben, you are living in an original! I would estimate this one to be built between 1920 and 1926."

In cultural matters, Dr. Westley always had to have the upper hand.

While I faxed the two documents to Michael, the Old Boy looked at my stack of scientific papers and at some library books on Brazilian Indians that sat on a small table beside my desk.

When the computer indicated that the faxes were dispatched, I turned to Dr. Westley and said, "Now for a spot of Rhine-Hessen Riesling?"

He agreed. I set the burners on simmer, then uncorked a bottle and poured two glasses. Somehow, the Old Boy didn't seem at ease. With glass in hand, I showed him around the house, then out the kitchen to the backyard.

"Oh, there is the vessel that I've heard so much about."

"The *Diogenes*. Thirty-six foot Cheoy Lee ketch."

As an old salt from Devon near Cornwall, the Old Boy knew a lot about sailing vessels. He commented on the rigging of the two wooden masts, and he expressed approval of the yacht's sloping lines and teak planked decks. I took him aboard, opened the companionway and invited him to take a peek below. He said nice things about the wood-finished interior. The late-afternoon sun was pleasant, the air was mild and there were no mosquitoes. And sitting in the cockpit, taking it all in, Dr. Westley seemed so much at home that I suggested we eat dinner on board. "That would be a capital idea," he replied.

I made a quick trip to the kitchen, completed preparations, and loaded everything on a wicker tray. I returned to find Dr. Westley standing at the helm. Yes, the open cockpit was the best choice. We took places, facing each other, the plates sitting on our knees.

Dr. Westley voiced approval with the first bite. "Mumm. Nicely done, the tortellini and shrimp. And the sauce is just right. You struck the Golden Mean there, I say. And then sprinkling it all with Parmesan. What a touch."

"Thank you. Have some more wine. I've brought a Tuscan white which should stand up to everything including the salad dressing."

"Quite."

The Old Boy was in a good mood. I went into the main salon and turned on some dinner music — a tape of the Turtle Island String Quartet. Dr. Westley had always laid classical music on me when he and Margaret had invited me for dinner. Turtle Island's exquisitely blended classically inspired craziness would be my answer tonight. The Old Boy seemed impressed but didn't comment. But returning tugboats stimulated maritime conversation.

Sunlight filtering through the live oaks played on the Old Boy's face. Tension seemed to dissolve. Eyelids half-closed under his fuzzy brows. His face relaxed into a contented, almost boyish, smile. "It brings me back to Exemouth. Oh, did we have some delightful sailing expeditions from there! Some quite exciting, too, when a storm blew up in the Channel."

He leaned forward, towards the center of cockpit, sliding his right arm over his knee until his hand almost touched the wheel. I was witnessing the reawakening of 50-year-old muscle memory — his memories of delightful hours spent holding the tiller of a small sailboat. To my questions about the boats, their headsails and keel shape, he gave such enthusiastic answers that he seemed to be getting younger by the minute. He had learned the ropes and knots in the British equivalent of a scout troop sponsored by a local rescue society. Later, he had served them as a "lead boy" in regattas and cruises along their rocky coast. "Yes, those were the days," he said.

A pelican glided by, turning his long beak as if asking us to toss him a shrimp.

We talked about Dr. Westley's childhood in Devon for a long time — all the way through dinner and halfway through that bottle of Italian white wine. It was nice to be able to picture him as a boy. An hour passed in what seemed a few minutes.

"Did you often rent a sailboat and go out when you were in your twenties?" I asked.

"Yes, occasionally . . . although the demands of career and the absence of money imposed some limitations."

"Did you get a chance to introduce Margaret to the wind and salt spray?"

"Yes. Once. Although, it was perhaps a bit much for her." He frowned. "One must remember that she's from London." He'd just referred to her in present tense. He shook his head sadly. "I do think that raft trips down a leisurely Jamaican river like the one near Port Antonio were more her . . . forte . . . if you catch my drift."

I remembered when he and Margaret had told me about their Caribbean vacation. "Yes, I catch your drift. Drift down the river. Catch a hanging vine and tie up the raft on the river's bank for the afternoon."

Dr. Westley smiled at the thought.

"I really miss her, Dr. Westley."

"I, too. God bless her soul."

It was getting dark

I recounted to Dr. Westley the English dinners Margaret had cooked for us. I reminded him of the delightful conversations that had taken place between the three of us at his table. The conversations were usually dominated by Dr. Westley's mini-lectures on Egyptology and were humanized by Margaret's common-sense interjections. Slowly, I had developed an affection for the Old Girl. Afterwards, Dr. Westley and I had always retired to his balcony where I briefed him on the clandestine murder investigation that he'd talked me into undertaking. I'd always regretted how Margaret's death had robbed me of the chance to tell her how much she meant to me.

And I felt a deep urge to tell Dr. Westley how much I appreciated the fatherly interest he had taken in me. I wanted to make sure that he was eating right; that he was able to keep up his condominium apartment; that he was enjoying life; and that he had things to look forward to. I fell silent, thinking how investigating the cause of death, day after day, must weigh heavily on his soul. Could I find a non-intrusive way to say any of these things?

Dr. Westley cleared his throat and shook his head. "So how is the young, attractive Dr. Rebecca Levis? Down on the Amazon, you say. Should I imagine *her*, on a raft, tied to a vine?"

His tone was formal now, properly English but mocking. He'd slammed the door shut. The magic moment was lost.

"She is working at a mission," I answered slowly, "on the *Rio Marauiá*."

"And where, exactly, is that?" he asked in a lecture-hall voice.

Verbally, I traced Dr. Westley a map, starting at the mouth of the Amazon, going west to Manaus and then up the *Rio Negro* 400 miles to the mouth of the *Rio Marauiá*. "She went up the river, north, in the direction of the Guyanan Shield and the Venezuelan border."

"Ben, from what you have described, your fiancée is in the heart of Yanomama territory! The fiercest, most uncivilized people of the face of the earth."

He made it seem like he was exercising restraint by not scolding me. I answered firmly.

"She's in good hands. She's going with Professor David Thompson. She's at a mission. He has been there before."

"Do you realize that this region is populated by savages. They are always at war with each other. Constant feuds, trying to collect the greatest number of wives." Now Dr. Westley was on a rant. He could be very passionate about things that didn't affect either of us directly. It was his way of blowing off steam. And I guess this was the only way he could be comfortable with me in an unstructured situation.

"Dr. Westley, I have read classic anthropological work of Napoleon Chagnon, too. But time has gone by. There has been a lot of change. And other people have gone into the region more recently, and they have reported differently."

"I would still worry. I would feel under siege by those savages."

On the other side of the river, 50 yards away, Haitian stevedores were loading the rusty freighter. They were loading it the old-fashioned way — with bent, sweaty bodies, straining under the load of hundred-pound sacks. Under bright deck lights, the men trudged along narrow planks. The occasional clang of an iron railing reported their descent into the bowels of the ship. Framed between the ship's high bow and stern, the action seemed like a morality pageant on an elevated stage — a sound and light presentation of backbreaking toil in the undeveloped world.

"Dr. Westley, I'm sure you know that the Yanomami are under siege themselves. You know about the invasion by the miners — the *garimpeiros*. You know how that brought malaria. You know that the Yanomama way of life was almost destroyed.

Dr. Westley had been gazing at the freighter, himself. "Their way of life will *have* to be replaced. It is impossible for them to go on that way. And they will not want to labor and starve with the old, inefficient methods, once they see power tools and modern conveyance."

Obstinate old Dr. Westley. So well-versed in anthropology and yet so ignorant: Willing to give the ancient Egyptians a mile; unwilling to give the present-day Yanomama an inch. Yet portraying himself as an expert in "cultural matters" from all over the world. I wasn't a defender of the Yanomama. I wasn't a great believer in "political correctness." But I hated to see people bowled over.

"So we have to destroy their belief systems and demoralize them?"

"One should rid them of those ridiculous belief systems. — That there is a forest spirit living inside your chest that will be scared out if someone uses your name!"

"They call it your *hekura*."

"That everyone has some sort of a forest animal as *doppelgänger*, which lives a parallel life!"

"They call it your *noreshi*."

As he stared at me, Dr. Westley's eyebrows came down like a hood. "Yes, I saw that stack of library books by your desk. I'm just surprised that you committed that infernal nonsense to memory."

My response was a little too sassy. "Isn't that in the great explorer tradition? Read about the place before you visit it. Richard Halliburton. The *Royal Road to Romance* and all that."

"Yes, very well. But you must keep in mind, Ben, that it is just prehistoric superstition. How primitive! How heathen!"

It was no use getting into a wrestling match in quicksand. But I didn't want to give him the final word, either. "They are the last living example of prehistoric thought. Their beliefs should be studied."

"Studied, yes. Revered, no! How ridiculous, to think that the center of the spiritual world is volcanic mountains, presided over by covens of spirits."

". . . Like the gods on Mount Olympus."

"And that they received fire from the mouth of an alligator."

" — Named Iwrame, who was like Prometheus."

"Or that *their* god could have created earth!"

"They call him Omam. For all we know, their creation myth may predate Adam and Eve."

I had to stop giving Dr. Westley smart answers because he was getting worked up. My answers were creating too much conflict with his Anglican beliefs. He was a vestryman at Trinity Cathedral.

"Ben, I see that you have been reading up on their religion — if you can call it that. But think of it! Grinding up your father's bones and drinking the powder!"

I stopped myself from saying anything about Communion.

"To think of it. — A belief system that condones infanticide, polygamy and barbarism to fellow man. One cannot allow it to remain. The greatest betrayal of civilization was that so-called cultural relativism doctrine of Margaret Mead. The savages must be civilized."

"I can see your point of view."

End of discussion.

Thinking about the constructive things we could have discussed, I felt disappointed in my old mentor. We could have talked about whether scarcity of food was the reason for their fighting and territorial wars. We could have speculated about how and when they discovered curare. Was their possession of this magic bullet comparable to Western Man's possession of nuclear weapons? Was it a chemical weapon so terrible that you don't dare to use it against your enemy? Had this special knowledge contributed to their dark mythology with *porés* or *onkas*, painted black from head to toe, wandering in the forest looking for people to kill with special poisons. Was this why one village had feared black magic and guerilla attacks from another? Was this why they had to announce their visits with loud voices and make many assurances of non-aggression before entering?

Why hadn't we been able to discuss any of this? Was it too hard for Dr. Westley to treat me as an equal? Was the possibility of logic in primitive mythology too threatening to his belief system? Had his medical examining profession already shown him too much horror?

I pressed the glow button on my watch. It was around 10 o'clock. Shouldn't have done it because Dr. Westley noticed.

"Yes, Ben, it is getting a bit late for me, too. Thank you ever so much for having me." He rose slowly to his feet.

"It was my pleasure. I hope to have you again."

"You are an excellent cook. It has been a long time since I

have enjoyed such a . . . ." He cut it short while stepping to the dock, and didn't resume.

"You are remembering to have balanced meals when you eat at home, aren't you? Fresh vegetables and fresh fruit." I was starting to sound like Rebecca.

"Quite. Yes, I manage."

He uttered that telltale word with much more determination than on the phone that morning. Thus, my invitation had been good for him. But as I guided him through the house and out the front door and into his car, I felt aged — like a 50-year-old man looking after a 75-year-old father. I pointed towards the arched concrete bridge and told him to follow the River downtown and then pick up Brickell Avenue. I gave him a lot of hand signals to help him maneuver the old Rolls through the narrow gate, but he came close to scraping a fender, anyway.

When he was pointed in the right direction and squared away in the broad, deserted street, he looked back at me through the open window. "Thanks again, Ben. And my love to Rebecca, when you . . . communicate . . . with her again."

And that was exactly what was on my mind. Back in the house, I turned on the computer and wrote Rebecca a long e-mail. It was probably much too long. Before clicking the send button, I said a little prayer, asking that David Thompson would remember to plug in his satellite dish when they had electricity at the Mission.

I should have prayed for good luck for the next day.

7   Locks, Keys and the DEA

It happened the next morning while I was working at my desk in my usual outfit — shorts and T-shirt. The Thomas Edison buzzer blasted me out of the world of diagnostic microarrays and DNA chips. The unannounced visitor was about my age and he looked like a magazine salesman. He was tall and gaunt, and he wore a beige tropical-weight suit. He had thin, stringy, red hair that came up in front like a cow lick and came out in back like a rooster tail. His skin was light and freckled. Maybe I opened the screen door because I felt sorry for him.

"Are you Dr. Candidi?" he asked in a querulous, high-pitched voice. As fast as I could say yes, he pulled out a leather-framed badge and said, "Phil Henderson, DEA."

I let my eyes ask the questions and received no answers. He elbowed his way past me and sat down in one of the rattan chairs. Then he flipped open an imitation leather holder to reveal a yellow tablet. He rested it on his lap, ready to write. "Just some routine questions."

I hadn't moved from the doorway. "Mr. Henderson, I do not remember asking you to sit down."

"It's okay. It won't take long. Just some routine questions."

I gestured to my computer. "I'm right in the middle of an important project. I've just blocked and cut a paragraph which I have to move into the right place. Then, I'll need a couple minutes to readjust the context while it's fresh in my mind." I shut the screen door and returned to my chair in front of the computer. "You are welcome to wait in this room if you confine yourself to the chair you picked out." Fuming, I hid my face behind the oversized screen.

"Just routine questions and it shouldn't take too long."

Do these guys get their inspiration from Friday night cop shows? I ignored him and took my time — four full minutes of it.

DEA badge-flasher Henderson spent the time doing a visual inventory of the room. When I pushed back and met eyes with him, he acted like I'd given him the go-ahead. "Just some routine questions. I hope I can have your cooperation." He said it with unfocused cockiness, then crossed his leg and looked down on a thick-soled, brown, wingtip shoe. Bare-footed, I was at a podiatric disadvantage.

"Well, Mr. Henderson, I suppose that will ultimately depend on your definition of 'routine.'"

My answer left as much of an impression as water on a duck's back.

"Your occupational license with the City of Miami lists you as a 'consulting pharmacologist.'" He dropped his voice like it was a statement but raised his eyes in question. They were bluish gray and hard to interpret.

If I asked whether that was a question, he'd probably turn hostile. "That's correct." He said nothing. Now was the time to strike. "As an example, I consult for the legal profession. As an example, my expert testimony upset the careers of a couple of incompetent cops who hogtied a man who was overdosed on cocaine, contributing to his death."

"Yes, thank you, but I do not need that question answered in so much detail." He made it sound like I was an ignoramus in need of instruction.

"As you wish. Just trying to simplify your visit."

"Are you engaged in the sale or distribution of drugs?"

"No."

"Do you keep any drugs on this premises?" He had an irritating way of staring.

"No, not really." Damn! Why did I say "not really"? I should have asked him to say what he meant by drugs. These petty bureaucrats love to trap people on the wrong side of a definition.

He subjected me to a gray gaze and asked, "What do you mean by 'not really'?"

I reached into my desk drawer and shook a small plastic bottle. "I keep a lot of aspirin around . . . for headaches and muscle soreness after karate practice."

He clicked his tongue and tapped his black government-issue ballpoint on the yellow pad, which now held four lines of notes. "Dr. Candidi, do you want me to record a frivolous answer?"

"Frankly, I wouldn't be able to say *what* you would consider frivolous. Were you asking about over-the-counter drugs, prescription drugs, Schedule One or Two drugs?" No use saying "illicit drugs." He'd just ask to define them.

DEA Agent Henderson rolled his eyes up into his forehead for a few seconds. Probably needed to think. "You can answer for Schedule One and Two for right now." He was asking about if I had any illicit or tightly controlled drugs.

"I don't have any Schedule One or Two drugs."

Henderson wrote that down, then looked up and stared at me.

I felt an urge to continue. "That takes care of illicit drugs and 'narcotics' as your agency calls them. And I don't have any

Schedule III or IV drugs either, although it would be my right to have therapeutic quantities if prescribed by a physician."

Henderson took a long time writing notes on this. I bided my time, thinking up a sassy answer in case he asked me if I had any Schedule V drugs — which are over-the-counter remedies.

"Could you describe for me your activities as a consulting pharmacologist?"

"I give expert advice on drug-related matters to the legal profession — either plaintiff's or defendant's attorneys. I advise the pharmaceutical industry on FDA-mandated testing pursuant to pharmaceutical development." I paused. "And I advise attorneys, as I did the plaintiff's attorneys who got a couple of Miami police officers demoted after they hogtied a man who was in a cocaine delirium. It was a wrongful death. And I think that case might have something to do with your — ."

"Are you involved in drug testing?"

"I have arranged for the testing of drug levels in blood."

"Have you ever done any drug testing here on-site?"

"No." The answer was truthful; my HPLC machine was not yet functional.

"Do you have equipment on the premises which can be used for drug testing?"

"I have a high pressure liquid chromatograph and that can be used for assaying drugs in blood samples."

"And is it true that this equipment could be used for determining the purity of illicit drugs."

My heart skipped a beat and then raced out of control. "Do you mean, 'Could *my* equipment be used for determining the purity of illicit drugs for a seller or buyer?'"

"Yes."

"Well the answer is 'no.' I repeat, '*no.*'"

"And why is that?"

The red-headed SOB reminded me of Woody Woodpecker — a bird-brained pest that you can't get rid of.

"My equipment could never be used for that purpose because I would never *permit* it to be used for that purpose."

He wrote that down. "Dr. Candidi, I have some more questions."

What more did he need? If he was working on a "hot tip" from a couple of rogue police officers, what else could I say that would make him discount their tip? And if this was only a "routine call," then what more information did he need?

"Questions of a *routine* nature?" I asked.

Sarcasm rolled off this guy's shoulders like water off a foul weather jacket.

"You made a trip to Brazil and returned two nights ago." He was playing that trick again, pronouncing it like a statement but acting like it was a question that had to be answered.

"Was that a question or a statement?"

"Let's call it a statement. What was your purpose for visiting Brazil?"

"Tourism."

"Is it not true that Rebecca Levis, who cohabits this house, also went to Brazil?"

"Yes, but I don't see how any of this concerns you or your agency." I reached into the aspirin drawer and found my hand-held tape recorder. Should I use it now? No, I shouldn't go off half-cocked. I'd give this guy three more chances before striking him out.

"It is no concern of yours what concerns me or the Agency," he replied.

Strike One.

"Sorry. Can't fathom your logic. It's sunk deeper than you in my chair."

That had as much effect on him as shooting a BB gun at a Terminator. He just asked another question. "Do your answers to my questions on drugs in this house also hold for Rebecca Levis?"

"Yes."

"Are you sure?"

"Quite sure."

"But she is a physician and might have drug samples. Does she have a black bag?"

"Yes."

"Then your statement about not having drugs in this house would be incorrect."

Strike Two.

"As I understand it, my physician fiancée's black bag carries first aid equipment and drugs for medical emergencies."

I heard a cough through the open window facing the street.

"And Dr. Levis is not here?"

"That is correct."

"Dr. Candidi, I would like to see Dr. Levis's black bag and your drug testing equipment."

Strike Three.

I pulled out the hand-held tape recorder and flipped it on. "From now on, Mr. Henderson, anything you say will be recorded. And your continued presence here will constitute consent to my recording."

"Put that away."

"You will not order me around in my own house. You have just asked to see my physician financée's medical bag and my scientific instruments. I, Benjamin Candidi Ph.D., am willing to grant that request if you make it in writing and state for what purpose and what lead you to come here in the first place."

"*Please*, turn that thing off for a second."

I flipped the switch with my thumb. "Okay, it's off."

"You look old enough and smart enough to know that you should cooperate with Federal authorities."

"I have been cooperating. I've told you we aren't doing anything illegal and you don't seem to believe me."

"Do you know that it would take less than a day to get a team in here under a court order to haul away your computer and pull up every floorboard."

"That does it. The tape recorder goes back on."

"Don't you threaten him, buster." It was Pops, coming in through the screen door. A second later he was standing over Henderson. "My name's Ted Harvey and I'm Dr. Candidi's landlord. I own this place and you aren't going to tear up any floorboards in this house. And you're not going to take his computer because it is storing information that he needs for a report he's making to a big-time pharmaceutical company." Pops whole body was shaking. Henderson had pressed himself back into the chair and was trying hard to stare back. "And if you come in and mess up his work, you're going to owe him forty thousand dollars and I'll see to it that every cent of that comes out of your hide and not out of the honest taxpayers' dollars." Pops stepped forward, leaving Henderson nowhere to go. "And it doesn't make any difference if any tape recorder's on or off because I heard every word you've said since you pulled up here in your fleet Chevrolet."

Henderson wriggled out of the chair. He headed for the door then turned to make a stand. "You are obstructing justice."

Pops shook a finger at him. "What a load of B.S. Should have run you off the first time you came here. You aren't a man enough to hear an honest man out. And since you were making such a big deal about Dr. Candidi cooperating, I'm going to make a big deal out of you cooperating — right now! I'm telling you to your face that I think you're a fake, impersonating a Federal officer. I'm telling you I want to see your badge so I can write down your number and get hold of your boss who'll see some real sparks flying."

Henderson went out the door. I said so, into the tape recorder. Pops followed him out. On the porch, Henderson turned and said, "Due to your advanced age, I'm going to overlook your interference with my official duties."

Pops stepped up to him like a batter arguing with the umpire. "Advanced age, my foot! Official duties, my foot! You and your kind don't know a damn thing about official duties. I was risking my life for my country thirty years before the best part of you dribbled down your father's pant-leg. You want to know about official duties, you learn what it was to fly a B-17 for twenty missions straight. And I didn't do that to have the likes of you bullying my tenant from behind a tin drug enforcement badge." Henderson retreated to his car and Pops followed him. "You want to enforce drug laws, you go over to the other side of the river and flash your badge around that Haitian tramp steamer. You get over there and . . ."

Pops stood there at the curb, shaking and wordless. There was nothing more to say, because Henderson was already in his car.

Henderson drove off. I kept the recorder on. It wouldn't hurt to get more of Pop's reaction.

"I hope I didn't make it worse for you, Ben. He got me so ticked off. He stands for everything that's wrong with government today." Pops was shaking all over. So was I.

"I agree. Thanks for your support. Come on in. It's time for a gin and tonic. It's early in the day, but today will be an exception."

It would be important to get that shaking under control. It was as bad as advanced Parkinson's disease. I've often wondered if that disease isn't self-catalyzing.

Pops accepted my offer. I made mine light and his double strength. We tossed the drinks down quickly and Pops' shaking subsided after a few minutes. With the tape still running, I took Pops upstairs and showed him the lab instrumentation. He appreciated the HPLC and helped me to tape-record an inventory of Rebecca's black bag. While we had it open, I talked Pops into trying on Rebecca's blood pressure cuff: I read blood pressure of 140/90 and a heart beat rate of 105. This didn't qualify him for a visit to Baptist Hospital or even for a nitroglycerin lozenge from Rebecca's black bag. But when we returned downstairs, we did re-medicate ourselves another gin and tonic. I made his plenty strong.

We chatted for a long time about government, bureaucrats and law enforcement professionals. When Pops said he'd better be going, I thanked him again and told him not to worry. I suggested that he take a nap.

I thought for a while about what to do with the DEA. A few months ago, Rebecca and I had done them a big favor out in the Bahamas. They owed me, even if they didn't want to admit it. I guessed that Henderson was new on the job. He had a lot to learn about professionalism.

I decided to keep it low key and unofficial. I put in a call to the Miami office of the DEA and asked for the public affairs officer. I used the hold time to fix lunch. After 25 minutes of waiting I got dumped. I called back and asked the operator for the voice mail of the public affairs officer. A recorded female voice invited me to leave my message for extension #463. I said that I needed to speak to someone about an unannounced visit from an Officer Henderson and that if I did not hear back from them, that I would assume that the matter was *completely resolved.*

But it would never be resolved in my mind until I knew for sure why Henderson had been sent to me. Was it really the work of a couple of rogue police officers? Had they told the DEA that I was working for a drug smuggling syndicate, working in a riverside lab, checking the purity of their cocaine shipments? How did they know that I'd visited Latin America? Had the DEA looked it up? Or was the visit triggered by my association with Michael? Maybe he was doing drug deals on the side. Maybe his dealings with legitimate drug companies were just a cover for a cocaine smuggling operation. I tried to get back to work, but these questions bothered me for the rest of the day.

The next morning Pops dropped in on me looking relaxed, alert and a little sheepish. "I was wondering whether I could keep you company," he said.

I had a good idea what he had in mind. "Sure, Pops. You're welcome to stick around while I work on my report. Grab a book from the shelf and you're invited for lunch."

Pops didn't get a chance to block any Swat team that morning, but he did get to hear me fielding a phone call from Michael, who made me explain the drug receptor biochip idea again. Then we played through the scenario with a diver bringing up coral scrapings for testing.

Over lunch, Pops lost no time putting in his two cents' worth. "It sounds like what you've got on your drug-sensing biochip is a miniaturized drug discovery institute!"

"Yes," I agreed, "that's what it will be after it's developed. I'm estimating that it will take ten years for someone to get one up and running. But — I'm sorry if I said this before — please don't talk to people about the idea. I have to keep it confidential for my client."

"I'll keep it under my hat," Pops promised. "But, boy, it'll really be something to see when you have it up and running." His enthusiasm was palpable. "Say you squish a drop of coral scrapings onto it and one of the spots on the chip lights up and tells you've got a better aspirin. What's your next step, then?"

"Get bigger samples of coral scrapings and start isolating the aspirin-like compound."

"Would you use a . . . HPLC machine for that, like you've got upstairs?"

"Exactly."

Pops would have made a good student. For the rest of the week he dropped in several times a day, keeping an eye on me, and picking up tidbits from the project when Michael called with technical questions. Michael's questions were becoming more reasonable. And since he offered no more objections to the points made in my executive summary, I was able to use it as a framework for organizing the three-foot stack of information.

And I heard and saw nothing of the DEA, which was just fine. But I did hear from Rebecca:

From: RLevis@tropmed.epi.bryanmed.edu
To: ben-candidi@netrus.net
Subj.: Love You

I am sorry for the long delay in answering you. We can't receive long letters and I can't write them. The satellite link is finicky. David had to try five times to download the packet with your message. So we can send each other our love with only seven lines. I'm working hard and learning a lot. The padre teaches only Christianity and the Indians are quite acculturated. It seems like nobody teaches them anything useful.

Love you. — R.

I printed it out and read it several times. I typed her a short message echoing her love and expressing enthusiasm for my consulting job.

Over the weekend, I did more of what I'd been doing in the evening: listening to jazz on public radio and reading about the Yanomama Indians. And I spent a lot of time mulling over the problem of how to make the drug receptor proteins glow when the test drugs bound to them. No, that would not be as easy as with the DNA chip.

Monday marked the start of my second week away from Rebecca. The week's first three days went by smoothly, with Pops keeping an eye on me and with Michael calling with questions about things like "genomic libraries" and "combinatorial libraries." I told him that the "libraries" are kept in test tubes. I explained that the genomic libraries will be a good source of drug-receptor proteins to go on the chip and that the combinatorial libraries of small molecules are what we want to test for candidate drugs. I followed up by faxing him a memo.

Pops was around on Wednesday when Michael called up with questions about the uses of synthetic chemistry. I told him how synthetic chemists saved a lot of trees from being cut down in the

Washington Pacific rain forest to extract from their bark the anti-cancer drug known as Taxol.

After I hung up, Pops said, "You know it's real interesting watching over your shoulder while you're playing this game."

He was so full of barnstorming enthusiasm that I had to smile.

"You know, Pops, maybe we should put on an Elderhostel right here. I'll be the instructor and you can be the demonstrator!"

Pop's face clouded over. "That's what I wanted to talk to you about, Ben."

"Yes?"

"I'm scheduled for one starting this Friday."

"That's right. Toronto. Have fun!"

"But I hate leaving you here to face the music with the DEA."

I laughed and told him why I thought it was all over. "So go, or your lady friends will be pining away for you. What's the Elderhostel in Toronto about, anyway? Playing the bagpipes?"

"Don't have the wind for that. But I'll be twirling the lassies and drinking Scotch whisky."

The next day, Thursday, Michael called to ask if you could get drugs from insects. I said, yes, and told him about the so-called defensive compounds secreted on small hairs of the pupal stage of the E. borealis beetle. They are macrocyclic polyamines that deliver a nasty sting to any predator that tries to eat them.

Friday was the day of Pops' departure. I rode with him to the airport then drove his car back. I learned that after the Elderhostel in Toronto, Pops was going to one in Monterey, California. He wouldn't be back for about three weeks. I promised to keep an eye on the *Alabama Tiger*.

When I got home, I received another e-mail from Rebecca:

From: RLevis@tropmed.epi.bryanmed.edu
To: ben-candidi@netrus.net
Subj.: Love You

Just a short note to say that I'm well and in love with you. I am learning so much here. There are so many important health problems that need simple solutions. An old Indian woman has to stay at the Mission because she is diabetic and her insulin has to be refrigerated. Maybe you could find a way to freeze-dry it so that we wouldn't need that silly old refrigerator that isn't working right anyway because we don't have electricity more than an hour a day.

Love — Rebecca.

I wrote back that I loved her and, yes, I would look into the question. I wrote that she could count on me as her partner for the rest of my life. I wrote that I could hardly wait through those 14 long days until she was back in my arms.

Through the weekend, I worked hard on the report — and almost forgot an important promise I'd made to Rebecca.

An Afternoon with Edith Pratt   8

It was the anthropology conference that Rebecca wanted me to attend. What saved me was a glance at my office calendar at a quarter after eight, Monday morning. I rushed up to Rebecca's study and found the notice: "Indigenous Peoples and Sustainable Development," a one-day conference at the Knight Center and starting in 45 minutes. In less than 10 minutes I was on the front porch, tossing the *Miami Standard* into the living room, setting the alarm and locking the door.

I picked up my black attaché case, now filled with library books and a couple of hastily made sandwiches, and set off on foot. Eight minutes later I was at the Culmer Station which sits, underutilized, above a stand of live oak. Seven minutes after that, I was getting off at the downtown Government Center Station. From there it was down one flight of steps to the Brickell Loop of the MetroMover whose rubber-tired robot train appeared promptly. It zig-zagged us around some old low-rise commercial buildings at roof level and to the Miami River. Then it climbed steeply to its next station built into the sixth floor of the Bank of America Tower, where I got off.

With 20 minutes before the conference start, I took a few seconds to admire the pleasure boats transiting the Intracoastal Waterway, the cruise liners along the distant docks of the Port of Miami and the sparkle of the morning sun on the Miami River below.

I took the escalators to the ground floor lobby and opted against the glass tunnel, taking instead the sidewalk to the pompously elevated, semi-circular "motor entrance" of the Hyatt Regency Hotel, passing through its elongated registration lobby and through its high atrium lounge to the Knight Center.

The Conference registration was two tables wide but very slow. The people in line seemed an equal mix of middle-aged academics, students and interested lay people. But the Conference had some international draw. One tall man who was ahead of me wore a three-button suit and, when he reached the front of the line, spoke stiffly with a Germanic accent. He paid cash from a flat, oversized, black patent leather change purse that seemed to contain more multi-colored "Euros" than American greenbacks.

It was two minutes before nine o'clock when I reached the front of the line and received a charm school smile from a primly dressed middle-aged redhead. But her smile disappeared when I gave her the letter confirming Rebecca's completed pre-registration and asked that the registration be transferred to me. Her answer was a categorical "no." And it didn't help matters when I pulled out my driver's license to prove that Rebecca and I shared the same address. For an embarrassing minute, it looked like we had reached an impasse: no transfer and no refund, either. My only option was to take a soft approach. I said, "I understand that rules are rules. Can I just pick up my wife's registration materials for her?"

The smile returned and she gave me a program booklet plus the badge that had been prepared for Rebecca. I thanked her and went to the literature table which was manned by a nice lady who didn't mind giving me a piece of adhesive tape. I pulled a sheet of white paper from my attaché case and snipped off a small piece, using the scissors attachment of my Swiss Army pocket knife. I flipped open the badge's clear plastic cover and made a minor modification. Now, I could attend the meeting as "Dr. R.   Levis".

Quickly, I leafed through the program book until I found Edith Pratt, the anthropologist that Rebecca wanted me to cover. The big rush had been for nothing: Pratt wasn't talking until late that afternoon. So I spent the morning attending small sessions on topics such as "The effects of deforestation on hunting and gathering among the Bataks of Indonesia." They managed to keep themselves fed, but had to work hard at it. And here in the conference, a free lunch wasn't part of the program, either. So, during the noontime break, I unpacked my sandwiches at the edge of the riverside café attached to the Knight Center and amused myself watching tugboats maneuvering freighters between the raised halves of the Brickell Avenue drawbridge.

After lunch, I did my own anthropological study, getting a close-range look at the muscular Tequesta Indian standing high on the 30-foot bronze column. His bow was drawn taut and his arrow was pointed high in the air and his back was turned to the Tequesta archeological site — a circular arrangement of post holes dug in the coral rock where the Miami River meets Biscayne Bay. I returned to the café, opened the briefcase and read from the library books about the Yanomama Indians.

I sat there reading long enough to miss a couple rounds of afternoon mini-sessions, but not long enough to miss Edith Pratt, who was the main event. In fact, while hanging around the lobby I got a good look at her. The program said she was a professor of anthropology at Johns Hopkins University with a secondary academic appointment with the "*Iphae,*" the Institute for Prehistory, Anthropology and Ecology at the Federal University of Rondônia. And the program said she was an expert on the Yanomama Indians. I wanted to introduce myself and tell her about what Rebecca was doing. But she wasn't inviting eye contact and was already surrounded by an impenetrable group of admirers. And beyond them, a man seemed to be running interference for her: a thin, bald-headed, moustachioed guy in a dark blue sport jacket and yellow polka-dot bow tie with matching handkerchief fluffed in his breast pocket. He was orbiting the group and giving me signals that no further accretion was desired.

Observing Prof. Pratt from a distance, it occurred to me that she was massive enough to attract an orbiting planetary system. She was well on the short side of six foot and was very much on the far side of 200 pounds. I guessed she was in her late forties. Her clothes advertised her field work: a short-sleeved, long-legged khaki outfit cut from cloth that was heavier than a factory work suit but lighter than a safari suit. She wore brown leather sandals which revealed large puffy feet and stubby toes. Her toenails were cut long and square. Her thin, strawberry blond hair was cut short and square. Hanging over her left shoulder and clutched under her arm was an enormous canvas bag that must have served as a combination purse and briefcase. With its long straps, it reminded me of those mail bags they used to hang out on a hook in front of the station for the express train to pick up without stopping. Her other arm hung at her side, but she sometimes raised and shook it vigorously to emphasize a point.

Her abundant subcutaneous fat would be good protection against starvation in the jungle. But if she ran out of Avon solution, the mosquitoes and flies would have a field day on that light, freckled skin.

I was too far away to pick up her conversation but was close enough to observe the cadence of the exchange. Professor Pratt answered her admirers' questions in short sentences, treating the questions and answers as matters of fact, and seeming to be oblivious to any social significance of the situation.

While I observed Edith Pratt, the bald-headed guy was eyeing me like I was trying to crash the party. Actually he was only semi-bald. He had a handful of carefully trimmed black hair on each side of his head. And he was wearing a smile — the type you see at elegant social functions. He would fit right in with one of those before-the-opera quizzes you can see on public TV. He was smiling at the instant the photographer caught him looking on at Pratt and her throng. Funny that he wasn't smiling afterward because I felt sure he would love to get his picture in the paper. Maybe this photographer wasn't with a newspaper.

Anyway, I decided to not add to Baldie's problems by moving in to give Prof. Pratt one of Rebecca's cards. I moved on and found a good seat for the main event. The cavernous auditorium was one-quarter full with about one thousand people, most of them college age. I guessed that local profs had dumped classes on the event to pump up attendance so that the student camera operators could shoot over a sea of heads. Their camera and sound station was about 20 rows back. But a professional camera crew was also there, loitering in the left aisle along the wall. And from the logo on their camera, I knew they were from Channel Eight, a non-affiliated station known for its "fast-breaking, hard-hitting" local news. Was this event going to have shock value?

From the talk in the seats around me, I learned that Channel Eight's Sanch Riquez would be covering the event. His real name was Sancho. But like many Cuban-Americans in public life, he opted an easy-to-pronounce nickname: "Sanch" (rhymes with ranch). And it's easy to remember if you imagine a ranch that raises bulls for the ring. Sanch is the personification of Channel Eight's approach to the ratings war — TV journalism with attitude. Wherever there was a drug bust or domestic violence, Sanch and his cameras were always the first on the scene, ready, willing and able to convince us, night after night, that we are living in the most dangerous, crime-ridden, cocaine-soaked city in the U.S. of A. And if the Swat team goes in for a wrong-house arrest, Sanch and his team will reedit the piece in a flash, bemoaning the official injustice towards the little guy.

Sanch Riquez is his name, and in-your-face TV journalism is his game. Miami, he's got you covered — editorially as well as reportorially. After a hard day out there stomping the bloody pavement, he returns to the studio and anchors the six o'clock news, interjecting free-wheeling comments that only a home-grown boy from Miami Beach High School could get away with.

The stage setup was a lectern and a table beside it with three microphones. Edith Pratt took a place on one side of the table, and a short man with a broad forehead took a place on the other side. Behind the table hung an enormous projection screen.

The lights dimmed and a bearded, bespectacled Prof. Erickson from Florida International University welcomed us to this session titled "Preservation and Development in Amazonia." He said that there was no better place to consider these questions than the Brazilian Province of Roraima, whose highland rain forest is inhabited by aboriginal Indians, known as the Yanomama, with vast mineral deposits below.

"We are lucky, today, to have two experts . . . opposing experts . . . on these problems. Professor Edith Pratt, an academic anthropologist will go first. She will be followed by General

Eduardo Sosa-Pereira who is now retired but was once responsible for security in the Province of Roraima."

Pratt rose and walked stiffly to the lectern. She grabbed the goose-necked microphone and pulled it down, then pushed it back up to about where it was in the first place. "May I have the first slide. For the next forty minutes we will be examining the subject which is the title of my presentation, 'Social Structure of Brazilian Indians and Economic Development of the Amazon Basin.' That is, if the sleeping projectionist doesn't rob me of my forty minutes."

About one-third of the audience laughed. More of us would have laughed if she hadn't delivered the line in a serious baritone. She reached into a flapped pocket, pulled out a ruby red laser pointer, and flashed it on the empty screen. "Well, at least something is working here," she said, returning to her normal pitch — contentious alto. "I brought it myself."

Pratt's second remark produced no laughter but did have the intended effect: The screen filled with a photo of a throng of Amazonian Indians.

"It is not just the oxygen-producing rain forest that I want to save. It is these people — a people who have a right to their culture and their way of life. We have no right to destroy their culture. Centuries ago, the coastal Indians fled past the waterfalls because the whites could not pursue them there. We had no right to chase them with swords, then. Just like we have no right to destroy them by destroying their habitat today. Just like we have no right to ignore their wisdom. It is at our own peril that we ignore their culture, their forest wisdom and their folk remedies. Not everything that is good is sold in a spray can. Things cannot be judged wrong just because they have been practiced for hundreds if not thousands of years by people who have never seen a spray can. We must abandon our industrial arrogance and . . . ."

And so it went, haranguing an audience that probably agreed with her main points already. I felt ready to help preserve the Brazilian Indians but I didn't want to be held responsible for what the Portuguese did in the 16th Century. And although I was mildly interested in how the Indians weaned their babies and made their food, I resented anyone who would tell me I *had* to be interested in it. Pratt wasn't just preaching to the choir. She was haranguing us with unsupported doctrine and presumptuous insults. And this altar boy sitting in the 10th row was getting fidgety.

"May I have the next slide?" The photo showed a large semi-circular thatched roof in a forest clearing. From both the distance and perspective, I could tell that it was taken from an airplane banked at a steep angle. The frame of the airplane's large, curving window was visible in the left corner. "This is a communal dwelling of a tribe of Yanomama Indians. The Yanomama have been living efficiently and sustainably in the rain forest ecosystem for thousands of years, as have all Indians. But the Government of Brazil has been very stupid in its policies towards Indians and their lands. For decades, now, they have pursued a self-injuring policy of encouraging settlers to slash and burn rain forest to make grazing land for cattle who are not adapted to that climate. And after two years the soil will be washed away. Or they have harvested trees to make charcoal for cooking which could be done just as easily with solar energy or to make pig-iron that they cannot sell competitively on the world market."

She went on to describe the gold miner invasion that tore up the streambeds, brought disease and malaria and contaminated the soil with mercury. As she talked on, I was reminded of Klaus-Dietrich, the German pilot who flew the "Berlin Air Lift" that transported the men and equipment that did this.

"May I have the next slide? . . . The *next slide*, I said! This slide shows how Brazilian policy almost extinguished the Yanomama about ten years ago."

The slide showed crates stacked high at the edge of a jungle airstrip.

"Armies of rowdies moved in with high-pressure pumps and earth-moving equipment, fouling the streambeds and rivers in search for minerals. Next slide! This is what I fought. Here you see nomadic prospectors or *garimpeiros*. This one is blasting away a streambed with a high-pressure hose. He has created stagnant pools that will breed malarial mosquitoes."

As Prof. Pratt showed slide after slide of *garimpiero* atrocities, the Channel Eight cameraman stalked her in a crouching walk. He seemed particularly fascinated by her use of the red laser pointer as she described death by the *Falciparum plasmodia* brand of malaria which turns your urine red, then black, and then dries it up altogether.

Pratt said that international outcry forced the governments of Brazil and Venezeuela to set aside "Yanomama-Land" as a nature preserves. She said that the Yanomama are forming a loose federation of tribes to prevent the destruction of their land and way of life but that this is not easy because there are four dialects of Yanomami and travel is difficult. As she began talking on a more constructive note, the audience began to warm to her. It was interesting to hear her description of all the foods that could be produced in the forest. She received a lot of applause at the end of her talk.

Next, the moderator introduced Gen. Eduardo Sosa-Pereira. He said that the General took pride in being a member of an influential family that can trace its history in Brazil to the colonial period. He listed the General's educational pedigree which included a stint at the U.S. Army War College.

Gen. Sosa-Pereira moved the microphone a couple inches lower than Prof. Pratt had left it. He did it gracefully. He was no Mexican General with a puffed-up chest full of metals. He wore a business suit of conservative cut that harmonized his short arms and legs with his egg-shaped body. His elegantly combed, straight black hair was yielding to gray. His face looked more European than Latin American. Yes, I could believe that his family had not diluted its Iberian blood over all those centuries.

"I thank you so much, Dr. Erickson, and I thank your institution, the Florida International University for the chance to speak at this academic conference and to tell your learned audience about things for which I have devoted my life."

Gen. Eduardo Sosa-Pereira spoke smoothly, with enough Portuguese accent to be charming yet fully intelligible.

"I am especially thankful to you, learned colleague, for your kind mention of my education. I hold dearly to scholarship. And those of us who are devoted to scholarship know that it must stand firmly on the solid rock of correct specification, just as a civilized country must stand on its constitution and laws. What my esteemed colleague, Professor Pratt, a much learned doctor of anthropology, has described as 'Yanomama-Land' is actually the western part of the Brazilian State of Roraima as well as the southern part of Venzeuela."

He reminded us Venezeula and Brazil were sovereign countries whose borders must be respected.

"Twelve years ago, our armed forces expelled the *garimpeiros*. And our armed forces did a good job of keeping the area free of renegades ever since."

After the Channel Eight camera had locked onto him, the General began speaking with greater forcefulness. I looked around and saw that he had the full attention of most of the people in the hall.

"Please permit me, now, to put the problems in perspective. I was commander of the armed forces of the Brazilian Amazon, headquartered in Manaus. I was responsible for the security of almost four million square kilometers. For this I was given a force of 15,000 men. Our mission was to support the settlement of the Amazon — which is actually six different economic regions — to enable our country to develop to its full potential. This is not a new process. It started in the 16th Century. Our mission is to provide what you North Americans call 'infrastructure' . . . an infrastructure of security and to facilitate transportation . . . the security of waterways and the building of roads so that education and health care can follow. Although it is not our mission, we *do* help the Indians."

The General quoted some politician from an earlier century who said that Brazilians could not continue to live like crabs on the edge of the sea. They must move inland and occupy their land. And thus it had been government policy to encourage the poor to move from the coastal cities to the interior.

"Each zone has a specialty. In Roraima it will be minerals."

Pratt shook her head and made a dismissive gesture of the hand. Groans issued from the audience. The general noticed. "The specialties of the regions are not dictated by . . . *generals* . . . and not even by bureaucrats in Brasília, our capital city. The specialties of the zones are dictated by the geography of the land. In zones where the ground is covered with water, it might be fish farming or even rain forest preservation. In Roraima, which is also rain forest but where the ground is high and geological strata are exposed, the soil is poor because it is washed away by the rains. There the work destined for our people will be the extraction of minerals — titanium, tin, molybdenum, silver, gold, and perhaps even diamonds."

More groans from the audience. The general looked up from his notes and gazed across the auditorium.

"I know that what I say may sound unfashionable. But a people can not live on fashionable opinions. And in poor countries, fashionable opinions do not put food on the table. So I will ask you some unfashionable questions. Yes, it is fashionable to worry about the Indian. But why is it not fashionable to worry about the poor *caboclo* — the poor man who subsists by planting manioc in his garden and catching fish?"

The General was now speaking freely, with passion, looking directly into the audience.

"Who is worrying about helping this man and poor woman . . . to give them hope to educate their children and see something besides misery? Why are we not having a conference on helping them?"

He thumped a fist against his chest and the microphone picked it up.

"There are millions of people living in the Brazilian interior that no one worries about. Why is it so fashionable to worry only about Brazil's 200,000 Indians? If we give them any more of the undeveloped land, they will become the biggest landowners. And for what purpose?"

He scanned the audience as if seeking an answer.

"It is fashionable to say that only the Indian lives in harmony with nature — that their life is poetic. From my education, I believe this idea was started by Rousseau. But Rousseau did not live on the hot banks of rivers around the equator. Rousseau lived in French palaces. Well, my wife and I know something about poetry because we both write it. Her poetry is much better than mine."

The General acknowledged the crowd's laughter with a shake of the head and a shy smile.

"But I think that everyone will agree that poetry can exist only if there is food on the table. Poetry should not exist in the minds of North Americans to curse the fate of the children of the working people of Brazil. Maybe I do not understand all the rules of poetry but I understand the rules of human nature. The Indian does not live on poetry. He lives on birds that he can shoot with his arrows and by the fruit he can climb for in trees. Once he has eaten pork from a can, he is no longer satisfied with the meat of birds and monkeys. Once he has drunk Coca Cola, he is dissatisfied with squeezing juice from fruits. Once he has seen American television

— once he has seen 'Bay Watch' — he is no longer satisfied with his own life."

"Or his own wife!" someone called out from a back row. The audience burst into laughter. Even the moderator laughed. The General laughed, too. I laughed, too — at the thought of an Indian getting hopped up by TV images of Spandex-packaged, California-brand mammary perfection but ignoring two elongated, conical, fleshy examples of the real thing that were dangling in front of his face.

But Prof. Pratt did not laugh. She was trying very hard to look stern.

The moderator caught the General's eye and signaled that time was running out. The General shuffled his notes and continued, speaking rapidly. "The Indian doesn't have medicines and he cannot produce them."

Pratt cleared her throat and shook her head vigorously. For a second, it looked like she was going to speak into her microphone to contradict him. Then she nodded to someone in one of the front rows and leaned back in her chair.

"The Indian doesn't have culture," the General continued. "He is dependent on the groups that support him with food and medicine — church missions, the military and Brazilian colonists like *garimpeiros*."

The Channel Eight camera was moving in close, now.

"Indians will always be attracted to concentrations of wealth, knowledge, equipment and power. This is simply human nature. And there is no force on earth that can stop this."

The moderator pointed to his watch. The General acknowledged with a raised finger.

"What are we to do if we cannot use the wealth locked in that ground to help give them a better life? Can we finance a modern way of life for the Indians by giving them special license to have gambling which the others cannot do. Will tourists flock to their reservations to play bingo like they do here, on the edge of your Everglades? No, I think not. I think that would be shameful . . . I thank you for letting me share with you my experience."

The General bowed his head and received moderate applause which continued until he had taken his seat.

The moderator thanked the General and announced that the panelists would be allowed to ask a question of the other.

Edith Pratt tapped her microphone a split second later. "Although I was very distressed by the unkind things you said of the Indians, I was even more distressed by the *kind* things you said about the miners."

She left it at that.

The General waited a long time before realizing there wouldn't be a question. "After the decisions were made under civilian authority, we mobilized and expelled the *garimpeiros* from Roraima. But to address your question in greater scope — in scope of all Brazil — mining is an important part of the Brazilian economy. There are a million people . . . true entrepreneurs . . . working in *garimpagem*. Every year, they extract over two billion dollars worth of gold. They provide employment for a further five million people. Now it is my turn to ask you a question: Where else are we to earn the money to buy American diesel engines to provide electricity for the villages? Where are we to earn the money to buy Japanese outboard motors to put on the Indians' dugout canoes? Let me ask you, Dr. Pratt, how will you feed the people of Brazil?"

Pratt finessed the question by talking for a long time about feeding people through silvaculture — producing foodstuffs in the forest. But the audience grew restless as it became clear that she wouldn't discuss the economic viability of silvaculture. And the more she spoke, the more frustrated she looked. And that was when I noticed her semi-bald friend sitting in the second row. His face bore a pained expression. And he was sitting on the edge of his chair like he was worried that she might say something stupid.

I heard low rumblings from outside the building and noticed that the air felt cooler and more humid. I guessed that a thunderstorm was rolling in.

The moderator said that the discussion was now open to the audience. He urged us to line up and use the microphone standing in the center aisle. A lot of students took this as a signal that class was dismissed.

A middle-aged academic wearing a gray jacket and matching pleated skirt asked Pratt why she had not identified the location of the Yanomama tribe described in her several articles.

The question made Edith Pratt frown. Baldie, too. "I will not reveal this information at this time for the sake of the integrity of their endeavor."

A community college student asked how it would be possible to "stop progress." He received a blunt answer from Prof. Pratt.

Then a tweedy professor made an extended comment about "the economic benefit of silvaculture versus plantations and the lessons taught by the rubber economy." But we didn't get to hear if there was a question and how the Professor and the General would have answered it: Sanch Riquez had moved along the first row until he was standing in front of them. Sure, the stage was elevated, but Riquez' broad shoulders were impossible to ignore. And in the second row, the Channel Eight camera was lining up to put Riquez, the Professor and the General in a high-perspective shot.

Shoot 9

The excitement of TV news in the making silenced the room.

"Professor and General, Channel Eight News has a few questions if you don't mind," Sanch Riquez said.

The moderator took this as an invitation to get out of the way. The General, obviously no stranger to TV, presented his proud face to the camera. And Prof. Pratt acknowledged the TV journalist with a nod of the head and said, "Shoot!"

"We are shooting already," Sanch Riquez said without missing a beat. Then he made a quarter turn towards the audience and camera, waiting out their laughter and Pratt's embarrassed reaction, thus creating several seconds of useful lead-in footage that he could voice over back at the studio.

It would be a good profile shot of his big head with his black, wavy but square-cut hair framing his big forehead. His broad jaw was set defiantly.

"Now, Professor Pratt, we have both heard General Sosa-Pereira speak very eloquently about the development of a million square miles of Brazilian land and what I hear you saying is that it should be *saved* for the Indians, even though they are only a small part of the population of Brazil. Can you tell the Channel Eight viewers why you think it is important to reserve all that land for the Indians?"

I had to admit that he was good at what he did. It was a "hard-hitting" question delivered in a throaty voice and without a trace of Spanish accent, unless you count a slight lengthening of the "long O's" in "Professor" and "even though."

"Regarding the Yanomama Indians, I believe they are the natural custodians of their region of the Brazilian rain forest until more capable custodians emerge." Pratt clipped it off there. I guess she knew all about sound bites.

Sanch Riquez said, "When Columbus came to the Caribbean Islands, he brought in Spanish culture. And back then nobody was talking about saving it for a bunch of ignorant people living in the stone age. Wouldn't you agree that it is bad enough for history to have one ignorant peasant running an important part of Latin America now?" His derogatory reference to Fidel Castro brought several derisive whistles and some applause.

Yes, I could imagine Sanch scoring a lot of points with his viewers, tonight — middle-class Cuban-Americans whose parents had lost their shops to Castro — and Old Florida individualists who are quick to shun any form of "political correctness" prescribed by university professors.

Pratt flushed pink. And she was so flustered that she overlooked the anti-Castro angle.

"The *peasants*, as you call them, are not as ignorant as you think. European people received a lot of useful knowledge and inventions from the Indians. Medicine, like curare. And agricultural inventions like yams and corn."

Riquez ignored this.

"The General has also talked about the burden of educating the Indians and the other poor people living in the Amazon. But listening to your presentation, it sounded like you think they have enough education already." He had now fallen into Spanish rhythm but was still forming his sounds from the back of his mouth, with a lot of echo.

Dr. Pratt was regaining her composure and was now staring at Riquez like a worthy adversary. "When industrialized society makes contact with a hunting and gathering society, it usually crushes it under deadening pressure. But if industrialized society thinks it is smarter, then it should be able to find ways to make contact without destroying the indigenous society. I think that with proper introduction and education, it should be possible for the hunting and gathering society to skip the industrialization phase and go directly to a technological and intrinsically integrated society which may be superior to ours."

The hall fell silent, probably out of embarrassment for Prof. Pratt's overblown and clearly impossible statement. How the hell did she think that hunters and gatherers could skip over the Industrial Revolution and come out more advanced than the rest of us?

Baldie was sitting on the edge of his chair like he wanted to jump up and turn off the camera.

Sanch Riquez shook his head. "I am sorry, Professor, but are you saying that they are going to get an education by sitting in their thatch huts watching satellite television?"

"Not if they choose to watch your Channel Eight, which offers nothing better than teenage comedy and newscasts of the latest shooting in Hialeah."

Wow, did Edith Pratt score a big laugh with that one! And I laughed along, too. But she spoiled it by continuing with a strident recitation of the educational television programs that did have value. And she didn't pay the least bit of attention to the moderator when he returned to the table to announce that the session was over. In fact, she kept on answering Riquez even after he turned his back and dismissed the camera crew. What an attitude! She seemed to hold an irrefutable belief that only she was serving a higher purpose — a purpose so lofty that she didn't have to justify it to the rest of us.

As the hall emptied, a handful of admirers clustered around her. I debated about going up and trying to give her one of Rebecca's cards. But the decision was made for me when Baldie stepped in again to manage her. So I followed the crowd out of the auditorium, across the atrium and into the hotel lobby which was jammed because it was raining hard outside.

I worked my way to the circular motor entrance and watched the storm from under the tall canvas awning. The clouds were black and low, and the wind drove curtains of rain towards us at a

45-degree angle, soaking a black limo and a black BMW that were parked in the "valet only" zone by the edge of the overhang. Yes, a motor entrance is not a motor entrance unless it is jammed with expensive cars and valets to admire them. But the valets were shivering in their shorts and the hotel guests were more interested in finding a yellow taxicab than admiring jet black automotive grace. And the two cars weren't that easy to see anyway because the recessed lights in the overhang failed to turn on.

With a half-dozen people, I hung around watching the wind blow the rain. I occupied several minutes with speculation on two things: Who was paying these several Little Havana high school dropout types to stand here with their "No Castro, No Problem" placards? And why were those two nuts in the Beemer sitting there with the front passenger-side window open and with the motor running? They were Latin types and were dressed like playboys. Did they think we were going to admire them through the open window?

My question about the placards was answered when Sanch Riquez' crew came out, with the camera shouldered and its lights powered up. Edith Pratt was coming out, too. Maybe now was the time to approach her. I found Rebecca's card and walked toward the automatic glass doors just as Pratt walked through them. She had a couple of female admirers in tow, with Baldie bringing up the rear. While walking up to her, I noticed a red flash from the Beemer. Probably from a gimmicky cellphone.

"Dr. Pratt, I enjoyed your presentation and just wanted to introduce myself and — "

I stopped talking, distracted by a red flash in her red hair. And my heart stopped when a small red dot jumped onto her forehead and danced there, shimmering like a back-lit ruby — like a spot from a laser! It must have been a reflex. I couldn't have thought that fast. I swung my briefcase high to catch the dot. An instant later, my briefcase jerked back as if pulled by a magnet. It hit her in the face. But the swish and the thud told me it was not magnetism at work. And my legs followed as I threw myself into Pratt, trying to push her back into the crowd and bracing myself for what was to come.

But a second bullet did not come as we tumbled on the wet sandstone. Instead, I heard a squeal of tires and shouted protests of the people around us. The Channel Eight spotlights followed us down. And before I could turn in the Beemer's direction, it was gone.

"Stop that car! It — ."

But I never got to finish the sentence. A heavy guy threw himself down on me. He knocked the wind out of me. Another guy twisted my arm behind my back. "Don't resist and you won't get hurt," the arm-twister said.

"They fired at her," I gasped. "With a silencer. With a laser sight."

But nobody was listening to me. They were all listening to Edith Pratt who was screaming that I was crazy, that her back was hurt and could someone help her up. With my face pressed to the pavement, I was kept busy finagling my next breath.

The black leather, round-toed, rubber-soled shoes walking up to my face identified the guy faster than his first words. "Hotel Security. We're taking you into custody."

"No. I'm a Good Samaritan. Those BMW guys shot at her and I stopped the bullet . . . with my briefcase."

He grabbed one of my arms and I heard a click. "Sure, and we'll — ."

"If you handcuff me in front of this crowd, I'll have my lawyer sue you for ten thousand dollars." It was hard to argue with my face to the ground. "And get that damn TV camera off of me."

"Camera off!" The voice issuing the command sounded a lot older. I got a better look at him when they lifted me to my feet. He had the same type of shoes and he wore a fire-engine-red blazer over loosely knit black slacks. The camera lights went off. He walked up to me. "Come with me."

"Yes, I'll go with you. I'll go with you to where we can talk. I'll go when you get that cuff off of me. I'll go under my own steam. And if you so much as touch me, I'll sue you for assault and slander and —"

"Yeah, yeah, yeah, yeah! Take if off, Joe."

Joe released the cuff but didn't let go of my left arm. I didn't give him a glance. I kept focused on the guy in charge. "I'm Dr. Benjamin Candidi. I want back my briefcase. It is evidence of the shooting."

"Get it, Joe."

Joe released me. So did the guys who had jumped on me and held me down. One was a doorman. I brushed myself off. Edith Pratt had her sights fixed on me. She was half sitting with an admirer propping up her back. "You insolent young hothead, you!"

"I just saved your life. They fired at you with a gun with a silencer and laser sight. My briefcase stopped the bullet." She just sat there sputtering. I yelled out to the crowd. "I want the police here. And if any one of you saw the two guys in that black BMW or got its license number, identify yourself to these redcoats. The police will take your formal statements when they come."

Funny, how my words were having just the opposite effect on people — making them creep away. Joe came back with my briefcase and handed it to me. He wore a red jacket and a law enforcement style moustache. My briefcase was punctured and scuffed. The paunch-faced older redcoat collected me up with tired eyes and indicated that I should follow him into the hotel. I walked with him, past the long wood-paneled reception desk, past the atrium restaurant and through an unmarked door which led to a large room filled with monitors.

"You'll need to get the motor entrance surveillance tape out of there and get the license of the black BMW," I said.

"We're already doing that," he said, motioning me into his office. It had a moderate-sized desk and two visitor chairs. I laid my briefcase on his desk with the hole facing up.

"While we're waiting for the police, I think your assistant, Joe, should be asking people about the BMW."

"He's already doing that. Probably'll get the most outa the valet people." His face looked as battered as an old catcher's mitt . . . and it had as much expression. He was sizing me up with slow eyes.

I pointed to the center of the lid of my briefcase. The puncture was perfectly round and just big enough to stick my index finger into. "The bullet went in here."

"Yeah, but let's not open it up until the police come." He pulled a walkie-talkie from the right waist pocket of his jacket and squeezed down. "Joe, advise MPD to send a detective."

Joe acknowledged in a high nasal accompanied by squawks and clicks. Mitt-face just sat there, behind his desk, regarding me with tired eyes. It was time to let him know I wasn't just anyone off the street.

"Dr. Benjamin Candidi, formerly with the Miami-Dade County Medical Examiner's Office." I pulled a card from my breast pocket and presented it with a flourish.

Mitt-Face studied it for a second and then raised his eyebrows, giving me the silent treatment. I began to get madder by the second, and it was a good thing that he finally spoke when he did. "Rebecca Levis, M.D.," he read. Damn, I'd given him Rebecca's card by mistake. He grinned. "Well, this card fits with something — with the registration badge that fell off of you."

He flipped the badge towards me across the desk. There it was, the work of my own hand: "Dr. R.   Levis".

"Sorry. Wrong card." I fumbled in my breast pocket for the right one. "Here."

"But still, the wrong badge."

"She asked me to cover the conference for her, and they wouldn't transfer the registration."

"Is she here?"

This was starting to feel like a police interrogation. "No, Dr. Levis is doing field work in Brazil. That's why she asked me cover the conference for her." I flipped him my Florida driver's license, the same way he'd flipped the badge at me. "You're a retired police officer, right?"

He proved to me that a catcher's mitt can smile. "Dennis Hildreth, retired from the Tampa P.D. after thirty years."

He offered his hand and I shook it. Then he handed me back my driver's license.

"Nice city, Tampa," I said, "But I bet you didn't grow up there." He seemed to be in his late fifties and sounded Midwestern.

"Indianapolis, Indiana. I'm a Hoosier."

I'd only flown over Indianapolis, but this guy could use a little buttering up. "Nice state. Nice town. Hear they play a lot of good basketball there. And of course everybody loves the Indy Five Hundred."

After that, Security Chief Hildreth and I started to get along fine. He asked me to sit down, which I did. After a few more minutes of talk, we understood each other well. He understood that I wanted to protect my reputation and be sure that ball-breaking Professor Pratt understood that I'd done her the ultimate favor. And I understood that he wanted to save the hotel possible legal problems involving one body pushed to the ground and another one held down by force.

We were getting along with each other splendidly by the time Det. Sgt. Morales of the Miami P.D. showed up. Morales would have made a good TV cop. He was middle-aged, in good physical condition and seemed intelligent and well-trained. I gave him my formal statement of the events. I ended by asking if we could open the briefcase.

"Yeah, go ahead," Morales said. "Open it."

The bullet went through my yellow pad of notes, through two books and made a dent in Napoleon Chagnon's *Yanomamö: The Fierce People*.

Morales slipped on a latex glove and pulled out the bullet, and inspected it before putting it into an evidence bag. "It's a forty-five." He pulled out a short flexible ruler and measured the thickness of the pad plus books. "And the caliber and penetration are consistent with the impact you both reported for the briefcase. But what knocked Professor Pratt down, Dr. Candidi?"

"The force of my body. I was trying to diminish our target size and get us away from that car as fast as possible."

"And you swear that your briefcase and your books were not damaged when you came to the conference." He looked at me suspiciously.

"I swear," I said, with a swearing-in gesture.

"Well, from what you describe, the shot would be consistent with an H&K Mark 23 pistol. It has a laser designator built in below, at trigger level. It shoots forty-fives. Did you see a silencer? Did it have holes or rings around it?"

"I didn't see the gun. I just saw a ruby red flash from inside the car before I got to Professor Pratt. I first thought it was some kind of adult toy, like a cellphone that flashes colors when you talk. When I saw the same ruby red glow on Professor Pratt's forehead I first thought they were playing laser tag. And my next thought was that it was a gun sight. The next instant I swung up my briefcase to head level and became a hero. Does she know that I'm a hero?"

Det. Sgt. Morales was following me pretty well until I asked about being a hero. Now he was eyeing me suspiciously. "We will report the facts to her. Can you demonstrate how you swung the briefcase."

I told him yes, but suggested that we first record the positions of the books and measure the angles of the bullet holes. We did that with the help of a pencil and an old protractor that was kicking around in my briefcase. Visual documentation was by Polaroid, courtesy of Hyatt Regency Hotel Security. Then I demonstrated the swing of the briefcase. Morales nodded like it all checked out.

Security Officer Joe poked his head in the door and told us they had gotten the tapes lined up. We moved to the next room and watched the monitor. Playback from a high-mounted black-and-white camera showed an underexposed version of me walking slowly and then quickly into a collision course with Edith Pratt. The collision took place within a small area lit up by the TV camera. My briefcase swung up swiftly and smoothly. When it reached the top of its arc, it jumped backwards into her face, and an instant later I was pushing her back like an offensive lineman in a football game. I asked them to play it again, slowly. "See how it jumps out of my hands. I couldn't have done that myself. The thing's got a flexible handle."

They answered me with half-hearted agreement.

The tape from the second camera was so underexposed that we could barely see the black BMW, to say nothing of getting its license plate. But we did see it driving away and everyone agreed it was a jackrabbit start. I asked them to play it over again. "A faint white line will appear rapidly, from here to here. There it is! That's the laser beam scattered by the water droplets in the air."

This proved to be too scientific for them, but they did agree that a comparison of the time-date imprints showed that the BMW took off an instant after my briefcase flew into Pratt's face. Now it was my turn to stare them down.

Det. Morales was the first to respond. "Dr. Candidi, there is no question that what you have told us and shown us is consistent with a shot being fired from that car."

"Thank you. And will that be reflected in your police report?"

"Goes without saying."

I turned to Joe. "And did you question your valet people on the guys in the BMW?"

"They didn't get a look at them. What did you see?"

I guess it's only human to harbor a bit of resentment against the guy who had slipped a handcuff on you. I came down on him pretty hard. "You sure you asked them right?" I asked.

"Yes."

"You mean someone parks a car in their area and they didn't go up and offer to park the car? They didn't tell the guy he couldn't park there? Didn't try to hustle him for a five-dollar bribe? Hey, am I out of date on this hotel entrance and valet parking thing? Have they cleaned up their act or what?"

Security Chief Hildreth looked at his assistant, Joe. I looked at Joe, too. Hildreth shrugged and said, "I'll question them myself."

"Great," I said. "And will your report also reflect what I've told you and shown you?"

"Yes," he said, sounding reluctant.

"Then all we need to put this matter to rest is an apology for the knock-down and the handcuff bit."

Joe looked to Hildreth who had been listening to our conversation like a risk management expert. Hildreth nodded. Joe turned to me like he was ready to extend his hand. "I do apologize. And I hope you realize that in the heat . . . I mean, in the . . ."

"In the rush of the moment," I said.

"Yes, that in the rush of the moment it was . . ."

He looked to Hildreth who also seemed at a loss for words.

"Was not inappropriate," I added.

"Yes, that it was not inappropriate in the rush of the moment."

"Yes, I agree with that. You saw what you saw and you were trying to do your job. And you can quote me on that, too, in your report."

Everyone seemed to exhale at the same moment. The mood in the room lightened. I smiled and said, "Well I guess all we need now is for someone to invite Professor Pratt in here to say these words, too."

Joe frowned. "She left in a cab, half an hour ago."

"What?"

"But she did say she wouldn't press charges against you."

"Well that was very magnanimous of her! You have any idea where she went?"

"Probably to the airport."

I shot a glance at Sgt. Morales and Security Chief Hildreth. "Well, I think that each of you has your separate responsibility to set her straight. She needs to know that two guys waited outside and fired a bullet at her. It's a matter for both the law and for risk management of the hotel." I turned to Joe. "You might talk to that semi-bald guy in his late fifties who seemed to be playing social secretary to her. Did you get his name?"

"I know who you mean. Talked to him briefly but didn't get his name."

Morales asked, "How do you know about Professor Pratt and this man."

"I'd been observing her for over an hour," I said. This seemed to perplex Morales. "She was the main speaker at the conference," I added.

"What did the two guys in the car look like?" Sgt. Morales asked.

"Dark haired, Latin American, between twenty-five and thirty-five."

"Hispanic?"

"Yes, but probably not from Spain or Portugal. Wearing suits or sports jackets. Dark."

"What were they doing?"

"Before? They were sitting in their car. I thought they were just trying to act cool."

Morales wrinkled his forehead. "What's that mean?"

"That's my interpretation of their attitude. Like they had a right to be there. Like the expensive car gave them that right. You might look into recent BMW rentals and thefts."

"Were they doing anything that would call attention to themselves?"

"Good point. No. No loud radio. No rocking to the beat. For the whole ten minutes they seemed to be talking to each other, but mostly looking out the front passenger-side window like they were expecting someone — as it turned out they were."

"Why were you standing there, watching them for ten minutes?"

"I was waiting for a break in the rain. I wasn't watching them all the time."

Nobody had anything to say for a while, so I got up and put my briefcase together. "Well, glad to have been of help to all of you. You have my address to send the reports. And give Professor

Pratt my regards." I was probably a little too theatrical. I brushed myself off.

Chief Hildreth got the last word. "Dr. Candidi, the hotel has connections with a good tailor and dry-cleaning shop. If you would leave us your jacket, we would be pleased to . . ." He let the words dangle.

I accepted. Some dirt was ground in. And the fabric was scuffed and stretched around the left shoulder. I took off the jacket and left it with him.

Outside, the rain had disappeared. While waiting on the MetroMover platform, I placed a cellphone call to Alice McRae at her office at the *Miami Standard*. She wasn't there, but I gave her voice mail a full description of what had happened, saying she could use the story but not to identify me, please. Having known her for a long time as a fellow Mensan, I had a standing promise to let her know when I came across something newsworthy.

I got home about a quarter before eight. That left just enough time to heat up some food before turning on the TV and VCR for the Channel Eight's "News at Eight."

What a delight to have Sanch Riquez talking at me from his anchor desk, bigger than life, while I ate dinner. He put on the story right after a commercial, at the tail end of the broadcast:

"After speaking at a Miami conference on 'Indigenous People and Economic Development,' Baltimore anthropologist Edith Pratt found that controversy over her theories spilled out to the sidewalk in front of the Knight Center" — the picture switched from Riquez to video footage of Pratt with a sideways shot of me closing in on her at the motor entrance — "when a member of the conference raised his briefcase in protest, hitting her face."

The screen showed me raising my briefcase, which suddenly jumped back one-half a foot to her face.

"Dr. Pratt was rushed from the scene by an unnamed colleague, and her assailant was taken aside by Miami police officers for evaluation. Channel Eight investigation found that the assailant was registered for the conference under a false name."

The camera returned to Sanch Riquez, in studio. They cut to a wider shot. The attractive co-anchor turned her head and said, "And Sanch, you attended that meeting. Were her theories *that* controversial?"

"And, how! She was critical of the Brazilian development efforts and said that the rain forest dwellers of South America should be able to skip centuries of civilization and get a standard of living higher than ours. Tune in at eleven-thirty after the movie for the full details."

Then came a brass fanfare. The Channel Eight logo swept in front of the news people and expanded to fill the screen.

I hit the power button to kill the TV. Then I programmed the VCR to record the 11:30 broadcast. I wasn't really recognizable on the screen and I wouldn't get rich suing Channel Eight for libel.

I decided to go to bed early that night. I took along a couple of undamaged library books to read myself asleep. Alice didn't call but someone else did: a woman asking to speak with "Dr. Robert Levis." When I told her there was no such person here, she said, "Then Dr. Roger Levis." She got flustered and hung up. I went downstairs consulted my caller I.D. It was a local call.

I couldn't go to sleep. At 11:30 I went downstairs to see Sanch's encore. The promised follow-up story didn't make the air. It was bumped by exciting news stories about "a hostage situation in Hialeah" and "the dramatic ending of an eighteen-mile police pursuit recorded live by our Channel Eight helicopter."

For me, all the suspense was played out but still it was hard to get to sleep. As a sleeping pill, I internalized 20 pages of Napoleon Chagnon's Yanomama field studies and two ounces of gin. The gin was a mistake: I should have held myself fit for the next morning.

Brazilian Bicyclist   10

The *Miami Standard* didn't contain any surprises for me the next morning when it was thrown up on my porch. There was nothing about Edith Pratt and me. But I did find a surprise on my porch around ten-thirty that morning. She came on bicycle. Out of uniform, she was twice as good-looking as before. Her white shorts fit loosely around her well-proportioned thighs and tightly around her flat stomach. Her white, short-sleeved blouse bared about three inches of tummy, highlighting the pleasant olive hue of her skin and accentuating her hour-glass figure. Knotted snugly below the ribs, the blouse anchored and cradled her ample topside assets in a gorgeous "V." There she stood, framed in my screen door, bouncy in her low-cut tennis shoes. She seemed ready for any type of physical activity. And although she couldn't have seen me through the screen, she was smiling at me anyway. What a coy smile.

"Nica! Welcome," I said, stepping up and unlatching the screen.

She held my card in her left hand. "I just flew in last night and went for a ride today and . . ." Her smile dissolved into embarrassment as I opened the door.

"And I gave you my card and you wanted to know how *propolis* works," I rejoined. "It works fine."

A couple of steps inside the room, she turned to face me. "Well, I'm glad. I told you how it keeps me going in those stuffy airplanes."

"Yes, and it helped me last night after a stuffy conference." She searched my face for a several seconds. "A stuffy conference that I attended for my fiancée, I should add."

Her face relaxed. I gestured for her to take a chair. She said, "Well, I decided this morning would be a good time for a nice long bicycle ride along the Miami River and . . ."

"And you remembered my telling you I lived on the River and you brought my card along and . . . now I can tell you what I turned up on with my literature search on *propolis*." Why was I finishing her sentences for her? Why was I talking so loudly?

"Yes," she said shyly. "Tell me what you found."

Although Nica didn't look the least bit overheated from the bicycle ride, I clicked the controller of the ceiling fan up one notch. I motioned her to sit in the nearest rattan chair and seated myself in the other, about three feet away. Boy, did her legs look nice. "I found over five hundred scientific papers on propolis. It contains polyphenols and flavonoids that kill bacteria. I'm glad you use it as an over-the-counter drug in Brazil. Saves you buying chemical antiseptics from us. In fact, it might be better. Didn't see too many articles on controlled clinical tests but — I'll tell you what — I'll do some more anecdotal self-experiments with the bottle you gave me. It's sitting in the medicine cabinet upstairs."

I didn't have to point to the stairs because she was already looking up the stairway. In fact, she had looked over my whole setup while I was talking. And now she was beaming enthusiasm but saying nothing. Come on, Ben, I said to myself, isn't it possible for you to converse with her like a normal person?

Then the phone rang. I should have let the answering machine handle it. Bad decision, but Nica had put me off balance.

"Excuse me for a minute."

"Sure."

I picked up the receiver. "This is Dr. Candidi."

"Hello. This is Michael. I have something important to discuss."

"Michael, can I call you back? I'm . . . in the middle of something right now."

"I'm sorry. We must talk now. We have had a big setback with the client, and we are in danger of losing the contract."

I covered the transmitter with my hand. "Nica, I have to take this call. Maybe you should lock your bicycle." She nodded her agreement. When she was out the door I continued with Michael. "In danger of losing what?"

"In danger of losing the contract."

"Why?"

"Because one of their high level chemists took issue with your statement about proteins and polypeptides as drugs."

"Michael, with rare exceptions, my statement is true. Maybe if I could talk to the guy."

"That won't be possible. All I know is that he disagrees strongly. And he is their chief biochemist. He is also an expert on recombinant DNA and genetically engineered proteins."

"— who probably doesn't know a damn thing about non-protein natural products, which make up ninety-eight percent of all drugs."

"He didn't buy your 'small, sturdy molecule' argument," Michael said.

"Well, he's wrong. Wrong, wrong, wrong!"

"He knows all about the DNA chip," Michael insisted.

"Yeah, he's probably rooting for the DNA chip because a lot of people getting into it, nowadays. It's a diagnostic device, not a drug discovery tool. He probably does his thinking with fuzzy logic and plans on riding that damn thing into the sunset. All he's probably thinking about is ten quiet years before he retires!"

Nica returned towards the end of my outburst.

"That is not completely true," Michael said.

"Give me his name and phone number and I'll call him."

"No, that won't be possible. We have to go through channels."

"Then can I at least know how this guy thinks he has refuted me?"

Nica was listening with half an ear, like I was talking to the chief mechanic about how to repair my car and the conversation would be over in a couple of minutes.

"He said that . . ." Michael paused to read notes, "that erythromycin A and cyclosporin A are *peptide* drugs and that they *can* be taken orally."

Now Nica was sauntering around my office in an admiring mood, like she was visiting an art museum.

"He is right that they can be taken orally. And he can call them peptides if he means that they are made up of amino acids. But they aren't the typical polypeptide *chains* that can be manufactured from a DNA blueprint. They are polypeptide *rings* and are called *polyketides*."

I gave Michael a citation from *Science* magazine to prove it. I capped it off by saying, "Hell, it's the same deal as those drugs from insects that I was telling you about last week. And I bet that the 'high level chemist' and his genetically engineered protein boys couldn't even make those compounds."

"It's not a question of whether he can make them," Michael said. "It's a question of whether he can detect those ring polypeptides."

"Right! Precisely," I said, seizing the advantage. "Ask him whether he could *screen* for them and find them if doesn't know their structure already. And if he thinks he can, then we can discuss it further."

I was handling Michael roughly, but you have to make a stand when you're fighting for your life.

"And your drug detecting biochip will?"

"Yes."

"And it will be able to detect the polypeptide rings?"

"If they have antibiotic activity or bind on any one of the ten thousand pharmacological receptors, yes." Slowly, I was getting him turned around.

"And you would test coral extracts and pond scum for these polypeptide rings with pharmacological activity?"

Thinking of Nica, I chose my words carefully. Conversations with a client must be kept private, even from laymen who don't have the background to understand them anyway. "Yes, I'd test that. Along with extracts from other organisms like actinomycetes, bacilli and filamentous fungi. Yes."

"And you would test those organisms with your biochip?" he asked.

It sounded like he was making notes that he would read back verbatim.

"Yes, along with those beetles that we were talking about the other day."

"Okay. Good, Benjamin. I will call my contact back right now and say that it is a misunderstanding. I will assure him that you didn't mean to contradict his top genetic engineering scientist." He spoke with such deliberation and self-confidence. "And could you prepare for me, by the end of the day, a short summary of what you just said?"

"Sure."

I hung up the phone, and turned my attention to Nica. She was standing by the window, looking out. She turned her head and caught me with a whimsical smile. "You sound like a real high-powered scientist."

She said it teasingly. She must have been following the conversation with fuzzy logic, interpreting the tenor of my words but not really understanding. Style and flavor would be what this woman paid attention to.

I put on a mock frown before answering in kind. "Well, I'm trying to be high-powered. Sometimes you've got to kick butt or the project goes down the tubes."

She reacted with a sniff, then relaxed her face into an appreciative smile. "What kind of project?"

I tried to relax, too. "I'm advising a company on drug disc—."

I broke it off. "On drug development." Couldn't relax too much because confidentiality is important, even around lay people. I put together an all-purpose answer. "I'm advising a client company on how to use its resources in product development."

Those dark eyes were so charming.

"Discovering new drugs?"

And those dark eyes were intelligent.

"No. Let's say that I'm advising a company how to find out more about the drugs they already have."

"And the man you were talking to doesn't understand it as well as you do."

"He's the weakest link — like in the TV show. And that's why they need me as a consultant."

Nica's visit was helping to improve my mood.

"Helping the company to advance through science?" she said.

"Yes, you could say that."

"That is how Brazil can advance, too. Through using science."

Around those dark eyes, her skin seemed to glow. Well, that's the way it felt while I stood next to her, by my desk. It was like the warmth you feel on your forehead when a car's headlight catches you on a curve while jogging on a chilly evening. I answered her with a mini-dissertation on science and Brazil's economic development. I showed her an opinion piece in *Science* magazine by a Brazilian scientist José Goldemberg. He wrote that developing countries like Brazil should concentrate on applied science. He was for replacing gasoline with locally fermented ethanol and protecting the rain forest as a preserve of biological diversity.

The mini-lecture must have made Nica feel at home: She moved to the fireplace and picked up a picture of Rebecca on the mantle. She pursed her lips for a second while looking at it. "I have heard that there are lots of opportunities for getting new drugs from the rain forest."

"That's true, but I'm not the right guy to tell you much about it." The disclaimer rolled off my lips nicely.

"And you told me when we were together on the plane that your fiancée is on an expedition on the Amazon. Is this her?"

"Yes. Her name is Rebecca."

Nica wrinkled her nose. "She's very pretty."

"Yes. Thank you."

She returned the picture to the mantle. "Her expedition sounds very interesting." She came back to me, slowly.

"Yes. She is providing medical treatment for the Indians."

"Is she trying to find new drugs?"

"No. She's interested in using existing drugs, effectively and inexpensively. That's what she's doing with Indians in the rain forest." I remembered having told Nica that before.

"That's nice," she answered neutrally.

"She's also interested in anthropology. In fact, yesterday I had to go to an anthropological conference at the Knight Center and take notes for her."

Nica took a second to think. "That was nice of you."

Not wishing to play the hero, I didn't say anything about yesterday's incident. Why was Nica visiting me anyway? Her smile wasn't just a sealed beam that could warm my forehead from across the room. It had attractive force. She threw her head back and swept her shoulder-length hair to the side, revealing her left ear. It was charming, with many graceful curves and folds — charming like the silver earring that dangled from its pierced lobe.

Too bad that Pops was gone. He would have made a good chaperone. Nica was moving up close again. "Do you help each other a lot?" she asked.

So close. So poised, her eyes taking in everything and especially me. Standing inside my zone but making innocent conversation. Standing inside the zone in which the most natural thing for me to do would be to lean forward and kiss her. Would she respond with demure deflection? Or would she respond in kind, opening a physical dimension as intense as the visual intimacy she was offering right now?

Don't do it, Ben, not even as an experiment. But it was so hard, like holding two magnets apart at close quarters.

I pretended to have a tickle in my throat and turned to cough. "Sometimes I help Rebecca with pharmacology. Sometimes she helps me with facts about medical practice. She will be coming back in two weeks."

Nica stepped back, out of the zone now. But she smiled brighter than before. "Do you do a lot of reading on medical anthropology?"

"No, it's a broad field. I don't follow it. Sometimes the *Scientific American* has an article on it. I leave that to Rebecca."

Now was the time to set a new tone with a more formal style of hospitality. "Nica, can I offer you a glass of grapefruit juice or a cup of coffee?"

"Yes, please. Coffee. You know we have a lot of coffee in Brazil. There was a famous song."

I laughed and walked to the screen door and hooked it. Then Nica followed me to the kitchen like she was right at home. Of course, it wouldn't do to offer her freeze-dried like I did Pops. Nica acted like my bean grinding and paper filter routine was the most fascinating thing in the world. But when she looked out the back window, she spotted something still more interesting: the *Diogenes*. I took her to the backyard for a closer look while we waited for the water to boil. And when I poured the water on the freshly ground powder, she watched on like I was conducting a chemistry experiment. And after we returned to the living room — she selected the couch and I took a rattan chair — she made it seem like drinking coffee with me was the most interesting thing in the world.

I went along with all that, letting her take the lead. She waltzed us around the topic of boats (I liked them, she was a land-lubber), swimming (she liked it in fresh water, I liked both fresh water and salt water), and bicycles (we both liked them, especially around Miami). She talked a lot about her flight schedule and how she spent half of her time in Manaus and half in Miami. We talked about her neighborhood in Miami Springs. (No, she hadn't noticed if they still had that old-time Rexall drugstore in the town circle; yes, she liked to take walks around the golf course.) As our cups emptied, I was thinking up a string of friendly questions about her fiancé in Manaus. That would really end the visit on the right note.

But the ending note was provided an instant later — by the Edison buzzer. It jolted us like a door opening on a pair of illicit lovers. Of course the door was open already. That's why I'd hooked the screen door. And through that screen, I recognized the narrow silhouette of Alice McRae. She looked her lanky self in that beige pantsuit she wears when she's out on assignments.

Nica relaxed back into her cushion while I got up to let Alice in. As I opened for her, Alice said, "Ben, I'm hoping I'm not barging in on you and Rebecca but . . ." she glanced across the room at Nica, "I'm sorry, I saw the woman's bicycle outside and just *assumed*. I hope that I'm not disturbing anything." A true Daughter of the South, Alice is a master of nuance and pregnant pause. She knew damn well that Rebecca was gone.

"No problem. Alice McRae, this is Nica from Miami Springs." I realized I didn't know her last name.

Nica got up with a gracious smile, ready to extend her hand. "Nica Brasaro." Alice smiled and nodded, making no effort to close the distance between them.

"Nica, Alice, is a reporter for the *Miami Standard*. She's responsible for Miami-Dade County government."

"And keeping track of our hero when he makes the news," Alice added with a smile of proprietorship.

Nica didn't act like she understood. And I wasn't inspired to say anything else, either. It was Nica who finally broke the awkward silence. "Glad to meet you, Alice. I really have to be going, Ben. Thanks for letting me drop in on you."

"Sure, stop by again, the next time you're riding through the neighborhood," I said, feeling like a ham actor in a poorly written play. Probably looked the part, too, as I helped Nica take her bike down from the porch. As we said goodbye at the sidewalk, Nica fished a small item from the pocket of her shorts. She squeezed it into my hand which I had extended to her. It was a folded scrap of paper. I slipped it into my pocket while waving her off.

Alice threw me a glance from the porch as I returned. "I see she shares one of your passionate interests." Alice waited for me to respond, which I didn't. "Bicycling, of course," she clarified. I answered that with an idiotic grin. "Nice swaying style," she continued. "Ben and his Spanish beauties." She clicked her tongue.

"Portuguese. Brazilian. Flight attendant on the plane back from Brazil. Started chatting. After I told her what I do for a living, she started telling me about an anti-bacterial gargle extract from Brazilian beehives. She said it keeps her from picking up viral infections on those flights."

Alice rolled her eyes. "Quite a find, Ben. Virus-free."

"It's supposed to work against *airborne* viruses."

"So you gave her your card and she came for a visit?"

"Yes. Exactly."

"I can see why you are attracted to her. Nice figure. Plump

breasts and a flat tummy . . . for a few more years, anyway. Although I doubt that she's up to our level."

"Come on, Alice! Why are you making a big deal out of this, anyway?"

"Because this scrawny Macon County redneck is jealously guarding her place at the front of the line in case your fiancée-away defaults. But I'm not going to wait patiently if you're taking rumba lessons on the side."

She'd said it with a light touch, but I groaned anyway. "Alice, you've been out in the hot sun too long. Come on in. Nothing's going on. Cut me some slack. You haven't even given me a chance to thank you for what you've come over to talk to me about."

We came to a halt in the living room. Alice ran the fingers of one hand through her coarse, dark-blond hair with one hand and pulled out a pocket notebook with the other. "Yes, I wanted to check the details on the story. 'Scientist saves famous anthropologist from assassin's bullet.' In case the *Standard* does decide to use it."

"No question your story will be better than Channel Eight's from last night. They had me bashing Edith Pratt in the face with my briefcase. No grounds for libel, though. They didn't use my name and you couldn't make out my face. And I don't really want any publicity on this one, even if I did stop a bullet and save her life."

"Of course you do. Everyone wants her or his blazing 15 minutes. And you've had three big stories already, although I only got the scoop on two of them." She frowned. "You didn't give me a bit of help with the first one."

"But you got the best two out of the three — especially the last one when hell broke loose at the medical school." I drove the point home with a wink.

Alice conceded my point with a smile. "Okay, what's your take on what this Edith Pratt has done to earn a bullet in the head?"

How much more charming Alice was, now that she had slid back into her working-journalist mode.

"I've been asking that question, myself," I said. "Maybe you can tell *me*."

"But right now you know her better than I."

I told Alice all about the meeting, the debate with the *garimpeiro*-loving general and the taunting questions from Sanch

Riquez. I shared with her my impressions of Edith Platt, adding
that she hadn't called to thank me for saving her life.

"She does seem very ungrateful. Her behavior toward you
seems as much a paradox as the shooting itself."

"I agree with you on that, Alice. And here's another paradox.
Why did the General come to the conference at all? He's retired,
so he wasn't speaking in official capacity. Is he working for some
interest group, making a preemptive public relations strike? Is
Brazil getting ready to change its policy on mining in the
Yanomama territory? I can understand how Pratt has enemies. Her
attitude alone is enough to make her plenty of them. But I don't
see what is the purpose of shooting her."

"I agree. Shooting her wouldn't serve any purpose for anyone.
If the mining interests wanted to get rid of her, they couldn't have
chosen a worse time and place. It would make her a martyr. And I
don't see any anti-Castro angle to it, either. I know how these Cuban
hotheads think. I don't see how any of them could be confused
and think she's a communist." Alice had completely shaken off
her huff, now.

"There were several guys carrying placards that read, 'No Castro,
No Problem.' But I figured they were plants for Channel Eight."

"Agreed." Alice moved in closer and half-turned like maybe
she would start making notes.

"In the session, Pratt was very doctrinaire. Dripping with
reverse snobbery. Seems to enjoy rubbing people the wrong way.
But that was just expressing opinions."

"I agree, Ben. The only way the shooting would make any
sense is if she was really standing in someone's way — someone
other than the mining interests."

Now we were touching shoulders. I shifted away.

"So, what else have you done about the situation besides
thinking about it?"

"Nothing."

An impatient look came over Alice's face. "Ben, Ben, Ben,
dear Ben," she chided. "What did the police report say? Did they
get any information on the assailant's car? And have you looked
into the TV out-takes?"

I gestured to the papers piled high on my desk. "No, not yet
Alice. It's just that I have this —."

"Big important scientific report to do. But when it comes down to what *really* happened, you don't care. Yesterday, you were almost killed, but I'm the one who does the worrying about it." Her frown relaxed into a self-satisfied smile. "Now, the TV out-takes show that it was a black BMW three-twenty-eight, four-door. And the only reason why anybody knows that is because I watched twenty minutes of out-takes at Channel Eight. Had to make use of my special relationship with *El Toro* to get the station people to make me a copy."

"Thanks."

"And the hotel security cameras caught that Beemer speeding off right after the bullet was fired."

"I know that. I showed it to Detective Morales. Wasn't that part of the police report?"

"It wasn't going to be until I brought it to their attention."

"Gee, thanks!"

"Say nothing of it."

"It sounds like Detective Morales was doing a lazy job on his report."

"Maybe so. You should check it. But he did record the fact that your briefcase stopped a bullet."

"Great. I was beginning to feel paranoid about the Miami P.D. An expert opinion that I rendered a while back cost them some money."

"You mean that cocaine overdose thing? I don't think so, Ben."

I knew better than that. But I didn't want to get into it with her just then.

"Thanks, Alice. I owe you."

"Agreed. You owe me a kiss."

I gave her a quick one on the cheek and withdrew. "Are you going to use this stuff in a story?"

"Yes, but it won't be a very long one. Maybe four column inches. Nothing that I would submit for a Pulitzer Prize."

She was heading for the door.

"Thanks again, Alice. We'll keep in touch." I waved her off.

I fished from my pocket the slip of paper that Nica had given me. It was her phone number. I tossed it into the center drawer of my desk.

How nice of Alice to run interference for me! Looking into that police report would have cost me a lot of time. I used it, instead, to write an e-mail to Rebecca. Wrote her that I'd seen Edith Pratt, had taken a lot of notes, and had done the old girl a small favor. No reason to distress Rebecca, and we were restricted to short messages anyway.

I spent the rest of the morning and most of the afternoon working on the summary I'd promised Michael. Faxed it to him before the close of business.

Later, I received another visit — a hotel employee delivering my blue blazer. The dry cleaners had done a nice job; it was nearly impossible to see where it had rubbed against stone. The man also gave me an envelope which contained a security report from the hotel. I was satisfied with their summary.

The next morning, I checked the *Miami Standard*. It didn't carry any story about Edith Pratt and me. But a phone call later that day told me that Alice had made an effort.

"Dr. Candidi, this is Hal Brown from the Palo Alto News in California." He had a deep, raspy voice. "We're calling up to check on a story we got over the wire that you saved the life of anthropologist Edith Pratt."

"Yes. Mr. Brown, could I ask what number you are calling from?"

He gave me a number in the 650 area code and it agreed with what my caller I.D. was telling me.

I took a second to write the number down in my appointment calendar. When talking to journalists, it's a good idea to check phone numbers and take careful notes on the conversation.

"It's my cellphone" he said. "If it's not convenient, I could call you back."

"No, I should be able to talk to you now. But if I need to get back to you, could you give me your number at the office."

"Yes, sure." He gave me another number in the 650 area code which I also wrote down.

"Fine, Mr. Brown. Now do we have an understanding that everything I tell you is only background unless we agree on a direct quote."

"Well . . . well, yes."

"Okay, what are your questions?"

"Can you tell me what happened?"

I told him about the black car, the red dot, how I raised my briefcase to shield Pratt from the beam and how the bullet went into my briefcase, making it hit her face. Then I asked, "Is that what your wire story said?"

"Yes, essentially. It said you raised your briefcase and that stopped a bullet. It didn't say anything about a red dot or a black car. Dr. Candidi, are you an anthropologist or social scientist?"

"No, I'm a pharmacologist."

"Dr. Candidi, if you don't mind my asking this, isn't it a little usual for a pharmacologist to attend a conference on economic development in the Third World?" His voice seemed to be clearing up as he talked.

"Yes. I was attending it for my fiancée who was out of town."

"Oh, I see. Would that be . . . Rebecca Levis?"

"Yes. Now can I ask you, how you got that information? I'm sure that wasn't part of the wire story."

"No. We talked to the conference organizers. Just one more question, Dr. Candidi. Is there anyone else we can talk to that witnessed this incident?"

"Well, you might try Edith Pratt."

"Yes, we will. And is there anyone else with whom we can confirm the story?"

"Confirm the story?" I let him feel my impatience. "You might try making a Freedom of Information request with the Miami Police Department."

"Yes, of course. Thank you very much Dr. Candidi and I wish you —"

"Could I ask a question of you?"

"Why certainly!"

"I hope you don't mind my asking this, but why is a California paper so interested in a Baltimore anthropologist almost getting shot at in Miami?"

"It was reported to us by a University of California anthropologist, as well as by the wire story."

"And what did he or she say?"

"Not much more than the wire story."

"I have one more request, if you could."

"Yes."

"Could you send me a copy of the wire story and a copy of your story, if you run it? I'd like to show it to my friends."

"Certainly. I'd be glad to."
I gave him my address. I should have asked for his.

Mr. Hyde Is 11
the Mother of Invention

For the rest of that week, things were surprisingly quiet. There were no repercussions from the Edith Pratt episode. The police never called me. No more reporters called me, not even Alice. I never did get a copy of Alice's wire story from that California reporter. And I never got a call or even a thank-you note from Edith Pratt. Well, you can't expect everyone to be grateful.

I counted my blessings: There were no return visits from DEA Officer Henderson. I counted my friends: My friend and electronics expert Joe Kazekian sent me an e-mail suggesting we go out drinking on Wednesday night of the following week. Pops sent me a postcard saying he was having a good time in Toronto with "two girls for every guy." And I counted down the days of that week — my third week alone in Miami and Rebecca's last week at the Mission. On Saturday she would start the journey home.

That week was quiet but it wasn't easy. Michael made it difficult. Judging from his daily calls, his client company was developing a dual personality, like in Robert Louis Stevenson's *Strange Case of Dr. Jekyll and Mr. Hyde*. The Dr. Jekyll personality liked my advice and always came up with an interesting follow-up question the next day. And the Mr. Hyde personality thought he knew all the answers already and didn't need to do business with us.

The Dr. Jekyll personality was oh so interested in the "natural product libraries." He wanted to know all about the Analytica Corporation and its library of 12,000 natural product compounds. And he was enthralled with the idea of equipping scientists with field laboratories on a chip and sending them out on "bioprospecting" expeditions for new drugs. He wanted to know what companies were bioprospecting already. He wanted to know all about Shaman Pharmaceuticals, Inc. and its licensing deal with a tribe in India for rights to a herbal remedy.

Dr. Jekyll praised me when I delivered estimates of the number of possible drug candidates that might lie in the Brazilian rain forest with its almost two million species of plants and animals. He marveled at my analogies, comparing the tall rain forest with a three-dimensional ecosystem in which a single tree can host as many different species as a whole acre of North American land. Dr. Jekyll agreed there were four billion key-and-lock combinations out there ready to be tested and that hundreds of billions of pharmaceutical dollars would come to the person who could figure out how to do it.

But in the same conversations, Mr. Hyde raised his ugly head. Maybe he was the company's chief biochemist. Or maybe he was a group of rear guard scientists. In any case, Mr. Hyde couldn't imagine new drugs from a rain forest or coral reef. And he didn't agree that most of the new drug candidates are small, stout, pharmacologically active molecules synthesized by small, vulnerable organisms living in remote corners of our planet. Mr. Hyde was probably a protein chemist. His idea of a good drug was an injectable growth factor or a new clotting factor for transfusion into hemophiliacs. He didn't appreciate the lock-and-key analogy. He seemed to think that if you know enough about the locks, the keys will discover themselves.

But worst of all, Mr. Hyde remained stuck with the same misconception that Michael had on my first day back in Miami: He still thought the DNA chip would be the *best* way to discover new drugs. But he could never say how or why.

It all came to a head in the middle of that third week: Michael told me, once again, that the chief biochemist's objections were serious enough to threaten the whole project. That was enough to make me stop editorial work on the report. I spent the rest of the week thinking up better analogies to present to Mr. Hyde.

I could see why Mr. Hyde was charmed by the DNA biochip: He could buy them for about $250 apiece. It was simple and it worked. It was almost magical how those messenger RNA molecules, or their copies, sought out the DNA molecules on the spots — and on the correct spots, only. And there wasn't any problem making those RNA molecules glow. They were like pieces of chain and adding the fluorescent tag molecule was just adding an extra link. The fluorescent tag didn't get in the way.

I walked around my office, restlessly, thinking about a big problem: There was still no way to make the spots on my drug-receptor biochips glow. It was the same problem that had bothered me while flying home from Manaus: Most of the candidate drug molecules weren't big like the RNA molecules. They were "small, sturdy molecules":

Drugs are sturdy molecules without many handles where the fluorescent tag could be attached.

Drugs are small molecules, not much bigger than the fluorescent tag molecule, itself. I remembered the analogy that occurred to me in the plane: It would be like putting the key on a key holder that's so bulky that you can't even get it close to the lock.

The bulkiness problem rattled in my head all week. Friday noon the problem dizzied me so badly that I stumbled into a chair and sat down. The fluorescent tag had to be attached to the drug, that was for sure. Otherwise, the spots on the chip wouldn't glow. But how to attach it? Slowly, the idea came to me. To keep the drug/key from being messed up, it would have to use a *thin chain* to attach the tag to it — a thin *key chain* that won't get in the way. The key would be at one end of the key chain, and the bulky fluorescent tag molecule would be at the other end. After I came up with that analogy, the answer came quickly.

I remembered some work that a scientist named Richard Kramer had done at the University of Miami before he left to take up a more attractive position at Berkeley. Dr. Kramer's work showed what I could use for a key chain — a long, stringy molecule called polyethylene glycol. He had been studying the binding of a drug-like molecule to an enzyme which is active in cellular signaling. When he attached polyethylene glycol to the drug-like molecule, it didn't mess up the binding to the receptor. The key chain didn't keep the key from sliding into the lock. In fact, he showed that when he made the key chain long enough and put one key on each end, he could open two locks at the same time!

Eureka! I could adapt the Kramer method to make the spots

on my biochip glow. I would put a *known* drug on one end of a Kramer string and the fluorescent tag molecule on the other end. The drug-receptor proteins would be anchored in the spots like I'd been thinking before. We'd apply the Candidi/Kramer molecule and the spot would glow. Then, we would add a drop of coral juice. If the juice contained any candidate drugs for that receptor, they would kick off the Candidi/Kramer molecule — and that spot would *stop* glowing!

Eureka! We could make the spots glow. And we could screen for new drugs by seeing which spots stopped glowing.

My brain stormed. I paced around the house deep in conversation with myself, occasionally erupting with esoteric utterances: "And there won't be a damn bit of interference from nonspecific binding!"

My discourse took me into the backyard where I twisted an ankle in a crab hole. I wandered to the cockpit of the *Diogenes* and sat down. It was a good invention — useful, novel and non-obvious. If developed, it could make us rich. Rebecca and I could say goodbye to financial worries and spend a year sailing around the Caribbean.

Then a shadow came over me. Was something like this patented already? I rushed back to my computer and *http*'d to the U.S. Patent and Trademark Office website. After an hour of searching I knew my invention was free and clear. The closest thing to it was a dozen reports on "tethered ligand systems" that had not yet been used with fluorescent tags. But, hell, I would use them. I'd use them to produce all kinds of glows — red, yellow, blue and green dots. Hell, I could make my own biochip with a matrix of dots. I could pack them as tightly as beads on an Indian belt!

Next, I *http*'d to the National Library of Medicine website and searched the four decades of scientific literature archived there. Nobody had invented my invention. Yet, the literature had a lot of useful background technology. It looked like I could put every major drug on one end of the Candidi/Kramer string!

That afternoon I worked feverishly on the idea, making notes and writing down examples of different drugs and receptors with which it would work. I kept at it well into the evening until noticing that I had missed dinner.

I took a break long enough to heat a can of camping slop.

Took the top off the can, set it in a pan of water and turned on the gas. The procedure grosses out Rebecca, big-time, so I never do it when she's around. But it *is* the most efficient method to prepare camping slop. With all the heat transfer going through water, nothing is burnt. And eating the ravioli directly from the can, there's no waste and no dish to wash.

Half-way into my meal, a cloud came over me: What about Michael and the mystery company? Would they have any rights to my invention? I rushed to the files and pulled out his "letter of intent" which gave me my marching orders. Yes, Michael was paying me to figure out *how long* it would take for someone to come up with this kind of invention. No, he wasn't paying me to invent it.

I thought my argument through: If Michael wanted my invention, he would have to pay me the development costs I would be saving his client. Ten years of effort by a couple of groups would be worth $10-50 million. That's what I'd already estimated in the executive summary.

I opened my office calendar and wrote down an important thing to do: "Polish up argument that Michael doesn't get the invention."

Writing it down made me realize that the day it was indeed Friday — the end my third week since returning to Miami. And it was one day before Rebecca would be starting on her trip home! Could she have sent me one last e-mail? I went on-line to check for it and received an unpleasant surprise:

From: RLevis@tropmed.epi.bryanmed.edu
To: ben-candidi@netrus.net
Subj.: Love You

Just a short note to tell you that I love you and that I'm not going back with David. I'm planning to stay two weeks longer. I have an opportunity to investigate. I will take the dugout, the next time it comes, and get a freighter to Manaus. I'll call you from the airport in Manaus.

Love, Rebecca

I hit the reply button and composed a message, saying that I

116 AMAZON GOLD

understood that opportunities could come up, that I loved her and could she please be careful, especially along the *Rio Marauiá* and while waiting in Santa Isabel.

After hitting the send button, I sank back into my chair. Hopefully, David Thompson hadn't already taken down his satellite dish. I shut my eyes and imagined Rebecca alone with Hashamo in his dugout canoe. I had a troubling vision — of Klaus-Dietrich Grünhagen stumbling into her on the banks of the *Rio Negro*.

12   Sticky Consult, Sticky Jungle

There was only one way to deal with my worry about Rebecca — by throwing myself into hard work. I spent the weekend writing up a patent specification for my invention. My prior experience working at the U.S. Patent and Trademark Office came in handy. By Saturday evening I had scoured the research literature for drug/ receptor pairs to use as working examples. And by Sunday evening, I had drafted the text of the patent application and had even worked up a set of claims.

On Monday morning of my fourth week in Miami, I was working hard on Michael's project. And for the next two days, Michael worked hard playing both Dr. Jekyll and Mr. Hyde in the same phone conversation. Dr. Jekyll wanted my opinion on a 1,536 spot "microtiter plate" from Corning, and Mr. Hyde wanted to know why his DNA biochip "couldn't be useful" for discovering drugs. Then Dr. Jekyll wanted to know how to stick drug receptor proteins to the biochip's silicon surface, and Mr. Hyde challenged my estimate that less than ten percent of the existing drugs are peptides or proteins.

But we were both making progress. In fact, when speaking in his Dr. Jekyll mode, Michael was starting to sound like a chemistry major.

On Wednesday morning, Michael called up as Dr. Jekyll, sounding as sharp as a Ph.D. candidate. He said they had decided that fluorescent detection of drug binding was the way to go. "My client wants to know your ideas for detecting the binding of the candidate drug molecules on the drug receptor. Obviously, we would use fluorescence. But what fluorescent reporter group would be used, and how would it be chemically coupled?"

Damn! He was asking me for my invention. I must have paused too long before answering, but at least some words came out.

"Well, I have some papers on drug-antibody-coupled ELISA kits," I said. That was different from the invention. "Or you might couple a fluorescent molecule to the drug receptor." That could be done but it wouldn't be useful.

"You wouldn't couple the fluorescent molecules to the drug candidates themselves?" Michael asked.

Hell, he was getting close to my key chain idea! Well, I'd feed him a few facts and let him go off on his own, bumbling down the wrong path.

"Michael, the problem is that the fluorescent molecule is about the same size as the drug. It will be a problem to attach the two. And even if you could find some way to attach the fluorescent molecule to the drug, it will probably get in the way and keep the drug from binding to the enzyme or protein sitting on the chip."

"How so?"

"It's like a attaching a key holder that's so bulky that the key won't fit in the lock anymore."

"Okay, Ben, but we would like you to think about it for a few days."

I probably took too long to answer. "Sure, Michael, I'll think about it. But I can't guarantee you a workable solution. And you've got to remember that figuring out *exactly* how a new technology will work is outside the scope of the project."

"How so?"

"Our agreement is for me to assess *existing* technologies and to make some *rough predictions* as to how long it will take for . . . those technologies to . . . be adapted to solve the problem."

"Do you know the answer?"

Damn! I took a deep breath before answering. "No, I'm not saying I know the answer."

"But if you know the answer, you have the obligation to reveal it to me and my client." His voice was 20 degrees cooler, now.

I sure as hell wasn't going to let him weasel the invention out of me for 20,000 stinking dollars. It was time to draw a sharp line.

"Look, Michael. Any hunch or notion that I might be able to come up with for you would probably require a couple dozen turn-arounds with guys like your chief biochemist. And then, it wouldn't be anything more than a brainstorm. If they want to balloon this forty-thousand-dollar survey into a major project, then they must give us some major bucks and a long-term commitment."

"But if you have already found the answer while we have been paying you —"

"Listen, damn it! Your letter of intent says the report is to be a *survey*, nothing more. Now I'll get you those reports on time and you can sell it to that company for whatever you can get for it. If the company gives us a long-term contract, I would be most happy, from that day forward, to dig deeply into the fluorescence detection thing. I would consult directly with their scientists and even invent for them. But until I see their long-term contract and the color of their money, I'm not going to get involved in *creating* any new technology."

The line was silent for a while. "Do you have any ideas for an invention?" He was as cool and imperious as a hit man in an action movie.

"Nothing worth talking about."

"Does that mean 'no'?"

"Correct." No, I wasn't going to talk about it.

"Okay. But perhaps we should sign a secrecy agreement and a confidentiality agreement and a formal contract."

Sure, maybe he should come over and put a shackle around my neck!

"No, let's just keep on going like we've been doing — under our letter of agreement that got me started on this project. And we'll do a full contract for the next one when we get a full commitment from your client — when he shows us the color of his money."

"Of course, the report must be satisfactory."

"It will be," I answered. "You and your client will get an organized, highly documented report on everything that's out there as public knowledge."

"Fine."

"Is there anything more?"

"Yes, the chief biochemist still disagrees with your estimate of the percentage of non-peptide drugs."

I groaned. "Well, Michael, I can't help you any more with that S.O.B. You will have to get someone in the company to rein him in, or you'll have to do it yourself."

"What did you just say?"

I repeated what I'd just said, word for word. And then the line went silent . . . for a long time.

"Ben, these questions must be answered, or the project is in jeopardy."

When I did open my mouth, I was surprised by the unstoppable stream of words that came out.

"No, Michael, the project is not in jeopardy. You have made one project into two. Just one of our *two* projects is in jeopardy. You don't have just one company on the line, you've got two. The first company with the 'chief biochemist' — let's call him Mr. Hyde — doesn't like my results very much. But you're still trying to hook him. Now the second company — run by Dr. Jekyll — is already hooked and moving nicely towards a big deal. But you want me to give you two reports for the price of one. But I have only one report. And it's going to be my best estimate. And when I give it to you, and you give me the final twenty thousand dollars, it will be your property."

I stopped abruptly. Michael didn't respond right away.

"Ben, you're wrong about there being two companies."

"Okay. There's only one company and it's run by Mr. Hyde who sometimes lapses into Dr. Jekyll. You'll just have to tell your chief biochemist to shove it."

The line was silent for a long, long time. Neither of us said anything more. And I honestly do not know which of us was the first to hang up.

While my blood pressure was up, it seemed like a good time to deal with another irritating individual: David Thompson, the guy who left Rebecca alone at the Mission. I called his secretary and learned that he had returned from Brazil and was back in the office. Yes, she would tell him I'd be dropping by in a few minutes.

This visit required a change of clothes — to dress slacks and an Oxford cloth shirt. I set the burglar alarm and rode my bike north to Thompson's office. It was on the second floor of a 1950-vintage medical arts building that had been taken over by Bryan Medical School. I made my way through a warren of offices and small laboratories set up in converted examining rooms, working my way through a narrow hallway lined with a soft laminated beige material that harked back to the invention of plastic. The fluorescent lights in the ceiling might be meeting city building code requirements, but the light bouncing off the walls was a forest brown. A mild *aspergillus* infection in the air conditioning system added to the moldy forest ambience.

Since Dr. Thompson and his secretary were separated by a couple of dozen yards of hallway, I was able to go directly to his open doorway. I rapped the door frame with my knuckles and expended one ounce of willpower to suppress a frown.

He was standing over his desk, an oversized, battleship gray, metal relic that probably served in World War II. He caught a glimpse of me — he probably read me out like a billboard — and returned to a disorganized search through a tall stack of papers. In normal clothes and wearing a long tie, his appearance gave few hints of a four-week expedition. His gray hair was an inch or so longer than normal and an insect bite had swollen the skin over one of his high cheekbones.

"Ben," he said, glancing up for a second time. "How nice of you to stop by. But I have a Human Use Committee meeting in fifteen minutes. If I can only find that file!"

Playing the fuddy-duddy was a standard tactic for that guy. He used disorganization as a crutch like some people use a cellphone. It allowed him to be there without really being there. But I was determined not to be put off.

"Human Use Committee, huh? How apt! Maybe you could answer a question or two on the *use* of Rebecca Levis."

"What?" That got his attention. He stared at me under a loosely wrinkled and hooded brow. One eye was focused directly on me and the other seemed to be staring at my left shoulder. I never did figure out which of those two gray eyes was dominant.

"David, I don't see how you could have done that!"

His brows narrowed. "Do what, Ben?"

"Leave Rebecca there by herself."

He slouched and put on a scowl for several seconds. Then he

leaned over and shuffled his papers, shaking his head like he was scolding thcm and me at the same time. "Nothing will happen to her. Nothing's happened at that Mission for ten years."

"And on the way back?"

"Hashamo is trustworthy. He'll take care of her."

"What if they come across a boatload of renegades on the way back? Can he protect her?"

"There won't be any renegades. The river's off limits because it's controlled by the *Funai*."

"Sure," I said, "if your idea of controlling it is sitting in a shack, miles from the river's mouth. How will she get back to Manaus?"

"She'll take a freighter, just like you did."

"And what happens if someone starts messing with her?"

"She'll give him a karate kick. You underestimate her, Ben. Stop worrying."

But I couldn't stop worrying. "So how am I going to communicate with her?"

"The Mission has a shortwave radio which talks to the *Funai* office and the *Funai* office has a satellite phone."

"And do you have its number?"

He abandoned his papers and grabbed his desktop Rolodex with two hands and spun it with amazing precision. "There!" he said, triumphantly, plunking it down in front of me.

I checked, and the card showed the same number as I'd rccorded in my little brown book.

"Now, Ben, does that make you happy?" Thompson asked.

"Not really. Why is she staying two extra weeks?"

"There was something about a shaman going to come to the Mission." He affected an Ivy League drawl. "Something of that order."

"Something of that *order*! Don't you know? Hell, man, you were the leader of the expedition. You gave her permission to stay on. Why shouldn't you know?"

That really got his attention. Hc drcw himsclf up — all of the disjointed, loosely muscled six feet of himself — and he stared down on me like we were going to play a round of New England style touch football.

"Look, Ben, I'm not married to her like you. And I can't get into personal arguments with her like you. You know she's got her own National Science Foundation fellowship to do what she's doing. If she wants to wait an extra two weeks for an old quack medicine man to come out of the jungle with his penis tied up to his waist on a string and if she wants him to tell her how he cures diseases by blowing ebene powder up people's noses, it's not for me to tell her no."

"Is that what she's going to do?"

"That's what I understand." His eyes returned to his papers.

I was still mad. "So you're sure that she isn't planning to do something stupid like joining a trading party to visit a *shabono* that's several days deep in the jungle where she can be taken by force and wind up as a Yanomama squaw, or whatever they call them." I paused long enough to catch one breath. "I read a whole book on 'something of that order.' Thrilling biography. A woman was abducted by Amazon Indians from the edge of her village on a riverbank."

"Rebecca's staying at the Mission and there's no danger," Thompson said, impatiently. He locked onto me with one eye then turned it laboriously towards the door. It was like he was trying to drag me out of his office by willpower alone. But I wasn't leaving until all my questions were answered.

"Talking about medicine, does Rebecca still have anti-malarial pills?"

Thompson scowled. "Yes, she has a four-week supply."

"Okay, that will give her one week of leeway."

"Look, Ben, I promise I'll let you know if I hear of any problem."

I glanced around the room, collecting my thoughts. His obsolete satellite dish was sitting next to a backpack at the side of his desk. "There's no satellite dish at the Mission — right? — because you took yours back."

"Right."

"So the only way I get any news is if the priest fires up his shortwave radio and gets hold of the *Funai* office and they pass it on to me using their satellite phone. Which reminds me, why the hell didn't you break down and get a hand-held satellite phone like I showed you?"

Thompson snapped out of his slouch. "Like that GlobalStar

ad that you tore out of your sailing magazine and gave me a week before we left? It might surprise you, Ben, but those things don't always work like the ads say they will. We looked into something like that three years ago and the company had just gone bankrupt."

Thompson looked at the door, this time as a command. So I swallowed the comment that was building up pressure in my throat. What good would it do to tell a member of the rotary phone generation that three years is a short time? "Thanks for your time. Hope you find your papers."

Thompson answered me with a grunt.

While I was in the neighborhood, I could have dropped in on Dr. Rob McGregor, my erstwhile dissertation advisor. He was a good friend and I owed him a visit. But not wanting to spread my foul mood, I decided against it. I returned to the house, changed into more comfortable clothes, and went back to organizing the appendices of my report.

The work proved such a good coping strategy — that's what Rebecca would call it — that I didn't notice when it got dark.

In fact, the work distracted me so thoroughly that the loud knock on the door made me jump out of my skin.

Applied Anthropology 13

"What's the matter?" asked a familiar voice coming through the screen door. "Your head so full of science that you forgot about the drinking date with your old buddy?"

It was my friend Joe Kazekian.

I got up and opened the door. "Yeah, Zeekie, the stuff's hypnotic. Just like electronics."

Zeekie runs a TV and video repair shop out on Bird Road, on the west end of town.

"Yeah, Ben, I know the feeling."

"But after you've fixed an electronics problem, you at least have the satisfaction of seeing the machine run. And you can draw the line on a job after you've finished it. My problem's not fixed until the customer thinks he understands how everything works."

"Yeah, I can see how that could be frustrating." Sight is the sense that Zeekie trusts most. Feeling through his fingertips comes in a close second. He gave me a quick look-over to see if I was ready for the evening, then he tapped me on the shoulder. "Where you suggest we go?"

"If you'll be satisfied with a good fish dinner at a reasonable price, there are a couple of places within walking distance, here on the River. But if you want a place with a lot of action, we could try Bayside or Captain Walley's."

"Let's do Captain Walley's," he said, with South Philadelphia enthusiasm and lots of throaty echo. "Bayside's got a lot of action but the drinks are too expensive."

"Okay, but if we run into my friends Sam and Lou, we'll have to shoot the breeze with them for an hour at least. I haven't seen them for a long time. Sometimes they feel like I'm neglecting them."

"That the boat mechanic and the carpenter guy?"

"Yeah."

"They're cool. Barrel of laughs. Let's go."

Now, the evenings were cool enough for long pants to be comfortable at Captain Walley's — and that was how Zeekie was dressed anyway. He wore a loose-fitting tropical-print shirt over a pair of dark-colored Dockers, with leather boat moccasins and no socks. But I stayed with my khaki boat shorts, cobalt-blue T-shirt and canvas slip-ons.

"Just give me a minute to turn off the computer and lock up."

"Sure." Zeekie strolled around the room, giving everything a cursory inspection until his eyes came to rest on Rebecca's picture. "Nice chick. You guys are really solid, right?"

"Soul mates. Growing into each other's souls. Inseparable, now."

Zeekie frowned. "Sounds too metaphysical for me." He smiled. "But right now it's temporary separation and we're going to have a night on the town."

I knew exactly what he was getting at, and that demanded an answer:

"And Mona knows we're out drinking? Armenian marriages

might not be very metaphysical, but they're supposed to be very *theological*. Right?" Old-fashioned was what I meant, but I didn't want to come right out and say it.

"Yes. And she said to give you her regards. She likes you. You're one of my few friends she tells me she can trust."

"Tell her 'hi' and give the kids a hug for me." I flipped off the lights, set the alarm and we stepped out the door. Fifteen years of traditional marriage and two kids had puffed up Mona. She was too comfortable to exercise herself back into shape. And Zeekie had a roving eye — a lot worse than mine. He punched the button on his key chain and his van answered with a flash of lights and two polite beeps.

"Still prosperous with the repair business?" I asked, climbing in on the passenger side. I settled into the bucket seat beside him.

"Still prosperous." Zeekie turned the key in the ignition and got us rolling.

"And any new additions to the electronic warfare suite?" I asked, turning my head to the compartment behind us.

"No, I'm getting along fine with what I've got now."

He had around $15,000 worth of video equipment back there, including some remotely placeable cameras. His electronic wizardry had been very helpful to me a while back, when a project that I'd been doing for a Boston venture capitalist took a dangerous turn.

"And the Armenian wedding gigs are making money and keeping you well-entertained?"

The tires sang as they rolled over the honeycomb steel of the N.W. 5th Street drawbridge.

"The gigs aren't as entertaining as they used to be. With more of our friends getting married off, Mona's developed quite a spy network. Hard to make a move anymore."

"Maybe that's just as well. That Boca Raton stockbroker looked too hot to handle, even as a video image."

"She was a real estate broker," Zeekie corrected.

Good that he was speaking of her in past tense. It would be healthier for his marriage. I studied my old friend for a couple of minutes as he piloted the van west along Flagler St. and south along 12th Avenue. Nature had been good to him: big head of curly black hair; pilose masculinity sprouting from the backs of his hands and between the buttons of his shirt; swarthy good looks and a killer smile; and it all holding together through his mid-thirties. Yes, he was doing a good job conserving muscle and staving off fat. And if they ever decide to do a knock-off of "Starkey & Hutch," he could play the part. With all his film connections, he could have acted in commercials. But Zeekie's genius was behind the camera, capturing nuptial revelry on weekends. He was also damn good at repairing cameras. Most of his shop's business was repairing video recorders and TV sets, but he was working his way into DVD. Hopefully, all that was keeping his hands busy.

Yes, we'd renew our friendship this evening. But I wasn't going to supply the type of encouragement that might get him into trouble.

Zeekie threw me a glance. "So, how's Rebecca?"

"Working at a mission in Brazil, in the middle of nowhere, one hundred miles from the *Rio Negro*."

"Yeah, that's what you told me when I called last week. I guess she's really into that helping humanity stuff."

"Yes, that's what I bought into when I fell in love with her."

He shook his head. "Bought into it. That's a good expression."

No, Zeekie didn't understand Rebecca. He considered her a goodie-goodie. Once again, it was time to set him straight. "Rebecca and I made a long-term investment . . . in each other."

For the rest of the way, Zeekie was silent. The night air felt almost cool as it streamed over my arm and through the open window. It was the second week of October, the time when summer yields to autumn. The continental weather system kicks in, knocks the tops off the cumulus clouds, and sweeps the ground with reliable winds so that sunbaked concrete has nothing more to say about nighttime temperatures.

We crossed U.S. Highway One and descended to the Bay, taking South Bayshore Drive to Miami's Coconut Grove district. Zeekie parked in the lot in front of the Miami City Hall, an interesting two-storey art deco piece that used to be the terminal for Pan Am's Havana Clipper. From there, it was a short walk through a boat yard to Captain Walley's sea shanty restaurant and outdoor bar. We took a table by the seawall. The sea breeze was gentle and pleasantly cool. It splashed lazy waves against the seawall below us, it clanked halyards against the masts of the

docked sailboats, and it flickered the flame inside the orange goblet
that sat on our table. Across the dark Bay, the condominiums of
Key Biscayne shimmered and their lighted windows twinkled at
us through several miles of stirred-up surface air.

Our waitress approached with a springy step and announced
herself as Julie. The bright-spirited college-age girl looked good
in the Captain Walleys consensus uniform: white running shoes,
white short shorts and personal choice of topping. Her variation
on the theme was a black, knit tube top with horizontal green stripes
that went nicely with her light blond hair. Its thick, straight strands
were tamed in a rounded cut that fell diagonally across her broad
forehead. She had widely spaced eyes, a cute nose and thin lips
that formed easily into a perfect smile as she took our order. I
asked for a seafood combination, Zeekie ordered a grouper
sandwich, and we all agreed that an *haste pronto* pitcher of Becks
and a couple of chilled mugs would be just right. When Julie came
back with the beer, Zeekie started some small talk and we learned
she was a senior in English at Florida International University.
After she left to serve another table, Zeekie and I poured the brew
and clicked mugs together. Boy, did that cold beer taste good and
feel great going down.

Zeekie gazed out over the water for a while and then shook his
head before picking up the thread of our conversation. "Yes, you
and Rebecca made a long-term investment in each other. I know
how you feel, Ben. You're newlyweds. Actually, you aren't even
married yet." He shook his head again. "Things change after you
tie the knot."

"Yes, but I'm going to do my best to keep it fresh," I answered.
Of course, love has to be exercised to keep it in shape. You work
at it to keep the muscle on and the fat off.

Zeekie studied me for a minute. "But something's eating away
at you, Ben. I can see it. Admit it. What is it?"

I admitted it. I told him about Rebecca's decision to stay longer
at the Mission, without David Thompson. I told him how she would
have to take the dugout down the *Rio Marauiá* and would have to
take a freighter down the *Rio Negro*, alone. I told him of my fear
for her safety.

"Well, I guess it'll all depend on how wild those Indians are
around the Mission and that river," Zeekie said.

"According to the books, the Indians living within two days travel from a mission are supposed to be 'missionized.'"

"Meaning that they are safe, docile and worthless."

Although Zeekie is a high school dropout and doesn't spend a lot of time reading books, he knows a lot. He has a good combination of smarts and common sense. Like me, Zeekie was able to make good grades without really trying. But unlike me, he didn't even try a little bit. He quit school at 16 and started working full-time in a T.V. repair shop so he could first get a car, then eventually his own place. He always had lots of girlfriends. But he's never had a formal higher education. That's left him with diverse knowledge and no structure to hang it on. But I have to admit that he always asks the right questions.

"What's it like where they're more than two days away from a mission?" Zeekie asked.

"Pretty grim if you're a woman and almost as grim if you're a man," I answered. "The Yanomama Indians treat their women like dirt. And when they're past puberty, it's open season on any female that isn't under the protection of a strong male. The woman could be gang raped by every young man in the tribe."

"Any way to protect herself?"

"By playing the part of a shaman woman — tough and mysterious. But that's not Rebecca's nature. She's more of a nurturer."

"I know what you mean. I saw a Discovery Channel piece on that one night. Didn't see it all — just when the ball game had commercials. The Yanomama are pretty Old Testament. You kill my brother, then I organize a raiding party and kill you or a warrior from your tribe. And I kidnap a couple of women, too. That's what they said, but the film didn't show any of that."

"Rebecca told me they aren't raiding each other anymore. I hope she's right." I paused to give Zeekie a chance to say something comforting but he didn't. "The descriptions of the raids are from books by Napoleon Chagnon. He's a famous anthropologist who did some important studies in the 1960s. The way he described the raids, it sounded like aircraft carrier warfare in World War II."

"How's that?" Zeekie had been listening, but his eyes were wandering all over the place, sizing up everyone in the half-full restaurant — especially the females.

Hell, if Rebecca didn't want me to worry and my friend was acting like there wasn't any problem, either, then I'd be damned if I was going to cry in my beer tonight. I drew the analogy with humor.

"It's like World War II carrier warfare because they strike from a distance. A raiding party leaves the village at the crack of dawn all loaded up with food, spears and arrows. They make camp a couple of hours journey away from the target village and move in to attack at dawn. With luck, they pick off a man who's out hunting or kidnap a woman working in the garden. Then they retreat to their own village and brace themselves for when the other village decides to do the same thing to them. It might be in a couple of days. It might be in a year."

"Sounds more like gang warfare. Turf wars."

"I agree. But none of the anthropology books made that comparison."

"No, I guess that would make it all too easy. Better to draw it out and keep people writing dissertations," Zeekie said with a smirk.

"I agree. What the academics do seem to be studying is whether they were doing all this fighting to keep down the population density and to keep other villages from encroaching on their sources of food — monkeys, birds, peccaries and so forth. Different villages or *shabonos* relocate from time to time along a circular route. They do it when their gardens are exhausted and the dung beetles can't keep up with the turds that are being laid down on the perimeter."

Zeekie gave me a smile for that one.

"What did the books say about marriage?"

"It's marriage by proclamation. A man can have more than one wife if he can feed and defend them. But sometimes the women are dissatisfied. There are a lot of extramarital affairs. The illicit couples meet each other in the middle of the night out in the forest. They pretend that they had to go out to take a pee. When the guy who's cheated learns what is going on, or when he can't ignore it any longer, the problem gets settled with a club fight. If one of them is killed in the fight, then the *shabono* splits into two groups along kinship lines. The smaller group has to leave."

Zeekie wrinkled his nose. "What's a guy have to do to find a wife? Go out and kidnap her from another village?"

"No, every so often one village invites another for a feast. It goes on for several days. The older men trade bows and machetes and try to line up suitors for their daughters. And there's a lot of ritual dancing and the younger men engage in athletic contests."

"Sounds like a cross between a plantation cotillion and a track-and-field meet."

We laughed together, hard and long. Julie came with our food. She regarded me through a swatch of blond hair before putting our plates down. She was medium height and nicely proportioned. The waitress kangaroo pack didn't detract from her figure at all, nor did she make the slightest allowance for it. It dangled as she stretched to set the plates on the table. With a reach like that, she had to be a good tennis player.

Julie asked what we were laughing so hard about. I asked her to imagine a social event that was a combination of a plantation cotillion and a track-and-field meet. She said it sounded like a new survivor game show on TV. We all laughed at that. But when I told her we were talking about an anthropological study of South American Indians, she didn't bat an eye. She just whisked back a strand of blond hair and told me she was reading a book called *Guns, Germs, And Steel* by Jared Diamond. She told us a little about it. Zeekie said the food looked good and that she could bring us another pitcher of beer. Julie went off to get it.

Zeekie lit into his grouper sandwich. The beer had obviously depressed his blood sugar as much as it had raised his mood in the beginning. After a couple of minutes, he was smiling again and ready to go on.

"Now, tell me, Ben. What kind of athletic contests do they have for the teenagers?"

"You could call it 'pulping the pecs.'" The beer was affecting me, too.

"What the hell is that? — 'pulping the pecs.'"

I smiled and probably giggled. "Well, Zeekie, after a couple of days of trading, dancing, pigging out, and snorting hallucinogenic snuff, the party scene starts getting a little old, and the young machos start putting on a series of chest-pounding duels. Sometimes it starts with an insult, or sometimes it's just a friendly challenge to see who is the biggest macho. Anyway, the challenger has to stand there and take it like a man, presenting his chest while the challengee gets to hit him twice on the right side of the chest, on the pectoral. And if he is still standing, then it's his turn to throw the punches. And this goes on until they have pulped each other's pectorals."

"Sounds like an old John Wayne movie."

I snorted. "Or until they faint in each other's arms, blubbering promises of undying friendship."

"Sounds like that Al Pacino movie where he was an undercover detective."

Julie came with a new pitcher and poured the remnants of the old one into our glasses, shaking her head as if to say, "Boys will be boys." When she left, I continued. The beer was loosening up my brain and dispelling my worries. And I had enough pent-up frustration to power a sarcastic monologue.

"Anyway, if they aren't into pectoral pounding they can go into side-slapping contests. They don't give up until they start pissing red. There are always some good sports around from both sides to make sure everything is done fair and square. But sometimes even the good sports get into disagreements about what's fair, and people go back to their hearths to get their clubs, and then the situation really does resemble a saloon fight in one of those old westerns."

"Have some more beer, pardner?"

"Thanks, pardner. Anyway, the two headmen have to try hard to stop the saloon fight, so that their *shabonos* don't turn into enemies. That anthropologist described a feast where the mood turned sour around the third day. The guests started complaining that the spread was too cheap. They left in a huff, caucused outside and then came back and raided the host *shabono*." For some reason I laughed at the thought of it.

Zeekie was laughing, too. "That reminds me of how the guys trashed a girl's house after a prom party back in Philly." We pounded the table together.

"Hell, that's what happened at *my* high school," I said.

"Yeah, it's like we went to the same high school." Zeekie was getting loud. We both were. "Say Ben, do you think that big shot anthropologist named after Napoleon went to the same kind of high school that we did? I guess not, or he'd know that his highfalutin' anthropological findings are trivial. We already know that Man's a natural fighter — and fucker, too! That's why the jocks get all the broads."

"Agreed. I'll drink to that. Here's looking at you."

"Maybe that Napoleonic anthropologist didn't go to high school. Maybe he skipped it, like the rest of us Mensans."

Julie slid in, asked me if everything was okay, winked, and slid out. She did it all so fast that she hardly interrupted our conversation.

"Could be, Zeekie. The Society seems to have a lot of theoreticians." I paused while Zeekie poured more beer into our mugs. "You know, reading those books got me thinking up a lot of theories. Like why most of the men in those villages sit around in a hallucinogenic trance most of the day every day, just like in the inner city. And why they never use curare-tipped arrows against each other, even in warfare. It's like the chemical weapons ban they had after the First World War. And all that shamanism. I'm wondering if they need this nonsense to keep people from thinking for themselves. I mean, if they started thinking for themselves maybe the whole social structure would become unstable, or the women would . . ."

I stopped talking because Zeekie wasn't listening. His humorous mood was gone. He'd been paying all his attention to his sandwich and refilling our mugs from the second pitcher of beer. It was now half-empty and he just sat there, staring at me and shaking his head.

"Ben, you're too full of theory," he said with a strong echo of West Philly. "It won't get you nowhere."

I frowned. "Bullshit! If you don't have theory, you don't know anything. Without theory, you're just trying to pick up the pieces . . . of other people's messes."

"Bullshit," Zeekie shot back. "You think your theory's so good, you tell me this. Your wife's out of town and Alice McRae's been after you for years. Now what are you going to do about it? Tell me, right now!"

"Couldn't do it, Zeekie. Just couldn't do it."

"Why not? Just a little playing around. Playing the field, like we did in high school."

"I didn't play the field in high school. I was on the debate team and I played chess."

Zeekie clicked his tongue and regarded me with a knowing smile. "So Ben didn't get any in high school." He shook his head. "And it doesn't sound like you hung out with the guys, either." Now he was sounding thicker than Rocky.

"I hung out with the geeks and fought off the Newark accent twenty-four hours a day."

"Jees," he said, shaking his head like he was wondering what had become of me. "Well, at least I know that you were getting a lot when I first met you."

I smiled. "Yeah, I was playing Don Juan in Little Havana."

"Did you get any in that college you went to?"

"My college was Swarthmore," I said with pride. "Yes, I had a lot of fun at Swarthmore. It was full of girls that liked to curl up with a good book . . . or with a guy who read one."

"Jees, Ben. Sounds too nerdy for me. Doesn't sound like a healthy girl at all. Sounds like one of those slinky willow sticks that wears pointy glasses with black frames and shares a can of tuna fish with her cat."

Zeekie drove his point home with a laugh that could rattle trash cans. His humor was irresistible. After he got me laughing, he locked onto me with an all-knowing grin and wagged his head from side to side until I was laughing out of control. Then, as if to rescue me from hyperventilation, he reached across the table and put a hand on my shoulder.

"Here, Ben, I want to do a thing with you. You got one of your business cards along? Give it to me." I gave him one and he inspected it with mock admiration. "Pharmacology consultant. Expert evaluations. Due diligence. Wow! Now lets see if you've been just as diligent with your personal life. Put up both hands and spread your fingers."

We were interrupted by Julie, who came to take our plates. She looked at my spread fingers and asked, "What are you guys doing now?"

I kept my fingers up and replied, "We're playing paddy cake, paddy cake, macho man."

Zeekie didn't miss a beat. "Gotta get the girls, wherever we can."

"Wow, you guys ought to get a job at the Comedy Spot."

"I'm into video," Zeekie said. "They used some of my footage on Hard Copy a few months ago."

I gave Zeekie a frown.

"Awesome," Julie said, talking to Zeekie but looking at me. "And what does your friend do with you besides playing macho games?" Her question was addressed to him but she gave a wink to me. She may have raised her eyebrows, too. They were trimmed short and narrow so it was hard to tell. She didn't use pencil or even makeup, for that matter. Her style was a clean, wholesome presentation. I smiled up at her and shook my head nonchalantly. Hell, this was Zeekie's show.

Zeekie handed Julie my card. "Call me Zeekie. And his name's Ben. Ben is a big-time pharmacology honcho. An expert in drug intoxication. Makes his bread working for lawyers."

"Interesting!" She handed Zeekie back the card while looking down at me, speculatively.

I shook my head at Zeekie. "What he says is true, but right now I feel like the world's expert on alcohol intoxication."

Julie laughed it off. "Can I get you guys anything more?"

It was time to chime in. "Yes, Julie. You can get Zeekie and Ben two orders of french fries and then the bill."

When she left, I had words for Zeekie: "You shouldn't have done that."

"No, play along with me," he replied, "I'm on a roll. She thinks you're hot. And her friend working with her is twice as good looking. And they're both game. I've been *looking*."

"Zeekie, come on!"

"Hey, what do guys go out drinking for?"

"Male bonding," I answered, using Rebecca's terminology.

"Sure, using females as glue."

I passed on that one. I just laughed. I put my hands up like they were before the Julie came. "Okay. But first let's finish up that thing you wanted to do with me."

"Okay, Ben. Take another look at Julie."

I followed his orders. I turned my head and caught a glimpse of her by the waitress stand. She looked damn good.

"And now look down on those ten fingers."

"Okay."

"And now tell me if you can count on every one of those fingers a girl that you've made it with who is just as good as Julie."

My heart sank. I looked up from the ten fingers into Zeekie's eyes. He wasn't gloating. He wasn't laughing at me. He was just making a point.

"I'm not going to answer that one, Zeekie. But you've made your point."

Yes, to his way of thinking he'd made his point as solidly as a geometric theorem.

"Stick around for a minute," he said. "I'm going to set something up for us."

"Whoa! You tell her anything, you tell her I'm engaged. And don't say anything about my involvement in that Hard Copy story or that thing at the medical school."

"I promise."

And he was off. I have to admit that it was interesting to watch him doing his thing with those two girls at the waitress stand on the far side of the deck. The guy's a definite chick magnet. The first time the girls glanced in my direction, I smiled and waved back. Then I looked out on the water, listening with half an ear to the conversation of a couple of older guys at the table next to ours. It was about racquetball. The Germanic-looking one with the short, white hair was telling the long-faced, English-looking one why he'd been able to score so many points on him with his serves. They both had standard American accents but they peppered their conversation with fragments of German. The English-looking one made a joke about "winning the campaign by default" if the German-looking one's knee didn't mend in a month or so. It seems like they were professional colleagues who had been playing a weekly game of racquetball for years. When Zeekie returned with the french fries, a big yellow Labrador appeared from under the English-looking guy's feet. I gave him a few french fries. The English-looking guy said the dog's name was Scotty and the German-looking guy said that Scotty loved to run and didn't have a mean bone in his body.

After Scotty was pulled back under his own table, I asked Zeekie what was up.

"They get off in a little while and they want to see my video equipment. Might turn it into a little garage party."

"Do they know I'm engaged?"

"Yes."

"Okay, party master. I'll play along . . . as a favor to you."

We didn't talk any more. I ate all my french fries and walked along the rope railing to the "Buoys Room" for a necessary correction to my fluid balance. I'd drunk a hell of a lot of beer. When I returned, the old guys with the dog were gone. Actually, the whole place was pretty emptied out. Zeekie was at the waitress stand chatting with Yvette. She had a dynamite figure, a delicate neck, a cute pixie face, and lots of blond hair that was all piled up on the top of her head and shaped like a canoe stern in back. And she didn't speak a word of French.

Julie came bouncing out of the kitchen, minus her waitress kangaroo pack and Zeekie told me he'd taken care of the check. We took off as a footloose foursome. I let Zeekie do all the talking, opening my mouth occasionally to confirm what he said or to smile at the girls. We walked between the I-beam scaffolds in the deserted boatyard, dodging oily puddles. I waved to the night watchman. Then Zeekie led us between the Australian pines to the empty parking lot.

Zeekie opened the rear door of his van and flipped on the lights.

"Gee, you weren't kidding," Yvette said. "It looks like a network control room."

"Independent producer's control room," Zeekie said with pride.

He flipped some switches and the van started thumping with DJ music. He flipped some more switches and a flat, state-of-the-art, 27-inch monitor lit up in blue.

Julie grabbed my arm and hollered into my ear, "What is he going to do?"

"Take you for a ride on Joe Kazekian's magic Armenian carpet," I shouted back.

Zeekie jumped out of the van, holding a video camera that was tethered to the van's interior with a long umbilicus. The camera sprouted a small hemispheric reflector at the end of a short outrigger boom. When he turned it on, it flooded our dark corner of the parking lot with light, like one of those deep-sea exploration vessels. And that was exactly what the device was doing. It was swimming all over Yvette. And inside the van, the monitor's solid blue screen transformed into a high-definition picture of statuesque legs over gray asphalt. Yvette yelped in surprise and did a girlish hop like she'd discovered a mouse. The projected legs were ultra-charming. Soon Yvette caught on and started dancing to the music.

She was a natural dancer and she really got into it. Zeekie shouted to keep on going because a tape was running.

Looking at the monitor, I didn't have any problem imagining how Yvette looked to Zeekie's masculine eye. In fact, if there's such a thing as making love to a girl with a video camera, Zeekie was doing it then and there. His eye caressed her face, found the place where that spiral of blond hair dangled around her ear, and tickled it. He slid down the tendons of her neck and plunged into her blouse. Then he swarmed over her hips and thighs. And every part that Zeekie's eye selected, Yvette brought to life. It was like they were electronically connected — a positive feedback loop set to max out on hedonism.

Of course I didn't just stand there. I grooved to the music and flashed an occasional smile of encouragement to Julie who was grooving, too. The music was techno-rock — slow percussion interlaced with some repetitive electronic effects and held together by the continuous dirge of an electric guitar. The music provided an endless foundation for artistic overlay. Within 10 to 15 minutes Yvette had exhausted her repertoire of moves. And Zeekie had exhausted his, too. As I said, it was like making love to a girl with a camera.

Zeekie handed the camera off to me, indicating I was to do the same thing for Julie. She, too, squealed with delight and started dancing. But she was a lot shyer than Yvette, and I had to keep my masculine eye under control to record a good performance without getting too personal. Didn't linger on her breasts like Zeekie did with Yvette. But Julie had a lot of aerobic dance steps, and I picked up a lot of good calf and thigh action in addition to full-body shots from different angles. About five minutes into our performance, Zeekie turned down the volume halfway and guided Yvette into the picture with Julie. After I zoomed back, all three were in the frame. There was Zeekie, sandwiched between the two girls, dancing in place, holding a microphone, displaying his chest hairs through the unbuttoned top of his shirt and carrying on like a Las Vegas showman. The girls danced sensuously, with amazing coordination of moves. Zeekie sang a lot of Jim Morrison inspired phrases to the music. And that made a damned good show for five minutes. The background track kept rolling, endlessly.

Zeekie didn't give me much warning. He just put on that grin,

like before. "And now, from Newark, New Jersey, but without a
New Jersey accent . . . with a genius I.Q. and a literary B.A. from
Swarthmore . . . is Mister Super Geek, himself, Doctor Ben
Candidi!"

Zeekie rushed the camera, taking it away from me while
keeping it trained on the girls. He put the mike in my hand and
pushed me towards the girls until I was in the frame.

Hell, I hadn't counted on this. I worked up a tight pattern of
steps that put me in sync with the girls. I gave each of them a smile
before looking up at the monitor. Damn! I didn't look any more
impressive than Woody Allen. Okay, I thought to myself, when
life hands you a pail of lemons, you make lemonade. I relaxed my
face into a bored expression and tried to think of something that I
could squeeze for 10 minutes. The guitar dirge was steady and I
could build on it.

Literary nerd from Swarthmore, huh? Literary! Trying to bait
me in front of Julie, the English major. Like I was going to recite
some damn poem, huh? Well then that was exactly what I would
do. But the only memorized poem I could bring to mind at the
moment was "Richard Cory" by Edwin Arlington Robinson. Well,
to hell with trying to give any kind of dignified treatment to the
century-old poem. I selected a raspy, punk voice and kept the bored
affect.

I got the first verse perfect, putting special emphasis on "went
to town" and "gentleman from sole to crown." I stole from the
third verse to get "he made us wish that we were in his place." I
used that as a vamp, half singing it while trying to remember what
came next. The girls caught on quick and sang along, each trying
to outdo the other with a sassy pop tart voice. Great, now we had
a chorus.

The poem's ABAB rhyme pattern helped me along: By the
end of the second verse I had the perfect gentleman quietly *arrayed*,
most human when he *talked*, fluttering pulses when he *said*, and
glittering when he *walked*. In the third verse I laid it on nasty where
Richard Cory was richer than a *king*, schooled in every *grace*, and
where we thought he was every*thing*, and made us wish we were
in his *place*. I probably hammed it up too much in the last verse,
gyrating with the girls while waiting for the *light*, cursing my *bread*
and describing the summer *night*. Julie seemed to know the poem

and helped me work it up to a climax where the man "put a bullet through his head."

As if on cue, Julie vamped on "bullet through his head" and Yvette joined her. I traded off with the girls by reciting phrases like "schooled in every grace" and "everything in place."

As Zeekie gave me permission to quit by inching back the volume slide bar to produce a fade-away, I noticed that we'd attracted a sizable crowd. And they applauded like we'd just taped a real video. They wanted to know when it was going to be on MTV. Zeekie turned the camera on the crowd, taking them in with a slow pan. Then he handed out business cards, saying that advance copies would be ready next week. Then a City of Miami policeman drove up with flashing lights, clicked his PA at us, announced that we were causing a public disturbance, and gave us two minutes to disperse.

Yvette rode off with Zeekie. Julie offered me a ride home, which I accepted because the Metrorail was already closed.

Julie's car was a black VW Jetta. As she zipped us out of the parking lot, I complimented her on the most excellent pop tart voice she'd used in the choruses. She hit the button for an oldies station and told me she'd always liked to sing. So we went on a "Surfin' Safari" along South Bayshore Avenue and then did a close-harmony duet on "I'm Leaving It Up to You" while driving up 17th Avenue. The Jetta put us at close quarters. During the duet, Julie's hand came down on my forearm when she wasn't shifting gears. But a commercial put an end to all that about a mile away from my house.

Julie said she hadn't had so much fun since singing karaoke with a bunch of friends at the Mandalay Inn in Key Largo. Could I get her a tape of our "Richard Cory" performance? Yes, I promised to have Zeekie send her one. And when we reached my curb, I thanked her for the ride and said I'd be looking for her the next time I visited Captain Walley's.

When she presented her cheek, I leaned over to kiss it. And as I did, she turned her face to make it a kiss on the lips. And the instant that swatch of blond hair brushed my cheek, I felt like a teenager in Newark. Julie was turned on. She leaned back in the seat, wrapping her arms around my neck so I couldn't escape her lips. They were so thin but so full of life. Her blue eyes twinkled with the reflection a distant streetlight. She sighed.

I turned my head and whispered in her ear. "Thanks, Julie. I have to go."

She sighed again. "I know. Zeekie told me about you. You're engaged. Too bad. You're such a fun guy, Ben."

"You too, Julie."

I closed the door and she drove off. In my office, the answering machine was blinking. It was Mona asking me to give her a call when I got home because Zeekie was not answering his cellphone and she was worried. I decided to pretend to have not gotten the message if she called again. I went to the upstairs bathroom and washed my face, then my hands. I held them in front of the mirror and counted on my fingers. I tucked in a couple, thought a little, and then untucked them. What was the numerical answer to Zeekie's question, anyway? It was a stupid question — one that could only make a guy sad. There was a much better way to use my fingers to keep score. I looked at the ring finger of my left hand. That was the one I was reserving for Rebecca Levis.

14   Dream Machine

The next morning was Thursday — of my fourth week without Rebecca. Around breakfast time, Zeekie called to thank me for going out with him and to say that he'd gotten home at one-thirty. He needed me to cover for him if Mona ever asked me about the evening. He'd spent a lot of time with Yvette, jiggling the springs of his van at Kennedy Park. I told him thanks for dinner and beer and that, sure, I'd cover for him with Mona. I could promise that because there wasn't any chance that she would ask me, anyway. Zeekie wanted to know whether I'd made it with Julie. I told him I could have but didn't want to. Before he could chide me, I told him that he owed Julie a tape of last night's performance and that he'd have to deliver it to her at work because I didn't have her

Dirk Wyle 141

address. Zeekie said that was no problem; he'd just give Yvette an extra one, the next time they were together.

I told Zeekie it was time for both of us to get to work. I finished breakfast glumly, mulling over the DEA visit, the fallout from the Edith Pratt episode, Rebecca's decision to stay longer, and the new problem that had cropped up with Michael. But the good news was that my hard work had put me very far along with the report. I decided that the best way to spend the day would be to do more work on conceptualizing my invention. I dreamt away while scribbling on a notepad:

For my demonstration project — "the first embodiment of my invention" — I wouldn't use any super-miniaturization. That could come later. I would probably construct the drug receptor dots using regular hospital lab technology — a microtiter plate with maybe 1,000 large wells. And I'd use a simple fluorimeter to read how strongly my dots glowed. And I'd test out my concept using a couple dozen well-known drug-receptor proteins that I would beg off of scientists who worked with them every day. Then all I'd have to worry about was cooking up a dozen drugs on the ends of fluorescently labeled Kramer strings. I could probably pay a graduate student in the chemistry department to do that for me.

Yes, I should be able to reduce my invention to practice without any help from Michael and his elusive company. Hell, after I got that HPLC machine working in our upstairs room, I would be able to do all the crucial experiments under my own roof!

I dreamed on. After completing my first experiments and filing a patent application, I would publish my results. Publications would help to get investors and more scientists who would collaborate for free. The project would snowball. Eventually, every scientist with a specialized protein would be clamoring at my door to have it included on my drug discovery chip. Hell, it would be the biggest boondoggle since they started sending biology experiments up on the Space Shuttle! And if I couldn't get money from the National Institutes of Health, I'd bootstrap my way up to financial success by doing small drug discovery projects for pharmaceutical companies.

I dreamed on, in high gear. I imagined myself as a project manager with a history of success with microtiter plates and $10 million to spend putting the system on microchips. I leaned back and visualized my dream machine. I would use existing hardware, starting with the 10,000-spot silicon chip and chip-spotting technology of the Analytica Corporation of San Diego, California. I'd probably contract out to them the job of spotting the proteins on the chip. The chip would snap into their "Fluidics Station" which is half the size of a video cassette. And I'd use their Analytica Array Scanner" to read out the glow on the spots.

My dreams went global. I'd take my machine into the jungle and do bioprospecting. I'd take along a digital camera to photograph each plant specimen for complete identification. And I'd take along a GPS unit that would make super-accurate longitude and latitude measurements so that I could come back to the same plants, again and again. When I found several dozen new drugs in the rain forest, that would turn some drug company executives' heads! Hell, when the project reached its full potential, it would be worth 100 billion dollars!

My daydream was disturbed by a ringing telephone. It was Michael.

"Ben, I'm sorry that our phone call was interrupted, yesterday. It happened when I drove into the parking garage."

That was just a cheap excuse for hanging up on me. It was a lie because I hadn't heard any signal switching during that phone call. He'd been sitting in one place the whole time. But it was a useful lie because here we were, talking again.

"Yeah. I guess that all that steel in the parking garages scatters your signal. What can I do for you?"

"I'll be in your neighborhood and would like to stop by."

"Sure, chief," I said without a trace of rancor. "When do you want to come?"

"In about five minutes, if that's okay."

"Fine. See you then."

He must have been calling me from one-half a block away because the buzzer sounded one minute later. No problem: I'd been planning to receive him in shorts and T-shirt, anyway. He cut a fine figure with his European-cut suit and thin leather carrying case, standing in the doorway.

"Come on in, Michael. Take your jacket? No? Coffee, juice or mineral water? No? Well have a seat." I turned the ceiling fan a step higher and pulled my chair around the desk to be closer to him.

"We want to know everything on three companies, particularly one named Xantha." He handed me a sheet of paper with the address of Xantha and the two other companies.

"Well, I've visited Xantha's website already. And I've already written them into my draft report. They're privately held and seem to be playing their cards pretty close to the vest. But they do look well-positioned to become a drug discovery company."

"Good. We'd like you to look closer."

"Okay. What aspect should I be looking into?"

"Their chances of economic success, especially in the next two years. If you can find out anything about their equipment or testing paradigms, we'd like that, too."

"Do you want a deep dig?"

"As deep as you can go."

"Well, I'm really trying to finalize my interim report to be able to give it to you in smooth by the deadline. Now, I'd be glad to spend a few more hours on Xantha and those other two companies. Would I have your okay to bill for extra hours for anything more?"

Michael took that without batting an eye. "Yes, for Xantha."

"Great! You've got it, chief. Anything more I can do?"

He reached into his leather carrying case and pulled out a handful of diskettes. "These are blanks. I would like you to make copies of your files on this project and your interim report as it stands now. I can wait while you do it."

"But the interim report isn't ready, Michael. And the files have all sorts of notes to myself which would be inappropriate to transmit."

"I understand what you're saying. But I have a lot invested in this project and I want a copy for safe keeping. What would happen if you had a fire or if someone broke in and stole your computer?"

"I have a fire and burglar alarm system, plus one hell of a good neighborhood crime watch."

"Phone line or wireless alarm?"

"Phone line."

"Phone lines can be cut."

"But I've already backed up the files, Michael, in a safety-deposit box."

"I will need a copy, nevertheless."

How irritating, his quiet insistence. "I do not give out personal notes and half-finished documents."

"Why not?"

"Because I won't release anything before it's ready. After I have deliberated on something enough, I will write a final statement which will be my hundred-percent best assessment for that time. After that, I do not play games of second-guessing myself. Won't hand out tools for people to second-guess me, either."

Michael looked down at the diskettes in his hand and moved forward to give them to me. "I don't understand."

I showed him two flattened palms. "I don't want any half-baked stuff getting in the way of my final product."

We wrangled for a long time. Finally, Michael conceded but reminded me that the interim report was due in three weeks.

After Michael left, I put down the patent project and turned my attention to Xantha. I went back to their website: www.xantha-pharma.com. Their logo has Greek bow and arrow. They were located in Mountain View, California. They had several divisions. The oldest was in "regulatory affairs" — masterminding the submission of new drugs to the FDA. Their brag page on this listed several drugs they had ushered in. Two of the drugs had been discovered at the nearby Stanford University School of Medicine in Palo Alto. The company also offered services for hire: analytical chemistry and fermentation. That page had pictures of a lab and gigantic fermentation vats.

But the page didn't list any industrial clients. Maybe the company was running the show with investment capital. Obviously, they were expanding. Their "Opportunities at Xantha" page said they had open positions for three pharmacologists, an analytical chemist, a fermentation microbiologist, an information scientist and several software engineers.

I combed most of the site without getting much scientific information. But when I clicked on a link named "Spectroscopy," I got a trove of information.

It was strange information. Every data set had a seven-digit Xantha number. The data set was cross-referenced to a *jpg* file which had a secondary descriptor with a crazy format:

00 10 wx
64 91 yz

where the "wx" and "yz" numbers jumped around while the other numbers were constant. I never did find the *jpg* files. That was a shame because a picture is worth a thousand words. The data files contained a 100 x 100 matrix of pluses and minuses. Almost all the values were minuses.

There were thousands of data files like these. I saved a few hundred on my hard drive to analyze later.

With that done, I looked in my browser's address slot and noticed that the strange "spectroscopy" data was from another computer within the company. With growing curiosity, I began working my way up through the computer's file structure. I found a trove of *gif* pictures which I could actually download. These were pictures of chart outputs of analytical instruments — an HPLC machine which separates drugs from mixtures, and a mass spectroscopy instrument which identifies structures of chemical compounds. They were doing serious characterization work on drug compounds. I saved as much as possible, then sniffed around for another hour until I was interrupted — by a phone call from Rebecca's mom.

She wanted to know why she hadn't heard from Rebecca. I had forgotten to tell her that Rebecca's return would be delayed. And did I catch hell for that! She also blamed me for Rebecca's going to Brazil. Somehow, I had made the girl "adventuresome." She blamed me for Rebecca's staying in Miami after graduating from med school. Rebecca should have returned to the Northeast. She should have a regular medical practice by now. And why hadn't I gone to medical school and become a doctor, too?

Well, to be fair to my future mother-in-law, she didn't really say those things. She'd said them between the lines. I'd heard much of it before. I talked with her for a long time. We were talking amicably by the time we hung up. By then, my Internet access server had already timed me out. Since it was late in the afternoon, I quit for the day.

By the end of the next day, Friday, I had a good draft of my patent application. And by Saturday noon, my interim report for Michael was almost finished! This freed me up to spend Saturday afternoon studying the files I'd downloaded from Xantha. I worked on them that Sunday morning, too, without making any real progress. Sensing that I had been working too hard, I devoted

Sunday afternoon to a bike ride to Key Biscayne and spent the evening reading the last two editions of the Atlantic Monthly.

Then came Monday, the first day of my fifth week alone in Miami. It didn't turn out to be a very nice week. I woke up around six on Monday morning, just in time to see a van pull up to the curb in front of my house. I watched it out the window for several minutes. Nobody got out. I kept an eye on it through breakfast.

I turned on my computer, went on-line and down-loaded my e-mails. One of them was very disturbing:

From: RLevis598@hotmail.com
To: ben-candidi@netrus.net
Subj.: Love You

Dearest Ben,
An amazing opportunity has come up. It will take two months more, perhaps longer. Please know that I am okay and make a harmless excuse to Mother. I'm sorry that you won't be able to e-mail me back. It's too complicated and difficult to explain. I will e-mail you as often as I can, but if you don't get anything, DON'T WORRY. JUST TRUST ME, AS I HAVE TRUSTED YOU.

Forever yours,
Rebecca

Why did she have hotmail.com as a return address? It made no sense. But I did know the meaning of the capitalized last line: It was a message in code.

Unwelcome Attention 15

I reread the e-mail's last sentence — the one that Rebecca had written in capital letters. She was echoing words that I had sent her in a telegram when I had been hiding out in the Bahamas. My clandestine investigation for Dr. Westley had blown up in my face. I had no choice but to flee to the Bahamas, leaving Rebecca to take the heat. My telegram gave her no return address and no explanation, except that I loved her and please trust me. And she *had* trusted me for those two months. Now she was sending me the same kind of message, asking me to trust her.

I wanted to trust her, but it didn't make sense. Why couldn't she tell me something more about her opportunity? It would have taken only a couple of lines. And what was so special about the present situation that I would have to trust her? Why could our communication be only one-way? Whose equipment was she using to uplink the message to a satellite? It wasn't David Thompson's dish because he had taken that contraption back to Miami. Supposing that someone out there had the equipment to uplink to satellites and let her use it, then why didn't she use them as a return address? She had never used Hotmail.com before, so why was she using it now? And if satellite links were so finicky down there, then why had she put herself through all the data- and bandwidth-intensive *http* rigmarole that Hotmail.com requires to set up a new account? And thinking as hard as I could, there seemed to be only one reason for taking out a Hotmail.com account: So that I could not tell where in the world her message had come from.

And if the people she was with were friendly, then why did she have to keep secrets?

I hit the reply button and composed a message.

From: ben-candidi@netrus.net

To: RLevis598@hotmail.com

Dearest Rebecca:
I get your message, loud and clear. But where are you?
And how are your messages getting to me?

Love,
Ben

Agitated and in no mood for desk work, I walked out of the
house and checked out the van that had parked out front early that
morning. I took down its license number and gave it a good looking
over. It was a tradesman's van, with double doors on the back and
right sides. But it bore no company name or phone number and all
the windows were tinted, including the front. The left side was
custom-modified with a small hemispherical window that was
about the right size to hold a camera. Perfect for a surveillance
van: The occupant could see out but nobody could see in. On the
roof, a small yellowed Plexiglas hatch was half-opened, providing
ventilation. And mounted in the center of the roof were three antennas.
Probably had a car phone, CB and two-way commercial radio.

I went around to the front, put my face close to the windshield
and cupped my hand to shield the daylight. The light inside was
murky and I couldn't see the back window. They'd probably hung
a curtain behind the driver's and passenger's seats. Too early to
make a move on this intruder, but I'd keep a close eye on him.

I returned to the house. After going through my other e-mails,
I opened the summary file that I'd assembled on Xantha, Inc. Over
the last two days, I had compiled a long list of questions on them.
It was time for a second visit to their webpage. I went back to
www.xantha-pharma.com, found the "Spectroscopy" link, and
clicked. This time it didn't take me to the data trove. It just gave
me a dictionary definition of spectroscopy. I consulted my Internet
browser's "history" file and selected the address that had given
me those files of undecipherable numbers. I pasted the file's address
into the *http* slot and hit "Return." I got back a screen saying "access
denied" and would I please resubmit my password. I hadn't needed
one before. I typed in "guest" and hit "Return." It came back again
as "access denied." I tried out passwords for half an hour until I

got a screen that said I had made too many attempts and please contact the systems security manager to have my access reinstated.

It's just human nature. It's frustrating to be locked out of a place you've visited before. And it was frustrating to see that van sitting outside my door. It still hadn't moved. I picked up the phone and dialed my across-the-street neighbor.

"Hi, Gertrude, this is Ben. The cats okay?"

"Yes, we're all fine."

"Katja came around the back porch a couple of days ago. We had a nice visit."

"Hope she didn't make a nuisance of herself."

"No, she was delightful. How are you? Read any good books lately?"

"Well, I'm over my William James kick and now I'm on Balzac." Having spent her whole life as a librarian, Gertrude was now realizing a childhood ambition: to read every book in the library. And having dealt with people her whole life, she had a good sense of what they wanted. "Is this a Crime Watch call?" she asked.

"Yes it is. Have you noticed that van parked in front of my house?"

"Yes. I was just thinking about taking down its number and calling up our community relations officer."

"Thanks, Gertrude. That would be a good idea. It's one of those heavily tinted window jobs, which can mean one of two things."

"Then let's find out which it is."

I gave her the license number and asked her to let me know what she found out.

I spent the most of the afternoon looking for descriptions of Xantha's scientific work in public databases. There were none. They hadn't published any scientific papers, they didn't have any patents, and the archives of the Pharma-Projects Newsletter reported no clinical projects and no alliances with other companies.

So I went back to the Xantha website, clicking on every link and hoping to find another wormhole to their data trove. Finding none, I returned to their front page and stared at a large photo of the company's headquarters. It was an upwards-facing shot centered on four men standing at the top of a cascade of stairs before a two-storey building. The men looked so small and the building looked so large. These had to be the company's key personnel. Curiously, the website had no special page with information on the company's executives.

Absent-mindedly, I ran my cursor over the men's profiles. Their names and positions popped up. The president was a tall, portly, white-haired gentleman who looked capable of giving grandfatherly attention to the firm. Although their images were only a few pixels wide, I could tell that the vice-presidents for operations and for business development were somewhat younger and looked like MBA types. The vice-president for research looked like one of those gregarious, semi-bald guys who can be seen smiling at you through his moustache on the social pages of the *Miami Standard*.

Although the website didn't offer any biographical data on semi-bald George Griffin, Ph.D., Vice-President for Research, I was able to find a load of scientific papers by him in the MedLine public database. He had been a biochemist and plant physiologist at the Stanford Research Institute (SRI), studying cellular ion transport mechanisms in desert plants. His last scientific paper from SRI was on "tyrosine kinase" inhibitors in cactus, two years earlier. My cross-check showed that SRI had just been issued a patent for medicinal use of one of his inhibitors and that he was the inventor.

While I kept digging, the van just sat there. Gertrude called back around four o'clock.

"Ben, the sergeant said it's not one of theirs. But we can't be sure it's not Federal agents, being so close to the river."

"Then I'll put out my own feelers on that. I've had a little contact with a certain DEA officer."

"Yes, Ted told me about it before he left." Gertrude was close enough to Pops' age to call him by his real name.

"Thanks for your help."

And thanks, also, to Pops who had organized our Crime Watch with military efficiency.

I dialed the number of the public affairs officer at the Miami DEA office and told her voice mail that our neighborhood Crime Watch was concerned about a van with license plate number U82-LYH parked in our neighborhood, and that if it was theirs and was involved in monitoring river traffic or if it involved me, could they please call me because we wanted to spare the DEA any possible embarrassment. And could she please be sure to share this message with agent Phil Henderson.

I completed my report on Xantha and faxed it to Michael, with an invoice for the extra work. My report didn't mention what I'd downloaded from my accidental access to the Xantha database. It probably wouldn't be legal to sell that information. But I might use it later if I could figure out what it meant. I quit work for the day and made dinner. Just before sundown, I looked out the window and the van was gone.

The next morning the van was there again: same van, same license number, same place. I gave it three hours, then called Gertrude just before lunch.

"Gertrude, it's Ben again. I'm sure you've noticed the van's here again."

"Yes, I most certainly did."

"I want to go down and make a preemptive challenge. Want to do it with me?"

"No, I think I'll just stay here and watch through the window."

"Fine, I'm doing it now."

I pulled a useful item from my bicycle kit before walking out the door.

I walked around, inspecting the van closely. Same deal as before. Listening hard, I could hear a ventilation fan. I tried the doors. Locked. I banged on the side doors and shouted, "This is a neighborhood Crime Watch action. We know someone is in there and we know it isn't police business. My name is Ben Candidi and we're giving you five minutes to drive out of here or we're going to incapacitate this van. If you think you have legitimate business here, you can either tell me now or call me at the following number."

I repeated my number three times, then went back to the porch so I could hear the phone if it rang. It didn't. I went back to the van and took out a week's worth of frustrations on it, rattling the sheet metal. "We know the van is occupied. The van will now be incapacitated and will then be lawfully impounded."

There was no answer, although I sensed a shift of weight inside. I looked underneath to verify that it was rear wheel drive. I went back and let all the air out of both rear tires. Then I removed the valves with my lifter cap.

I went back to the house. While I ate lunch, a police car rolled up. A patrolman stepped out and issued a ticket. Around 1:30 p.m., a wrecker pulled up and latched onto the van. Gertrude called. "Well, congratulations, Ben. You are successful. I called in that it had been abandoned."

"Thanks." I looked out the window. "I see it's being recovered by Molinas Towing. They've got a yard up on Seventh Avenue. Want to get in the car and follow them and see what kind of people step out?"

"No, that would be too exciting."

"Could you do me a favor? I have to go out on errands for a couple of hours. Could you keep an eye on the house. I'll put the alarm on."

"Why, of course."

Before leaving, I copied all my important files onto diskettes. Michael did have a point. If the van had been sent by Woody Woodpecker from the DEA, he might get a warrant and send in a team and confiscate everything. And if it was some kind of private action — for whatever reason — it could be worse.

I went to David Thompson's office at Bryan Medical School. He wasn't there, but his secretary was. She said he was on a field study in Costa Rica. I turned on the charm and got her to let me into his office to double-check my memory of my last visit. Yes, sitting next to Thompson's desk was his three-foot-diameter satellite dish. And his secretary verified something else for me: Thompson didn't have two of them.

The question burned in my brain. How had Rebecca gotten her Hotmail.com message to me?

I pedaled down to Union Planters Bank in Little Havana and put my diskettes in the safe-deposit box.

Back at the house, I composed an e-mail to Hotmail.com, asking whether there was any way to trace the origin of Rebecca's message.

The next morning, the van didn't return. But Nica did — around noon. By the time I noticed her, she had already pulled her bike up on the porch. When I came out to meet her, she offered her cheek like we were old friends. She looked so pretty and fresh, like she'd never broken a sweat — the same as the last visit. I gave her cheek a perfunctory peck then returned my attention to her bicycle. I decided not to invite her in. It would be a lot easier to resist her charm standing out here. Also, I didn't want our awakened neighborhood Crime Watch to think that Nica and I were overly friendly. Yet Nica was acting like standing on my porch was the most interesting thing in the world. What was she after, anyway?

"Nica, good to see you. Where are you biking today?"

"Down this side of the Miami River, and then up the other side."

I stepped back from the bike. She was holding the chain and combination lock. "For the exercise?" I asked.

"And for the sights." She wrinkled her nose. "The River has such a Latin feel. It makes me feel at home."

That's what I didn't want at that moment — for her to feel at home. I went for a formal reply:

"Are you saying that you're homesick?"

"No." Her enthusiasm was unquenchable. Words didn't mean a thing to this woman. She was all eyes.

"When did you get in?"

"Last night."

Her posture was so forward that she might have fallen on my shoulder. And her smile was so engaging that I found it hard to meet her gaze for more than a second at a time.

"Do you fly *every* Miami/Manaus flight for Varig?"

"Every second one. There are two crews. When the plane turns around to go back, we stay."

I looked down on the concrete floor of the porch. Several weeks of frustration were churning inside me: Dr. Jekyll and Mr. Hyde, Mr. Henderson from the DEA, the van, and the thing that Zeekie put me through the other night. I didn't need any new problems. This conversation would most definitely be held on the front porch.

"So how is your fiancé doing? You never told me his name."

"Emilio. Emilio Ribiero He's spending a lot of time at his hospital in Manaus and not enough time with me." She formed her lips in a pout.

"Well, I hope you don't feel *too* neglected." I put on a frown so it wouldn't seem like a flirt.

She sighed, then her face relaxed into a wistful smile. "No, I am proud of *meu amor* for all the good work he is doing. I wish I were trained to help him." She looked toward the screen door. "Could I have a glass of water?"

"Of course." I couldn't help it. It was like a reflex. Ditto for opening the door.

Quickly, Nica chained the bike to the rail and followed me in. And on the way to the kitchen, I decided to find out the real reason for her visit. I changed my offer to a glass of lemonade and she accepted. She took it back to the living room and chose one side of the couch. I selected a nearby chair.

Nica took a shallow sip, winked her approval and set the glass down on the side table. She looked up at the ceiling fan and shook her hair loose and rearranged her blouse. "Now that I have told you about my fiancé, it's time for you to tell me about yours."

I glanced at Nica's lemonade. She picked it up and took a more generous sip.

"Rebecca's not back yet."

"But isn't she supposed to be back soon?" she asked, full of interest.

Was she cultivating my friendship so that we could go sailing as a foursome when she brings Emilio up for the weekend? Maybe. Or did she want us to play it as a Platonic twosome, turning off our animal magnetism and exchanging confidences and information on how her *propolis* works? Not likely!

I looked up at Nica. Her eyes were wandering all over my face. *Muy simpática*. No, that was Spanish. *Muita simpática* in Portuguese. I asked myself what was going on behind those dark eyes. I looked away and held a little conversation with myself about unleashed passion and about Zeekie's comment about my wasted geek years in high school. How could it be possible to be just friends with her?

My fingers took refuge in my palms. "Yes. Rebecca should have been back, now. She's overdue. She stayed on after the expedition returned. She'll have to come back down one hundred miles of river, alone except for the *caboclo* who's steering the dugout canoe. And after that, she's got to hitch a ride on a freighter and go another four hundred miles. And I'm growing concerned."

Oh, how rapidly Nica adjusted her mood to mine! "But maybe she feels the work she's doing is that important. Maybe this is the only chance in her life that she will get to do it."

"But could you think of anything so important that she couldn't describe it to me in a satellite e-mail?"

"I don't know. Maybe she is having success treating a tropical disease." For the first time in the visit, Nica's gaze became diffuse.

"And why couldn't she tell me about it?"

"Maybe she doesn't want you to worry that it is dangerous."

Her answers had no logic. Would she say just about anything?

"Listen, Nica, I can't figure out how Rebecca's even able to send me e-mails after the expedition leader took back the satellite dish."

"Maybe there is a new visitor at the mission who can send e-mails."

"Then why didn't she tell me that?"

"Did you e-mail her back and ask her?"

"Yes."

"And . . . ?"

"And I haven't gotten an answer back yet. Maybe you are right. Maybe it hasn't been long enough for me to start worrying."

"Yes. And *don't* worry. Brazil is safer than you Yankees think. And the *Rio Marauiá* is safe. It's inside a national park reserved for Indians."

I should have thought through the implications of what Nica had just said, but the image of Rebecca alone out there was very upsetting. I worked hard to dispel that image and to figure out why Nica was visiting me.

Was Nica trying to turn off memories of Rebecca and Emilio so that we could devote full energy to ourselves in the present? Was she coming on to me as the "Perfect Stranger" that Carmen Lundy sang about? — When two strangers meet at a unique instant in time and exchange love energy, unencumbered by inertia of the past and not threatened by hooks in the future. "You do it for me and I'll do it for you." We meet and unwind each other's everything — except for our DNA. Our love pact is to do it now, and to never seek that moment with each other again. It leaves a bitter-sweet feeling. I'd known it once with a married woman. But that was before Rebecca.

When my eyes returned to Nica, she was looking with enthusiasm towards my computer and the papers on my desk. "It looks like you are making a lot of progress with your report."

"Yes, that's true. But how do you know?"

"When I came last time, you had a big stack of papers on your desk. Now, the stack is smaller and you have cardboard dividers between them. It looks like you're ready to put those — I do not know how you call them — metal posts through them and turn it in as a big, important report." She delivered the words innocently, with a fatuous smile.

Yes, I had transformed that pile. And now I should be storing the Appendix in the lockable file cabinet.

"What is your report about, Ben?"

"It's about selecting the right instruments to test drugs."

That was a lie, but I couldn't tell her exactly what it was about.

For a few seconds, Nica seemed lost in thought. "Does your report talk about how to find new drugs?"

"No, my report is about drugs you already have and want to manufacture to Food and Drug Administration specifications." That was, of course, an outright lie. But my work for Michael was confidential.

"Oh, it sounds so interesting, so technical. Can you show it to me?"

Of course I wouldn't show her the report, but I could show her a part of the Appendix that was harmless — a part that had nothing to do with drug discovery. "Yes, let me think," I said. I got up, flipped through the pile, looking for a company brochure that was technical enough to bore her to death. I pulled out Appendix G: Methods of Chemical Analysis.

Nica made room for me on the couch and I sat next to her. "Here's a collection of literature and company brochures describing a method called 'GC-Mass Spectroscopy.'" I pointed to the cover of a brochure on a $100,000 instrument. Nica wiggled closer. I flipped through the pages, talking quickly. "It can give you very precise information on the molecular structure. It works by — here they've given us a diagram — by injecting a collection of drugs in a column with a moving gas that carries them at different rates because some of them bind better to the column packing material than others. So drug A comes out before drug B. And when drug A comes out it is pushed through a — let's call it a spark gap — which breaks the drug up into small pieces."

"It doesn't burn up the compound?"

That was an astonishingly good question.

"No, it doesn't burn it because there's no oxygen in the column."

She pointed to the part of a diagram that showed a stream of particles coming out of the spark gap. The big ones traveled in a straight line; the smaller ones curved to the left. "And what's happening here, Ben?"

"Electrodes accelerate the fragments of drug A out of the spark and then another pair of electrodes bends their path. This separates and identifies the fragments according to their 'charge-to-mass *ratio*.'"

Nica's eyes darted across the page. She was either a hobby scientist or a good actress because her enthusiasm was palpable. I felt it through movement of the cushion. Her knee was almost touching mine. She pointed to where the small particles went on the diagram. "How does identifying these fragments identify drug A?"

"For the smaller fragments where we know the *ratio*, we know precisely how many carbon, nitrogen, oxygen and hydrogen atoms are in them. So you can write them down as a chemical compound. And the larger fragments can tell you the actual size of the molecule." Interested in what she would say to that, I cut the explanation short.

"How do you get from the structure of the smaller fragments to the structure of the larger fragments?" She was a good student.

"I'll give you an analogy." I rattled off four numbers that were related by addition and subtraction: 12, 16, 28 and 56. "Suppose those were the sizes of the fragments from your molecule. And suppose you know the structure of the *twelve* and the *sixteen*. What could you say about the other two fragments?"

She frowned for several seconds, then said, "The twenty-eight is made up of the twelve and the sixteen. And I guess that the fifty-six is made up of two twenty-eights."

"Exactly! You understand it perfectly."

And how wrong Alice had been about this girl! She'd make a better student than Pops.

Nica was now holding the brochure, and her knee was touching mine.

"Thanks for the explanation." She was all smiles. "Can I ask one more question?"

"Okay."

"Why do you need a machine that will separate drug A from drug B when all you want to do is analyze drug A?" She laid a hand on my forearm.

I concocted an explanation as fast as I could. "Because . . . because, you have to be sure that drug A is pure. And . . . the FDA forces you to do a complete analysis of any impurity over zero-point-one percent."

Wow, she'd almost made me spill it! The mass spectroscopy instrument was actually more of a drug discovery tool than method for quality control. No, I couldn't afford any more questions like this one, even if she was a layperson. Now was the time for me to go on the offensive.

"Nica, you are the most technically interested flight attendant that I've ever met. Did you study chemistry?"

"Just freshman chemistry. Then I took a course called environmental chemistry."

"Where did you go to college?"

"At — In Maryland, actually." Her knee pulled away.

I retrieved the brochure. "What university?"

"At the University of Maryland, actually."

I wondered why was she adding 'actually.' "What was your major?"

"Social sciences."

"What was your favorite course?"

"Oh . . . it must have been . . . Social Problems." Her answers came so slowly. She gazed beyond the screen door, then smiled. "We have a lot of social problems in Brazil."

"Yes, like you have coffee." I laughed and set Appendix G on the floor beside me.

"Maybe I should be going. You probably have to get back to your report."

"That's true, I'm sorry to say. But it was a lot of fun explaining it to you. I haven't had anyone else to tell it to."

"I'm sure that you explained it to Rebecca." She threw her arm across the back of the couch and turned to face me, pinning down my thigh with her knee.

"No, we don't talk about science much." That wasn't true, but something told me this would be the right answer to give Nica.

"Rebecca's interested in hands-on work with patients and I'm interested in analyzing my chemicals."

"You don't talk with each other about the details of your work?" She regarded me closely.

"No, not much."

Nica tapped my shoulder and giggled. "Except when she sends you to take notes at an anthropology conference."

It was remarkable how she had remembered everything I had told her.

I laughed along with Nica. "Yes, I attend lectures for her when she's slogging around in the Amazon jungle."

Slowly, a far-off look returned to Nica's face. "Don't worry about her, Ben. I'm sure she will be alright."

So she was back to that, again.

"It's just that she's never gone off like this before. Not since we've been together."

Nica stared down at my hands which were crossed over my lap. "You mean that since the two of you have been together, it was always you who made the decisions." She moved her hand on the back of the couch and stroked the back of my neck. What the hell was going on with us?

"Rebecca and I have made our career decisions together. When we moved to Washington, D.C., I subordinated my career to hers. But concerning things we've done together that involved . . . physical danger and . . . calculated risk, I've always been the one to make the decisions."

"When did you make those decisions?"

"When sailing our boat on the open ocean."

"Yes," she exhaled. Then she breathed in deeply.

I turned to look her in the face. But this time she did not answer my gaze. Her downcast eyes seemed to have lost their sparkle. She laid the other hand on my forearm, but did not move it. She seemed lost in thought.

When she finally did speak, it was slowly and with effort, as if she had to pump the words up from a deep well. "Maybe Rebecca feels like this is something she wants to do on her own . . . to prove to herself that she can face a new challenge, too. I don't mean that it has to be danger. Maybe it's just being off, doing something on her own."

I thought about it. "How could you know, Nica?"

She looked into my eyes. Gone was the sexy élan. She answered slowly. "I can't know for sure. I can only tell you how I have felt, myself. Sometimes, I feel dwarfed by Emilio. He is the physician in an important hospital, and I'm the . . . flight attendant." Huskiness crept into her voice.

"If I know anything about the Brazilian economy, *you're* the one who's making the money."

"That's true. But, still, it can be complicated, being engaged to a professional."

I thought of another reason why she was coming on to me — something that I'd read about in a book by Margaret Mead. I'd even given it a name: prenuptial probe stone. Before committing to marriage, the maiden sleeps with a man that she cares nothing about, hoping that he will be no better than her fiancé. Did Nica want me as a prenuptial probe stone for her feelings towards Emilio? I looked down on my spread fingers and remembered a girl who had used me that way once before. Her probe stone had left a scratch. That was before Rebecca, but it still hurt to think about it.

I had to know. Where was all this familiarly coming from? Was I her perfect stranger? Her prenuptial probe stone? Or would she let me off the hook as a Platonic confidant?

Without looking away, I stood up slowly and carefully, leaving my arms at my sides. Nica did the same. Behind me was a stairway that we could climb together. In front of me was a screen door that I could send her out. And front of me stood Nica, seeking me out with dark, languid and unfathomable eyes. Was our equilibrium distance really this close? With conscious effort, I tried to turn off all animal magnetism and let her drift away.

"Thanks for coming to see me, Nica." It came out as a whisper.

Slowly, Nica closed the narrow gap between us. As our noses came together, I tilted my head slightly. Her lips were soft on mine. So were her breasts, nestled against my lower ribs. Her arms found their way beneath mine and encircled my waist, drawing our hips together. I put my arms around her, drawing our chests together and massaging her back muscles, my fingers finding her shoulder blades. She shifted her weight and moved her hips.

We sustained a long, open-eyed kiss. At first, her lips were full, soft and compliant. But as we lingered in the kiss, her lips seemed to dissolve into mine, like confectioners sugar in spilt water. I waited for her tongue to come exploring. I waited for her to show me what she wanted.

She sustained the kiss beautifully. She had invited me to dance and I gave her the lead. I responded to every nuance, answering her high-pitched sigh with a squeeze and answering the movement of her breasts across my chest with a massage of her lower back. I kept answering everything until she gave me nothing more to answer. The dance didn't take us up the stairs.

Slowly, I disengaged, smiling. "Thanks again, Nica, for coming."

"Can I come again?" she asked, as coyly as a teenage girl.

"Yes," I answered, softly. "Any time for any reason."

She didn't blush. She didn't try to kiss me again. She didn't say anything more. She just smiled, bathing me in afterglow. But what act had we consummated? She stepped toward the screen door.

Beyond that door, Nica made no problems for me or my Neighborhood Crime Watch. She exited briskly and unlocked her bike. I carried it off the porch and out to the street. There, she said goodbye with a businesslike shake of the hand — supplemented by a wink and an air kiss from a distance of several paces. I answered that with a casual wave of the hand.

I didn't go right back to work. I took a walk in the backyard to the edge of the Miami River where I held a conversation with myself:

Ben, if you were a perfect stranger then she just chickened out. If she used you as a prenuptial probe stone, then you didn't scratch her. And if she used you as a Platonic confidant, what did she confide?

As I thought this stuff through, my eyes settled on a bass boat tied up on other side of river and on the guy sitting in it. The sides were low and I could see him well. He wasn't dressed for fishing. He was dressed in street clothes. So where was his girlfriend? Or had he taken out his boat to impress the pelicans? Or was he stalking Pops' boat or the *Diogenes*? I wrote down the Florida registration number and memorized the boat and as much of his face as I could make out from 80 yards.

The telephone summoned me back to the office. It was Michael, calling for more information on Xantha. I told him what I knew but left out the part about discovering the wormhole in their website.

After Michael hung up, I checked my e-mails. I received one from Hotmail.com, informing me, in generic language, that they could not tell me the point of origin of e-mail messages handled by them. I wrote back asking whether it was technically unfeasible or just a matter of policy.

For what was left of the day, I worked on my patent application, redrafting it so that I wouldn't need to do my own experiments. Something told me that I might have to submit that thing in a hurry. As it grew dark, I went to the kitchen to fix something for dinner. But the refrigerator was empty. I had known that yesterday, actually. I set the alarm and rode my bike a few blocks north to the Winn Dixie and did a week's worth of shopping. I should have stayed home.

16   Miami River Scramble

As I wheeled my grocery-laden bicycle up to the porch, I noticed what was wrong: The house was completely dark. And while leaning the bike against the porch rail, I heard the persistent beep of my computer's backup power supply. That made no sense because lights were on in the rest of the neighborhood. I started to walk around the outside of the house then hurried to the back after hearing the kitchen's screen door slam.

He was half-way across the backyard, running towards the river with a large object in his arms. "Stop, thief!" I shouted and ran after him. Boy, was I mad! He would have gotten away with it if he hadn't tripped on a crab hole. He let go of it as he fell. He stumbled for a few steps, then continued running at full speed towards the dock, heading for the empty space between the *Diogenes* and the *Alabama Tiger*. By the time he reached the dock, I was only a couple of yards behind. He jumped into a low, broad boat.

Mad as hell, I cannonballed after him. I managed an excellent two-point kick, landing with both feet on his shoulder blades. I snapped my body straight at the instant his face hit the far-side gunwale. It felt like I broke a couple of his ribs. But before I could get my footing, the motor went into high revs and the bow rose high on my left. The pitch and acceleration threw me towards the stern which was digging in deep. My legs hit the outboard engine housing and I fell upside down into the propwash faster than I could get my hands to my face.

It hit me with the force of a fire hose. The exhaust-laden froth went up my nose, forced open my mouth and filled my throat faster than nerves and muscles could react. The ugly brew hit my stomach and an instant later the propeller whine receded like a near miss torpedo. My stomach wretched. I threw up under water, emptying my lungs in the process. I struggled to the surface. It took a lot of willpower to inhale slowly to keep the witch's brew from working deeper into my lungs. I gave up my frantic dog paddle and Australian crawled to Pops' boat with one held breath. While clambering up the stern-mounted dive ladder, I grayed out. Scrambling over the *Tiger's* gunwale, I banged my shins and tore my pants. Hurt both knees tumbling onto the fantail. But I blessed that fantail as I knelt on it, coughing my lungs inside out.

When I could breathe again, I stumbled back to the house. Entered through the open kitchen door and made way to the sink where I gargled the stomach acid out of my throat.

After spending ten minutes kneeling upside down on the stairway, coughing unproductively onto a kitchen towel, I realized that it was too late to call 911. The boat already had enough time to make it to the mouth of the Miami River. Yes, I could call the Marine Patrol, requesting that they look for a bass boat with an oversized motor and two guys — one with several broken ribs. But what if I'd broken his back? Maybe it was best to keep the police out of it. And why weren't the police here already? Was something wrong with my alarm?

I grabbed a flashlight from the hallway closet and inspected the outdoor utility boxes. The phone line had been cut; the alarm company hadn't gotten a break-in signal. And the master switch in the circuit breaker box had been thrown. That's why the house was dark. When I threw the switch on, the living room lit up and the internal alarm started screaming. Why hadn't it worked before? The backup battery was probably dead. I rushed into the house and punched code into the keypad by the door to deactivate the alarm.

While I was getting the bike and groceries in, Gertrude came running over with a flashlight and putting iron. I thanked her for the quick response and gave her a short version of the events. She said I looked horrible and she insisted on doing something for me. She wanted to call the police or drive me to *Dade County General Hospital*. We finally settled on her helping me search the house for signs of damage while I went out into the backyard to retrieve what was missing from my desk — my Dell tower. I found it where the guy had stumbled. It was standing on its back end. I brought it into the kitchen and wiped a lot of dirt from around its cable connectors before returning it to the desk.

Gertrude reported that they had pried open the kitchen door, defeating its deadbolt. My inspection of the office showed that they had gone through my file cabinets and had tried to open the locked file cabinet — the one that contained the hard copy of my draft report together with its appendices and diskette backups. Well, Michael had been right about one thing — the need to secure the report against contingencies.

"What do you think they were after, Ben?" Gertrude asked.

"My computer, I guess."

"But it seems like an inefficient getaway car — a motorboat."

"I agree."

We discussed whether the Crime Watch was driving burglars off the streets, forcing them to use the river. I told her about the loitering bass boat I'd noticed after Nica's visit. And, yes, I mentioned Nica's visit. I identified her as "the fiancée of a Brazilian physician." There was no getting around that.

Gertrude and I talked for a long time before she agreed to return to her house. I agreed that she could be a witness if the police needed one.

Figuring that it was more important to put the computer back into service than to hold it for evidence, I opened it up and gave it a thorough cleaning. It worked fine when I fired it up. And after grabbing a pan and setting my camping slop dinner to simmer, *en boîte*, I went outside and spliced the phone wires back together.

I ate dinner from a can while verifying that I could retrieve files. And yes, the modem worked, too. And while connected, I did one thing too many: I checked my e-mails.

From: RLevis598@hotmail.com
To: ben-candidi@netrus.net
Subj.: Love You

Dear Ben,
The messages come from the satellite dish at the Mission which doesn't always work. I know you like to be in control of our relationship, but you shouldn't be trying to do that now. I am working on an important project. Rebecca.

How could she write that? Was she delirious with jungle fever? Were amoebas crawling through her brain? But if that were so, then why wasn't someone helping her? Whose satellite uplink was she using, anyway?

Did I even know that the message was from her?

After thinking for a long time about how to get answers to these questions, I hit the reply button and composed a message.

From: ben-candidi@netrus.net
To: RLevis598@hotmail.com
Subj.: Love you and trust you

Dear Rebecca,
Just a short note to say I understand and will respect your career and all that you are doing. I won't write again until you write me. I will end with some happy news. Your cousin Irene has just delivered a 6 pound boy, Joshua. And Jason is very happy.

Love, Ben

I looked at my watch: 8:45 p.m. It was not too late to call the *Funai* office in Santa Isabel. I dialed up their satellite phone. No answer. Tried again. Let it ring up to the automatic cutoff. Well, I'd try again tomorrow.

I paced around the house for a while until a good idea came to me. I reached into the center drawer and pulled out the little scrap of paper Nica had pressed into my hand at the end of her first visit. I was in luck. The number was good and she was there.

"Nica, this is Ben."

She responded with a quick inhalation. It wasn't quite a sudden gasp, but it wasn't the beginning of an effusive greeting, either. And she took a too long to answer. "Ben! How are you?" It sounded overdone.

"I'd like to say I'm doing fine, but I had to chase away a burglar tonight."

"Did you lose anything?"

"No. And I'm in okay shape, too."

"Good."

"The reason I'm calling has . . . uh . . . to do with . . . your visit this afternoon." I was drawing it out on purpose.

"Yes?"

"Well, it had to do with something that you said and it really got me thinking."

"Yes?" The word came out twice as cautious, this time.

"Well . . . I was wondering . . . since you . . . come from Brazil and . . ."

"Yes?"

I blurted the rest out. " — and know the language, maybe you could make some telephone calls for me down there."

She laughed, explosively at first. "Of course, Ben. Who do you want me to call?"

"The main office of *Funai*."

"Fine, I can do that. What do you want me to ask them?"

"Who else has satellite communications capability where Rebecca is."

"On the *Rio Marauiá*?" she asked.

Everything was going so fast.

"Yes, and especially at the Mission one hundred miles up the river. That's where she is supposed to be."

"Okay, I'll ask that. But you have been getting messages from her. What's the matter?"

"I haven't gotten any new messages from her." It was a white lie; Nica didn't need to know everything. "I'm very worried."

"I see. Okay, I'll ask them."

"And I have some more questions. Maybe you could write them down."

"Yes. I'll have to find a pen and some paper."

When she returned, I dictated my wish list. "Ask whether Rebecca is at the Mission. Ask who the other people are. Ask how long they will be there. And whether the *Funai* is informed of Rebecca's plans. And ask if they have a way for me to contact her if the other people leave."

"I'll see what I can do," Nica said.

"Great. You're a real friend. When are you leaving?"

"Tomorrow night."

"Good. I'll keep the phone line open the day after that. And tell me, when will you come back?"

"I don't know for sure, Ben. I'll let you know when I call."

"Good. And can you give me your phone number in Manaus?"

"Ben, it would be better if I just called you. I promise to call."

"Okay. And thank you so much. I don't know what I would do if I hadn't met you. You're something really special."

"Thanks. You are, too, Ben. But I have to hurry and can't talk any more now." She hung up before I could ask her what she was doing.

I went upstairs, looked through Rebecca's black bag and found what I needed: a small bottle of a floxacin-type antibiotic — a class of broad-spectrum, bacterial "gyrase inhibitory" antibiotics that are especially effective in treating pneumonia. The pills would wipe out my digestion but that was a lot better than getting pneumonia. I washed the first pill down with a good quantity of gin to make me sleepy. Before going to bed, I drove a screw into the kitchen door to secure it against another visit. And I set the alarm — the first time I'd ever armed the alarm when I was inside the house.

The next morning, I concentrated on that satellite phone in Santa Isabel. I dialed it every 15 minutes, getting no answer. Around eleven in the morning, I called the Brazilian Consulate in Miami and asked them to do the same things I asked Nica. A little after one o'clock, they called back and said that they had confirmed with the main *Funai* office that the satellite phone number I was trying was correct. I said that nobody was answering it, and could they arrange for the Santa Isabel *Funai* branch to call me and I'd pay for it. And I renewed my request for information on any satellite-communications-enabled people presently on the *Rio Marauiá*.

I decided not to report the break-in to the police. There simply wasn't time for it. But I called the alarm company, explaining how their system had been defeated and insisting that they replace the siren's backup battery. And I asked the phone company to send a man to do a professional job of repairing the cut line.

I spent the rest of the day working on the report. I worked fast and efficiently, but not for love of the project. I had to get the damn thing off my desk so that I wouldn't have to worry about it the next time they attacked — and so that I'd be free for Rebecca. For the rest of the day there was no news. I worked long into the night and set the alarm before going to sleep.

The next morning a guy from the alarm company came to replace the backup battery. I worked hard on the interim report, intending to finish it by the end of the day. Impatiently I worked on, hoping for Nica to call me from Manaus and checking my e-mail every hour. I didn't get any e-mail from Rebecca, but I got one from Hotmail.com. They wrote back that it was not technically feasible to determine the point of origin of Rebecca's e-mail. By late afternoon, the report was almost done. Just a few little things to do and I could print it out.

Nica's phone call came shortly before six:

"Ben, this is Nica. I've got some news from you. I checked with the *Funai*. They told me that a German medical team has permission to visit the Mission. Rebecca must be sending her messages through them."

"Great. Did they say when the German medical team arrived and when they will leave?"

"No. I couldn't get into that. You know how hard it is to get information from bureaucrats."

"Well thanks a lot for your help. You've taken a load off my mind. How are you doing?"

"Fine, but I can't talk for long."

"No, I can imagine. And I bet the international long distance rates out of Brazil are expensive. Just tell me, when are you coming back?" I was clutching at straws.

"I'm not sure." She sounded so distant, now. So tentative

and unsure.

"You're not coming back tonight?"

"No. Maybe tomorrow night. Maybe a day later. I'll let you know when I get back. Goodbye." (Click)

Nica's information put me in a more optimistic mood. Maybe Rebecca had just had a frustrating day when she wrote that e-mail. I decided to turn off the computer and call it a day. Of course I couldn't resist checking my e-mails just one more time.

From: RLevis598@hotmail.com
To: ben-candidi@netrus.net
Subj.: Love You

I'm doing fine. Tell Cousin Irene I'm so happy for her. Love you. — Rebecca

My heart sank. This e-mail did not come from Rebecca: She doesn't have a Cousin Irene. Rebecca doesn't have *any* cousins.

Northwest by North River Drive   17

Was Rebecca alive but held incommunicado? Was she alive but someone stole her identity? Who would do such a thing? Or was she dead and someone was trying to make me think she was still alive? And what could I do about it now?

I spent an hour on a fax to the main *Funai* office in Brasília. I composed it in English and translated it into Portuguese as best I could. Transmitted both versions, stating that it was urgent and asking them to insert handwritten answers to my list of questions.

It took another hour to delete all stray ends from my interim report and to print out four copies. It was time to get that thing off my desk.

It was past midnight before I finished. I turned off the computer, went upstairs and climbed into bed. But sleep didn't come.

Thoughts bounced around in my skull like a wild monkey in a cage. There were too many strange and unexplainable things to deal with: Rebecca's strange e-mails, Nica's strange appearance at my doorstep, Nica's strange attraction to me, and her phony assurances that everything would be right. What did I know about Nica, anyway? I knew that she was a flight attendant on Varig between Miami and Manaus. And I had a Miami phone number for her. But did I know that her information on the German medical team was correct? No, not until the main *Funai* office answered my fax. What else did I know for sure about Nica? Nothing, really.

I went downstairs, pulled out the telephone book and looked for Brasaro, Nica. No listing. I dialed her number and listened to her voice on an answering machine telling, in Portuguese, how I'd reached the Brasaro residence and could I please leave a message. I left a cheery message asking her to call me as soon as she got in.

I turned on my computer, went on-line and visited a very useful website: an Internet crisscross directory. I typed in Nica's phone number and got her name, plus an address in Miami Springs. Well, at least that part of her story checked out. I wrote down her address in my little brown book. Before going off-line, I checked for another e-mail from Rebecca. Nothing.

Reluctant to turn off my computer so quickly, I sat down and stared at the screen, pondering an old paradox: how to discern truth in the Land of Liars. My eyes drifted to the lower-right corner where the time was displayed. It was 2:15 a.m. — early in the morning, just like when I had stepped off that Manaus-to-Miami flight, four weeks and four days before. Then it occurred to me that a Varig flight would be coming in from Manaus in one hour! Yes, I could go out there and meet it. I wouldn't be able to sleep anyway. A couple of minutes on the phone was all it took to verify the flight. I had a little less than 60 minutes to intercept it. And it took me only three of those minutes to get dressed for business and wheel my bicycle out the door.

How to catch a liar in the Land of Liars? Catch him in a lie — him or her.

It was strangely exciting, pedaling at break-neck speed through sleeping Miami under a three-quarter moon, crossing poinciana shadows on the bumpy street and running through puddles of orange-yellow sodium light that didn't splash. I pedaled hard up

Northwest North River Drive, past the criminal court complex and crossed the Miami River on the 17th Avenue drawbridge, pumping hard against its steep incline and holding tight as the coarse steel honeycomb vibrated the handlebars. And I held the handlebars tightly while pedaling over the broken pie crust of Northwest *South* River Drive, working my way past that neighborhood's motley collection of old houses, shacks and apartment houses. I slowed for the low, short drawbridge that crossed the south arm of the Miami River until my tires told me that the old wood planking had been replaced. Stacks of shipping containers marked the beginning of the warehouse district. The bows of ocean-going freighters nosed between them like friendly dinosaurs.

I followed the River's south arm, dodging potholes and eruptions from the roots of Australian pine, and racing through two blocks of warehouses and three blocks of Bertram Yacht yards. Upon reaching 37th Avenue, it became clear that I'd be okay for time.

I pedaled hard up the wide bridge over LeJeune Road and merged on the downswing with a lot of fast, impatient airport traffic trying to sort itself between the arrival and departure lanes. I steered close to the wall, ready to ditch in a split second. It had felt strange, making that high-performance run in a buttoned-down dress shirt, slacks and leather shoes. But my critical performance would be here at the airport, before third parties who didn't know me.

Parking Garage A in front of the terminal was the most convenient location to leave my bicycle. I locked it to a palm tree. After crossing several arrival lanes full of slow-moving, exhaust-spewing vehicles, I walked through the automatic doors into the international arrival area where floor-to-ceiling glass plates separated the arriving passengers from their waiting parties. It didn't take long to verify that this was also the exit for the flight crews. The crowd of waiting parties was just dense enough for me to hide in and watch. When the monitor announced that the Varig flight had just arrived, I started looking hard for the woman who said she wouldn't be coming back this evening.

Nica came out about 20 minutes later in a group of six — two pilots and four flight attendants, all pulling wheeled suitcases. After they emerged through the automatic doors, I fell in a couple dozen steps behind. They all stopped at the curb of the inner pickup area. Nica chatted with them for a minute and then waved goodbye.

Through a jumble of parked cars she dragged her gear — a suitcase with built-in wheels and a slide-out arm. Strapped onto the arm and sitting on top was a large, black camera bag with many zippered pockets. And strapped on top of that was a leather-encased 35-millimeter camera.

The suitcase scuffed and rocked as Nica pulled it off the safety island and dragged it across four slow-moving lanes of traffic. She was heading for the parking garage. I hung back, using cars and pedestrians as shelter from her occasional backwards glances. My tactic worked, all the way through the open short-term parking lot and into Garage A. This was not the carefree Nica who showed up on my porch by whim. This wasn't even a tired version of a carefree Nica. This was Nica on a mission. She moved with vigilance. As pedestrian traffic thinned out, nobody within a hop, skip and a jump of her escaped her notice.

Nica walked up to the elevator and pushed the button. I hung back behind a pillar, escaping her 270-degree sweep. When she looked away, I made my move, closing most of the distance quickly, before she looked my way again.

I addressed her from a dozen steps away, walking towards her slowly. "Nica, I've got to talk to you."

As she turned to face me, her eyes told it all: I was the last person on earth she wanted to see. But she recovered quickly. "Ben! You shouldn't have come." She put on her *simpática* smile. "How nice of you to think of me, but it's so late. And I have my own car."

I spoke gently. "Nica, I really need to talk to you."

"But I have to get home right away now. Maybe I could call you or come by tomorrow."

The elevator door opened. We both got in. A guy about my age stepped in after us. He was wearing a designer shirt under a black leather jacket with a sports-coat cut. He had black hair and his cheeks bore acne pocks. Nica pushed the button for six. The guy didn't push any button.

Nica's reaction didn't surprise me. But the next couple of minutes would be crucial. I'd already decided how to play this interview: stupid and candid. "I need to talk to you now. Those people on the German medical team are answering Rebecca's e-mails for her. It's not Rebecca on the other end."

The door closed. The elevator started. Under the fluorescent lights, Nica's face looked drawn and pale. "How do you know that, Ben?"

"I just know. It's not her." I didn't move my eyes from Nica for even an instant. And she didn't look at me for even an instant. She stared at the floor, throwing an occasional glance towards the elevator buttons. As we approached the sixth floor, she tipped her suitcase onto its wheels and moved towards the door. Our fellow passenger made room for us.

The door opened and I followed Nica out. She handled the suitcase briskly, jumping it from the elevator island and walking purposefully along the length of the garage. She hardly looked at me. The man from the elevator drifted off at a right angle to us, like his car was on the down ramp.

"I told you that she's okay," Nica said, over her shoulder. "Why won't you believe me?"

"Well, I'd like to believe you, Nica, but I need to know *how* you can be so sure. And I need to know more about that German team at the Mission."

Nica was walking faster now and glancing furtively over her shoulder. We passed a businessman walking in the opposite direction.

"Who did you talk to at *Funai*, Nica?"

"I can't remember the name," she said with annoyance. Her steps quickened.

"*The* name?" I said, impatiently. "Not, his name or her name?"

"Why are you cross-examining me?"

"Because the more questions I ask you, the more inconsistencies I uncover."

"Inconsistencies?" She spat the word. She passed a down ramp and turned left onto an up ramp, walking towards a white Chevy Cavalier. It wasn't more than five yards away and she had her keys out like she was going to jump right in and drive away.

I hurried to catch up with her. "Yes, *inconsistencies* like your not even knowing whether the *Funai* official you talked to was male or female. And nagging little questions like how you managed to look so fresh when visiting me after a seven-mile bicycle trip."

She hit the car's alarm deactivation button and popped open the trunk. "Ben, you shouldn't talk to me like this. It will destroy everything."

I stood beside her. "What's it going to destroy? The cosmic parallelism between your life and my life — with our wonderful but absent fiancées? Will it destroy all our shared idealism for anthropology and ecology in Brazil?"

"Didn't you hear that the lady doesn't want to talk to you?" The voice was male and Latin-accented, and it came from two dozen steps behind us.

I turned to face him. It was Pock Face, walking up like I was trespassing on his property.

"No, I didn't hear her say that. And for the last three weeks we've been talking all the time. How does this concern you?"

"It concerns me." He kept coming.

"No it doesn't. You don't even know her." If he came within range with that attitude, I'd knock out his teeth with a side kick.

He slowed. "I know her. And I'm telling you to get out of here."

Nica's eyes told the story. Her eyes ditched me like I was beyond redemption. Her eyes locked onto him, beseeching him not to do it. And when I caught my next glimpse of him, the gun was already halfway out of his jacket. I gambled that he wasn't bad-assed enough to use it. Not yet, anyway.

I took one step backwards toward the driver's side door, locking eyes on Nica but keeping track of him. "Is this your Emilio? Your fiancé and benefactor of mankind? Or is he just another guy that you spend your afternoons with when you're laid over in Miami?"

"Leave me, Ben, or you'll get in deep trouble."

Pock Face was about four steps from her and six steps from me, swinging out at an angle to get a clear sight on me and handling the revolver like a pro. It looked like a .38. He held it close to his jacket at rib cage level, making it invisible to a passerby and impossible to kick out of his hand.

But somehow, I wasn't afraid — not if this encounter would bring me closer to Rebecca.

I kept walking backwards, away from them. "What kind of trouble, Nica? The type of trouble that Rebecca got into?" Her eyes were screaming at me to shut up. "Walking into someone's smuggling operation? What are you carrying that you need an armed escort to walk you to your car?"

"Shut your fucking mouth or I'll blow your fucking brains out. Nica, load up and drive off."

She hesitated. "But . . ."

"Just do what I say." He was standing a couple of steps to the side of the car, even with its rear bumper.

While Nica loaded the trunk, I inched away. In front of the car were restraining cables, strung like guitar strings. Behind them was a seven-foot drop-off to the down ramp.

Nica loaded her bag in the trunk.

Pock Face said to her, "Go home. We'll take care of things later." To me, he said, "And you, come here, slowly. We're going to take a ride."

At that distance, his first shot would wound me for sure and might even kill me. But if I let him get closer, he'd be able to kill me for sure. As a kid, I'd already worked through the logic of this situation: The few extra seconds of guaranteed life aren't worth it. Never ever let them increase their control over you.

Nica tipped the odds in my favor:

"No!" she yelled, stepping towards him. "Leave him alone. He won't hurt anything."

I dove for the front bumper, rolled, and then crawled under the cable, banging an already-sore knee in the process. I dropped four feet to the hood of a car parked on the down ramp. Rolled off and ran like hell between the front bumpers and the cables. Didn't slow down until I'd scrambled far enough to deny him a good shot. Then I dove under the cables again, landing on another hood, one full level below their ramp.

I crouched behind a SUV and listened, clutching my banged and bleeding left knee. Heard nothing but the rumble of a nearby air conditioning cooling tower, the whine of taxiing jets and the buzz of the transformers on the mercury arc lights. No, he hadn't fired at me. And no, he couldn't be running towards me. I remembered he was wearing leather shoes that would make noise.

Silently and breathlessly, I waited. Heard the click and grind of a starter motor. An engine revved. Then a second vehicle started up. I took a quick survey of the building's layout and the pattern of arrows and exit signs.

Clicks of metallic spacers between the concrete plates overhead told me that the cars were rolling towards the ramp that I'd just run down. I moved to the front of the SUV and climbed the steel cable. I put my chin to the ramp and looked out from under a

parked car. Nica's white Chevrolet came first, followed by Pock
Face in a black, late-model Pontiac muscle car. I got both of their
license numbers in the turn that took them onto my ramp. At first
a thick column hid me from view, but then I had to scramble down
the wires quickly to get out of sight. Pock Face was looking hard
for me as he drove by. Nica wasn't; her eyes were glued to the
road like a driver's ed student.

Catching them again at the next level down, I was able to verify
their license numbers. I did feel a certain power over them, being
able to climb down those six levels faster than they could drive
down the switchbacks. But as I stalked them to the toll booth, it
became clear that I had no power to stop them. No Metro Police
were around. Little chance of getting the Haitian cashier to keep
the gate arm down. And a strong-arm citizen's arrest of Pock Face
would be tricky, and would probably backfire if it turned out that
his gun was registered.

But as they drove off, I promised to not give up on Nica
Brasaro. Her address was in my brown book. I would pay her a
visit. And for that, I would need a car. I limped back to my bike
and pedaled hard in the direction of the warehouse district. While
coasting down the LeJeune Road overpass, I caught a glimpse of
the old floodgate standing in the moonlight. It looked so serene
and inviting — the Everglades water cascading down its sides to
the south branch of the Miami River. I descended into the gritty
warehouse district.

At SuperValue Car Rental, I dealt with the grit. I took a few
minutes in their men's room to wash it from my bleeding knee. At
the counter, I asked for their biggest sedan. While the clerk ran my
credit card, I used her stapler to repair the three-inch tear on my
pant leg. After driving the car out of the lot, I returned on foot to
retrieve my bicycle which I then stashed in the trunk.

The drive to Nica's took me past a second ancient floodgate
— the one forming the junction of the main branch of the Miami
River and the Miami Canal. I took Okeechobee Road which runs
parallel to the Miami Canal. On the right, Hialeah showed her
ragged edge — a couple of miles of warehouses, junkyards, decrepit
motels and lunch counters interspersed with patches of gravel and
weeds. On the left, behind the coral and fern-lined banks of the
Canal, Miami Springs was showing its backside — rough cinder

block walls, utility sheds, and parking lots of low-rise apartment houses.

Not knowing the neighborhood very well, I crossed the Canal into Miami Springs on the third bridge — the funky old drawbridge with the silver-painted steel beam superstructure that probably hadn't raised the bridge for sixty years. The country club oriented municipal management had torn down all the landmarks on the old town circle, but I found South Royal Poinciana Boulevard on the second pass. It still had its royal palms and a couple of poinciana trees.

Nica's address led me to a U-shaped three-storey building, a couple blocks north of the second bridge that crossed the Canal. It was gratifying to see her name on one of the mailboxes in front and her white Chevrolet parked in the lot at the side of the building. The hood was still warm so I couldn't be that far behind her. I was especially pleased to not find the black Pontiac anywhere near. Obviously, they had already made the transfer; hopefully Pock Face was long gone.

I walked to the back of the parking lot where the property abutted the Canal. Looking over the chain link fence and Canal, I located a clump of bushes by a warehouse on the far side of Okeechobee Road where I could stash my bike. Swimming across the Canal would take only 30 seconds, if I had to make a second escape. Everything was quiet except for the transformer buzz of the mercury lights. The thirty-unit buildings were too small to have security guards, and nobody gets arrested for trespassing at places with so much junk furniture lying around. Hell, with my cellphone along, maybe *I* would be the one to dial 911 tonight.

I returned to the car, got back on Okeechobee Road, drove a half-dozen blocks south, and parked next to a Latin diner. Took out the bike, rode to the place I'd located across the Canal from Nica's, stashed and locked it, and set out to visit her on foot.

Behind the mailboxes was a six-foot iron fence, an electrically activated gate and an array of buttons to ring each of the apartments. But with half of the buttons unlit and the gate unlocked anyway, I just walked into the courtyard. It was dominated by an undersized pool. The names on the mailboxes suggested at least five different languages. I guessed that the rental policy was "no children" and that the tenants' main interests would be grass, coke and casual sex.

The layout was motel-style, with wrap-around balconies for second and third-floor access and with stairways starting near the pool's edge. I climbed the stairs to the third floor. What distinguished the apartments from motel rooms was the absence of large, motel-style plate glass windows and heavy drapes. The windows were of frosted glass and were set well above eye level. I walked along the balcony, checking door numbers, dodging the crowns of palm trees that grew up from the courtyard, and dodging the low-lying room air conditioners installed though the apartments' walls. They were all running and dripping — nourishing patches of slime mold on the balcony's slanted concrete floor. Nica's apartment #310 was at the far end of the building, close to the Canal. Light in her frosted window told me she was still up.

I knocked on Nica's door with businesslike strength and tempo. The door opened on my third set of knocks. It opened only three inches, held back by a chain. It opened just wide enough for a glimpse of Nica's face.

I started out softly. "It's Ben. I need to talk to you."

"I'm sorry, Ben, but I can't."

"Yes, you can. And you owe it to me."

She tried to close the door and failed because I'd wedged my foot in. The door was wooden, weathered and rickety. The brass chain slot seemed to be secured by only one screw. Forcing my way in would have been a simple matter.

"Ben, leave me alone or I'll call the cops." She yelled it like she meant business. But so did I.

"Sure, Nica, let's get the police. I'll make a nine-one-one call on my cellphone." I raised my voice so that it echoed across the courtyard. "When they come, I'll make a formal complaint about how your pock-faced friend threatened my life with a thirty-eight. I got his license number, incidentally. I'll tell them that I have evidence that you were importing contraband from Brazil — that I saw you handing it off to him. I'll tell them how I ran for my life while he chased me with a pistol. I'll show them my busted knee and they will verify that it's my blood back there on the concrete."

"Shut up, Ben!"

"No, I really do think you should make good on your threat to call the police, Nica. I'll stick around, cooperate with them, and give them probable cause to search your apartment. They can bring in a drug dog to sniff around."

"Okay, I'll let you in," she said, sounding desperate. "Just shut up!"

When I eased my foot from the door, she tried to slam it shut. When I convinced her that wouldn't work, she took off the chain. She stepped aside as I walked in. It was plain to see that I'd given her the jitters.

"Are you alone?" I asked

"Yes."

I walked in, cautiously, past the small, starkly lit Formica-top kitchen on the left. The living room was straight ahead. At the end of it was a sliding glass door leading to a small balcony that faced the Canal. Off to the right, a short hallway led to a bedroom and a bathroom. Nica's rolling suitcase stood in the hallway, its carrier handle retracted and the camera bag nowhere in sight.

"I need to go to the bathroom."

"Sure," she sighed.

I went back and poked my head in bedroom to make sure nobody was lurking there. Nica's camera sat on the dresser. The camera bag was on the bed, empty and lying on its side next to Nica's uniform. None of this surprised me. Neither did the automobile bike rack sitting in the corner. I went into the bathroom and ran some water in the sink, then returned to the living room. It was dominated by two low couches separated by a coffee table. A state-of-the-art TV stood near the balcony door.

Nica gestured me to one of the couches. After she committed to one, I sat in the other one. She was in shorts and a mostly unbuttoned white blouse. That seemed to be her favorite color. She now seemed to have gotten her jitters under control and was doing a pretty good job of projecting languid sexiness. "Ben, you've just got to trust me. Everything will be all right for everybody if you just sit still."

How the hell could she promise that?

"Okay, I'll try to trust you."

"Good, can I get you a drink?"

"No, thanks. But you can tell me who you talked with at the main *Funai* office."

Her blouse was held together by one lower button. Her shorts were too tight to be hiding any sort of weapon. "I don't remember. It was a woman. I know it's important for you to know but I can't remember."

"Okay, then let's talk about something harmless. How's your painting?" On the airplane, she'd told me it was a hobby.

Her first expression was bafflement, but she recovered quickly. "Fine, but I don't paint here. I paint in Manaus. I'm sorry, I can't show you any pictures."

"But I bet you could show me some photographs. What about the one you took of me in the Manaus airport?"

"No, I'm pretty sure that one's in Manaus."

"Why?"

"That's where I keep my photos."

"It looked like a pretty fancy camera. Do you have a telephoto lens and a lot of filters and stuff?"

"No."

Distracted by the wide slit between the two halves of her blouse, I did my best to press on. "Of course, you get your film developed here because it's cheaper."

"Yes." She was sounding impatient, now.

"So, why *did* you take my picture in the Manaus airport?"

"For the same reason I told you before. Because it's my hobby, studying people's faces and painting them. And when I took that picture, it wasn't just of you. There were a lot of people in it."

Maybe yes, maybe no: The camera she'd used in Manaus had a built-in zoom, I remembered.

"So it was just a coincidence that you happened to be talking to me on the plane after you snapped my picture at the gate."

"Yes," she said with conviction. "I'm always friendly. And you're an interesting guy." She smiled.

"Okay, I'll try to believe that was a coincidence. But it was no coincidence when that pock-faced macho showed up at the airport. Is he an interesting guy, too?"

"Not as interesting as you, Ben."

"And I don't think he is a love interest, either."

For a second, Nica looked like she wanted respond to that.

"Can I take that as a 'no'?" I asked.

She remained silent, but the effort she was making to suppress a smile was enough to tell me I was correct.

"And you think Rebecca is okay."

"Yes, I told you."

"Yes, you did. You even told me you were *sure* she's okay. How can you be so sure Rebecca's okay?"

"I . . . I just *feel* that she's going to be okay."

"Do you know anything about her that you haven't told me?"

"No."

"But you just *feel* that she must be okay, so you told it to me like it was a fact."

"I guess."

"Why are you so interested in the work I'm doing?"

"I'm interested in people learning new things, Ben."

"Because it reminds you of when you studied anthropology at Johns Hopkins University?"

"Social science at the University of Maryland," she corrected.

"And you want me to believe you are being truthful with me?"

"Yes."

"Then tell me the real reason you came to visit me?"

"I was . . . attracted to you Ben." Her eyes turned moist. "I still am." She leaned towards me, her eyes downcast.

What had she been carrying tonight? Could I rule out cocaine? I put on an expectant smile. "Are you attracted to me enough to offer a line of cocaine?"

She stiffened. "Right now?"

"Yes. What could be nicer than doing a line before making love to you?"

Slowly, she got up and came around behind me. Slowly, I raised my hands to guard my neck against a karate chop. She massaged my neck with her fingertips. I held her wrists lightly, responding in kind. Her massage went deeper.

"But I thought you were a natural type, Ben."

"Look, if you guys thought I was trying to mess up your cocaine run, I apologize."

My accusation didn't break the rhythm of her caresses. She answered me in a firm, insistent tone. "Ben, I didn't . . . I don't smuggle cocaine."

She pushed her body against me so that my head was between

the parted halves of her blouse. Still holding her wrists, I turned my head and kissed her right breast. "Then what were you carrying in your camera bag?"

She stiffened.

"What did you hand off to your pock-faced *goucho*?"

She emitted a tiny screech and pulled back. "Ben, it's harmless, but I can't tell you. You just have to trust me."

I didn't respond but kept holding her wrists. Slowly, she relaxed and moved back to me, cradling my head between her breasts, a nipple at each ear. What a simple polygraph machine! The arrangement was as sensitive as the pen on a seismographic recorder.

"Just trust me, darling," Nica purred.

The baseline was flat.

"Did you feel turned on by our long kiss at my house, Nica?"

"Yes," she said with a coy laugh that tickled my ears.

"You were turning me on, then . . . the natural way. But right now, I can't keep from thinking what would happen if the police came in with a cocaine dog and sniffed around your suitcase and camera bag."

"They'd find nothing. The dog would find nothing to sniff at." The seismograph pens were stable until she laughed. "I'm a natural kind of girl. I don't use it and I've never carried it." She snuggled closer. The seismograph would need to be recalibrated.

What was she smuggling if it wasn't cocaine? Diamonds? And how could I trick an answer out of her? Maybe it was time to thrown logic to the wind and change the game to Ouija. "And it was just a coincidence that you came to visit me the very next day after I saved the life of Edith Pratt?"

Nica took a deep breath and moved back an inch or two. She worked harder on my neck. "Who is Edith Pratt?" she asked. Her body felt stiffer, now.

"She's a famous anthropologist who works in Brazil. Didn't I tell you about her, darling? It was when I went to an anthropology conference at the Knight Center to take notes for Rebecca."

"You told me about going to a conference but you didn't say anything about saving anyone's life."

"My briefcase stopped a bullet that was intended for her. And it was shot by a guy who didn't look much different from your pock-faced friend."

I overstated the similarity, but pressure had to be kept up.

"I don't know anything about that anthropologist, Ben."

That was a lie. I was 100 percent sure. She'd moved her hands to my shoulders where her strokes could be coarser. But her attempts to control her breathing gave her away.

Keeping hold of one hand, I turned my face up to her. "And after you started visiting me, Nica, a surveillance van spent several days in front of my house. And after I chased it off, a man broke into my house and ran off with my computer and almost got away with it."

"But what's that got to do with me, Ben?"

"You tell *me*."

She pulled in a deep breath. "Nothing! It's got nothing to do with me." She sighed. "You've got to believe me. Trust me." She worked hard to breathe normally.

"I'd like to trust you. And maybe I can, if you can give me one legitimate reason why Pock Face met you at the airport and thought he had to point a gun at me." I looked up at her.

Nica's face screwed up horribly. She screeched: "Ben, I was ready to do anything for you. But you keep asking questions I can't answer. Don't fight things. You are making trouble where there isn't any." She shook her hand free and turned away. Worrying she might grab something and hit me, I got out of the couch. But when she turned towards me, her face was full of sad resignation. "Now I see that all we can do is hurt each other." She broke into tears. "Don't destroy me. Ben, I'm going to ask you to leave, now. You promised."

I got up and headed slowly to the door. "I'm going. You won't be any help to me with Rebecca. I won't come back. But I don't want you and your people coming around my place, either."

"I won't."

I went out the door, closing it behind me. I walked back to my bike, deep in thought. Yes, I'd learned some interesting things about Nica tonight, but they didn't seem be any help with finding Rebecca. When I reached the center of the bridge, I took a couple of minutes to look down on still water of the Canal, observing the slow movement of Australian pine needles on the water's surface and thinking about the adage that still waters run deep. Logic can take you only so far. Use it on an airhead and it generates more new questions than answers. I wondered if Nica was more a child of impulse than a student of logic. Mindless optimism might be a sufficient explanation for most of what I'd learned about her. Well, right now it would be a waste of time to try to learn any more.

I walked to my bike, unlocked it, pedaled to the car, loaded it up and drove away. Well, at least the trip to the car rental place wasn't wasted. I would put that car to a lot of use before returning it to the airport.

18   Miami and Manaus

The sky was growing lighter as I drove home. Walking in the door, my first thought was to get rid of that damn report. I sat down and composed a cover letter. Then I scooped up the Appendix and drove off to a 24-hour copy service. Told the clerk to make two copies as a rush job to be picked up that afternoon. Got back home just before 9:00 a.m. It was an okay time to ask for some help from Alice. She would be up, but wouldn't have left yet for work at the *Miami Standard*. Felt sorry for the girl, working for a morning paper with a midnight deadline. I dialed her at home and she answered with a yawn.

"Alice, this is Ben. I need your advice."

"Sure, Ben. What can I do for you?"

"It seems like my whole world is crashing down. Rebecca's missing, I had to deal with a surveillance van that's been parked in front of my house, and last night they broke in and tried to steal my computer." Forgetting my advice to myself, I continued. "And this morning at the airport I had trouble with Nica — she's the Brazilian flight attendant you met — "

Alice cleared her throat. "I'll give you a simple piece of advice concerning her, Ben. Stop encouraging her."

"Look, you won't be able to understand it until I tell you the whole story."

"Well, I hope you can tell it all to me in fifteen minutes, because that's when I have to leave for an assignment."

I gave her a very short version, telling how I knew the last two e-mails had not come from Rebecca. I told Alice about taking down the license number of the surveillance van and getting it towed away. I told her about the motorboat burglary and how it couldn't be a coincidence. But she cut me off when I started to tell her about Nica's strange visits.

"That's not strange, Ben. You just told me you gave her your card on the plane and she knew Rebecca was away. She visited you for a little *divertissement*."

"I like your French, but that doesn't explain why she waited for two and one-half weeks to visit and came right after the Edith Pratt episode. And it doesn't explain why she was so interested in the report that I'm working on. She asked some real good questions about it. I had to work damn hard to keep her from finding out what I'm actually doing — working on new paradigms for drug discovery."

"You think her questions about your report weren't just her way of keeping up a conversation with you? Okay, let's assume that she wasn't just attracted by your pheromones and your good looks. Maybe she wanted to check you out for some other reason — like how you happened to stop the bullet for that anthropology professor. You said, her first visit was on the very next day."

"Exactly. And when I asked her about Edith Pratt this morning, she said she didn't know anything about her. But I'm sure that was a lie."

"Maybe she's in with the people who were trying to kill Dr. Pratt. Maybe she wanted to find out your connection to Pratt and why you were defending her."

"That could be."

"Maybe Pratt's standing up for indigenous people's rights is costing certain people millions of dollars in lost opportunity."

"Could be. Pratt was a real terror on the podium. But somehow it seems like Nica would be more on the side of the little guy than . . ."

"What were you doing with her last night, anyway?"

I told Alice about meeting Nica's flight and how Pock Face

drove me off with a gun and how I got the license number of their cars.

"Ben, it sounds like you're idealizing the girl. If she keeps company like that, I'd say she's more likely on the side of the hit men. It sounds like she's smuggling coke and her only interest in science is as a cover story."

"I thought that, too. But when I threatened to sic a cocaine dog on her luggage, that didn't seem to bother her."

"Look, Ben, I have only have a couple of minutes. Then, I'll be busy until eleven tonight. What can I do for you?"

"I don't know. I'm going to ask for the Department of Motor Vehicles for the tag history on the surveillance van and for the Pontiac that Nica's pock-faced escort was driving. That will get me names and addresses."

"What? You want to send a written request and get your information in two weeks?"

"Is it that slow?"

"Yes. Just give me the numbers. I'll use my connections."

I gave her the tag numbers for the surveillance van, Pock Face's Pontiac and Nica's Chevrolet. I threw in the Florida registration number of the suspicious boat for good measure.

"Alice, I don't know how to thank you."

"No thanks necessary. Glad to bounce that Brazilian bedroom bunny out of the waiting line."

I ignored that comment and pressed on. "And thanks again for looking into the shooting."

"That's okay. I spend lots of time pursuing leads on stories that my editor decides not to run."

"Well, at least you put the story out on the wire."

"Ben, I didn't put *any* story out on the wire."

"You sure?"

"Yes."

"But — ."

"Ben, I've got to go." (Click.)

I printed out my patent application, put it in an envelope together with a check to cover the application fee, and drove to the post office where I sent it off by certified, return receipt mail. On the way home, I started thinking about the call from a reporter in Palo Alto, California, who claimed to be following up on a wire story that Alice had not sent out.

When I got home, it was still too early to call California but it wasn't too early to call Michael. And, by amazing coincidence, he called me that same moment.

"Ben, how are you doing?" He sounded businesslike.

"Not too great, Michael. How are you?"

"Fine. Ben, the reason I called is that our client wants an add-on — a search of patent databases for any patents that might have resulted from bioprospecting in the last five years. Money is no problem, just bill us for the extra hours at time and a half."

"That's very generous, Michael. But I can't do it."

"No?"

"No, I can't do it. Got some bad news. But I've got some good news, too. The interim report is finished. I want to drop it off to you this afternoon."

"That's fine. I'll come by to pick it up at five o'clock. But please tell me — why don't you have time for the patent database search?"

"I'll need two weeks for a serious personal problem. Maybe more."

"I'm sorry to hear that, Benjamin. That will be very bad for the project. Maybe it is something that can be put off."

"No. It can't be put off. Rebecca Levis — maybe you noticed her name on the door — she's a physician and she happens to be my fiancée. She's on an anthropological field trip and she's overdue. Everyone else came back but she stayed on. I'm concerned. I will have to go in after her."

"Where is she?"

"Brazil."

"Really!" For some reason, Michael sounded genuinely interested.

"I got an e-mail saying she had some big opportunity. Then the e-mails . . . well, I'd have to say they stopped."

"Where in Brazil is she?"

"Amazonia. At a mission on a river off of the *Rio Negro*."

"Interesting. I'm sure that my . . . what I mean is that I'm sure my client will *understand* your situation. When are you leaving the country?"

"I plan to fly to Manaus tomorrow night. Then I'm going up the *Rio Negro* on a freighter, just like we went up on the last trip."

"Okay. I'll see you this afternoon at five." (Click)

I spent an hour making a list of things to do before I left. Then it was time for the call to California. I went to my office calendar and found the phone number I'd jotted down for Hal Brown, the dubious Palo Alto journalist. I was just about to call him when the Edison buzzer went off. A repairman from BellSouth had finally shown up to redo the wires that the motorboat burglars had cut. I showed him the terminal box and told him to check back with me when the job was done.

While the man was working on the line, I used my cellphone to call the number that Hal Brown had given me. That turned out to be the main number for the *Palo Alto News*. I worked my way through their menu to the editorial office and finally got an irascible male voice that answered, "City Desk." No, they didn't have any Hal Brown writing for the paper. When I asked if Hal Brown could be a "stringer," he said, "No way!" And when I told him about Hal Brown's call about the "wire story," he laughed me off the line.

I was still pondering this when the telephone man came back. I asked him in.

"It wasn't any trouble to splice those wires," he said, "but I had some, figuring out what this is."

He held out an open palm with a plastic module with four miniature alligator clamps protruding. He gave it to me, and I examined it.

"What is this?"

He raised an eyebrow. "It's *unauthorized* equipment."

My sleep-deprived brain was not functioning well. "I didn't put that on, and I don't have any idea what it's for. And that's not why I asked for today's service on — "

He stopped me with a shake of the head. "It's the type of equipment that you wouldn't authorize, either. It's a bug."

"A bug. Can you show me how it was attached?"

He took me out there and showed me where they'd tapped in. The box was accessible to anyone with a screwdriver. The repairman couldn't tell me much about the device — how it worked or whether it was government or private. He just left it with me.

I returned to the problem of the pseudo-journalist from California. I searched my office calendar for the number I'd copied from my Caller I.D. when "reporter" Hal Brown called me on his cellphone. I used my own cellphone for the call.

"Hello." The voice wasn't as raspy as I'd remembered it. The background was full of highway noise.

"I want to speak to Hal Brown."

"Sorry, you've got the wrong number."

It was hard to tell if he was the guy who'd called me three weeks earlier. His voice was rather nondescript, like a character in one of those made-for-TV movies.

"Well, I'm sorry, but I talked to him on this number three weeks ago." I repeated the number to him.

"Sorry. He must have had the number before me. I just got this phone."

"Can you tell me your name?"

"Joe." (Click)

I looked up the number by Internet crisscross and I learned that it belonged to Joe Keverson. Luckily it's not a common name. I found another listing for a "J. Keverson" in Mountain View. I dialed it and got a woman who sounded like she had a baby hanging from one arm and a toddler hanging on her apron.

I said, "I'm sorry to bother you at home, but I can't get Joe on his cellular. Is he here? This is Bob."

"No, Bob. I don't know where he is. Have you tried the agency?"

"No. Sorry. I seem to have lost the number."

She gave it to me and went back to her domestic chores. When I dialed "The Agency," a woman with a scratchy voice answered: "Sequoia Investigative Services."

I told her I was Bob and asked for Joe. She said Joe was out on a case but could she take my number and he'd call back. I said I'd just call Joe on his cellphone.

I took a couple of minutes to think about this — the phony journalist was actually a detective. Why would a California detective be interested in how I saved Edith Pratt's life?

I did a lot of phoning that day. My next call was to Security Chief Hildreth at the Hyatt Regency Hotel. I asked if there had been any fallout from the episode with Edith Pratt. He said that everything that was going to fall out was pretty well "shaken out" already. I pressed him on this. "What kind of an understanding did you reach with Edith Pratt?" I asked.

"You want to know if we relayed your message to her?"

"Yes."

"Well we did."

"And what did she say?"

"Well, she didn't say much more than hello and goodbye in the whole conversation. Her lawyer did all the talking. It was a conference call."

"What did you tell them?"

"That she was one lucky lady. I think I called her a lady. I said that she should thank her lucky stars that you were there and did what you did. Her lawyer, Wagner was his name, kept asking what we knew about you. I told them both that you were a fine, forthcoming young man."

"Thanks. Did they agree with you?"

"After I read them the police report. Faxed Wagner a copy, too. You sound like you didn't hear from them at all."

"No, I didn't."

"Well, I'll be doggone! Talk about ungrateful!"

"I would like to talk to her. Do you have a number for her?"

"I'm sorry, but hotel regulations don't allow us to give out guests' telephone numbers. But if Professor Pratt ever calls me again, I'll give her a piece of my mind."

I thanked Security Chief Hildreth and we wished each other well.

My next call was to Gisela at Blue Lagoon Travel, for a flight to Manaus for tomorrow night and not on Varig. I didn't want to see Nica again.

But I did spend some time on a question that was still nagging me about Nica: how strangely she had answered when I'd asked about her college studies during her last visit at my house. What had she studied? "Sociology, actually." Where had she studied? "At the University of Maryland, actually." Why had she said "actually"? Because she hadn't, *actually*? Sure, she had wasted no time correcting me when I had purposely said it wrong during last night's interrogation. But it's always easier to tell a lie the second time.

I called up the registrar at the University of Maryland, asking for confirmation that Nica Brasaro had received a bachelors degree from them in the last five years. I said that she was a job candidate

191

and, unfortunately, her graduation date wasn't legible on the copy that I'd received. A few minutes later, the clerk came back on the line and said they had no record of any Nica Brasaro.

While I was on the subject of institutions of higher learning in the State of Maryland, it occurred to me to call Dr. Edith Pratt. I dialed long distance information and got the number for the anthropology department at Johns Hopkins University in Baltimore. When I dialed that number, the departmental secretary answered. She told me that Dr. Pratt was "unavailable and will be for some time." When I asked her what that meant, she said that Dr. Pratt "is not coming into the office." She made it sound like Dr. Pratt was a touchy subject. When I asked whether Dr. Pratt was out sick or out of the country or what, she treated me with suspicion. She claimed to be "not authorized to give out personal information." I resisted the impulse to compare her department to the C.I.A. I also resisted the impulse to call back and ask for another professor in the department. But with so many other important things to do, I had exhausted my time for inquiries at Johns Hopkins University.

I called Zeekie and made an appointment to see him at the shop at 3:30 p.m.

And I called my old mentor Rob McGregor at Bryan Medical School and told him I would be out of the country for a while.

"Hey," Rob said, "I hope you get that job you're applying for. It sounds like a big deal."

"Who was it and what did they say?"

"I forget the name of the company. They were from New Jersey. The guy said he was calling up 'for verification purposes,' but you know me — I made him tell me about it. Sounds like a real executive position. Drug discovery, huh?"

"What did you tell him, Rob?"

"That you were a great guy to have around the lab. A problem solver. An inventor."

"How long ago was that?"

"About four days ago."

"Did you get a phone number? Write down a name?"

"Sorry, Ben. Just went back to my experiment. Did I do something wrong?"

"No. You did fine. But if anybody calls, don't say anything

about my going out of the country." I managed to end the conversation without telling him where or why I was going.

I ate lunch, then made two diskettes of my report and printed out some important phone numbers and addresses. I checked my e-mail one more time. Nothing from Rebecca. Unplugged the computer and took out the hard drive. Took it out to the car, with a bunch of other stuff. Drove to my bank and put the report, one diskette and the hard drive in my safe-deposit box.

My next stop was L.B. Harvey Marine on 27th Avenue. David Holland sold me a GlobalStar satellite phone for $495. Now I could call home from the jungle. Next, I visited Radio Shack and picked up a hand-held GPS receiver for about $100. Now I would know where I was, in the jungle.

Next, I went to Zeekie's repair shop and showed him the bugging device that the phone man had removed from my line. He said it was a high-frequency radio that could transmit my phone conversations and modem communications for about one city block. He agreed that the van and the loitering motorboat might have carried the receiving equipment. But he said the receiver could also have been a dedicated cellphone hidden somewhere in the bushes. He couldn't tell whether it was a government or a private job. He was concerned. He listened patiently while I told him about my serious problems and how I needed his help. I gave him my laptop computer for safe keeping. He agreed to handle communications and look after my interests in Miami. It took us an hour to go over everything. When I offered to pay for the time it would cost him, he refused to even consider it.

Then, as a bonus, he put together a small hand-cranked generator for recharging my satellite phone. And he downloaded a lot of satellite maps for where I was going. The *Rio Marauiá* was sometimes visible as a crack in the green canopy. Zeekie was a real pal.

On the way home, I picked up the copies of the Appendix from the photocopy shop. After returning home, I received a call from Gisela, saying I was set up for a flight leaving 7:55 the next evening.

The next incoming call was a strange one. "This is Dr. James Woodruff calling from the National Institutes of Health. I would like to speak to Dr. Rebecca Levis."

My caller ID was registering a 301 area code, which checked out for the NIH in Bethesda, Maryland. I said, "Dr. Levis is away for a few weeks, but if you leave a message I will be sure to give it to her the next time she checks in."

"If you could give me a phone number and location, I could call her myself."

He sounded more used to giving orders than receiving them. And since he might be a bureaucrat calling up to invite Rebecca to apply for a grant, I couldn't just brush him off.

"I'm sorry, she's in the field — doing tropical medicine in Brazil."

"Interesting. And right up our alley. Can you tell me a little more about it?"

"Dr. David Thompson can tell you a lot better than I can." I gave him Thompson's number."

"Great. Thanks."

"Could you give me your phone number to pass on to Rebecca when she checks in with me?"

He gave me the number that my Caller ID was showing. Then I cut off the conversation, saying I had to take part in a conference call.

After my experience with the "California journalist," I was suspicious. Ten minutes after hanging up, I thought up an excuse to call Dr. Woodruff back and punched in the number. The phone was answered after 15 rings by a nice woman from "housekeeping service." She explained that I had reached a pay phone outside a cafeteria at the National Institutes of Health. I thanked her and hung up. I called the main number at NIH and asked for Dr. James Woodruff. They didn't have any such person.

A few minutes later, Michael came to pick up the report. He looked his usual playboy self, dressed in an Italian-tailored suit.

"Have a seat, Michael. Here it is. Three copies of the Interim Report and the Appendix." I handed him the documents. "Two for them and one for you to keep. The report is in excellent shape. We can call it interim, but it is really final. All that's needed to make it into a final report is to insert the hypertext links."

Michael hefted the documents and flipped through the pages. They looked nice with their stiff maroon covers. And the Appendix added a lot of weight. He nodded his head approvingly. He was probably just looking at the format. He put on a neutral expression, looked at me and said, "It looks fine. I'll send it to them by express, tomorrow." He produced two diskettes. "All I need is a copy of the files." He gestured like I was supposed to pop them into my computer and make copies.

"Sorry, Michael. I can't do that. My hard drive is in a bank vault, along with the backup copies on diskette."

"Well, then you can give me one of the diskettes you are keeping here."

"I'm not keeping any here." I paused and studied his face for a reaction. There wasn't any. "I'll need the second payment before I hand out any electronic copies of the report."

Michael stared at me for a long time. I stared back, neutrally. Michael was the first to blink. "But it could be awkward if the company decides they want to get going on this fast and you aren't back. Or if something happens to you down there."

"Michael, if that happens and you really need the diskettes, here's what you do. You cut a cashier's check for twenty thousand dollars and give it to Mr. Joe Kazekian. He is acting as my agent while I'm gone." I wrote down Joe's address and phone number and handed it to him.

Michael sat there for a long time, thinking but saying nothing. He didn't let off any steam. He was a cool operator. Finally he smiled. "Okay, we can play it that way. I just hope you get back here in two weeks so we won't lose headway on the project. Three weeks at the latest."

"I'll try. I'm not going down there for vacation, you know. And I really *do* want you to hook those *two* companies on the project." I smiled. "I have a big stake in our projects. We should be able to make a lot of money."

Michael took that without a blink. I guessed that he had hooked Dr. Jekyll and wasn't in that much danger of losing Mr. Hyde.

In fact, Michael looked quite relaxed, now. "Good luck on your trip to bring back Rebecca. You said she is interested in medical anthropology."

"And providing health care for Third Worlders."

"On what river did you say she was?"

"The *Rio Negro*."

"But that's a long river. You said she was at a mission that's up a shorter river."

"Right."

"What is it's name?"

"I can't tell you the name of it right now. Getting too upset to think. I got absolutely no sleep last night. I still have a load of stuff to do before I leave."

"When are you leaving?"

"Seven fifty-five, tomorrow evening. Hope I can get everything done in time."

"Flying Varig direct?"

It seemed like Michael couldn't resist playing the cosmopolite.

"No, I'm taking another airline, flying through Caracas."

"After you hook up with Rebecca, could you call or e-mail me so I know everything is okay."

"Sure. Wherever I find the first phone or Internet café."

Michael thought this over for a minute. Then he rose and extended his hand. "Well, I wish you a safe and successful journey."

We shook hands on that. I helped him carry the reports to his car.

Returning to the house, I grabbed a can opener, circumcised a can of Dinty Moore beef stew, and performed my *in situ* heating trick. And while the can of stew rocked gently in the pan of boiling water, I stewed about my business relationship with Michael: First there was one company, then it became obvious that there were two companies, and he still wouldn't admit it. And after I told him to tell Mr. Hyde to go to hell, Michael stopped relaying demands from him. And when Michael got an inkling of my own invention, he first made a big play about owning rights to it. But then he backed off. And yesterday the patent search on bioprospecting was so damn important, but today he was wishing me *bon voyage*.

With the water at a sustained and vigorous boil, the stew was now undergoing intermittent volcanic eruptions. I made a lettuce and tomato salad and pulled a yogurt from the refrigerator, then terminated my science experiment on the stove. Tired and hungry, I sat down to eat.

The phone interrupted my dessert. It was Rebecca's mother. Why hadn't Rebecca called her? What, she's not back? Why didn't she come back? Wasn't I worried? Was it right that she was more worried than I was worried? Wasn't I wrong for encouraging her jungle medicine? What's Rebecca think she is — Indiana Jones or something? The girl might be a doctor but she isn't normal. Maybe she wasn't *ever* normal. When she was 14, she was already filling her head with all that psychology and anthropology. No, that wasn't normal.

And, between the lines, she said I wasn't normal either. Otherwise, I would have put a stop to it.

And, she wanted to know, what the heck was so important that Rebecca had to extend her stay down there, anyway?

I almost lost patience with the old gal. I almost told her that Rebecca was waiting for an old medicine man to come out of the jungle with the tip of his penis tied to his bellybutton.

But I didn't say that. I couldn't deal with an escalation of complaints and questions. Although she had never raised her big questions, I could feel them ready to erupt: When would Rebecca and I finally settle down and get married? Would there be grandchildren? Would my Catholic background cause problems? Couldn't I get a "real job" in a blue chip pharmaceutical corporation in New Jersey, not far from New York?

Sorry, Mom, I thought. I can't promise you anything that Rebecca can't promise me.

I just kept on listening, respectfully, until Rebecca's mom was all talked out. We ended the conversation with my promise — that I would go down there and return Rebecca "by the crook of the neck." And I would make Rebecca call her from the first available phone.

After that conversation, I felt weary. I drifted aimlessly around the house before realizing that I had gone 34 hours without sleep. I set the house alarm and went to bed.

The next morning, I woke up in a panic. Would the remaining 12 hours be sufficient to get everything done? There were so many things to do. Two incoming phone calls kept me pinned me down at the house for a half hour.

The first call was from a Dr. Gerhard Kaufmann from Wiesbaden, Germany. He wanted any non-confidential information that was available on my consulting company. After promising to mail him a brochure, I asked if he had any special interests. He said he maintained a pool of consultants and that he was especially interested in ones with expertise in drug discovery. I admitted to being such an expert but informed him that I was tied up with a project and wouldn't be free for one month.

The next call came from Alice. The surveillance van was licensed to a corporation in Hialeah. Nica's car was licensed to herself, listing the same Miami Springs address that I'd visited. And Pock Face's car was registered to Abelardo Requejo with a residential address at 7975 Biscayne Boulevard. We both agreed that had to be a business address. I thanked Alice for the information and told her I was going down to Brazil to bring Rebecca back. I promised Alice that if there was a story behind it, she would be the first to get the scoop. Told her that I'd be using satellite phone to keep in contact with Zeekie. She said she knew Zeekie and had a rather low opinion of him.

Alice was a good friend. She spent a lot of time analyzing my problems from a lot of angles before concluding that she couldn't make heads or tails of it. Her voice cracked while saying goodbye. I promised to do my best.

My plane left the tarmac at 8:20 p.m., bound for Caracas. Through the starboard window, Miami looked like a microarray of 10,000 glowing orange spots — the streetlights receding and the grid contracting as we gained altitude and passed over the high rises of the Brickell Financial District lining the water's edge. Biscayne Bay was as black as ebony. Key Biscayne glided under us like a thin strip of light. And the Atlantic was completely dark, except for widely spaced patches of woolly clouds reflecting the light of the three-quarter moon. Occasionally, a white dot slipped along below us — the deck lights of a freighter. Unlike the stars in the sky, the freighters were few. Could a lonely mariner look up and see the light from my window? No, my portal was too small and dim.

Maybe that's the definition of loneliness: when you radiate into a cold, empty universe and not a single photon bounces back to you. Or maybe loneliness is what comes when you hang suspended between your future and past — the future unknowable and the past irretrievable.

I'd left a day late. The past two days were a blur of logistics problems: getting traveler's checks, cash, flashlights, batteries, Avon solution to keep the mosquitos at bay, disposable cigarette lighters to make fires, chlorine-generating tablets to sterilize water, salt tablets and Gatorade to keep my electrolytes balanced; finding a drugstore that could fill a prescription for a two-month supply of mefloquine; typing up a handbill for Rebecca in Portuguese and English and making 100 copies; and doing non-essential things, like buying tape for my hand-held tape recorder.

I'd bought a lot of things at Quartermaster Sales, Miami's foremost military supply store located way down south where U.S. Highway One cuts through the bean patches. There, I bought mosquito netting, a mess kit, two tough duffel bags and a hammock. I didn't buy a high-powered sling shot, a Crocodile Dundee size knife, nor that $278 Russian night-vision scope, although I spent a lot of time looking at it. It made my head look like a stalk-eyed snail. Hopefully, I wouldn't have to creep up on someone in the dark to find Rebecca.

When I leaned back in my seat and shut my eyes, I was haunted by two images from Quartermaster Sales. One was of a painting of the half-track on the building's outside wall. The other was of their real half-track standing near it at the edge of in their parking lot. The one painted on the wall looked so gallant, rearing on its hind tracks as it leapt over a sand dune, its anti-aircraft gun blazing. The real one looked so immobile and rusted. Why is glory so easy to imagine and so difficult to achieve in real life?

Then came another sad memory — of hanging around the County firing range located along Tamiami Trail at the foot of the Everglades, looking for someone to teach me about guns.

Ned Johnson was a nice guy. After squinting at me through his yellow-tinted shooter's glasses, he sensed that I was in trouble and adopted me like a stray dog. He let me shoot his .38 revolver and his .45 semi-automatic, then gave me a lot of fatherly advice. His age fit the relationship. He was somewhere between 50 and 70. It was hard to tell exactly. His skin was stretched tight over his face but his body was lean.

Ned's friends had a lot of advice, too. Some said that for the jungle rivers you really needed a rifle. But I wondered if a rifle would be too conspicuous and might actually bring me trouble. The consensus was that the best pistol for me was a .45 because it throws a lot of weight and does a lot of damage, especially when it hits bone. It ejects the casing after each shot, but that would be no problem since there "won't be many crime scene investigators down there." Ned's friends advised buying a spare magazine so I wouldn't have to stop shooting. Everyone was so friendly. It felt strange, how talk about killing people can bring people together.

Killing is against my nature. Maybe that's why I was actually relieved when I went to 7975 Biscayne Boulevard looking for Pock Face and found nothing more than a mail drop.

In the jetliner, I willed myself to sleep. I spent the next few hours chasing away dreams involving a thatch-roofed bar on the *Rio Negro*, a crazy German pilot, and a lot of dusky guys in the background.

I didn't wake up for the landing in Caracas. I didn't have to get out because the plane flew on to Manaus. I half-slept while the other half of my mind planned my steps in Manaus. We descended on that equatorial city about an hour before dawn.

I felt rested enough while shouldering my backpack up the aisle, through the jetway and to the baggage area. A baggage carrousel delivered my two heavy duffel bags. The sleepy customs inspector took no special interest in me or my bags. I listed tourism as the purpose of my trip. Out on the curb, it did take a while to get a cab. But having remembered the names of a couple of hotels in the old Central District, I could offer him a destination.

At $15 per night, the *Estadista* was a lucky choice. On street level it had a small reception — a combination front desk and bar. Above, accessible by rickety wooden stairs, were four storeys of rooms. Mine, located on the back end near the toilet serving the third floor, had a sink with a broken bowl and a window looking down on a cluttered alleyway. In places, the plaster was deeply cracked and the floor creaked under my step. But the door lock was secure enough to protect my gear.

Down the street from the hotel, I found a restaurant. After a heavy breakfast of omelet and ham, I headed for the market area near the floating docks. There I spent the morning shopping for trade goods. An hour of searching yielded a hardware store that had what I needed: three machetes, one hatchet, a hundred fish hooks of various sizes, fishing line and several meters of stout cord. I would use these items to purchase information and guide service. At another shop, I bought a dozen packs of domestic cigarettes, also for trading purposes. On the way back to the hotel, I located a grocery store which had the right look — like a warehouse. After stowing my purchases in my hotel room, I returned to the grocery store with an empty duffel bag. I bought a four-week supply of canned sardines, crackers and canned fruit. These, would not be for trade. These would sustain me while searching for Rebecca. I returned to the hotel, stowed the bag, and headed out to the restaurant for lunch.

It took the rest of the afternoon to line up my next purchase: a serviceable .45 with two boxes of ammunition. The owner of the third shop had what I needed and was willing to accept a $200 bribe to relieve me of impossible paperwork and a two-week waiting period.

With my .45 semi-automatic, my extra magazine and two boxes of ammo packed in a brown paper bag and tucked under my arm, I descended the seawall's 30-foot stairs and sought out a secluded area between two derelict boats. There I test-fired the .45, using a soggy burlap bag as a muffler. Satisfied with my purchase, I made my way through the crowded streets and back to my hotel. When I got there, I asked the guy behind the front desk for my key. Actually, the front desk looked more like a bar right then: Several cane-backed bar stools were set up before it and the liquor bottles were more prominent. It adapted to the time of day. And the guy standing behind it didn't snap to attention when I asked, in Portuguese-flavored Spanish, for the key to Room #29. And that seemed to amuse a guy sitting in the corner. He addressed me in English.

19   Up the Lazy River

"It looks like you are doing the same kind of traveling as I am."

His words came out in English, but it wasn't an American, Canadian or British variety. It wasn't a French accent. Too stiff for that. He didn't sound German either, although he did say *trafeling* for traveling. I took a second to look him over and decide how to reply. He was short-haired — so blond that it looked almost white — and his face was long and sun-damaged. It didn't look like it did much smiling, although it was smiling now. He was dressed much like me, but with black leather ankle-boots and long khaki pants without cargo pockets. He probably kept his stuff organized in his photographer's vest which he was now flapping with one hand to demonstrate what he meant by his kind of *trafeling*.

"No," I replied, "it doesn't look like we came here to attend the opera."

He rolled his eyes to the side, slapped his knee and laughed like I'd told a damn good joke. Then he pushed off from his bar stool and closed the distance between us with a couple of quick steps. He was probably around 50. Straightened up before me to his full height, he was about six-foot-one. While extending his hand, he deferred to me with a slight bow of the head and made like he was clicking his heels. "Jos van der Hoek," he said.

The pronunciation of his first name caused me some confusion. "Glad to meet you, Mr. van der Hoek," I replied. "I am Doctor Ben Candidi." While shaking hands, I matched the strength of his grip. "Are you from Holland?"

He nodded. "Photojournalist for *Elsevier*." He repeated the head-bow and heel-click gesture. "Call me Jos." He repeated it, spelling it out and explaining that the *j* is pronounced like *y*.

By European standards, he seemed to be making a special effort to be friendly. That's how I interpreted the stiff smile on his broad face and the forced gaiety in his deep voice. But the half-dozen Dutchmen I'd known had always looked me in the face while talking. This guy's blue-gray eyes kept sliding away from me.

"Interesting," I said. "Sounds exciting, too — photo-journalism." I was making an extra effort to be friendly.

"And I am sure that what you are doing is just as interesting." He said *watt* for what. "Why don't you sit down and I will invite you for a beer." He moved back to his bar stool and half-sat, half-stood there, with his left hand in the air like he was hailing a friend at a street carnival.

The barkeeper/deskman set down a cardboard coaster, creating a place next to Jos. I did some quick thinking. Would it be comfortable sitting there with my gun and ammo on the bar? Well, it was double-wrapped and probably wouldn't show. And wouldn't it be an insult to refuse this guy after he'd put himself out on a limb? And I didn't have a ready excuse to say "no."

"I would be glad to accept." I said, pulling a stool to a comfortable distance from him. I set my package on the bar. Hell, I deserved a beer tonight. Hell, I deserved two beers: the one he would buy for me and the one coming in the second round that I would buy.

In broken Portuguese, Jos ordered me a Brahma Chop. We lifted our glasses to Brazil. As his guest, making the conversation was my job. And I was interested to know how a middle-aged Dutchman makes a career in international photojournalism.

"What kind of assignment are you on, Jos?"

"A free assignment. Their idea is that I get a lot of nature shots and maybe some stories about the Indians."

"You're not working with a reporter?"

"Not this time."

He answered earnestly now, without the forced gaiety with which he'd greeted me. His eyes focused on his glass.

"But you usually work with a reporter, don't you?"

"Yes, usually."

"Do you know a lot about Brazil?"

"Very little." He raised the glass to his mouth and glanced around the room.

"Are your assignments mostly domestic, in Holland?"

"No."

Was he having trouble giving answers because English was not his first language? My eyes fell to his photojournalists vest which looked like it had seen more of the world than Holland.

"So, tell me some countries you have worked in."

"I have had assignments in Germany and Switzerland."

"But you wouldn't dress like we do to go there." I slapped a cargo pocket on my pants.

Jos stiffened for a second, then relaxed. "I have had assignments in Africa."

"What did they have you do there?"

"Human interest shots in South Africa. There is interest in how our . . . in how the country is working after *apartheid*."

"Did they ever send you to Somolia?"

"No. And I never saw anything bloody, like what those . . . *people* did to that American soldier."

"Did they send you to the country, I forget the name, that produces the so-called blood diamonds?"

"No. No, *Elsevier* is not as — how do you say? — not as sensationalistical as *Stern*. That is the big German magazine that has many photographers which they send out to get mostly that type of pictures. We Dutch are a friendlier people."

That might be, but this guy looked like he'd do fine in hostile environments. Yes, I could imagine he'd be one tough son of a bitch — all 210 pounds of him, most of it muscle — if someone pushed his back against the wall. I asked him a lot of questions about magazine photography without learning much more.

With the first round of beer exhausted, I offered a second round and Jos accepted.

"To the success of our business," he proposed, as we raised our glasses and clinked bottoms.

"Yes. I hope you get a good story."

"So what brings you to Manaus, Dr. Candidi?" He turned toward me like it was now time for him to interview me. "I would guess that you are an American who has had a lot of experience with Spanish-speaking Latin America but maybe less with Brazil."

"That's true," I said.

"So what brings you here? Not photojournalism, I would guess." He talked loudly and ended abruptly, looking at me with a wooden face and wide, unfocussed eyes.

"I'm going up the river to pick up my girlfriend." I said that as if it were as simple a matter as picking her up after work.

"Which *one*?" he asked, like it was a schoolboy joke.

That sounded a tad too familiar for my taste. For the first time, I looked him in the eyes and stared. His irises had the texture of a frozen daiquiri. What was going on behind those pupils? Was he putting himself out on the limb, making a conscious effort to be friendly and entertaining? Was I talking to a Pinocchio doll? A Dresden porcelain soldier? And how long would he hold my gaze with that wide-eyed smile?

"Are you asking me which girlfriend, like the sailor with a girl in every port?"

"No, no, no," he laughed, rolling his eyes upwards to the right. "I mean which *river*." He made it sound like we were engaged in high-level repartee.

"Up the *Rio Negro*," I answered.

"Oh, well that's the same river that I'm going up. With a freighter tomorrow, if it works out."

"Great. How far are you going?"

He pulled a long chug before answering, "Calanaque." That was about three-quarters of the way to Santa Isabel. "I will see what I can see. If not, I will go a little further."

"Why Calanaque?"

"I have a contact there."

"What do you expect to photograph there?"

"Birds, monkeys, peasants and the fish they pull from the river. And how far are you going up the river, Dr. Candidi?"

"Farther than you."

I left it at that. He looked at me, expectantly. I finished my glass with a couple of gulps. Now we were even. I set a foot on the floor.

"Maybe we can share a taxi to the docks, tomorrow," he said.

"That's cool, but first I'm going to scout out the boats myself on foot, without my gear."

"That is good thinking. No use carrying all that heavy stuff around."

"I'm leaving early tomorrow morning." I planned to leave at six, but didn't say so.

"Good. I will see you then."

I picked up my heavy paper sack and went to my room where I ate a dinner of sardines and crackers. I got everything into the duffel bags and went to bed early.

The next morning Jos was waiting for me in the lobby. Can't say whether I was happy to see him or not. It's good to have a fellow traveler when operating in a strange environment. It's especially good when he knows the place better than you. Jos strode through crowds of shoppers, merchants and street urchins with a don't-mess-with-me attitude. He proved a capable navigator with a good sense of direction and an uncanny ability to read the small street signs from far away. Soon, we were walking westward along the *Rua 10 de Julho* and crossing the bridge over the São Raimundo inlet.

Riverboats were nosed in, side-by-side, for 150 yards along its steep, muddy bank and the narrow dirt road serving it was already jammed with trucks, some of them careened at dangerous angles. The steep hillside behind them was covered by rough cinderblock houses with jutting wooden balconies. And the narrow stretch of red clay bank below the trucks was a beehive of stevedore activity. Laden with eighty-pound bags of cement, manioc flour or loads of beer and soft drinks, they walked up 40-degree gangplanks to deposit their loads.

"How is your Portuguese?" I asked Jos.

"Good enough to say, 'Up the *Rio Negro* to Calanaque.'"

"Make it to Santa Isabel for me. I will need a separate cabin and am willing to pay for it."

"Yes, it is no good sleeping on deck with a hammock. You will get no sleep and your equipment will disappear."

"Okay. I'll start inquiring on this side, and you start on the far side. And we'll meet in the middle."

I learned a lot more Portuguese in that hour. I also brushed up on my playground skills, walking steep gangplanks and sometimes even climbing between boats. When Jos and I met up again, I had a 100-footer that would leave the next day and Jos had a 120-footer that was leaving in the early afternoon. I opted for his find. His was a triple-decker that was taking on a load of cement, building materials, canned food and beer. We went back, plunked down the equivalent of $80 on the cargo master's table, and got lockable, adjoining staterooms near the bow on the third deck.

I told Jos I'd meet him in one hour at the hotel. After we split up, I searched for a public phone. I spent a lot of time calling the *Funai* office in Brasília. The *Funai* bureaucrats had no information on Rebecca, didn't know about any German medical team on the *Rio Marauiá*, and couldn't help with communicating with the Santa Isabel office.

When I arrived at the hotel, about ten minutes late, Jos was waiting at the reception with his gear, two duffel bags and a long, cylindrical camo bag, looking worried. I told him not to worry. I dragged down my gear and paid my bill while he was outside, flagging down a cab.

Jos helped me load my stuff into the taxi and then onto the boat and finally into my cabin. Yes, it was good to have a fellow traveler on this trip — someone to watch out for my interests. He made sure the boat didn't leave without me while I delivered my handbill to the other captains. It listed the number of my satellite phone which was now helping to bulge a pocket on my left leg.

Of course, I had to give Jos some sort of explanation for the handbills. I told him I was keeping an eye out for Rebecca to make sure that we didn't cross paths on the *Rio Negro*. For some reason I couldn't let him know the depth of my concern.

Because the captain wanted a full load of cargo and hammock passengers, we didn't get underway until sundown. During the waiting time I learned that Jos wasn't much of a conversationalist. Several times I tried to start up a conversation on photography and didn't get much out of him. Maybe he had trouble finding things to say. We ate separately and privately, each in his own cabin. But I did notice that his cuisine was a level above my sardines and crackers. He had pre-packaged MREs — "Meals Ready to Eat."

It was interesting to watch the captain navigating the boat at night through the finger islands without a depth sounder, positioning instruments, or even a chart. At sunup, the boat stopped at Novo Airão to discharge cargo and take on passengers. I got off to show the flyer to people at the landing. They hadn't seen Rebecca. Jos got off too, and took some photos with a 35-millimeter Nikon. Half an hour later, we were underway again. Shortly before sundown, we landed at Santo Antônio where the boat tied up for the night. We retired to our separate cabins. I went to bed early. Jos did not.

With little to do, my brain put on a slide show. I saw images of multi-colored pharmacological keys that would open locks in living cells. This mixed with images of garbage dumps and junkyards with poor people crawling around, looking for food and spare parts for machines.

The next morning I thought about how much the river had changed in the last six weeks. Thunderheads were replaced by wispy clouds. The distant beaches looked larger and brighter. The sandbars were more frequent. The river level had dropped. The currents were slower and the breeze was faster, but the temperature was still brain-deadening. I pulled out the phone, folded out its cylindrical plastic antenna arm and dialed Zeekie. He read me loud and clear. He said that my answering machine had not recorded any important news and that there weren't any e-mails from Rebecca, either. I kept the conversation short to save the battery.

Jos climbed down the stairs, camera in hand. He said hello, then drifted off to the starboard side where he occupied himself with his photography.

I spent the day trying to find logical connections between the strange things that had happened in Miami. And I thought about Rebecca. Had she walked into Jonestown, a place where they take final communion with cyanide-laced Kool-Aid? Was she already brainwashed? No, brainwashing wouldn't explain her flunking my test about the baby of her non-existent cousin. It had to be someone else answering for her.

Why would someone else answer for her? Had they killed her and were trying to cover up the fact? Where were the Hotmail.com e-mails coming from? The first ones sounded like her; the last ones were from someone else. They must have had her confidence before they took over.

Rebecca is not afraid of physical danger. And she does the right thing when in a tight spot, like the one we found ourselves in during our last cruise in the Bahamas. But her trusting optimism might get her into trouble, especially if it was connected with healing. I remembered that night in South Miami Beach when she walked into the middle of a fight to help a man who was down and bleeding. "Stand back. I'm a doctor," she said. "This man needs medical attention."

Sure, normal people would understand this — but not people zonked on methamphetamine. Luckily, they did move back. Luckily, a couple of plainclothesmen arrived a minute later.

Rebecca stayed with her patient until the paramedics came to take him away. On the way home that night, Rebecca and I had a long talk about guns and knives. She wouldn't agree she was wrong to jump in that time, but we did agree on one thing. When a bad guy threatens, you never let him increase his control over you.

In the middle of the day, our freighter pulled in at Moura. Jos got out to take pictures and I talked to some people and left some handbills. Nobody had seen Rebecca. Same thing at Carvoeiro, where we tied up for our next night. And after our separate dinners, Jos surprised me by knocking on my door.

"Ben, I am going to have a drink on the roof. Would you like to join me?" He had a bottle, two glasses and a couple of limes. It would have been a rebuff to turn him down. Europeans are so formal. He'd probably agonized over the invitation all day.

I picked up a couple of cloth sacks for us to sit on, and I

followed him up the outboard ladder. The captain didn't let the hammock passengers up there so we didn't have to share the space with anybody. We leaned against the top section of the back wall of the empty pilothouse. The sun had just gone down and it had gotten dark in a hurry. The shore was dotted with light from small fires and kerosene lanterns. Some 20 feet directly below us, the water was a milky glow — reflected light from our cabins. And deep within the boat, the diesel generator throbbed, massaging my back and obscuring the jungle noise.

Under the light of a tropical half-moon, Jos poured three fingers of rum into each of the glasses. He pulled out a jungle knife from its holder on his belt and halved a lime with a fast twisting motion. He squeezed a half-lime into one of the glasses, threw the peel overboard, lifted the glass and swirled. He handed me the other half-lime and indicated I was to do the same. He waited until I had finished, then saluted me with his glass. "To the success of our missions."

"To success," I affirmed. We were only two days away from relative civilization, but the rush of the rum and the aftertaste of the lime seemed like a real luxury. "Thanks, Jos. This really hits the spot."

"You are a good fellow and it is right that we should have a drink together."

"Well thanks, Jos. Tomorrow noon we hit Barcelos and by this time tomorrow you will be on shore at Calanaque. You said you've got a contact waiting for you there."

Jos half nodded and half shook his head. "I have a name of a person who will take me in. But he will not meet me at the dock like it was an appointment. You know how it is in the uncivilized part of the world."

"What are you going to do?"

"I will pay him some money and he will take me in his canoe and I will take pictures of the fish he catches. And then I will set up my camera on a tripod with my telephoto lens, and take pictures of birds."

"So that's what's in that long bag of yours."

"Yes. And then I will take pictures of dirty-face children and palm thatch huts and maybe when I get enough pictures I can come back and my *redakteur* will assign some lazy Dutch boy to make a story out of it."

"Well happy fishing. I hear they pull some really strange-looking fish from the river around here."

"Yes, thank you." His voice was soothing, like the rum. I guessed that Northern Europeans are just like the rest of us once they break through that crust of stiff formality. "Ben, would you like another one?"

He didn't wait for my answer. He just pulled out his knife and halved the second lime. I said, "Yes, please," and he poured me four fingers of rum.

"And what will you be doing one and one-half days from now?" Jos asked.

"Why did you pick that time?"

"Because that is when you will be in Santa Isabel."

"And why did you pick that town, Jos?"

"Because that is the one you said you were going to . . . when we were trying to pick out a boat."

That was right. I had told him. And the answer to his question was that I'd be grasping at straws, asking the *Funai* couple of hundred questions. But I didn't want to tell him that.

"I'll be making arrangements for a dugout canoe to take me to my girlfriend."

"Yes, Rebecca Levis. I have seen her picture. She is quite pretty."

I searched his half-shadowed face.

"It should not be such a big surprise, Ben. I have seen the *blat* that you have given everyone, everywhere this boat stops. Either she is missing or there has been some big problem with your plans. You are afraid she is lost. You are afraid she is in danger." He paused and I said nothing. "I can see it on your face when you talk to them. I notice such things. I am a photographer." His face looked warm and sympathetic in the light of the half-moon.

"You're right, Jos. I didn't say anything about it because I didn't want to bother you with it. She's out of communication with me and she's long overdue. But she's at a mission and they're usually safe. Just have to get a dugout canoe and go up there."

Jos kept asking questions and I kept giving him answers that made it seem harmless.

"Maybe I should go with you and help you."

"No, thanks. I can do what I have to do by myself."

"But you never know when it is good to have another white

man there. It is a big strain out in the bush by yourself. You want to lie down and go to sleep but you can't trust yourself to sleep because maybe someone sneaks up to steal your gear or maybe even kill you."

I thought about this. I would have to hire Hashamo and his dugout canoe to take me up the *Rio Marauiá*. I could trust him to get me to the Mission. But what if they tell me that Rebecca trekked off into the forest? I couldn't hunt for her all by myself.

"I don't know, Jos."

My denial was weak and he must have sensed it.

"But I want to help you with your search." His face looked so open and earnest.

"Why?"

"For . . . one reason, because you are a good fellow and I want to help you. But another reason is that it might make a good story . . . a lot better story than the one I have about these lazy *caboclos* and their fish and the jungle birds."

The more I kept denying, the more persuasive Jos became. "Together, we both have a better chance to succeed. You find your pretty 'Doctor Without Borders' and I get the story about how you seek her. And, you must remember, searching for her might be expensive. Maybe you can do it with a dugout canoe or maybe you can't. And, of course, I would pay half your expenses. If you have to organize a trek, with a lot of people, or if you have to go searching for her with a helicopter, that can be expensive. If your situation is desperate — and I do not like to say it but it could be — then I can get on my satellite phone and get the okay from *Elsevier*, and then we get a helicopter for free. Your story could be that important."

I thought about the Rebecca's admonition to just trust her. And then I thought about the false e-mails.

"I don't know. If you want to go to Santa Isabel with me and if there's enough room on the canoe, I guess you can come. But no promises."

"I understand. And maybe I cannot go, anyway. I will know after I see my contact at Calanaque, tomorrow night."

As we talked on into the night, it seemed like we had switched roles, with him playing the friendly one and with me playing the stiff, stand-offish one.

The next day, my third day up the river, we kept to ourselves. In the middle of the morning, Jos went to the rear of the boat and made a satellite phone call. That night, when we arrived at Calanaque, he went off to find his guide, telling me they would return for his gear. Since I was planning to go to bed early, I shook his hand and wished him luck. The next morning, the beginning of my fourth day, I was awakened by the sound of the freighter's motors. We were underway. And when I went down to my place on the bow, I found Jos sitting there.

Santa Isabel   20

I went up to him. "Jos, you're still here!"

"Yes, I am going with you to Santa Isabel."

"What about your contact in Calanaque?"

He extended his hand, palm down, and rocked it, his face slipping into a disdainful expression. "One day is no different than the other for these people."

I thought hard for a full minute. "Okay, you can come with me. But there's one thing you have to understand. This is my show. I do all the talking, I make all the decisions. You are just along to take your pictures. Is that a deal?"

"Yes, of course."

I told him my plans for the day.

We pulled up to the dock across from Santa Isabel shortly after noon. Actually, it was good to have a second pair of hands to help carry my gear down that 40-degree gangplank and up the path to the *Funai* station. But I didn't want his help with the interview with the Campos de Carvaloh couple. I made Jos stop 25 yards short of the house and watch our gear.

Both Marcello and Lucia were at home. And they were delighted to see me — for the first few seconds. They must have read the situation off my face. And my language problems didn't help the situation any:

No, Senhora Doutora Rebecca has not returned. Yes, we knew that she wanted to stay. Yes, we are sure that is what she did. The satellite phone? We are sorry but it has been impossible to receive calls on it. The *Funai* budget had been reduced and we cannot afford batteries. No, it is impossible to get an adaptor to run it off of electric power. And the power is not available to us, anyway.

Just as before, Lucia did most of the work on the conversation. Marcello volunteered much less, this time. He stood back with his arms crossed. Looking at both of them, I asked how they powered the shortwave radio. Marcello said it was powered by a lead-acid battery, recharged by a solar cell. I asked why they couldn't use that power for the satellite phone. They said they didn't have an adaptor for it. It was hard to suppress my frustration. Of course, undermining their hospitality would serve no purpose, but a part of me wanted to scream out that the use of a ten-dollar voltmeter and a soldering iron belongs in everyone's education.

I asked Lucia who was going up and down the *Rio Marauiá*.

No, Senhor Doutor, nothing new is happening on the *Rio Marauiá*. No, there is not a German medical expedition up the river. No, there is no expedition of any kind that went up the river since you were here. Yes, we are sure, Senhor. Why does that make you so excited, Senhor?

I told them about Rebecca's strange e-mail message.

No, we do not know much about e-mail. We do not know how she could be sending messages. No, the Mission does not have its own satellite dish. Yes, again, we are sure that nobody else went up the river.

It was a long, strenuous conversation for all three of us. And they couldn't help from noticing Jos, standing conspicuously at the bend in the path. But it was too early to factor him into the equation.

I asked them to call the Mission on the shortwave radio.

Yes, Senhor, we will try to call the priest on shortwave. We will do it tonight. That is the only time to do it. The Mission does not run its generator during the day. But I should not hope too much, because the priest doesn't turn it on very often. He speaks good Italian but poor Portuguese. The last time we spoke to him? It must have been 10 months ago, don't you think, Marcello?

Yes, you can stay here in the tent, for as many days as you like. Your guide, too. He can come, too. We are hospitable.

Could you go up the river? Officially, we have to deny you permission. But Hashamo went up two weeks ago. And he will be going up next week to supply the Mission. What we do not see happening we cannot forbid.

What? You want to pay him to take you tomorrow? You would have to talk to him. How much would it cost? You can offer him 70 American dollars. But you would have to get 120 liters of gasoline plus oil.

I waved Jos over to us and introduced him as "Jos who is helping me find my way around here." I told him to move our gear into the tent.

While Marcello went off to get Hashamo, Lucia showed me a map that had the locations of the *shabonos* that could be accessed from the *Rio Marauiá*. I copied them onto the maps that Zeekie had downloaded for me. When Marcello came with Hashamo, I had him ask if he'd seen Rebecca at the Mission on his supply run two weeks ago. He said he didn't see her.

Hashamo spoke a broken Portuguese that barely had a future tense, and had no subjunctive tense whatsoever. Yes, he would make an extra trip for me. No, there wasn't anybody with 120 liters of gasoline around San Isabel. Marcello said we would have to take the next freighter to Calanaque where there was a floating gas station where we would probably have to buy a whole drum. Then I remembered the German pilot.

First, I had Hashamo show me his own hut. Jos followed along. Then we walked along the riverbank to Amazon Touristic. As Klaus-Dietrich's shed came into view, it was clear that he still had plenty of drums of gasoline. I told Jos to stay back, out of sight.

I walked up and knocked hard on the door. "Hey, Klaus-Dietrich, this is Ben." I heard movement inside. "This is Ben, the *Amerikaner* that you had a drink with a few weeks ago."

"*Warte, warte.*" He sounded irritated for having been disturbed. He came out in shorts — shirtless and shoeless. He had bushels of chest hair and his skin looked reddish, like it didn't take a tan. He didn't pay any attention to me at first. In Portuguese and in a scolding tone, he reminded Hashamo that he was never supposed to set foot in his camp.

In halting Portuguese, Hashamo protested that he didn't come on his own accord, but because of me. Klaus answered that with a scowl that could cook flesh. Hashamo slinked off in the direction we came from. Happily, Jos was still out of sight.

Klaus-Dietrich turned to me. "*Ja, mein amerikanischer Freund.* You come visiting. We go drink another beer, tonight?"

"Yes, I'd like to do that. But I also want to hire your plane."

"*Ja*, I take you back to Manuas. Four hundert dollars, American, tomorrow."

"What I would really like to do is have you fly me to a mission to check up on my girlfriend."

"*Ja*, maybe I can do that. Where is the mission?"

I pulled out a map. "Here, on the *Rio Marauiá*."

"*Du Idiot*! Do you think that I am going to try to land on that narrow river with trees all around?"

"No, I know you can't land there. But I thought that you could circle around over it so that everyone will come out. Then when my girlfriend comes out, I will see her. Maybe I can drop a message."

"Yes, I could do that. It will cost you three hundert dollars, American."

"Okay, and if we add another fifty dollars, could we fly over some *shabonos* in case I don't find her?" I showed him the map.

He looked at me suspiciously. "Why do you want to fly over *shabonos*?"

"Just in case we don't see her at the Mission."

"But she will be at the Mission."

"That is what everybody tells me."

He thought for a few seconds. "Yes, we could do that."

"And after we find her, could you sell me one hundred and twenty liters of gasoline and four liters of oil? That's so Hashamo can take me there with his dugout canoe?"

"Yes, I can do that. But you do not need one liter of oil for every thirty liters of gasoline. I will give you two liters of oil. It is aviation oil. You do not need a one-to-thirty mix for the *scheiss* motor boat engines around here. They will fall apart anyway. One-to-sixty is enough."

He apparently knew what he was talking about. Around the

corner of the shed, I caught a glimpse of a long aluminum canoe with a motor mount. "Okay," I said.

"The fuel will cost you one hundert and fifty dollars, American."

"Okay," I said again. "Can we start tomorrow morning at ten?"

"*Ja.*"

Wc shook hands on it.

On the way back I found Hashamo with Jos, who had been waiting about 70 yards up the river. I told Hashamo that I wanted him to take me up the river the day after tomorrow. I told Jos I'd be doing air reconnaissance tomorrow. We returned to the tent where we ate our separate rations. I spent the time thinking about how to get the most out of tomorrow. I don't know what Jos spent his time thinking when he went for a long walk. I spent the evening working by candlelight on a project involving my handbills, two cut-up T-shirts, small rocks and lots of string.

The next morning I got up early. So did Jos. With his camera over his shoulder, he followed me to the *Funai* shack where I got the bad news: The Mission had not answered our wireless calls. I returned to the tent, picked up a plastic bag filled with the fruit of the last evening's labors, and set off for Klaus-Dietrich's. Jos fell into step along side of me.

"Hey, Jos, there was no arrangement to take you along."

"I know, Ben, but I need some good pictures for my story. I will ask to go along and it will probably be okay." He rubbed his thumb and forefinger together to indicate that the problem could be overcome with money.

But when I arrived at the shack, I found Klaus-Dietrich half-awake. And hc was in a foul mood, even after I gave him the $300. He scowled at Jos, who was loitering a few steps behind me.

"*Was ist dass*? I said yes to you, but I will not load up my planc with a lot of people."

"Klaus-Dietrich, this is Jos. He is a Hollandcr that I met on —"

Jos stepped forward and did his heel-clicking thing with a slight bow. "Jos van der Hoek from Amsterdam." He had a clip full of money in his hands, which he held together, almost beseechingly. "I am willing to pay to come along. It would be good to take a few pictures."

Klaus-Dietrich regarded him with crossed arms. "*Drei hundert, amerikanisch,*" he replied. He made it sound like a command.

Jos pealed off six 50s and handed them over. Klaus-Dietrich disappeared into the shack for a few minutes before locking up and taking us down to his floating dock. This time, I took a better look at it. Sure, it floated on tree trunks like all the docks around here. But the deck of this one was of regular wood planking. Although Klaus-Dietrich looked wasted from the previous evening and had hangover breath, he ran a taut ship. He stared at Jos's boots.

"You will not wear those heavy boots on my plane," he said.

Jos looked back at Klaus like he was suppressing a smart reply. Klaus tapped his temple with a forefinger in a *Dummkopf* gesture and said, "I do not carry weight which is not necessary."

While Jos stowed his boots along the side of the shed, Klaus readied the airplane. He opened the window-doors, swinging them high over the cockpit, and untied the far-side mooring lines that were holding the plane from the dock. I held it off, myself, until Jos returned in his stocking feet. Klaus ordered him aboard, indicating he was to sit in the back. No sooner was he seated than he turned around and inspected the back corner. A small collapsible grappling anchor was attached to a thin rope that was spooled on a winch bolted to the airframe. A sausage-shaped canvas bag sat to the side. Jos hefted the grappling anchor. "Maybe if you are worried about extra weight you — ."

"Shut up or I will throw you out," Klaus spat. "Sometimes you have to *schlepp* this thing through the *Wasser*," he added, like an afterthought.

Funny the types of things that bush pilots will improvise. Funnier still was the sensation after Klaus closed the window-door, started the engine and taxied out into the middle of the river. It was the sensation of water gurgling around me at waist level. And at low power and slow speed, the tiny water rudder didn't give the plane a lot of directional stability. We kept slipping sideways, to the left and right. And to correct the slippage, Klaus kept his booted feet busy pushing the pedals back and forth from one extreme to the other. It felt like one of those the little paddle boats in the pond at the amusement park. But this all changed after Klaus lined us up with the river, gunned the motor and improvised a takeoff.

It felt like the takeoff would depend on our willpower in

addition to the power of the little engine mounted on the pylon above us. First we were pushing water, making a big bow wave. Gradually, the plane climbed up that bow wave. Then we were skimming along the water. But it took so long to pick up additional speed, and it didn't seem like we'd climbed an inch higher in the water. Sitting in the right front seat with the controls in front of me, I had to concentrate to keep my hands away from them. I turned my attention on the air speed indicator. Its needle crept up slowly while a broad island was coming up fast. Would Klaus steer the plane around the island or try to hop that rapidly advancing line of trees? After it seemed too late to do either, Klaus pulled back on the controls. We rose fast and cleared the tops of the trees with maybe 40 feet to spare.

Klaus dipped the left wing and headed north, following the general direction of the *Rio Marauiá*. The river was visible as a dark and muddy groove whose edge had a lighter shade of green. Before us, it turned and twisted through the forest as we flew towards the steamy horizon. Over the next half hour, I used airspeed readings and my digital watch to track our progress and plot it on the map. Every once in a while I could make out a hut. And five times during that half hour, the dark river turned white. Rapids. How had Hashamo, Rebecca and David gotten the dugout canoe through those rapids?

Jos seemed to be reading my thoughts. At the first rapids he shouted, "White water. Not easy." He was taking pictures through his window in the rear. It was smaller than mine.

I went back to navigating for another 15 minutes. A few minutes after that, I made another entry on the map. Klaus watched me, shook his head and snorted. "*Falsch!*" he yelled. "The Mission is right here." He pointed out the window ahead of us. "What do you want me to do, now?"

The first thing I saw was a semicircular brown area on the inside of a sharp bend in the river: a sandbar that gave the village convenient access to the river.

I shouted back, "Circle the Mission . . . clockwise so that I am on the low side."

Klaus-Dietrich did what I said. I could make out a small white church and a prefab aluminum shack that made up the Mission. It had attracted a scattering of thatch huts along the river's banks.

Our first pass over the Mission caught the attention of a handful of children at the river's edge. I told Klaus-Dietrich to keep circling until adults started coming out. My big, round side window was excellent for viewing the landscape below. But, unfortunately, there was no way to stick my head out — just a small vent which I could slide open. I put my mouth to it and shouted out at the top of my lungs, "Rebecca! Rebecca!"

We did get the natives' attention. With every round, more people came out from under the thatch. And they waved back at us. By the fifth round, the crowd had maxed out at a couple dozen. If a padre was among them, I couldn't recognize him. Some natives were naked and some were partially clothed with boxer shorts and maybe a T-shirt. None looked like Rebecca. Hoping against hope, I concentrated on those two dozen mopheads with half-naked bodies. I could make out plenty of females, but their bellies were large and their hips were narrow. Where was that thin, broad-hipped girl with her hair tied in a ponytail?

I shouted until my vocal cords were ragged. "*Médica* Rebecca! *Doutora* Rebecca!"

Jos's face was buried behind his camera and Klaus gave me no moral support. His attitude was impatient and cynical. "Now, what do you want me to do?"

"Fly directly over them. As low and slow as you can go. Perpendicular to the river."

He did what I said. I reached into my plastic bag and pulled out a message-on-a-parachute: one of the devices I'd worked so hard on the night before. I prayed that they would work as planned. Each carried a written message on the handbill I'd made for Rebecca. It was wrapped around a rock, tied on with four strings, each of which was tied to a separate corner a patch of cloth. From two T-shirts I'd been able to make 10 such parachutes. Hadn't made one of those since I was a kid, and I'd never thrown one from an airplane. Timing would be everything.

Klaus swung us out to the east until the church became very small. Then he turned and lined us up for a run on the Mission, perpendicular to the river. He descended to about 40 feet over the forest canopy. Tree crowns were whizzing under us at 80 miles per hour. We were so low that I couldn't see the groove of the river ahead of us. For a few seconds, I panicked. Then my eyes located a frame of reference — the edge of the river, visible only far to the right. Like the cutting point of an opening scissors, the edge slid towards us. With my nose to the window and my hand near the vent, I counted down to the imagined zero.

Before my eyes, it flew up in an instant the groove and the church on the other side of the river. NOW! I threw it out. Everything whizzed under us in a second.

Klaus pulled back on the controls and applied more power, putting us into a climb.

"Now turn right and circle," I shouted.

I looked back. My parachute was an aerodynamic success! It was coming down at just the right speed. Yes, the people could see it coming down. It was coming down slowly. But . . . but it was coming down wrong. It was coming right down . . . it came down in the middle of the river. Several kids ran to the bank, pointing to it. Well, at least I'd gotten their attention.

"What now?" Klaus shouted.

"Line up again and fly over . . . exactly like before."

"*Jawohl!*" Klaus shouted back, as if confirming a military command. He flew with military precision, too.

"*Exactly* like before," I shouted. "Same course. Same height. Same speed."

"*Zu Befehl*," he acknowledged.

My brain was swimming. The parachute had fallen about 60 yards short of the church.

I had to aim for the church. Eighty miles an hour. Call it 60. A mile a minute. That was 5,280 feet per minute. That's a little less than 100 feet per second. Sixty yards is 180 feet. You need to hold the parachute back 1.8 seconds longer than before. But we're going 80 miles per hour, not 60. Make the time shorter. And 1/60th of 5,280 is less than 100 feet. And subtract about 15 percent because the airspeed readings are in knots.

Damn, those calculations: We were already in the middle of the next approach! We were low over the trees. They were whizzing under us. We were too low to see the river ahead of us, only its groove off to the right. And the groove was scissoring in fast. Hell, make the delay one and one-half seconds. Tense as a coiled spring, I set my internal metronome for one beat per second and stared ahead, at exactly as before. I mouthed the seconds while watching for the church to pop up from the trees.

"One and, one and, one and, one and, coming and, *church* and, one AND!"

I threw it out so hard it hurt my wrist. The Mission whizzed below us. I didn't have to tell Klaus-Dietrich to turn.

Jos was the first to spot my parachute. "Coming down on the . . . beach . . . no . . . right in front of the shack!"

And so it did. I told Klaus to keep circling. I watched. A crowd of children ran up from the beach and made a circle, like a football huddle. And old native woman in a floppy dress walked over up to them, waving her arms. The children dispersed — all but one. The one walked up to the old woman, slowly like a dog that was going to get a beating. Their hands touched. Yes. He had given it to her. Other adults gathered around her slowly, all of them Indians. Could she loosen the strings without ripping my note to shreds?

Klaus was holding us steady in a tight turn, thank goodness. "What did you write?" he asked.

I didn't remove my eyes from the spot. "It has a picture of my girlfriend and a notice that she's missing. I wrote that she should radio the *Funai* office."

"Maybe one of those *Affen* can read it."

"Just keep circling." I was watching the old woman as best as I could. Some of the Indians standing around were waving to us, some were focused on her.

Jos said, "It is hard to send any message to those people. Maybe it would work better if you throw down a Coke bottle. Maybe they would *worship* it." He laughed like he'd made a joke. I could have thrown him out of the plane.

"Keep circling, Klaus. Give her a chance to read it."

"*Jawohl.*

By the time we had circled a dozen more times, half of the people had lost interest in us. Some children fell into a game of throwing sticks and leaves into the air. Eventually, the old woman looked up at us and opened her arms in a "U" pattern. Then she closed them. If she were an American, I'd interpret it as "I don't know."

"Klaus, wiggle your wings."

He did.

The woman repeated the gesture more vigorously for several seconds. She held the remnant of my parachute in her right hand.

"Klaus, make your circles bigger, like we are slowly going away."

As our radius increased, the woman stopped gesturing.

"Klaus, wiggle your wings again."

The woman with the same gesture, but faintly this time.

My heart sank. My message had been delivered to intelligent hands, my question had been understood, and an answer had been returned. They didn't know where Rebecca was.

"*Dshungel-Affen*," Klaus said.

"We should put it in a coke bottle," Jos shouted.

I had to take it from Klaus, but not from Jos. I turned my head to the rear, hooked my eyes into him and spat out, "Shut up, asshole."

Jos raised his camera in time to catch me in the middle of the epithet.

I leaned towards Klaus and showed him the nearest *shabono* on my map. "I want to go here and do the same thing."

"I cannot. We do not have enough fuel."

"Bullshit! The indicator shows the tank's three-quarters full. I'm paying you an extra fifty dollars. A deal's a deal."

"*Jawohl.*"

Yes, a command voice was the way to deal with that guy. And he worked hard for me for the rest of the flight. The *shabono* was harder to find because it was on a creek, not a river. We might not have found it if it weren't for the smoke from their cooking fires. It was a U-shaped, thatched affair with a small dirt courtyard and a small path leading to the creek. Our circling generated a lot of interest and no sign of Rebecca. My second parachute made it into the courtyard. We flew tight circles but nobody answered with any sign language. All we got was a lot of waving and brandishing of bows and arrows.

There were six more *shabonos* on our map and I let Klaus pick out them out in his own order. I ran out of parachutes after the fourth. Everyone who ran out was naked and there was no sign of Rebecca. And after flying over the next to the last *shabono*, Klaus told me we were running out of gas.

"Come on, Klaus," I wheedled. "The gas gauge says over half-full and the last *shabono* is only forty miles from here. And it won't take us any farther away from home."

Klaus' look told me he was deadly serious, now. "I am the pilot, you are the passenger. I say that we have enough fuel to get back with forty miles to spare. I need those forty miles in case we have to go around a thunderstorm."

I felt desperate enough to argue with him, but reason took over: We had covered six of the seven *shabonos*. Dejected, I sank back into my seat.

My eyes were too tired to look down any more into that green blur of rain forest. And my eyes were too wet to look either of my fellow travelers in the face. I hardly noticed when Santa Isabel came into sight. And I wouldn't have been interested in Klaus-Dietrich's landing maneuvers if they hadn't been so spectacular. He flew down on the river at a steep angle, pulled out at the last minute, glided ten feet above the surface then cut the power, landing finally with a controlled stall that felt like a "cannonball" and splashed water all over the windshield. Klaus taxied skillfully to the dock. There, my seaman's instincts took over. I jumped out and secured the plane.

Klaus gave me an approving nod and climbed out after me. He was less approving of Jos who was fingering the rope and grappling anchor again. "Now you get out, too, you *Schlapschwanz*."

Literally, the expression means "floppy tail." Figuratively, it means that the guy has trouble getting it up. And Jos acted like he knew both meanings.

After getting both stocking feet on the dock, Jos crouched to examine an alteration of the tail end of the fuselage: a small improvised sheet metal door that opened inward. "And what kind of a *Schwanz* is this?" Jos asked, speaking to neither of us in particular.

Klaus hurried to tie up the last line, then hustled over to Jos and stood over him with balled fists. "Enough! You have had your ride and you have taken your pictures. Now you must leave."

Jos looked up at him, coolly, for a few seconds. Then he brought himself up straight and rearranged his photojournalist's vest. For a moment, it looked like the two were ready to come to blows. Then Jos turned and walked away. "*Danke schön*," he said over his shoulder.

"*Scheiss Süd-Afrikaner*," Klaus replied, under his breath.

But I'd be damned if I'd let antipathy between a couple of European machos mess up my plans.

"Jos, I'll see you back at the tent," I said, as a command.

I worked on a jovial mood before approaching Klaus and handing him the extra 50 dollars.

"Klaus-Dietrich, you are one hell of a flyer. Thanks a lot for helping me."

"You are welcome. I am sorry that we could not find your girlfriend."

I pulled a handbill from my pocket and gave it to him. "But I'm sure that if you see this black-haired, light-skinned woman the next time that you are counting Indians for your organization, you will let me know."

"*Jawohl!*" He folded it and put it in his shirt pocket.

"Thanks. And I want to buy gasoline and oil from you tomorrow morning, like we were talking about."

"But you said they signaled she is not there at the Mission."

"That's right, but I still have to talk with them and ask them where she went."

For a few seconds Klaus frowned, like this might be a problem. He thought for a few seconds more. His answer came abruptly, in staccato rhythm. "*Jawohl.* One hundred and twenty liters of gasoline and two liters of oil. Tomorrow. One hundred and fifty dollars, American."

"Right. Tomorrow morning at eight."

It was all profit for him; his Indian-counting organization was probably supplying him with fuel. And Jos had gotten his money's worth, too And he still was. He was taking a rear end shot of the amphibious plane. I walked up to him quickly.

"I told you to get going."

He fell into step next to me. "I was just waiting while you made arrangements for our fuel for tomorrow."

"Forget it, you're not going with me tomorrow. You're more trouble than you're worth."

"If I said or did something wrong, I am sorry. What did I do?"

"It's bad enough that you don't even know."

And that was enough conversation to take us back to the tent. I ate a late lunch of sardines and crackers. Jos ate his military MREs and then went for a walk. I knocked on my hosts' door and told them about the flyover and asked them to *please* radio the Mission that night and to please monitor it for the whole evening.

21   Up the *Rio Marauiá*

The outboard motor turned out to be a 10 horsepower Johnson. It putted steadily, pushing the dugout canoe across the *Rio Negro*. I sat on my duffel bags, a couple of feet behind our pointed bow, looking down on the dark, acidic water. Like a smoked mirror, it reflected the morning sun but revealed nothing below the surface. The water occasionally splashed over the low sides a couple of feet behind me and trickled back along the floor to the low spot in the center where Jos was kept busy bailing to protect his own gear. In the back, Hashamo presided over the putting outboard and five red neoprene tanks of gasoline. He was steering us towards an ever-widening gap in the opposite shore — the mouth of the *Rio Marauiá*.

No, the Mission had not answered our calls on the shortwave radio last night. The *Funai* couple had shared my grief and frustration. They accepted my gift of batteries for their satellite phone and promised to turn it on between eight and eight-thirty every night in case I called. Now I had one contact down here. Not wanting to put their jobs in jeopardy, I promised to call only in an emergency. Funny how bureaucracy works down here. They didn't know about Klaus-Dietrich's Indian counting operations. Maybe the organization that sponsored him was not part of the Brazilian Government.

Klaus was a good fellow and might have been even a friend if I had gotten to know him better. He'd made good on the gasoline deal. While Hashamo and I were transferring it from his fuel drum to the neoprene containers, I thought about how much nicer it would have been to have had Klaus-Dietrich's aluminum canoe. It would carry only two people but they would be high and dry.

And it would have been light enough for Hashamo and me to portage around the rapids. I noticed that Klaus had a five-horse outboard in the shed. But I didn't get the impression that Klaus wanted to talk with me about his equipment, to say nothing of lending it to me.

Of course, I didn't take Jos along when we swung down to pick up the gasoline. The antipathy between those two was all to obvious. And I had developed a certain antipathy to him as well. Told him so last night. Told him I didn't appreciate his pissing off Klaus-Dietrich and his second-guessing my decisions in the air. And I didn't like his sarcastic joke about Coke bottles. I told him I couldn't afford any jokers in the deck.

Hearing this, Jos turned contrite. He said he was sorry, he would just follow me and try to be helpful. And wouldn't it be useful to have a third man to drag the dugout canoe around those rapids that we'd seen from the plane? That was a convincing argument because the canoe — which was nothing more than a sculpted tree trunk — must have weighed a thousand pounds. Communication with Hashamo was not easy and I had no idea how he'd managed to get up the rapids with Rebecca and David Thompson.

Jos also argued that we could guard each other's flanks. There was something to that. He showed me his .38 revolver. Adding it to the .45 that I carried in the Velcro-flapped pocket of my "cargo" shorts, we had enough firepower to fend off outlaws along the river. There would be someone to guard me while I slept. The extra satellite phone would be useful in case mine went on the blink. He also used an emotional argument: He couldn't turn his back on my story.

Well, if I died trying to find Rebecca, at least it would be written up in a Dutch magazine. I caved in. I told Jos he could come along if he brought his own food, if he didn't bring too much gear and if he would agree to follow my orders. So far, today, he had followed all my orders except one: I couldn't get him to leave behind the long bag containing his tripod. He claimed it was necessary to take pictures of the three of us.

Now, we were entering that gap in the trees. The *Rio Marauiá* was about 100 yards wide. We traded a broad horizon for a water ride through the forest. I peered into the water, watching for snags beneath the surface. Sometimes they were betrayed on the water's smooth surface by ripples that distorted the otherwise perfect mirror image of the trees and sky. The river's banks were lined with a thin rock and gravel beach that was strewn with fallen and washed-up tree trunks. Then came forest wall — a thick overgrowth of sun-loving bushes, many covered with thorns. It would be next to impossible to make this trip on foot. The bushes gave way to small trees whose leaves partially obscured the trunks of 40-foot trees of the forest core. In many places, vines crept along the bank and climbed the trees. The forest glided by hypnotically.

An hour later, we landed on a patch of beach to stretch our legs. I walked through the bushes and into the forest. It was a strange, beautiful world. The tree-tops spread out to make one continuous canopy high above me. The space below it was filled with brown tree trunks and was permeated with greenish light. The light was bright near the tops and grew darker below where the trunks were covered with moss. The forest floor was covered by a springy mat of decaying vegetation.

I returned to the canoe and we resumed our journey. The longer I stared into the cross-section of forest green, the more often I could make out differences in that color: the chartreuse green of new leaves, the dark green of the moss, the waxy green of the fronds of the açia palm and the brown and green crisscross of the vines, some bearing red and purple flowers.

And each time I returned my eyes to the dark water's reflective surface, the easier it became to judge the water's depth. Sometimes, in the shallows, I could make out a catfish, an electric eel or an electric ray.

Our first human contact was an hour later when we came across a thatch hut that sat on stilts. On its long porch, which jutted out over the river, sat a naked woman breast feeding a baby. Two small children looked down at us with curiosity.

I gestured for Hashamo to steer towards them. I gave my orders in pidgin Portuguese. "I show picture of Rebecca. You ask if she see her."

Hashamo slowed the motor and threw it out of gear. I held up the picture. Hashamo yelled to her in a Portuguese Creole which I could only half-understand even though he said a lot of the words double. The woman listened hard, nodded and finally answered.

"She say she see your woman."

"Ask her how long ago."

He asked and she answered.

"She say long ago."

"Exactly how long ago?"

"She say very long ago."

"Which way did my woman go?"

Hashamo asked the question and the woman answered, pointing upriver.

I bowed my head in thanks and looked back to Hashamo. "Ask her if she see my woman come downriver."

She answered no. I put my hands together as in prayer and looked up to her in thanks. She made the sign of the cross. Hashamo threw the engine in reverse to get us clear, then motored on.

It was another hour before we came across the next human habitation. A man was fishing from a small dugout canoe and a woman was cleaning a catfish near a small fire on a patch of beach. A thatched hut stood a few yards back. Another woman was sleeping in a hammock and children were playing in the water along the shore. We beached the canoe. Hashamo and I got out and asked the same questions. None of these people had seen Rebecca at all.

After we pushed off, Jos said that we couldn't stop so many times if we were going to make 100 miles in three or four days. I took off my shades and turned to face him. I reminded him that he was here as my guest and if he didn't agree, he was welcome to get off, make a raft and float back to Santa Isabel. He apologized, explaining that he was just trying to be helpful.

For the rest of the day, we made good progress against the slowly flowing river. We didn't come across any more settlements. Toward dusk, we found a large sandbar at a bend in the river with many overhanging limbs to tie up on. We collected driftwood and made a fire which I used to boil water to replenish our canteens. Jos ate his MREs. Hashamo and I ate my canned sardines and crackers. The remnants of the fire helped to keep the mosquitos away while we were up. I strung a mosquito net over the bow and crawled under it. I set earplugs against crawling insects and succumbed to a cramped, bone-crunching sleep.

We set out early the next morning for our second day up the river. As the morning progressed, the river became narrower and the water swifter and the snags more frequent. We reached the first rapids before noon. It was about 150 yards long but steep. Hashamo had us unload the canoe and portaged all the equipment including the motor to above the rapids. Then we pushed and shoved the heavy dugout canoe along the gravel bank. It was backbreaking and exhausting work and I was secretly angry that Hashamo hadn't had enough sense to bring along a winch or at least a makeshift pulley.

Later in the day we came to the second rapids. It was marked by a sign stating that this was an "Indigenous Area, prohibited to all unauthorized persons." But the sign wasn't the only thing that would keep people out. The rapids were steep, flowing through a canyon of granite rock. And at one point it was actually a waterfall. The granite pathway up the side was narrow, steep and slippery. Jos shook his head and grumbled; Hashamo grabbed a couple of gasoline tanks. I grabbed a couple myself, and we trudged up the path. Jos just waited there.

At the top of the rapids, I told Hashamo that it looked impossible. He smiled and disappeared into the forest. A minute later, he called to me. I found him standing beside another canoe stuck in the bushes and stored upside down to keep it from collecting rain water. I went back down for the next load and told Jos the good news. Within three-quarters of an hour we had our old canoe secured and hidden, and had our new one ready to go. Nobody broke his back and the experience put me in a happier mood. Just as Jos had to stop second guessing me, I would have to trust Hashamo's experience.

As the day progressed, the river ran faster and it felt like we were gaining altitude. The forest was changing, too. Fewer decaying logs, more moss-covered rocks and thinner ground cover. It was as if the rain washed away the soil faster than it could form. We were entering a "land of minerals," to quote Gen. Sosa-Pereira's speech at the conference in Miami. Along the shore, rocky outcrops and jagged boulders stood like heralds announcing the fact.

That evening, we stopped at a settlement of three houses sprawled along a wide shoreline. The inhabitants were pure-blooded Indians who had adopted Western dress — boxer shorts or underpants and T-shirts. With Hoshamo's help, I questioned everyone about Rebecca. Most of them recognized her because

Hashamo had encamped the expedition there on the way up. None of them had seen Rebecca go down the river. Yes, they would be able to see anyone going up or down the river. No, she couldn't have gone down the river without them seeing her. It was a real effort to communicate with them in the subjunctive tense, but I had to get solid information.

That night, some men were hunting along the river for *iwan* — alligator. They shined flashlights on the river until they found yellow, glowing eyes looking back. Then they shot them with rifles. Jos took along his camera and his tripod bag. I hoped he got some good glow shots with slow exposure and telephoto lens. Being tired from my second day up the river, I went to sleep early that evening.

At the Mission   22

We set out early on the third day, making good progress but coming across no settlements. We portaged three rapids before nightfall. At the beginning of the fourth day, the only thing unusual was a sizable tributary going off to the east. I asked Hashamo where it went and he said it went nowhere. We reached the Mission shortly before two o'clock in the afternoon. It was on the left side, on a large, high clearing in the forest. I immediately recognized the church, with its small wooden bell tower and thatched roof. Its whitewashed plank walls rested on a waist-high foundation of stacked and cemented flat stones.

Behind the church was a cottage with screen walls and next to it was a prefabricated aluminum hut. I guessed that the Brazilian military had once helicoptered in a load of light-weight building materials. Behind the Mission and along the riverbank was a sprawl of inhabited shacks. The riverbank was littered with dugout canoes and fishnets hung up to dry.

We were greeted by a mob of mostly naked children who called Hashamo's name and splashed into the water faster than he could cut off the motor and beach the boat. They stayed with him while I trudged off to the Mission with my duffle bags and backpack.

Lacking the emotional strength to go running and calling for Rebecca, I decided to look around first and ask questions later. Yes, the church was the central point of this operation. The front doors were made of cross-braced tongue and groove. They were suspended on heavy hinges, reminiscent of old-style garage doors you see in New England. They were padlocked. I walked around to the side and looked in through the screened but otherwise open windows. The sanctuary had six rows of pews, rough-hewn from split logs and doweled legs. There was room for maybe 40 people. At the front was an altar, sheeted with white marble and draped with heavy cloth. On it sat a brass cross and a communion cup, capped with a small square of purple felt. On the wall behind was a crucifixion statue, one-quarter scale. Hoping to purify my thoughts, I said a little prayer.

I went around to the other side of the church. There, I found a prefab aluminum shed. On its wall, a red cross was painted against a white circular background. The shed was made of corrugated gray aluminum set on a crumbling concrete slab. Its roof was also of corrugated aluminum, set on a slant, about six feet high in the front and about eight feet in back. It was small, only 12 feet wide and maybe six feet deep. Access was by two hinged aluminum doors which were locked. Construction had probably required less than 50 board-feet of lumber and half a pound of nails. It was about right for storing gardening equipment and a riding lawnmower on a large estate. A thin electric line arched from a high pole in back towards the screened bungalow farther inland.

So this was where Rebecca had practiced medicine. And the screened bungalow behind it was the parsonage. A glance at my watch told me it was five minutes after two o'clock. Siesta time was over and I could come calling. The priest's bungalow was built on a carefully sloped concrete slab, 30 by 30 feet. The structure consisted of four corner poles and one center pole which held up the palm thatched roof. Several flat boards formed the corners, to which were stapled a dark screen which wrapped around the structure. And to the side was a wood-framed screen door. It was an efficient structure that would protect the priest from rain and insects while remaining open to air and daylight.

I walked up closer to the screened wall. Inside were several chairs fashioned from log and reed, a low bookcase with maybe four feet of books, and a desk on which sat a shortwave radio equipped with earphones and microphone. Next to the desk stood a small refrigerator and a food preparation table on which rested several fruits and a water jug. The bungalow was subdivided by a partition of woven reed. In a corner hung a hammock, and in it slept an old man.

"Padre, padre," I called. But he was sleeping deeply and my words could not awaken him. I let myself in through the framed screen door and placed my gear on the floor. I walked up to the hammock. The padre must have been 65 — yes, a flabby, obese 65 with wispy white hair. Unhealthy skin bore evidence of a body that had struggled long against infection and tropical disease. He was wearing gray boxer shorts, a black T-shirt and a crucifix. I shook the hammock. "Padre, padre, I need your help. Help. *Ajuda!*"

He awoke slowly and resentfully. I repeated my words until he was aroused.

"Do you speak English?" I asked.

He shook his head and started to sit up.

I spoke to him in Spanish. "I am Doctor Benjamin Candidi. I am seeking my loved one, Rebecca Levis."

"Rebecca." He uttered her name in repetition, not in question nor in affirmation of my words. With considerable effort, he sat up straight. With greater effort, the struggled to get one leg over the side.

I steadied the hammock and lowered the side to make it easier for him. "Yes, yes. The loved one of me. The Doctor Rebecca Levis who came here in September and ministered to the sick people of you." I said it in Spanish but it felt like praying in Latin.

I steadied the priest at the upper arm as he leaned forward and put his feet on the floor. And with both hands, I helped him to straighten up and gain his balance. Could he have done it without help?

"Father, I ask your help to find my beloved Rebecca. I fear she is lost or even dead." I repeated these words many times

"I do not know." His words came out drunkenly but there was no alcohol smell on his breath.

I let go with both hands and carefully unfolded the soggy

photocopy that I had been carrying. I held it close to his face. "Rebecca. Rebecca Levis. You know her."

"*Sim*," he said. That is Portuguese for "yes." Then he said, "Yes. *Si*." He repeated it several times.

I turned my eyes to heaven, threw my hands into the air and tried my best to speak to him in Portuguese. "We called you and asked you on radio." I gestured to the shortwave sitting on the desk.

"No function more," he said.

Was he speaking Portuguese-flavored Italian or Italian-flavored Portuguese? Or was it church Latin? No matter, I would keep talking. "And I came . . . come . . . four days before with airplane." I acted it out, making the noise of the motor. "I drop this note and the people take it to you."

"Yes, you brought message. No, I do not know where she is." He made his way to one of the chairs and sat.

I went to his desk and shuffled through a small pile of papers. They were mostly handwritten letters. Under a pair of glasses and a Latin prayer book was a church calendar from a town in Tuscany. And on it he had inked in notations under some of the days. While reading it, I heard children's voices drawing near. Hashamo was approaching with all the village children in tow. He entered through the screen door. The children stayed outside, strangely quiet and observant, now.

"Hashamo," the priest said, greeting him with open arms.

Hashamo knelt before him, then leaned forward to kiss the priest's crucifix. The priest put his hands on the boy's head and uttered a blessing in Latin. He motioned for Hashamo to rise, which he did. He moved several steps to the side, then sat on the concrete floor.

I handed the priest his glasses and pulled a chair next to him. I showed him the calendar. "September. This day. Hashamo come."

"*Si*."

"Hashamo come with my beloved Doutra Rebecca Levis and with Doutor Thompson." I showed him the picture of Rebecca, again.

"*Si*."

"My beloved Doutra Rebecca Levis and Doutor Thompson stay these days," I said, pointing to the calendar.

"*Si*."

"Then Hashamo come take Doutor Thompson to Santa Isabel."

"*Si*."

"And my beloved Rebecca stay here on this day." I pointed to Thompson's departure day on the calendar and then clamped my thumb on it.

"*Si*."

Then I pointed to today's date. "And this day . . . today . . . I come and Rebecca not here."

"*Si*."

"Then what happen to my beloved Rebecca here?" I ran my index finger back and forth between the dates.

"I do not know."

"When did Rebecca leave? Disappear? No more here?"

"I do not know."

"When is last day you see her in clinic?" I pointed to the shed. "You see her this day? This day? This day?"

It was laborious but we were finally able to fix Rebecca's last day as five days after Thompson left. That was three days before I got the first e-mail from her with the Hotmail.com return address.

An old Indian woman entered the enclosure. She seemed to sag inside her faded floral-print dress. She was carrying a lidded pot which she set down on the food preparation table. She went to the refrigerator and removed a small rubber-stoppered bottle from the refrigerator and shook it. She pulled a wet syringe from the pot and drew an aliquot from the bottle.

An Indian boy in his mid-teens entered and greeted the priest. Like the priest, he wore boxer trunks, a dark T-shirt and a crucifix. He put his hand on the priest's neck as if to judge his condition.

The woman used water from the pot to wash her left arm. Then she injected her arm with the syringe. Her arm was thin. Her skin looked old and unhealthy; her face looked wrinkled but intelligent. She never returned my glances. She returned the small bottle to the refrigerator.

I looked at the acolyte and the old woman, holding up the picture of Rebecca. "Where is she?" I asked.

And no one looked at me or said anything. It was as if I wasn't there.

I buried my face in my hands, trying to fend off a sarcastic analogy — that I was searching for a thimble full of practicality under a haystack of religion. I wrestled with myself. After all, I didn't know how many days or years this priest had labored here, fighting off tropical infections. I did not know how many decades he had spent here, lonely as a star, radiating his knowledge and receiving nothing in return. But on the other hand, I did know that Rebecca had stood in that tin shack under the tropical sun for over a month, doing good in the name of his mission. I stopped fighting with myself: The priest's few remaining brain cells owed me an explanation.

I looked into his eyes, deeply and intensely. "Who took Rebecca away?"

He did not answer.

I pointed to Hashamo. "Hashamo did not take her away?" Hashamo understood my words and made clear his denial.

Acolyte approached me as if I were threatening the padre. "Ask him," I said to Hashamo. "Ask everyone here."

Hashamo spoke to Acolyte and received a short answer. "He say she leave one morning early when everyone still sleeping."

"Ask him who she left with," I said.

Hashamo asked, received an answer and told me. "They do not know. May be no person."

The old woman was busying herself at the table.

"Did she leave any of her things?"

"No."

"Did a group of foreigners visit this camp? Could she have gone with them?"

Hashamo's eye's widened. I repeated my question. He asked Acolyte who answered "no."

"Then go to everyone in this village," I ordered, with exasperation. Ask questions. Did any strange people come here before she disappeared? Did anyone go with her? Did they take a canoe?"

Hashamo left to carry out my instructions. Acolyte fussed around the priest. The old woman busied herself with food preparation but kept track of me with intelligent eyes. Was she the one who had signaled me from the plane? She looked the same size, but the dress was different. Did she understand a word I'd been saying?"

I sat down on the floor and buried my face in my hands. I

stayed that way for a long time until I was finally roused by Jos. I
didn't hear him come in. "I have asked everyone in the village
where is Rebecca," he said. "Nobody knows."

"How did they know it was Rebecca you were asking about?"

"I showed them her picture on your sheet."

"Oh. And how could you ask where she went? You don't speak
their language."

"I used sign language."

He laid a hand on my shoulder to comfort me. I didn't stir.
There comes a time when you have to believe the bad news that
people bring you. I didn't say a thing. I just slipped inside myself.
Catatonia is Nature's way of keeping the animal from killing itself
by unnecessary struggle.

"We will sleep here tonight," Jos said. "You rest up and I will
have another look around." He left.

I sat there for a long time in the lotus position, oblivious to the
other people. And they seemed oblivious to me. Finally, I got up
and looked around the enclosure. I opened the refrigerator. It was
not stocked and its interior was warm. The old woman had probably
injected herself with rot. I asked the priest for the keys to the clinic
shed. Neither he nor his helper understood what I wanted. So I
went through his desk drawers until I found them. The old Indian
woman, who was now sweeping the floor with a home-made broom,
watched me but said nothing.

The shed contained bandages, drug store remedies and a small
assortment of prescription medicines. It didn't contain Rebecca's
field kit nor any other personal belongings. That meant that she
was not abducted in her sleep. She had planned to leave and she
took everything with her. I tried to feel good about that.

Next, I wandered around the village, showing everyone
Rebecca's picture. Everyone knew her and their smiles told me
they liked her. But nobody knew where she went. How could that
be possible? When I found Hashamo, he hadn't learned anything,
either.

At nightfall I returned to the priest's enclosure. It was
illuminated by a single naked lightbulb that cast long shadows.
The priest was asleep in his chair. Maybe he had been lulled to
sleep by the purring of a gasoline generator some 25 yards from
the building. Acolyte was in the corner, head bowed over a small

gilt-leaf book that had to be the Bible. Jos had made himself at home and was eating from his mess kit.

"That old Indian woman brought us this," he said, gesturing towards a cast iron cooking pot sitting on the table. "It's manioc root. She and this boy take care of that zombie," he said, gesturing to the priest.

The manioc root was as good as potatoes. It went well with my sardines. When I was through, I went to the refrigerator. It was running, now. I took a look in and examined the small bottle. As I suspected, it was insulin.

"Stupid operation," Jos said. "The old fool has no idea of how to live in the wilderness. Probably uses the refrigerator to cool his communion wine. He probably drank it all up. Better that he use his gasoline for a lantern that makes *real* light. His helper boy will ruin his eyes reading his prayers under that low-watt light bulb."

I didn't want to get into a discussion of the efficiency of gasoline lanterns. I didn't want to think about whether chilling insulin half the day was better than not chilling it at all. The generator was working now and the shortwave radio was sitting on the desk. I pulled up a chair and sat down to study it, then turned it on. After noting its dial settings, I turned the knobs until I started picking up transmissions. Yes, its receiver was working okay. I was getting all kinds of signals — conversations in Portuguese, military transmissions in Spanish, ship to shore and even some high-strength yammering in some Indian language.

I went back to the original settings, pushed the microphone button, and called for the *Funai* post. The power meter did not register. I went to the back of the set and unscrewed the microphone plug, generating a lot of aluminum dust in the process. I cleaned the male contact and then used it to renew the female contact, working the pair in and out for several minutes. After putting it back together, I was pleased to be able to make the power meter swing to my voice. For good measure, I cleaned the contacts on the antenna output.

The *Funai* station answered after one-half an hour of hailing. I told them I was at the Mission and that Rebecca had left without a trace. They had no news. I told them to forget about the satellite phone but asked them to monitor the radio every night. Said I'd call again when I learned something new.

My conversation half-aroused the priest. Acolyte helped him out of the chair and back into his hammock. With sign language and facial expressions, he indicated that the priest was in very bad health and that today was typical. He invited us to make beds from the stuffed sacks that were stacked in the corner. He would be leaving soon and would cut off the generator.

Jos and I used the last minutes of light to lay out our bedding next to each other on the floor.

"Thank you for helping me today," I said. He had been so sympathetic. He was showing his human side, again.

"Think nothing of it. Tomorrow, we will find out more from them." He sounded almost fatherly.

I sighed. "But all three of us have asked everyone here. Nobody knows anything."

"No, someone knows something," Jos insisted. "It is not possible for Rebecca to trek out without someone knowing. And there are methods for finding out."

I thought about the possible methods. "I'm sure that all the people here have contact with at least one of the nearest *shabonos*. Maybe I can get a person to guide me to them."

"Or maybe I can start twisting people's arms. Then they will tell us *which shabono* to go to. Or which ones are not civilized enough to treat a white woman like a lady. You have not had as much experience with coloreds as I have, Ben. It never works to go begging. It only works when you deal with them from a position of strength."

The lights went out. Slowly, my eyes adapted to the darkness. Slowly, my ears started picking up rain forest noises in the silence left after the generator was turned off — the whistles of far-off birds, the buzzes and chirps of nearby insects and croaks and clicks of reptiles. There was so much to be heard under the priest's snoring. The wilderness was so vast and I felt so small.

"Jos, the only way it will work is for them to help us *willingly*. There are too many square miles and I have no local knowledge."

"*Ja*, you can wait around here for a month being nice to them," he said in a tired monotone. "You can give them your fish hooks, one every day, and maybe after a few weeks they will be nice to you. Then you will run out of food and you will have nothing. And those *kleurlingen* — those coloreds — will get away with it."

"Get away with what?"

"Whatever they are doing with your woman while they are keeping her."

"And what do you think they are doing?"

"I have no way to know, Ben. But I know that when your woman disappears, you do not stay in the compound and be nice to everybody. As we say, you put the squeeze on and see what comes out."

"Goodnight, Jos. We can talk about it tomorrow." I surrendered myself to the rain forest noises and I slowly dropped off to sleep.

It was a light sleep. Every night since leaving Santa Isabel my sleep had been lighter. Now, it seemed like part of me was sleeping and another part of me was drifting through the village like the smoke of the dying campfires, picking up wisps of the spirits living in one family hut and then another, floating over the river and the alert eyes of *iwan*, the alligator. And somehow, I felt that a pair of eyes was watching me — the eyes of the jaguar, the one who sees all and hunts at night.

It was the call of nature that wakened me. Slowly, I got up and let myself out though the screen door. The night air was cool and crisp. In the last four days we must have climbed one thousand feet above the steamy valley of the *Rio Negro*. The tropical sun might have its way with us during the day — hell, my map showed us right on the equator at 00.08 degrees — but the nighttime air temperature is also determined by altitude. The moon was now shrunk to a quarter. I walked by its light to the bank of the river and emptied my bladder. The river would carry away all traces. And as I tinkled in the river, I heard rustling nearby. But I didn't turn around until I was done. — Which was good because I would have pissed my pants.

When I turned around, the apparition shocked me speechless. It seemed to speak to me without words.

Walk In the Forest with You   23

"Rebecca is safe and happy," the apparition said in a faint voice that sounded as old as the grave.

And as hard as I tried, it was impossible to bring a single word from my throat.

"But if you keep looking for her, you will destroy it all." The voice was female and was speaking to me in English.

My mouth was as dry as first-aid cotton. "I cannot . . . I cannot . . ."

"Of course you cannot understand. You are impatient, as almost all of you are." She was speaking with an English accent that seemed to strengthen with every word.

"I'm impatient out of my love for her. Where is she?"

"Stand back or I sha'n't be able to help you."

I stopped in my tracks. I recognized her shape. It was the old Indian woman with the insulin.

"But I love Rebecca," I said.

"Yes, I have seen *that* in your eyes. And I have felt your distress and agitation. But I cannot tell if you can be trusted with our secrets . . . and with Rebecca's secrets. I have not been able to look into your eyes as I have looked in her eyes . . . as I looked while she was healing our children's sick bodies. She will become a great woman shaman. She can look into the sick and make them well. While she was looking into them I looked into her . . . into what you would call her soul. It is clear and clean, like a pool in a forest stream. Rebecca can be trusted. That is why I told her our secret. That is why I took her away."

"You took her away!"

"Oh, how you threaten and posture, like a warrior at a feast. Do you think I carried her off with a raiding party? Rebecca wanted to come to minister to the sick at my *shabono*. And she wanted to see the work of the Great Shaman. Rebecca *asked* me to take her there. But before I could take her, Rebecca had to promise not to reveal the *shabono's* secrets. Those secrets must be kept or the magic will be lost, perhaps forever."

How, I asked myself, could this Indian woman conjure up an English accent to tell me fairy stories? Had she served me an hallucinogen with those manioc roots? Where was Rebecca? Who was this "Great Shaman"? What was he doing with her? What was the magic and why would it be lost if Rebecca had told me what she was doing?

The old woman laughed. "I can see you are impatient. You are doing what Western Man always does when he cannot understand. Your impatience could destroy the Shaman's work and could bring death — even here."

She was right about my not being able to understand. And as if to test me, she stepped back slowly. I fought the urge to rush forward and grab her by the arm. And I felt so ashamed of my feelings towards her and the priest. And I was afraid — afraid of what I would have been doing tomorrow. I would have been twisting people's arms. And I felt ashamed of what I was about to do: embrace paganism to find Rebecca. I dropped to one knee and held up my hands, clasped together. It felt like someone else was talking for me.

"Please, please wise woman. I can feel your wisdom through your understanding of Rebecca. I will make all the promises that Rebecca has made. If I must keep secrets as the price of seeing her, I will."

How strange it felt to be governed by fairy tale logic.

"Then I will try to help you," she said, "although it will damage me further. But I cannot allow you to put our quest in jeopardy. You must promise to do exactly as I say. Will you?"

"Yes, I will do exactly as you say."

"Then return to the priest's dwelling and collect up everything you have brought and return here. Do not waken your companion. He must not see you go. He must not question you. Leave him a note that says only this — that you have found Rebecca, that you will not be coming back for a long while, and that he should return to Santa Isabel with Hashamo and tell them all is well."

"Yes, I promise."

I returned stealthily, under the cover of the priest's snoring, but I awakened Jos nevertheless. He rolled over and asked, "What are you doing?"

"Took a leak. And now I've got to find the anti-malaria pill I forgot to take." I sat cross-legged on the floor facing away from him and unzipped my backpack. I found pen, paper and flashlight. "Shut your eyes, I've got to use my flashlight." Hastily, I wrote the message. I also used the opportunity to check that everything was in my duffel bags and that they were pushed away from Jos. Then I turned off the flashlight and lay down.

It was hard to just lie there, pretending to be asleep and listening to Jos's breathing. I didn't dare touch the glow button on my watch, but it must have taken three-quarters of an hour for Jos's breathing to go into deep rhythm. Slowly, I got up, put on my backpack and carried my two duffel bags to the door. I rolled on the balls of my feet, Iroquois style, and coordinated the door opening with the snores of the priest.

When I returned to the bank, the Indian woman was there, sitting in a dugout canoe. "Load your things in the center and climb in the back. Paddle us silently for one hour down the river."

I did what she said. After I started to paddle, she lay down in the bow, looking at me. The village floated away until it was distinguishable only as a white patch of reflected moonlight from the church. I could deduce the direction of the river only as an ill-defined notch in the forest that surrounded us. When I thought we were far enough away, I pushed the glow button and marked the time. And I unzipped my pack, turned on my GPS unit and marked our position as a waypoint. It was hard to know whether she slept or just lay staring at me. But when I pushed the glow button half an hour later, she told me to lie down and sleep until dawn. I tried to comply.

When the sky lightened, she told me to paddle again, quickly this time because we had to make haste. And as it brightened, I could make out more and more of her form, wedged as she was in the bow of the dugout canoe. She was not wearing the old house dress like before. She was wearing nothing but a loincloth and a string of beads around her pendulous breasts. At first, they looked like three breasts, but the one on the side proved to be a leather bladder for drinking water. It hung by a thin leather strap over one shoulder. The skin around her chest and stomach sagged in horizontal folds, reminding me of an old, undernourished elephant. It looked like obesity had once stretched her skin so far that it could never pop back in her lifetime. Remodeling of collagen is a slow process.

Her hips were narrow and her legs were short, with adequate muscle. Her face was unadorned, but her ear lobes were now stretched by the weight of two brass rings that had the diameter of coffee cups. With quiet, unfathomable, black eyes, she observed my rolling glances as I paddled. Occasionally, she lifted and turned to look forward. After a quarter of an hour, she pointed to a small stream flowing into the river. She told me to paddle into it.

Past the gravel bank, the inlet was occluded by thorny bushes and by a crisscross of vines hanging from the trees. After a dozen yards, stone outcropping and protruding roots made it impossible to advance the canoe any further. The woman got out. She told me to unload the canoe, haul it up the bank and turn it upside down. I did as she said. With gut-busting effort, I hoisted the bow over a moss-covered log and manhandled the canoe to the other side. The stream cooled my legs. The mossy forest floor felt spongy under my feet. I maneuvered the overturned canoe against a massive rotting log and searched for a smaller one. I used it to fill the open space between the forest floor and the exposed side of the canoe. To a casual eye, the canoe would look like another log.

The old woman smiled as if observing a little boy at play.

"My companion Jos did not see me go. I told him nothing."

"I know," she said.

"And I left the note as you said."

"I know. I saw you writing it by flashlight."

"My name is Ben."

"Yes, I know. I know much about you." But she volunteered nothing more. She reached down and filled the leather bladder with water from the stream.

"What name can I call you?"

"You can call me Owani. You must continue to do as I say. You have brought many things, which you must now carry. Load yourself up as best you can, for now we must walk."

I tied the two duffel bags together and tied them high to my backpack. Owani walked away from the stream. I loaded up and followed her. I might have enjoyed the hike if my burden hadn't been so heavy. The forest floor felt spongy as I walked along, stepping over mossy logs and sometimes grabbing vines for support. The cool, damp air trapped the smell of decaying leaves. It seemed like a fun house in green.

Owani was in her element. Lithely, she walked before me, naked except for her leather loincloth and sandals woven from palm fiber. With little more than a sideward glance, she dodged around boulders and the buttressing roots of large trees. She flowed gracefully through the forest with her hands at her side except when it was necessary to part the branches of large bushes. Doing my best to keep up with her, I felt like a clumsy robot.

"Do not break branches," she said. "Do not leave footprints. You must leave no trace of yourself."

That was easier said than done. It was hard to lift my feet high while struggling under my heavy burden.

Gradually, we gained height over the stream, and moss gave way to moist, rotting leaves. And as the sun rose, the moisture diminished and the forest became lighter — an endless green room with a 40-foot ceiling, permeated by soft green light. Occasionally, a ray of light shot through the ceiling and lit up a patch of brown bark or a spider's web glistening with dew. And sometimes I didn't see them and the thin strands tickled and teased my face.

After half an hour, Owani's course became less meandering. The shafts of sunlight were more frequent and their slant was always the same. The signs of the trail were almost too subtle to read. The scatter of dead leaves on the forest floor between the bushes seemed less random. There were fewer tree branches to dodge and unanchored vines were encountered more frequently, swinging overhead.

After picking up the trail, Owani quickened the pace so much that it took most of my attention and all of my lung power to keep up with her. Sometimes we walked over bare rocky ground. Sometimes we descended a stairway of exposed roots and rocks, arriving in a mossy bog or a stream bed. When the stream was small and shallow, we slogged through. Sometimes, when the stream was larger and deeper, we crossed it by walking over a felled log. When the stream was still deeper and wider, the bridge was often two logs, side by side. And once the trail brought us to a small river which we crossed on a suspension bridge. It consisted of a thick liana stretched between the two banks, held up by crossed poles, with handrails formed from thinner lianas, similarly suspended and tied down to the main liana with small fibrous ropes. The suspension bridge was so wiggly that I had to break down my load and go back and forth three times.

After crossing that river, the terrain became more difficult. We pressed on in an easterly direction, going up and down hills. When the hillsides became steep, Owani took off her sandals for better traction. Sometimes I could see deep indentations where she had gripped the soil with her big toes. In those places, I often slipped and stumbled in my tennis shoes. Sometimes a fallen log became part of the trail, notched by previous travelers to create stairs. Halfway up a particularly steep hill, we came across a resting place and stopped. It consisted of a couple of fallen logs in front of a stand of bamboo. A hole in the canopy from two fallen trees allowed me a narrow-angle view of the undulating landscape that we had just traversed. It was a welcomed stop. The sun was high and I was hungry and tired.

I broke out a ration of unsalted crackers and sardines which I shared with Owani. Although I had contributed the meal, Owani didn't contribute any conversation. And she didn't respond to my attempts to strike one up. In fact, she gave me the distinct feeling that I was on probation. What a shame, because I had so many questions. Why all the secrecy? Why had she forbidden me say a word to Jos? What was the great work of the Great Shaman? And how had Owami learned such excellent English, with an English accent, nonetheless? When she was speaking to me last night, her voice reminded me of dear old Margaret Westley.

But I did know a few things about Owani: that she had to be the one who had read the flyer I had dropped from the airplane. That she had understood it and was logical enough to signal back that she did not know where Rebecca was. And that she had not helped me when I struggled to ask my questions of the priest. And that she was the Indian woman that Rebecca had mentioned in her e-mail asking about freeze-dried insulin that wouldn't have to be refrigerated.

How was Owani treating her diabetes now? Did that bird skin pouch around her neck contain tablets of oral hypoglycemic drug? Rebecca once told me that diabetic symptoms are easily seen in the skin. But it was hard to look at Owani without staring at her nakedness. Her breasts hung flattened under many loops of beads.

These must have given some protection against the hundreds of bushes that we had crashed through. But she wasn't scratched anywhere. Under the morning's exertion, her skin looked healthy. Maybe she was only borderline diabetic. Maybe her body worked fine after her metabolism got reved up with a morning's walk, burning fatty acids.

When she noticed me looking at her, I turned my attention to the hole in the tree canopy. My eyes were now able to pick out a few unusual features in the textured green hills that stretched before us. I made out the red and blue of a perched squadron of macaws. And the dark reddish spots moving in the trees had to be a family of monkeys. By listening hard, I could make out their screeches over the hum of insects. And in the trees before me, I was able to make out black and yellow beaks belonging to a pair of toucans.

Owani watched me as my eyes explored the forest. And as soon as I finished eating, she got up. I took a big drink from my canteen, buried the empty sardine tin and then we were off.

For the rest of the day, we trekked through streams and up and down the sides of steep hills. I drank liberally from my canteen but didn't sweat. Although we were close to the equator, our green room was naturally air-conditioned at room temperature. The multiple layers of branches and leaves of the green canopy did a good job attenuating the sun's rays. And on the ground, saprophytic plants held down the temperature by evaporating water.

As the sun sank in the west, I wondered how we would spend the night. Owani chose a spot with a carpet of moss under a bromeliad-loaded tree. The water from the nearby stream was refreshing after the long march. I asked Owani if I should cut limbs for a shelter and she said it would not be necessary. It would not rain tonight. When I asked her if I should make a fire, she replied, "What for? Are you going to cook tea?"

"The smoke might help to drive away insects."

"And the light will attract them, too."

We ate sardines and crackers for dinner.

It was getting dark. I extracted the hand-held GPS apparatus from my backpack and took a reading. We had traveled almost 40 miles. I returned the apparatus to my backpack. Cautiously, I attempted conversation with Owani. I started by talking about immediate things — my thankfulness for her taking me along, how I loved Rebecca and how I spoke Spanish and was trying to learn Portuguese and how good it was that she could speak English with me. When she didn't react, I told her about reading books about the culture of South American Indians and how I was trying to learn more about it. But somehow, I couldn't bring myself to say anything good about their culture.

It was getting dark fast, now. Owani looked at me for a long time. It was hard for me to hold her gaze, even in the dim light. Finally, she shook her head slowly.

"Yes, we will need a fire for tonight."

I went around our spot, in ever-widening circles, gathering dry sticks and twigs and finally palm fronds until I had assembled enough for a small fire that would last the night. I tore the dried fronds into small strips which I piled and surrounded with twigs and sticks. I inserted my lighter and gently blew life into the little tepee until it smoked, heated and burst into flame. By that time it was quite dark and several degrees cooler. The flame cast flickering shadows on the tree trunk and on Owani's face.

Finally, she spoke spontaneously. "You want me to take you to Rebecca. You want to learn our secrets. But you have not shown me your secrets. If I am to take you to her tomorrow, you must show me your *hekura*."

She opened the bird-skin pouch hanging around her neck and poured several grams of black powder in her hand. "You must inhale this deeply."

24   Hekura Analysis

"Owani, I will be open with you. You can ask me any question, and I will give you an honest answer. You do not need ebene powder to get the truth from me."

The fire flickered in her dark brown eyes. "You have quick eyes and quick hands that can fix radios. But you are unable to find a path in the forest. Your *hekura* is like a wild monkey in a tree. It will not come down by itself. It must be shot with *mamucori* to bring it down."

"What will you do with the monkey? Run a sharpened stick through it and roast it in the fire?"

"No, the monkey will be returned to the tree."

"Okay, I will relax and answer all your questions."

"You say that, but you are not relaxed. Your *hekura* is like a clever fish swimming in on the bottom of a muddy river. It cannot be coaxed to the surface and it is too smart to bite my hook. We must pour *ro-ton-ton* in the water and bring the clever fish to the light."

"What will you do with the fish? Fry it?"

"No, the fish will be thrown back into the river."

Her black eyes were as unfathomable as the *Rio Negro*. And they did not blink in the flickering firelight. I felt like a monkey trying to hide in a solitary tree. I felt like a fish out of water. Owani had all the control. And if I didn't go along with her mumbo jumbo she wouldn't take me a step further.

But I didn't feel threatened by her. She sounded so much like Margaret Westley. And somehow this moment felt so much like the time when Dr. Westley and she had intoxicated me with her rum-soaked "trifle" — that sweet bread and fruit pudding she had served so festively from a large jar. Oh, how we had joked and laughed that night! The alcohol had dissolved away all our rough edges and had coalesced us into a family. How unfortunate that fate had taken Margaret away before I'd had a chance to tell her how much she meant to me. But how fortunate that Margaret had magnetized me by her good example. She had strengthened my moral compass and it had served me well through a spiritual crisis. And here, now was Owani, Margaret's *doppelgänger*, risking her health to lead me dozens of miles through the forest. I would just have to trust her, as she was trusting me.

"Yes, I will do it."

Owani extended her palm and I bowed my head. I inhaled deeply through the nose. Like ground pepper, it stung in my sinuses. I inhaled again. My eyes watered. My nose ran. This was enough; I let it drip. My stomach convulsed and the sardine-and-cracker mash came halfway up my throat. I swallowed it back down and fumbled for my canteen to wash the acid from my vocal cords.

My eyes wouldn't focus. Owani wiped my nose with a leaf.

"I am the sister of a shaman. I have learned to see into people's souls. I can see through the paint that men wear on their faces and through the masks that they put on to look ferocious. You squint. You think that what I say is foreign. You blink that it is untrue. But I have also flown to lands where women paint their faces to look beautiful and where men button their bodies in tight cloth to look ferocious behind their desks and counters. Their *hekuras* were not different from ours. They hold restless monkeys, lazy turtles, slithering snakes or cowardly peccaries. Some are even crouching jaguars. But their *hekuras* are no different from ours.

"I saw into the *hekura* of little Shaman Woman Rebecca. No, I did not make her sniff ebene powder. She was always open. I could see it in her face. I could see into her eyes when she was looking into theirs, trying to heal them. I could see it when she looked at me. Her *hekura* holds no animals, only the pure spirits of the earth. Her spirit is nurture. I could feel her spirit in her questions about our shamans and their healing. I knew I would have to show her to my brother, a shaman of great power. Just like I had to show him to the Great Shaman who is finding even greater power."

The drug was loosening the layers of my brain. Her words penetrated deeply.

"I do not know what spirits you bring. But I know your yearning for Little Shaman Woman is strong and passionate — so strong that it brought you here . . . and so passionate that you threw yourself down before the priest. I could not bear to see you suffer. But before I bring you to Rebecca, I must see into your soul. I must know you will not do us harm."

"I won't hurt anyone." My head was swimming. My arms dangled, lifelessly.

"Your eyes move quickly. Your hands are fast. You climb and leap, aimlessly. Your *hekura* holds a monkey."

"Okay, I'm a monkey. But I won't hurt anybody."

"You say that. And for many years your people have been saying that. And look what harm they brought to us . . . first the diseases that sickened our strong ones and killed our weak ones. Then they brought in your tools and guns. They made us all feel ashamed of the things we have always made for ourselves. They said they were bringing progress, but they often brought destruction."

"I don't want to destroy anything. I just want to find Rebecca."

Owani moved her face closer, searching my eyes. She seemed to have the aura of a rainbow. The aura was real. The rainbow danced around the fire, too. The powder was playing tricks on my eyes. I shut them and the aura swam through my brain. I was hallucinating.

"No, none of you Englishmen want to destroy anything. But you can destroy it without thinking. Let me look into your eyes. Do not look away this time. You have shy eyes, like my Derek. I believed him when he came to our *shabono*. I loved him. I was a young woman. I followed him, down the river to the big cities, onto the aeroplane and over the big ocean to his country where the grass was green but you are not allowed to walk on it, where people cover their bodies with clothes and hide their *hekuras* behind cold masks. Those people were as cold and barren as their winters.

"I followed him back to his people where I was a curiosity . . . to his university where they studied me . . . until I became like a pet bird with clipped wings who could not fly. I could not move my body freely. I grew fat. I became sick from their food and dependent on their medicines. And when I finally learned how to look behind Derek's eyes, I found nothing. I found only a peccary. And he had no love for the things that could sustain me . . . and no honesty to tell me his thoughts. His love was not deep enough to put himself inside me and cry for joy. It was not a love that would make children. Look at me, I must see into your eyes."

Her face was close to mine, now, filling my entire field of vision. Firelight bounced between our cheeks and foreheads like flashes of lightning deep within clouds.

"I'm sorry it turned out that way," I said. "The English are so formal."

"Yes, that is what he said. His language has so many ways to say that you are sorry . . . and all of them false." She said it with resignation.

I could understand. I could understand Derek and Owani. The gulf had been too wide to be bridged. The disparities were too great. Like the disparity I heard and saw before me — the language

I had been conditioned to hear as elegant and a face that I had been conditioned to perceive as savage.

"I am sorry Derek couldn't . . . open himself up enough to love you. Maybe he was too . . . proud. No, he was probably unsure. Even with his own people."

"You are all unsure. You have walked on the moon. You go to places in the sky. You can send your voices around the world. But you have nothing to say. You are confused. There are so many things you do not know. You destroy the earth. You, Ben Candidi, must promise me that you will not destroy what you see."

"Yes, I promise. I've always loved the Earth. I do not waste it or pollute it. I ride a bicycle. I don't even own a car. And I already know some of your customs. I — "

She cut me off and asked forcefully, "Do you know the Rebecca you seek?"

"Yes."

"Do you cherish her?"

"Yes, with my heart and soul."

"And you must also honor and respect her. She is not an ordinary woman. She will become a great woman *shabori*. Do not look at her with a warrior's eyes. She is skinny but strong of will. She knows how to find the *hekuras*, to take away pain and suck out sickness. She has told me how she is learning to hunt for lost souls of children and the lost *hekuras* of men and women — what you call mental illness. A woman *shabori* can have only one kind of husband — a husband who will serve her. You must follow her."

"I will. I am."

"How deep is your love for your Rebecca?"

"It is deeper than my body has been inside her. Deeper than you can walk into the forest. It is real, like you said."

"Tell me how real." Her voice was insistent. She was squeezing my arm.

"Real, like I want the explosion inside us to bind us forever."

"*How* real?" Her fingers pierced my arm like claws.

"Real, like I want the explosion to make . . . children . . . who can walk with us . . . on the forest floor . . . and sail with us on my boat on the ocean . . . who can swim with us over the reef and look down on the fish through clear water." I was losing it. "When

Rebecca tells me that it is time to have children." Mucus streamed from my nose; tears streamed down my face.

"Rebecca will not have children. She is becoming a great woman *shabori*. When they have children, they become like ordinary women."

"I will follow her anyway. If we can't have children because of her career . . . ." I broke down, crying.

Owani leaned forward and hugged me. "I believe you. I will take you to Rebecca tomorrow."

I kept on sobbing. She said nothing for a long time. Then she cradled my head and spoke softly. "You are confused. You were once gentle. But you turned into a warrior who is too restless to grow plants in his woman's garden — too impatient to know the healing spirit that dwells in a small flower high on a tree. You come seeking your loved one, I must warn you that Rebecca is now a keeper of our *shabono*'s secrets. Betray these secrets and the *shabono* will be endangered. And you have endangered us already. That man you brought could be very dangerous. And you, yourself have brought a gun and a satellite telephone. You must promise that you will not use them."

"I promise."

"When you see her tomorrow, you must obey the Little Shaman Woman. We will sleep, now. As the fire goes out, let the spirits enter you deeply so they will not be driven out by the light of day."

She withdrew. I leaned back and saw the dancing shadows that the fire cast on the underside of the trees. I plugged my ears against scorpions, beetles and stinging ants. Laying on a bed of moss, I watched the shadows of forest spirits, *doppelgängers*, jaguars, monkeys and alligators dance on the underside of the canopy. Gradually, I crossed to the other side, a world full of vivid dreams that lasted the whole night.

25   Yanomama Maiden

The next morning Owani made me scatter the ashes of the fire and cover the spot with fresh moss. Breakfast was the same as last night's dinner. I buried the sardine tins in the forest. When Owani wasn't looking, I reached in my pack and stored another waypoint on the GPS. And I transferred my compass to my pocket. We trekked in a northeasterly direction all morning. We stopped only for lunch, then trekked onward, still harder. The farther we went, the more easily I could make out the trail. It now ran like a shallow groove in the forest floor on a path free of low-hanging branches and bushes.

We made our first contact that afternoon. I was hurrying to keep up with Owani who was traveling so far ahead that she was sometimes out of sight. When I caught up with her, she was standing in front of an Indian and engaged in excited conversation. And he was holding a six-foot bow at half-draw, aimed in my general direction. I stopped in my tracks. The warrior's face was the picture of painted-on fierceness. Vertical red stripes on his cheeks contorted as he spoke.

Owani was standing in front of him as if to block an attack on me. She concluded her argument by putting her hand on the bowstring. The man let loose a mouthful of resentful gutturals then returned the arrow to its quiver. Owani stepped past him and motioned for me to come. I approached cautiously, doing my best to appear confident and trying hard to provide the right amount of eye contact. The elaborate face paint made his eyes hard to find and interpret.

The thatch of black hair overhanging his face bounced in agitation. His lower scalp was shaven all around, an inch above ear level. He was slightly shorter than me but very muscular. He was completely naked except for a bone necklace and what he carried — a leather water bladder, a quiver, and a leather string that encircled his waist. From it hung a loop which held up the tip of his penis. That part of his anatomy wasn't all that impressive; I averted my eyes and tried to suppress a smirk.

He stood his ground in the middle of the trail, forcing me to go around him. While doing so, I put my hands together and nodded my head in an oriental greeting. After I was a few steps beyond him, he growled some words at my back. When, after several dozen yards, I did turn to catch another glimpse of him, he was peering in the direction from which we came, as if worried that more intruders might be coming.

A ten-minute hike brought us to a Yanomama man and woman standing near the trail. When Owani called to them, the man answered in what sounded like pleasant surprise. He was naked, with the same bow, quiver and waist string arrangement as the first Indian except that his penis was not tied. His hair was also bowl-cut, but his face paint was limited to a couple of vertical red lines on his temples. He was about my size and build. I guessed he was in his mid-twenties. And in his right hand was a sleek black piece of electronic equipment, from which a short antenna projected.

Standing behind him was a Yanomama woman about the same age. She had a short, oval body with a slightly protruding stomach and a smooth, filled-out face with few markings. Her breasts were high, small, and strangely shaped — conical with finger-width nipples. They pointed to the sides at an unusually wide angle. Between them were hung several intertwined strands of glass beads. She also wore a waist string. From it hung a small patch of thin leather which obscured her pubis from frontal view. While approaching, I tried not to stare. She had shy eyes, and hung back behind the man.

I fell in several steps behind Owani and rendered my oriental greeting to the pair. Owani identified me a "Ben" and started telling a long story that made the man smile and the woman giggle. The man made a loud call into the forest. As Owani continued the story, the man looked me over. Two more Yanomama men emerged from the forest, similarly dressed and armed. They were followed by three women.

The first two women had ovoid bodies. But the third woman was thin and slightly taller. She had broader hips and walked with a looser gait. Trying to be polite, I did not look at her for too long at a time. Her skin was a different color. The others were light brown — hers seemed to have no underlying color but bore a strong blueish cast. Her cheeks bore vertical stripes which emphasized the narrowness of her face. Her hair was also black, but was longer than the normal bowl-cut. Her breasts were small, at normal height and were covered with many strings of multi-colored beads fashioned from seeds and nuts. She stopped in her tracks, a dozen yards away. It was not shyness that made her put a hand to her mouth. It was surprise.

Then she took her hand from her mouth. "What's the matter, Ben? Don't you recognize me?"

My ears were telling me it was Rebecca, but my eyes were still deceiving me. Everyone was laughing. I looked again, hard this time. Yes, take away the stripes on her cheeks and it was Rebecca. But parts of my brain still hadn't caught up.

I stammered, "But . . . but . . . but . . . ."

Her cheek markings stretched. "You *did* get my e-mails, didn't you?" She approached, her hips swaying and her little patch of loincloth flapping.

"Yes."

Her loincloth was no larger than her hand. "So you knew that you didn't need to come . . . But I'm so glad that you did." The cheek marks were now rounded in a smile.

I dropped my gear and ran up to throw my arms around her.

She extended her arms out straight before her. She had one of those black electronic devices in one hand. "Careful, the blue stain is very strong. It won't come out of your clothes."

I hugged her anyway. The little group laughed and teased in their nonsense syllable language. And the things I blubbered probably made no sense to anyone, either. I must have lost face in front of all of them. But it was so good to have Rebecca safe in my arms. And it was such a relief to not have to search any longer.

I did mess up Rebecca's paint job. And the little group squeezed closely around us. Obviously they were curious about western kissing. The movement of our tongues sparked a play-by-play commentary that caused us to stop. We disengaged and I looked down, embarrassed. I looked at the men's hands. They were holding those electronic boxes. Everything seemed so incongruous.

"Rebecca? What are you doing here?"

"I came here to provide health care. After that, I got involved in a project that's really amazing. But I can't tell you about it." She glanced to Owani as if seeking guidance or approval.

"Why can't you tell me about it?" I asked.

"Because the Great Shaman ordered that I can't tell anyone for two moons. I can't leave for two months. If I tell you what I'm doing, you will have to stay here with me and promise to keep it secret."

Owani was translating our words for the benefit of the others. That just added to my confusion.

"Who is this Great Shaman? Do you mean to tell me that because of some witch doctor, you're running around with these . . . people . . . naked in the forest? And you won't be able to quit for two months! Have you been chewing ebene seeds? Are you out of your mind?"

"No, Ben. This is very important. You've probably seen too much already. You'll have to promise to keep it secret. If I tell you anything more, you'll probably have to stay these two months with me . . . until I get permission to leave."

"Permission to leave? Big secret? Like hell!" I took a couple of steps back and looked around. Then I started putting two and two together, thinking out loud as I did. "Those boxes have antennas, so you are using some kind of electronic communication, probably digital. Yes, the big one this man is carrying has an infrared port. So it's getting its information from the palm computer you are carrying. Yes, and that's a digital camera."

I looked around and drew myself up to make the pronouncement. Owani looked at me disapprovingly. The Indian we met on the trail was approaching. "You have hooked yourself up with some sort of anthropological field survey. You are running around with these . . . people . . . taking digital pictures of plants and animals. You are doing it for an anthropologist who has made a deal with a shaman."

Rebecca was shaking her head at me. She didn't like my tone.

"The anthropologist is probably dealing with that 'population density and food scarcity as a cause of ferocity and war' theory that they've been debating for decades. Can you guess how I know that? Because that stuff has been my sole bedtime reading for all those nights that I've been waiting for you to come home. I guess that your anthropologist got carried away with this stuff. Wants to keep his results secret for a couple of months so he can make a big splash at the next anthropology convention."

I waited until Owani finished translating for her clansmen. Her face looked glum. Her people obviously didn't like what they were hearing. She looked at me, shaking her head. Everyone else was looking at Rebecca. She threw back her head as if to cast off my words, then looked me in the eye.

"Ben, I'll have to ask you to respect these people and to not undermine my status in the tribe."

Owani translated this, too. All around us, the people stirred.

"But what *are* you doing here? I was right, wasn't I?"

She smiled. "Good guess. Close, but no cigar." She turned to Owani. "He doesn't understand our work here."

Owani translated, and everyone laughed.

"I think it will be okay for him to turn around and go back," Rebecca said to Owani. "He doesn't understand."

For me that was pushing the wrong button. "Give me that thing and I'll figure it out." I took it from her before she could protest. "Look, it's just an oversized palm-held device. It has an LCD display and a couple of polyethylene tubes dangling —"

The Yanomama from the trail snatched it away and banged me on the chest. He yelled, flailed his arms and stomped the ground.

Owani said, "He says that you will not steal their secrets from their forest. If you run away or try to take Little Shaman Woman from the forest, they will hunt you with arrows."

"Little Shaman Woman?"

"Yes," Rebecca said. "That is what they call me. That is my status with the tribe. I'm the adoptive daughter of Yakgamu, the head-man of the tribe. I'm not leaving before my time. Please don't make a scene. My brother-in-law will take it seriously and get physical."

The women murmured in agreement as Owani translated.

My eyes sank to the forest floor. What would make this project so important that Rebecca would cast me off from a continent away? Why was she taking the side of these savages when I tried to reason with her?

Somehow I had just collided with the hard core of her idealism.

It had been years since we'd disagreed on anything this strongly. And as I stood there, trying to think, I felt more naked than the Indians around me.

"Rebecca, I can't promise to stay two months with you. Back in Miami, I have a report due."

"Then I'll kiss you goodbye and promise to come back in two months, when the project's finished. And try harder this time to remember that I love you."

I searched her eyes for sympathy and found none. She had already made her watershed decision. Now it was up to me. Everyone was watching me closely as I dangled like the polyethylene tubes from the electronic unit in the man's hand. Why would anyone outfit a palm-held computer with polyethylene tubes? I glanced at it again. Yes, polyethylene tubes. That could mean only one thing — liquid going in and out of it. And the unit's shape was familiar. Suddenly the whole answer came to me.

"Rebecca, give it to me straight — no details. Is this project really worth it?"

"It is amazing. It is revolutionary! You won't believe it, even after I tell you."

"But you can't tell me unless I decide to stay."

"That's right, Ben. Like I wrote in the e-mail, you just have to trust me."

I looked again to the unit, and did a quick mental calculation.

"And you're sure that gadget's doing awesome things?"

"Yes."

"And we're not walking into a Jonestown? Nobody's going to make us drink cyanide-laced Kool-Aid?"

"No, I promise you."

"If I stay here for these two months, I won't be able to submit the final version of my report. And I might lose the chance to get a regular consulting contract with the company. My expert witness business will be set back for months. I might lose thousands of dollars in billable hours. And the word might get out that I'm unreliable."

But Rebecca wasn't impressed with my barrage of business jargon. A faraway look came over her face. She smiled, diffusely. "Decide for yourself, Ben. But the money is nothing in comparison to what we're doing here."

"People will miss me. They will worry about rescuing me, like I worried about rescuing you."

"We can get word to them."

"What am I going to do during the two months?"

"You will live the most exciting time of your life. But before I tell you any more, you must sign a non-disclosure agreement." She said it with a sassy smile. Several months ago I had given her a mini-lecture on non-disclosure agreements.

"Who will I sign it with?"

"With me. Owani and our tribesmen will be the witnesses."

My head was spinning. One part of me was lured by the thought of it — thumbing my nose at civilization, taking off my clothes to scamper around the rain forest with my fiancée and her new friends, and collecting some sort of scientific data with biochip reading machines. The other part of my brain was saying it wasn't science if you didn't devise the experiments yourself and perform them in a laboratory.

Rebecca seemed to be reading my thoughts as I struggled with the dilemma. Her eyes were so full of sympathy. I took a deep breath and raised my shoulders.

"Rebecca, I have to tell you that I recognize the unit as an Analytica 503. I've never had one in my hand but I've read the description. It accepts biochips with up to two thousand spots or micro-wells and is theoretically capable of reading out the activity of two-thousand types of genes using a few drops of fluid. It is described in the scientific literature, and would thus not fall under our non-disclosure agreement."

"Okay," Rebecca said, "But you must not disclose the fact that we are using it here."

"Okay. If you're using it to read DNA or RNA samples, I do understand that your work could have some utility . . . as a *genetic archive*."

"We aren't reading DNA or RNA samples."

Damn! There was only one logical alternative: Her people had adapted it to hunt for drugs like I'd written in my report! Had they scooped my invention? Had they already made the same invention that I'd filed with the patent office? My next words came out cautiously. "Before coming here, I was aware that the instrument *could* be adapted to read pharmaceutical activity in a few drops of fluid."

"Duly noted, Ben. But *our* instrument is already doing that."
She said it so firmly. My head was spinning and my knees were
getting weak.

And how funny it felt to be negotiating business terms with
my fiancée while she stood in front of me naked, together with a
bunch of naked tribesmen.

"I agree to never disclose the fact that you are using the unit
here — apparently for a pharmaceutical survey. And I agree to
keep secret everything I learn about how you are doing here. But
this does not include any documents that I have already created in
Miami. Is that good enough?"

"Yes. It is enough that you know I am safe. And you know that
what I am doing is important. You know enough." She took a step
back. "I'm sorry to say this, but now you will just have to trust me.
If you ask another question or take one step forward, you must
agree to stay with me for two months and to follow my instructions
on everything — *everything*, Ben. And no arguing!" She looked
to Owani and received a nod of approval.

The forest seemed to darken. It felt like reality was imploding
on me — the cosmic big bang in reverse. The only thing left in the
universe was our love. I swallowed hard. It was such a big decision
to make.

I swallowed hard, again. "I agree. I'll stay. I promise. Where
do I sign?"

"With a kiss." Rebecca stepped up and kissed me on the lips.
She whispered, "Trust me. Here comes a Yanomama kiss." She
blew a trumpet call on my cheek.

Everyone laughed in approval. Sheepishly, I turned to Owani
and asked her to tell the group that I agreed to keep their secrets,
and that I would live with them for two moons as the Little Shaman
Woman's assistant. I slapped my left breast for emphasis.

One of the men let out a whoop. There was instant jubilation.
The men kept repeating "*shorima,*" which Owani translated as
"brother-in-law." Even the guardian of the trail was saying it. Owani
identified him as the first son of the *shabono's* headman. I made
an oriental bow to him and repeated the word. First Son stepped
forward and hit me on the chest as an expression of friendship. I
hit him back. We slapped each other on the shoulder. This kindled
a spontaneous celebration on the forest trail. After my new brother-

in-law stepped back, he seemed to be holding a conversation with himself. Then, I saw the walkie-talkie hanging between his shoulder blades. A tiny earphone was plugged into one ear. A microphone was hanging in his bone necklace. When First Son stepped back to me, he made an announcement which Owani translated for my sake. They had received permission to bring me into camp. But the party should first complete today's survey.

It seemed like all my problems had disappeared, like I'd awakened from a bad dream. Rebecca and the rest of the party disappeared, too, returning to their work in the forest. When I told Owani that I needed to make one call on my satellite phone to ensure that I would not be missed, she agreed.

I pulled out my satellite phone and called Zeekie.

"ABBA Radio and Video," he announced. His voice came through so clear that it sounded like he was talking from a few yards away.

"Zeekie, this is Ben. I've found Rebecca and everything is okay."

"Great. Tell me where you are."

"In the jungle about two day's trek from the mission where she was working."

"So, what's the story?"

"She's onto something very important here. She has to stay two months more to see it through. And I'm staying with her."

"Sounds great. Tell me more."

"Can't. I had to promise not to tell anything about what she's doing. But don't worry. We're not in danger."

"Yeah," Zeekie said with suspicion, "that's what Rebecca was telling you in those e-mails, too, and you didn't believe her. And now I'm supposed to believe the same thing from you."

"Yes, believe me, Zeekie."

"Like what am I supposed to believe? That they've got some kind of black hole down there that you two have fallen into? A black hole that things can fall into but can't come back out of?"

"No, it's a matter of keeping a sensitive and important secret. And I can't tell you more."

Zeekie was silent for a long time. "Okay, what am I supposed to do to cover for you?"

"Send a message to the *Funai* office that the search for Rebecca was successful. Call and tell her mother in New York that Rebecca is deep into a project that will take another two months and that I'm down here taking care of her."

"All right, I can take care of that. Anything else?"

"Call Michael Malencik and tell him that I'll be delayed for two months, and that if he wants to prepare the final report himself, he can hire himself a word processing expert to put in some hypertext links. But be sure to collect the twenty thousand dollars from him before handing over the diskettes."

"All right. Anything else?" I gave Zeekie instructions for handling my e-mails, telephone messages and mail.

"That shouldn't be too hard," he said.

"Great. When I come back, I promise you a digital photo of every set of knockers in the tribe."

I was lucky. Zeekie was a great pal, the type of guy who would do anything for a friend. When it was all over, I'd offer him a couple of thousand dollars for his effort . . . and he would decline them. Then I'd make it up by buying him the latest electronic gizmo he'd had his eye on. His latest interest was fast acquisition and manipulation of video images.

"Zeekie, there's just one little wrinkle on the deal. I won't be able to call you back again while we're at this location. That's part of the promise I made to Rebecca and her tribal brothers and sisters."

"Sheesh, Ben."

"I know it's putting you on the spot. Just do the best you can. I'll stand by any decision you make."

Then I remembered to ask him to tell Alice I was okay. He said that would be a little harder.

Owani was acting like it was time to end the conversation. I asked Zeekie to get my friend Sam to take a look at the *Diogenes* and the *Alabama Tiger* once a week. Then we said goodbye and I returned the telephone to my pack. Owani said I'd have to give her the phone when we reached the *shabono*. I agreed.

I went into the forest, looking for Rebecca. When I caught up with her, she was with the husband and wife team. They were kneeling over a small shrub growing from the base of a moss-covered log. On the ground before her was what looked like a small chemistry set: an array of small, plastic-capped test tubes, small glass dispenser bottles for solvents, syringes, and one-inch diameter plastic Millipore filter disks. She was squeezing a twig sample in a pliers-like contraption similar to what they use to squeeze slices of lemon into tea. Except she was squeezing it into test tubes containing a few drops of the solution.

Rebecca sensed my presence and looked back at me. "We are screening for a lot of things. We assayed this shrub two weeks ago and it tested positive for a lectin against *Entamoeba histolytica*. It might clear the intestinal tract of parasitic amoebas. That's a big problem down here. The lectin might even become an IV product."

"And you've come back to verify it, now?"

"Yes, and to see if the lectin concentration is reliable or if it varies with the growth cycle of the shrub."

"And you used the GPS coordinates to find your way back to this very same plant. And your teammate just took a digital picture to correlate your chemistry with any changes in the plant's appearance."

"Right. His name is Shamki."

I looked over Shamki's shoulder. The machine showed the following numbers:

00 10 15
64 91 73

That was our longitude and latitude. And beyond that, there was something vaguely familiar about the format of the numbers.

It was easy enough to see how Rebecca analyzed the leaves after Shamki photographed them. She squeezed them to collect drops of juice which she distributed into several different test tubes. One held clear solution, another was soapy and still another had a layer of water over chloroform. Then she put some of the leaf pulp in a separate test tube, added water and agitated it with a machine that looked like an electric screwdriver and made a high-pitched grating noise. I recognized this as a "sonicator" which uses ultra-high-frequency sound to bust up cell membranes. That releases molecules trapped in the cytoplasm. And the detergent releases molecules that are bound to the solid parts of the cell.

Like a skilled technician, Rebecca shook the samples and drew them up into syringes. She fitted Millipore filter discs onto syringe tips and squeezed the syringe contents into fresh test tubes which she labeled. Then she dipped the polyethylene tube from her biochip machine into the first test tube and punched buttons. The machine sucked up the solution.

For a minute or so Rebecca relaxed.

"Very impressive," I said. Rebecca didn't answer, but responded to the machine's beep. The Indian girl at her side activated an instrument that looked like a palm held computer, fitted with infrared port and stubby radio antenna. She nodded to Rebecca who pushed a button, and after a few seconds, both devices beeped. Rebecca said I had just witnessed the performance of 1,000 pharmacological assays of leaf juice. And now the results were being transmitted to the palm-held computer and by radio to a central station.

Rebecca dipped the polyethylene tube in a larger bottle labeled "wash-out" and the machine started slurping. I looked to the Indian girl and said, "*Bom instrumento!*"

She looked away.

"You won't get very far with her in Portuguese, Ben."

"Not in English, either," I replied. "So how do *you* communicate with her?"

Rebecca said a few words to the girl in what could have been Japanese. The girl smiled shyly, gave a short answer, and held out the computer to me. I looked at the screen. There were no words, just graphic icons.

"Awesome, Rebecca, learning Yanomami in a few weeks. But you can't be talking science with them in Yanomami. They won't have any words for concepts like detergent extract, serial dilution and effective concentration."

Rebecca smiled and said, "Very good, Ben." She waited until the machines had reported the second assay before answering me in full. "We have screen icons for all scientific operations. The language was developed by Ken Lee. He runs the communications shack. He's an expert at visual basic and he's good at pictographs because he reads Chinese."

"Really!"

Rebecca said more words to the girl in Yanomami and she responded by pointing to an icon on the screen.

"What would you guess this means?" Rebecca asked me.

Looking at the screen closely, I perceived the icon as an arrow shooting upwards out of a leaf.

"Is it *leaf extract*?"

"Yes."

"Awesome!" I couldn't find any better word for it. "And what is your symbol for pharmacological activity?"

"An arrow coming out of an arrow-head. And we have symbols for muscle, gut, brain and so forth for the different types of pharmacological activity."

This really was awesome. Trying to think about it set my head spinning. Maybe that's why my eyes grabbed onto the woman's breasts. They were high on her chest and pointed upwards, bringing to mind an icon for an observatory turret with partially protruding telescopes. I didn't realize I was gawking until the woman tittered. She wiggled, and dug her toes into the forest floor, pigeon-toed.

Damn you, Ben. Your eyes seem to be completely under hormonal control.

To cover up my faux pas, I tried to use sign language to describe the magnificence of what they were doing. I directed most of my attention to the woman's husband. All three of them accepted my virtual apology. I withdrew to a nearby log where I sat and watched them work for the next hour.

When Rebecca finally capped her test tubes and folded together her chemistry set, Shamki put his hands to his mouth and let out a call like a howler monkey. Within a few seconds an answering call came from a distance. A few minutes later, we were joined by First Son. For some reason he didn't look as friendly as when I saw him last.

Rebecca interpreted for me. "First Son is responsible for the *shabono's* security. He's a believer in the old ways and takes his duties very seriously."

We began a fast trek to their camp, the first of several tests that I would be put to.

Hearth and Home 26

It was a fast trek for me and a glide through the forest for them. They moved efficiently, fleetly. The Indian women and Rebecca carried all of the equipment on their heads. It was interesting how Rebecca imitated the Indian women and Owani, walking perfectly balanced with turned-in toes that grabbed into the forest floor, especially where the trail was steep and muddy. The men, carrying only their bows and arrows, seemed to be skating along on out-turned feet, leading with their knees and ready to change direction in a split second.

For two hours, I did my best to keep up, frequently slipping out and stumbling — to the great amusement of the men and to the derision of First Son who brought up the rear. He divided his time between dropping back to peer into the forest and following close behind me, running up on my heels every time I made a false step.

The first sign of the *shabono* was its smoke. We arrived a quarter of an hour later. We were greeted by a gaggle of noisy children. As we walked into the clearing, we were greeted by an old man with a proud demeanor. He raised an arm to salute the men of our party. He hugged Owani. From the way he talked to her, it was clear to see that she was his sister. He gave Rebecca a noisy kiss. After she introduced me to him, he made a loud noise and slapped me hard on the shoulder — a greeting that I didn't dare return. Rebecca said he was the headman. She didn't have to tell me that he was not the Great Shaman.

Headman appeared to be around 60 years old. He was quite healthy for a Third World person. He had all of his teeth and his only affliction seemed to be a bit of stiffness in his lower back. He was lean and athletic and favored his left leg when he walked. From the circular scar below his left rib and old slash marks on his shoulders and arms, I deduced that he had engaged in mortal combat in his younger years. Also, his cheeks bore circular scars, but I took these to be remnants of holes that once held ornamental sticks. Later, I noticed these marks on other older men in the *shabono*.

Headman's main sign of age was graying of hair — it was almost white — and lightening of skin. He wore no body paint. Age showed on his face the way it does with all races — with loss of fat and underlying muscle, and with stretching of the skin.

There was nothing static about Headman. With noisy gesticulation, he called out to the *shabono* dwellers. He fell into a wide-kneed gait beside his son and led us to the *shabono*. It was build in a semi-circle probably 70 yards in diameter with a large central open area. The palm-frond thatched roof was 15 feet high in the front and sloped down to about three feet at the outer perimeter. It was held up by large poles between which were hung hammocks. From my bedtime reading, I was already familiar with this type of layout. You might say that I'd already done my homework on these people.

The front of the *shabono* was studded with hearth fires which would "belong" to individual family groupings. But otherwise, the *shabono* would be completely communal, with no privacy. In fact, the only things resembling walls or partitions inside were steamer trunks stacked between the hearths. And these were the only modern-looking objects except for the walkie-talkies of the men — scouts, warriors and bioprospectors — that hung from the ceiling by their hearth or from leather straps around their waists. Obviously, this was an important status symbol.

As I followed Rebecca, the women watched me curiously, but didn't abandon their cooking or basket weaving. First Son took me to his hearth where he introduced me to his wife, and to his three sons who seemed to be twelve, five and two years old. He indicated that I should drop my gear under Rebecca's hammock which was strung on the edge of his area. Rebecca gave me a kiss and told me to make myself at home while she went off to return her equipment. I kept myself occupied with my host's youngest son. He had invented a game involving a beetle and a stick. He was a gentle soul; the beetle survived.

In the adjacent area, Owani was chatting with Headman and his wife. It was getting dark. Most families were gathered around their hearths, eating. Rebecca returned and told me that Ken Lee at the "Technical Center" had talked to the Great Shaman and it was okay for me to stay. However, I was forbidden to go out with the bioprospecting parties and I had to stay away from the Technical Center as well.

"I agree. Those are your trade secrets. I have no need to know." But the thought of spending two months of playing games with two-year-olds must have put a sour expression on my face.

"Don't worry, Ben. The time will go quickly for you if you spend it learning their language and culture."

First Son's wife must have heard the noise my stomach was making. She gestured us to the hearth where a cast iron pot was steaming and giving off good smells. She scooped its contents out into clay bowls which she handed to us. And she gave us clay utensils that were a cross between a scoop and a spoon. Nothing ever tasted so good. It was like a beef stew, but of lighter texture where manioc root was substituted for the potatoes, where slithery plantains were substituted for carrots, and where capybara was substituted for beef. The flesh from the world's largest rodent tasted a lot like pork.

After scarfing down my bowl, I looked up and noticed that many people had moved close to our hearth to get a look at me. My hostess made a comment with a bashful laugh.

"She said you have a good appetite," Rebecca told me.

My host stood up and made a pronouncement in staccato tempo and guttural tones, punctuated with lots of glottal stops and arm movements. At the end of the oration, he fell clumsily to the ground. The whole *shabono* laughed at once while my host picked himself up and stared at me, haughtily.

"What did he say, Rebecca?"

"He said that you had a good appetite because you had a hard day falling down on the trail . . . Wait, Ben! Don't do it."

Rebecca reached out to hold me down but I was already on my feet. No, I wasn't planning a face-off with Headman's First Son. I faced Owani who was sitting at the next hearth. "Headman's Sister, thank you for bringing me here so that I can be with Little Shaman Woman. It is true that I fell down many times on the trail today." I hammed it up, pretending to slip and fall. "But it was not because I was trying to keep up with the men. It was because I was trying to keep up with you, Owani, Headman's Sister."

I sat down. Owani laughed and translated my words for the

whole *shabono*, identifying me as "Ben." She added some flowing body movements to illustrate her own speed and grace on the trail. When she finished, the whole *shabono* was up in arms.

Everyone was laughing — except Headman's Son. He glowered at me, unamused by his elderly aunt's grace and insulted by the idea of coming in second place to her. He stood up, beat his breast and made a short, guttural pronouncement. Then he took a couple of steps forward and stood over me.

"Ben, don't get up," Rebecca warned. "You have no idea. It could get very dangerous."

Yes, I had promised to obey her. But no, I hadn't promised to endure humiliation. There was no alternative if I was to stay here for two months. I got up, again facing Owani. Her face also warned me of a serious situation.

"Owani, what did Headman's brave and fast son say?"

"That he never falls down on the trail, even when someone pushes him."

"Then tell him I agree with that. And I thank him for accepting me to his campfire."

Faster than Owani could translate my words into Yanomami, First Son pounded his chest and yelled at me.

"He wants you to try to push him. But don't do it," Owani said. Her voice was grave and her face was full of concern.

Rebecca was pleading for me to sit down. But to me it was clear there would be no escape. I said, "Don't worry, I've dealt with worse situations around Newark."

Headman's Son stuck out his chin and braced himself. His back was to the clearing and nobody was behind him. Remembering my bedtime reading, I wound up like a New York Yankees pitcher and landed a stiff-arm onto his left pectoral, hitting it with an open palm that made a big slap but delivered no force. He rocked a little but didn't fall over. He laughed and let loose with a torrent of words that could mean only one thing: that I had to stand there and let him do it to me.

I looked around and behind me to make sure there was space to do what I wanted to do. Rebecca was trying to get up and interpose herself between us. I pushed her back down and to the side, telling her to trust me. I braced myself, presenting my left pectoral. First Son came in hard with a fist. The instant it struck, I spun counterclockwise and rolled over backwards, and, in one continuous movement, regained my feet, sprung into the air and struck a hanging basket with a side thrust kick. It sent a cache of manioc roots flying every which way. After landing on my feet, I went through my full repertoire of karate moves, including the *kiais*, working my way towards First Son with special emphasis on power punches and front thrust kicks.

As a die-hard macho, he stood his ground, ready to take whatever I had to give. When I got within striking distance, I made like I was standing on a log and losing balance. Then I went down in a mess of flailing arms.

The whole *shabono* laughed and howled. Finally, my worthy opponent figured out it was supposed to be funny and started laughing, too. As the laughter subsided he pulled me up, made a noisy pronouncement, and hugged me. Rebecca told me later that I was welcomed at his campfire as a brother-in-law. I pulled a machete from one of the duffel bags and presented it to him as a gift.

Levity and good spirits continued for another hour while the children played a new game called "push me down and see me act tough and crazy." The adults cheered them on. One old woman walked around dishing out a pail of casava beer, fermented from her own spit, no doubt. I accepted a gourd full, made a show of drinking it and flung it back into the shadows when nobody was looking.

As the festivities died down, Rebecca climbed into her hammock and invited me to climb in with her. I inspected it first. It was a combination of braided hemp fiber rope and webbing that was stiffened and bulked out with long, thin inserted cane stalks. The overhead beams seemed sturdy enough to support our combined weight. I climbed and wiggled in, and the hammock pressed us together. Together we hung there, entwined in each other's arms. We talked softly and languidly, feeling each other's breaths and heartbeats while *shabono* life went on around us like a sound-and-light pageant.

I asked Rebecca about Owani. Rebecca said, "I met Owani at the Mission. We became good friends. She told me I was a good healer and was doing good for her people. We talked every night. Every time we talked, I learned more about her *shabono*. I also learned that they have a high rate of infant mortality. I suspected that from the babies that the mothers brought to me at the Mission — dehydrated. I said if she took me to her *shabono*, I would give lessons on infant care. At first she was hesitant, but then she took me into her confidence. She told me that a great shaman was helping her *shabono* to organize its future and that I would have to promise to keep their secrets. I agreed and Owani agreed to take me here. That's when I wrote you about the great opportunity and how I'd be coming back a couple of weeks late. And I told the same to David."

"Okay."

"We left very early the next morning. We walked two and one-half days. Owani introduced me to Headman. He introduced me to First Son and to the *shabono*. And Owani did help me to interview the mothers and to give them advice on infant care. They were doing a lot of things right but a lot of things wrong, too. I showed them some simple ways to treat fever and dehydration. I didn't have to relate my teachings to their mythology because they are pretty well tuned to Western ways. Of course I couldn't help noticing their walkie-talkies. I noticed the survey instruments as well, but I didn't let on that I did. When Headman's second son saw me at the *shabono*, he was upset. He scolded Owani for bringing me here and went off to tell the Great Shaman. He came back and told me that the Great Shaman had forbidden communication with the outside world. He asked if I would agree to stay for the next two months."

"How did he tell you this? Did he get Owani to interpret for you?"

"No, Second Son speaks excellent English. He said that if I stayed, I could take part in all aspects of village life and that I'd be known as Little Shaman Woman. As you can see it was such an opportunity, to be part of a *shabono* that was making the transition from the old ways to the new ways. So much I could do and so much I would write about. And it was so exciting that they were doing a survey project with modern equipment. And, as you see, they finally let me work on the project. But first, I had to promise not to take any information out of here. I promised, but I *told* Second Son that I had to send a message back to you. And they let me send it. They have a satellite dish here. You did get the message, didn't you?"

"Yes," I said. "I got your first messages." I would talk to Rebecca about her final message later. "So tell me about this Great Shaman. Is he a Yanomama or a Brazilian?"

"I don't know. I didn't actually talk to him. I talked to him through Ken Lee at the Technical Center. It's not far from here."

"Were you there while Ken Lee talked to him?"

"I was outside the Technical Center. Ken went inside and talked to him on the radio, then came out and asked me questions."

Flames danced in the hearth and visions of communion at Jonestown with cyanide-laced Kool-Aid danced before my eyes.

"And what language was he talking to the Great Shaman in?"

"I don't know. The door was closed most of the time."

"And what language did you hear him speaking when the door was open?"

"English. I've only heard him speaking English."

"Do you think the Great Shaman is a Yanomama?"

"I don't think so. I have heard them call the Great Shaman a foreigner — 'not of the village' or 'not of our people.' I'm guessing that he's a Brazilian."

"And you don't know where he got all this scientific equipment? You don't know what organization he's working with?"

"No. Owani said what they were doing was top secret, and it was in a critical phase. She made it clear that I wasn't supposed to ask a lot of questions about the surveys. What she wanted me here for was to serve as a physician. Great Shaman brought in a lot of scientific equipment but didn't bring in any medicine."

"Strong in science but short on medicine."

"Yes, I think he is a scientist. And very concerned with secrecy."

"Keeping the secrets of the Great Shaman . . . or the Great Shaman Corporation." I exhaled deeply and said nothing, although I had some ideas.

Rebecca propped herself up on an elbow. "But I made him — them — promise that I could communicate with you by e-mail. And we did write each other, until you stopped writing."

"I didn't stop writing. You did. Or you tried to, anyway."

"What?" Rebecca shifted in the hammock so she could look me in the eyes. I looked in her eyes, too. With our faces so close, she seemed to have four eyes.

"You wrote back telling me that I was trying to control our relationship, and that it wasn't possible to write any more."

"I didn't write that!"

"Well, someone sure as hell did!"

The hammock swung as we tried to lift ourselves on an elbow at the same time.

"He censored it. He changed it," Rebecca exclaimed.

"Yes, either he or his organization did it . . . an organization that we know nothing about."

"Maybe they thought there was a good reason. But still, it wasn't right."

It was good that I'd brought the .45. It might come in handy if we had to void the promises that Rebecca and I had made. But just then, I kept calm for Rebecca's sake. "I guess that this Great Shaman figures that deception is justified when big money is at stake."

"When the future of the Yanomama People is at stake," Rebecca added.

"Okay. But where is this Great Shaman, right now?"

"Away. But he's supposed to come back, soon." Rebecca relaxed into the hammock and hugged me. "I'm so glad you're here, but you shouldn't have come for me."

"Well, maybe I could have stayed in Miami after getting the false e-mail about being controlling. But I couldn't stay after getting your last one."

"What did that one say?"

"Well, first I wrote you that your cousin Irene just had a baby."

The hammock rocked.

"But I don't have any cousin Irene! I don't have any cousin at all."

"Right. But the answer I got back was you were delighted and give them both a hug and kiss."

"Burr! That's not fair. They had no right to do that."

"And that's why I set out to find you, darling."

Rebecca took a minute before answering. She didn't answer with words. She answered with a kiss — a very long one. And it would have lasted much longer if we hadn't gotten a visit. It was Owani, bathing us with a crinkly smile. "You two are so much in love. You should go into the forest together."

We promised we would. But we didn't. The hammock was

so comfortable and my body was so tired. And my chest was sore.

After Owani left, Rebecca told me about her. "She was once married to an English anthropologist. He tried to bring her back to England."

"I know. She told me some about it last night."

"It didn't work out, and she came back here — with diabetes. It must have been a reaction to the Western diet, because diabetes is unknown to the Yanomami. Diabetes is why she has had to stay at the Mission."

"Yes, I saw her pulling her insulin out from the priest's refrigerator . . . which is cold only a fraction of the time."

"That's where you can make a difference, Ben, if you want to. You could find some way to keep insulin in the tropics without refrigeration."

I had shifted my gaze to the *shabono*. Half the hammocks were occupied and many hearth fires were vacated. "Do we even know if she's insulin-dependent? She looked pretty good on the trail these last two days."

"No, we don't know. I just have this information secondhand — from her. The insulin is from the Brazilian Army doctor who comes to the Mission once a year. Maybe she could be controlled by oral hypoglycemics. I wish I could do a lab workup on her." Rebecca sighed, then relaxed in my arms. "Ben, I'm so glad you are here with me."

"I am, too." I relaxed, letting my head sink into the scratchy hemp fiber.

Slowly, Rebecca's naked body dissolved against mine. I wouldn't be able to ask her any more questions that night. Slowly, the *shabono* fell silent and the hearth fires shortened and transformed into glowing red holes in the ground. Forest noises came out like stars after a setting sun. And between our thatch eve and the tree line, a patch of sky was visible. It was full of bright stars — the same stars that we had seen outside the bright lights of Miami, but shifted 25 degrees northward. We were a world away from Miami. Although my body was tired, my brain was restless. I searched the stars for familiar constellations — connections between stars. If you can connect the dots you can draw a picture.

The last several weeks had given me many dots to connect:

the DEA interview, the veil of secrecy Michael had hung between me and his clients, the near-deadly incident at the anthropology conference, Edith Pratt's ungrateful behavior afterwards, the spontaneous visits from Nica, the strange story of Dr. Jekyll and Mr. Hyde as told by Michael Malencik, my strange findings at the Xantha Corporation's website, the surveillance van, the break-in, the strange calls and the ugly way it ended between Nica and me. Could I connect any of these dots to what I had just learned?

I relaxed my body against Rebecca and the coarse hammock. A strong wisp of smoke drifted from a neighboring hearth. My thoughts turned to the strange spirits that lived on this continent — the transiently ischemic priest, the swashbuckling German pilot, and the Dutch photojournalist who had followed me to the Mission, seeking a human interest story. And the latitude/longitude coordinate on the tribesman's survey machine. Could I connect these dots any better than the ones from North America?

I didn't.

Maybe if I had written it all down and had examined it under the light of day, I might have made sense out of it. But I wasn't sitting at my well-lit desk in Miami. I was hanging in a hammock, giving warmth to my naked loved one, communing with her, feeling the beat of her heart and the depth of each breath. We were succumbing to sleep. And like the smoke, my thoughts diffused into the forest.

I felt secure. I had found my lost lover and still had my GPS, my satellite phone . . . and my .45.

27   Open-House

At dawn, Rebecca awakened me with a kiss. She was already out of the hammock. Tucked under one arm was her chemistry equipment. Slung over her shoulder was a net filled with bananas and manioc roots.

"I'm going to work today. I'll be back around sundown. Left

you lunch and dinner." She pointed to a net like her own hanging directly above my head. I must have grimaced. "If you have to eat your canned sardines, take them into the woods. Otherwise you'll have to share them with the whole tribe. First Son's Wife will feed us tonight, just like last night. They are glad to because I am working for the tribe."

"All right," I said with a big yawn. "I'll just stick around and make myself useful here around the *shabono*."

"And remember our agreement. Stay away from the Technical Center by the garden."

"Yes, sir!"

Rebecca left to join three tribesmen waiting at the edge of the *shabono*. They walked away through the morning mist and disappeared into the green wall of forest. I dozed off for a while, reliving last night's dreams. Finally, hunger and children's voices awakened me. It didn't require too great a stretch to pull down the web net from the thatch of the ceiling. My breakfast in bed consisted of two small bananas and several slices of dried plantains, strung like figs. I washed it down with water from the pig stomach hanging from a secondary beam.

When nature called, I made my way some 50 yards into the forest where I found the communal WCs — potty chairs fashioned from sticks and woven reed. Each sat over a shallow pit and had a hinged lid to keep the flies away between visits. The one I picked bore my weight okay, but the layout was unisex and the protocol was first-come-first served. I kept my eyes averted from my *shabono*-mates and spent my potty minutes pondering a question: Was this the new Yanomama style or was it the invention of the Great Shaman?

I decided to put off work on connecting the dots until that evening. I could learn a lot around the *shabono* and would have a new set of questions for Rebecca when she returned.

Back at the hearth, First Son's Wife was nice to me. We could communicate some with gestures and it pleased her to see me playing with her two-year-old son again. Her five-year-old son was mostly off with his friends in the forest. Every once in a while, he came back with a bug, leaf or flower that he would show to his mom. He made a big deal of inspecting it under a plastic magnifying glass that hung from his neck. She told him the name and he repeated it, then went running off for his next find. All of the younger children around the *shabono* had a magnifying glass hanging as a necklace. Forest exploration seemed to be a big part of their play. Older boys seemed to be more into archery and spear throwing in the clearing. And as many times as I held my breath, not once did I see a little kid endangered by a big kid's arrow.

When I walked out into the clearing, I collected an entourage of kids, aged four to eight, who talked to me incessantly and amused themselves by emulating my karate moves. I looked back at the *shabono* and counted about three dozen hearths. What an interesting social arrangement: three dozen extended families with father, mother, children and sometimes grandparents; three dozen nuclear families who had arranged themselves by kinship and lineage. All of that under one thatched roof! And everywhere I looked, it seemed to be functioning, with women at work and children at play.

I studied the layout carefully. No, this *shabono* was not one that I'd flown over. Either it wasn't on my map, or it was the seventh, which Klaus didn't have the gas to fly to. When I had a chance, I would make a GPS reading and locate it on my map.

This *shabono* was larger than the others and it had a different layout. Its courtyard was crisscrossed with the stems of vines which hung from the nearby trees to a large maypole in the center of the clearing. The vines were not alive, and I wondered why the tribe had gone to so much trouble to hang them there.

A bunch of kids invited me to follow them into the forest. They showed me plants and had a lot of fun teaching me their names. It was a strange feeling, learning things without writing them down. A couple of hundred yards from the *shabono* was a small stream where the women fetched water and washed their cooking utensils. The adolescent girls among them tittered when I came near. And my boy guides laughed like we were playing a big joke. We moved on along a forest path. After several minutes we came to a large clearing. One of the boys pointed to it and said, "*Hikari täkä.*"

The clearing was substantially larger than a football field and was filled with fallen trees. The boys scampered over the trunks, jumping from one to another and never stepping on the ground between them. I followed. One of the boys pointed, with an expression of pride, to a trapezoidal area between four trunks. Then it became clear: This was the tribe's produce garden and this small section was the plot owned by the boy's family. I sat on the log beside him while he showed me more plants and named then. With memory of my bedtime reading plus concentration, I was able to see this motley array of plants as something other than a patch of weeds. In the soil, under a cluster of stringy leaves, I could see a fleck of the purple. It was the skin of a cara potato. And at the base of a green stalk, I recognized a manioc root. It could be boiled and eaten whole like what Rebecca had left me for lunch. Or it could also be ground to make the flour called farinha.

On the edge of the clearing were palm trees, none of which bore coconuts. Their fruit was orange-red with a leathery skin that looked like a hand grenade. Another type of palm was covered with thorns. A woman was digging around a fallen palm and collecting grubs. Other women were scattered around the clearing, weeding their plots and selecting plants for tonight's dinner.

Like a Canadian log roller, I jumped from one log to another, making my way across the clearing. In the center stood the trunks of two tall trees that were stripped of their branches. They stood straight, about 70 feet apart and 40 feet high. At their peaks was a curious arrangement: an inverted triangle formed by a thin rope that was attached to the top of each tree. The triangle's low point was formed by the weight of an elongated canvas bag. The rope was attached to two metal rods which projected horizontally from the peak of each tree. A red scarf hung from the top of one of the trees, fluttering slightly in a light breeze. Was that their idea of a scarecrow? When I asked one of the kids, he walked along a log, growling and dipping then raising his hand. This seemed to amuse an Indian man who was standing with bow and arrow near the base of one of the trees. What was he doing? Waiting for birds to shoot for dinner?

Another curious feature of the garden caught my eye. At the edge of the forest, on the far side, was a large green disk. Surrounded by juvenile palms, it hadn't been plainly visible. But as I approached, it was clearly a satellite dish. And it wasn't just one of those little dish antennas for satellite TV. This one must have been 12 feet in diameter — the type that you see around TV stations, the type that can pull down a signal from a geostationary satellite and send up a signal, too. So the Great Shaman Corporation had a satellite uplink for its scientific field work.

I made my way to the base of the dish and followed its cables along the ground and into the forest. Only one of the boys followed me. So the area was taboo. Well, nobody told me where the Technical Center was, so what was to keep me from blundering into it? A few minutes into the forest, I picked up a hum. As I followed the cables snaking through the forest, the hum became louder and recognizable as a stationary motor — a generator. A few minutes more and I came to the origin of the wires: a prefabricated sheet metal building that resembled a large house trailer. Its windows were small and were outfitted with vertical blinds which obscured any view of the building's interior. Through-the-wall air conditioners whined and dripped water onto mossy pads that had formed on the ground below them. Nestled between the trees, the building rested on piles, mortared stones and on the stumps of trees which had been cut down to make room for it.

Nobody could blame me for lingering a couple of minutes to get a look at the setup. The generator was probably 50-some yards on the far side. Power lines projected from a mast on the building's roof and were strung to the trees behind it. Another set of lines projected from the side of the building and went straight up, ending in a collection of antennas mounted on the top of a tree. This would be their wireless communication with their field parties.

My speculation was cut short when the door opened and a man came out. He was a Yanomama Indian. With an amazingly fluid combination of a jump, run and walk, he closed the distance between us faster than I could compose myself.

"You promised to stay away from the Technical Center, Ben."

Having been forewarned by Rebecca, this wasn't a complete surprise. But it was strange how he was talking like he knew me. And it seemed strange that he was speaking to me in fluent American English.

"I'm sorry. I saw the children playing by the garden and then I heard the motor and wandered over here."

He was about my age and size. His body bore neither paint nor puncture marks. His black hair hung like a thatch, but it was not in the typical Yanomama bowl cut. With his high cheek bones and dusky skin, there was no doubt that he was one of the clan.

But he had the speech and demeanor of a California surfer boy. And he was dressed like one, too, in shorts and an open floral-print shirt.

Then he surprised me. He turned towards a boy who was lingering a stone's throw away, put on a fierce look and chased him off with a string of angry gutturals. He followed that up with something that sounded like an instruction. Then he resumed talking to me like he was guarding the door at a fraternity party.

"Look, Ben," he said in a scolding tone, "before Owani took you here, you promised to follow Rebecca's instructions. And Rebecca told you to stay away from the Technical Center. But here you are, spying on us."

It was hard to look him in the eye while answering him. "She didn't tell me where it was so I could stay away from it."

"But you know now. Stay away from the garden and from everything on this side of it."

"Okay. I'm sorry."

"And behave yourself while you are here. Be a good guest and don't make us any more trouble. And one more thing. It was pretty dumb, that stunt you pulled with my brother last night. He could have hurt you badly. He hasn't learned to think in the new ways."

"I think he and I understand each other now. I'm planning to hang out with the children . . . and learn your language and the ways of the forest."

"That's good. But don't you go around trying to learn our science. And you'd better not try to leave before we give you permission, or my brother and his men will hunt you down like a peccary."

As he said those last words, his face turned savage. How mercurial!

"Hunted down like a peccary," I repeated. "Yes, I've heard that before."

"Then believe it." He delivered orders like a *sensi* to his karate cult.

"I'll keep the rules. I understand that it's important to keep the secrets of the Great Shaman." I suppressed a wisecrack about the Great Shaman Corporation. It would be better to take a soft, submissive approach to this guy. I smiled. "You speak excellent English."

He smiled back. "I studied at an American university."

"Cool. I went to Swarthmore. Where'd you go? What was your major?"

"Can't tell you now." His look told me I'd gone too far.

The trailer door opened and another guy poked his head out — non-Indian, possibly Chinese and about my age. My conversation partner noticed this and yelled to him, "I'll be right back, Ken." Then he said to me, "You've got to leave, now. And don't ever come back here. And stay away from the garden. I'll see you tonight at the *shabono*."

"Good. What do I call you?"

"Call me 'Second Son of Headman.'"

My bedtime reading had already taught me that name etiquette is a complicated deal with the Yanomama. So I let it go at that. I waved goodbye and walked back in the direction from which I came.

Making a beeline back to the *shabono* would have taken me straight through the garden. Instead, I made an honest effort to keep away from it, staying ten yards inside the forest. But that didn't keep me from witnessing a very interesting event. It started with the distant hum of a propeller airplane. Curiosity drew me to the edge of clearing where I'd have a chance of seeing it. As I lingered there, the engine noise got louder. The plane overflew the field at about three times treetop level. I'd seen this plane before — its large, rounded fuselage with boat-like bottom, its tapered rear, its high wings, each with pylon-mounted pontoons, and its cowled motor mounted on a pylon high above the wing. And, yes, "Amazon Touristic" was written on the side. I had to resist the impulse to run out and wave at Klaus-Dietrich — German flyboy and Indian counter. In the middle of the garden, in clear view, were Indians for him to count: one man, a scattering of women and a handful of children.

The pass lasted only a couple of seconds. As the engine sounded more and more distant, I walked back into the forest. But when my ears detected a change in pitch and the sounds started getting louder again, I rushed back to the clearing's edge. Got there in a nick of time. The Lake Amphibian was coming in low and slow, and it was trailing something behind. It looked like Klaus was going to fly between the two stripped-off trees in the center of the garden. But the space between them was filled with that inverted triangle of rope holding the canvas bag. Then I saw what was going on: He was trailing a hook at the end of 30 yards of rope. It hung low.

It was his grappling anchor. As he flew over the two tree trunks, the anchor swept through the middle of the rope triangle, collapsing it into a straight line. The canvas bag was jerked high into the air. Immediately, Klaus applied power and sent the plane into a steep climb. The bag cleared the treetops over my head with several dozen yards to spare. The plane roared off and did not return.

Ingenious! It was like an on-the-fly mail pickup from the old days of steam locomotives. I remembered the canvas bag and the winch setup that Jos was so interested in when he sat in the back of the plane when we went hunting for Rebecca. But it wasn't a mail sack that Klaus-Dietrich had just picked up. It would be a bag full of biological samples. Klaus would winch in the canvas bag and deliver it to a laboratory.

So there! I had learned something more about the Great Shaman Corporation already. Klaus-Dietrich ran a courier service for them, picking up small vials of leaf extracts from plants that tested positive for pharmacological activity uncovered by the bioprospecting team's biochip readers. I guessed that Klaus-Dietrich would deliver the samples to a lab with HPLC and GC mass spectroscopy machines capable of figuring out the actual structure of those small, sturdy molecules with drug activity. If this operation was as successful as it looked, it would have serious impact on the pharmaceutical industry.

I sat down and started to work on my connect-the-dots project. Then I remembered that I wasn't supposed to be here. I hurried back to the *shabono* and ate a quick lunch. Then I fell into watching an archery contest that a group of teenage boys was holding on one side of the clearing. Their target was a crude basket made of palm fronds. They had two types of contest: one against a stationary target, and another against a moving target pulled by a line. Surprisingly, most of them were better at hitting the moving target than the stationary one. In one fluid movement, a boy would lift his bow, lay in an arrow, draw it back, and loosen it on the target. Their bows were as long as I was tall. Their arrows were almost as long. As soon as they noticed me watching, they invited me over to have a look.

One of the older boys handed me his bow. It was made from a very tough, dense and resilient wood which was worked to a perfect surface and stained with tree bark. The hand grip was made from a pig jaw. The bowstring was made from fibers of long strips of tree bark, twisted around each other. I expressed my appreciation and handed it back to him. The other boys showed me theirs. Every bow was customized by its owner with bird feathers, leather windings and even inlaid stones. I guess that's the way they show class.

The older boy handed me his bow again, indicating I was to try it out. It had a 60-pound draw. The length of the arrow made it easy to aim at the basket. Feathers were inserted in its notch to keep its course true. I almost hit the basket at 30 yards on my first try. I retrieved the arrow and examined it. The arrow was tipped with a removable palm wood point. My new friend noticed me inspecting it. He reached into a gourd that hung from his shoulder on a leather strap. He extracted another tip. This one had several circumferential groves, each a millimeter or two deep. He clicked a fingernail over the grooves and said, "*Mamucori*."

I repeated his word and then said, "Curare." With gestures, I gave him my understanding of how that they filled the rings with curare paste and how it dissolves in the monkey's flesh to cause paralysis that drops him out of the tree.

A half dozen adolescent girls walked by, carrying firewood and pots of water. Some of the guys got excited and started making jokes. The girls responded with negative answers and mocking laughter. It felt like being back in junior high. One of the guys concentrated on the cutest girl and made like he was shooting a blowgun into her butt. When I asked him if he had a blowgun, he ran off to the *shabono* and pulled one out of the ceiling. The thatch and beams of the ceiling are the storage trunks of the *shabono*.

Soon, our archery contest turned into a blowgun contest. From an overhanging branch, the boys suspended the basket embellished with leaves to serve as an *ersatz* monkey. And they strung up a banana to serve as a bird. The blowguns were about six feet long and shot a sharpened bamboo sliver which was wrapped with cotton thread to make an air-tight seal inside the tube. The hole was amazingly straight. I never did learn how they drilled it.

As the sun sank into the trees and more hearths were lit, the young hunters' interest began to wane. They drifted back to the hearths where evening meals were being prepared. Since Rebecca and First Son were still out, I spent the time visiting different hearths. At one, a man was playing with his newborn baby. His wife was preparing a fish. I gestured to ask if her husband shot it. She gestured "no" and showed me the net she had used. It hung from the bamboo rafter along the boundary of their area, like a privacy curtain.

In the next hearth, a mother was giving her son a haircut. She used a blade of razor grass wrapped around her index finger. She cut and scraped away all the hair on the lower half of his head, sculpting him to look like Moe in the Three Stooges.

When I smiled in admiration of her skill as a barber, she put down her work and approached me. She spread the open halves of my safari shirt and inspected my curly black chest hairs. In mock exclamation, she described this masculine attribute loud enough for everyone to hear. Soon, the *shabono* was awash in waves of call and response from the womenfolk. I joked with the woman for a minute or two before returning to my own hearth. There, First Son's Wife insisted on pursuing the subject in depth. I allowed her a short glance and then quickly changed the subject to "what's for dinner."

Thus we made small talk in sign language for about half an hour until her husband and Rebecca came home. Darkness had set in. We ate dinner with them and their kids. Rebecca said it had been a productive day. I told her about playing with the kids and competing with the archers. Rebecca said that her group would not be bioprospecting tomorrow. First Son would be leading a party to patrol the perimeter of their territory. I proposed to go romping with the teenagers and maybe one of them would show me how to make a bow and arrow. Rebecca interpreted that for our hosts. In a not very friendly way, First Son said that staying with the boys would be the right thing for me. I smiled back at him and said that everyone has to start at the bottom.

After we had finished eating, Owani came over from Headman's hearth and said some words that made Rebecca and First Son's Wife laugh. Then she turned to me and said, "I told Rebecca that she should eat more or you will find her too skinny." She winked an eye. "And I told her that she was spending too much time in the woods looking for plants and not enough time in the woods with you."

"I agree," I replied. And grabbing Rebecca by the shoulders, I said, "And I think it is time to do something about it."

Rebecca giggled as I lead her off. Judging from the reactions of the people around us, the whole *shabono* knew that we were going for a walk in the woods.

By now the forest was quite dark. But that didn't stop us from finding a good spot. It was a joyous reunion on that forest floor. At the moment of rapture, my retina played tricks on me and the black forest seemed to come alive with a million points of light. And afterwards, our little patch of forest seemed to be aglow with the diffuse light of one hundred fireflies. Time seemed to stand still. I could have held my Little Shaman Woman in my arms there forever. But Rebecca hadn't lost her sense of time.

"We'd better be getting back, Ben, or we'll be missed."

"No we won't. Let's stay here a bit longer."

"No, Ben. Think of my position in the tribe."

"That Little Shaman Woman loves her Fall-Off-The-Trail Ben so much that she's in danger of losing her magical powers?"

Rebecca tried to shake loose.

I pushed the glow button on my watch. Its soft green light cast interesting shadows on blue-dyed skin around Rebecca's neck and gave her face an exotic look. "Now listen here, my enchanting Little Shaman Woman. My liquid-crystal-photodiode firefly says that it is only eight thirty-six. That's only twenty short minutes from the time we walked out on the party."

"So?" she asked, with teasing inflection.

"So what's going to happen with *my* status in the tribe? Am I going to become 'He-Who-Falls-Off-The-Trail-And-Can-Please-Woman-For-Only-Twenty-Minutes'?"

"Well, I'm sure they aren't all watching a clock."

I had to laugh. "I'm sure they are counting burnt-out embers, the number of times Headman has coughed, the position of the moon, rotation of the stars and every other damn thing they have to measure time."

"Don't be paranoid. I just think it's time for me to get . . . mmm . . . . Maybe we *could* . . . Ben! What are you doing?"

"Anointing myself with the protective essence of our love."

"Ben, you crazy —"

"Salving my wounded chest. Setting up a chemical shield to

repel the local maidens and bored Yanomama mamas who seem to be very interested in my chest hairs."

Rebecca laughed. "Ben, you can be so crazy!"

I grabbed her up by the shoulders again. "Okay, my Mount-Venus-shaven, mini-loin-cloth-wearing Shaman Woman and seductress, you're ready to return to the party. And I'm ready, too." I lead her by the hand.

And yes, our return was met with a strong mix of cheers and catcalls. I might have been responsible for some of them myself because I left my shirt unbuttoned.

But speculation about Rebecca and Ben had not been the only entertainment during our absence. Headman had set up a shortwave radio on a steamer trunk by his hearth and was talking to other Yanomama tribes. He had told them our news of the week and was giving individuals a chance to send news to their relatives. And the answers that came back were played on a loudspeaker for all to hear. Sometimes the whole *shabono* cheered; sometimes they sighed. And from the tones and frequent overlaps of the answering voices, it was clear that this was more than a two-way conversation. It was a party line conversation, with many tribes taking part. It was amazing what people could do with a solar collector, a lead-acid battery and one thousand bucks worth of radio.

After listening awhile and watching the faces of my fellow tribesmen, my perceptions shifted: The angry-sounding gutturals and foreign-sounding palatal stops and clicks transformed into a language with a rich vocabulary of human emotion.

Headman clicked off the loudspeaker, held up a set of earphones and spoke to the *shabono* in fatherly tones. At the far end of the *shabono*, a middle-aged woman stood up, tentatively at first. Then, by the encouragement of Headman and her neighbors, she was coaxed to the microphone. Her eyes glistened in the firelight. She spoke into the microphone with a sorrowful voice.

Owani caught my eye and explained it to me in a stage whisper. "She is speaking to her brother who is a member of a distant tribe the one in which she grew up. She is saying that she misses him every day and that she hopes that she could see him next year. She says that she has never seen his sons and his grandchildren and that she wants to see them before . . . they grow up and before she . . . turns into a frail old woman."

As the message became more personal, Owani made her way to me until she was finally whispering her translation in my ear.

"She says that when her brother comes to see her, she wants him to bring her father's ashes for her to drink. She is glad that the tribes are living in harmony and that the Great Shaman brought us the radio so that we can talk to each other because she is so lonely."

Finally, the woman was sobbing into the microphone. A little circle of friends lent her support and helped her to find the words to say goodbye.

I had to swallow hard to keep my own composure. Headman held the microphone and asked for the next volunteer. A young woman came with a baby on her hip.

I turned to Owani, whose eyes were also glistening. "It's nice that the tribe can use the shortwave for personal communication."

"Yes, but it has other uses, too. We use it for security. We compare notes. If a tribe's patrol discovers rubber tappers or *garimpeiros*, they will use the shortwave to report it."

"Do the other tribes know what your tribe is doing with the scientific instruments?"

"Not exactly. Some know that we are studying the forest. Not everyone in our own tribe knows exactly what we are doing. Old minds work differently than young minds. Every member has a different understanding."

"Who among you has the best understanding?"

"Headman's Second Son. He is the only tribal member who knows how to run all the machines in the Technical Center. He and his wife, Kurn, work with Ken Lee."

"Is she a Yanomama?"

"Yes."

"Do they have a hearth in the *shabono*?"

"Yes, but they do not use it every night. She is working hard to perfect her English. She is taking correspondence courses in business administration. She does not have time for traditional women's work. She studies by day and they sleep in a screened room by the Technical Center."

That was as many pointed questions as I could ask Owani in one conversation. We went on to talk about bows, arrows, blowguns and the natural curiosity of children. Finally, she returned to Headman's hearth. Rebecca was in conversation with First Son's Wife. I rolled into our hammock and listened to the shortwave radio transmissions and murmur of conversation across the *shabono*. Slowly, I let my mind replay the events of the day and play another round of "Connect the Dots."

A few moments later I was taken by surprise. The whole *shabono* let out a tremendous whoop. I looked around and saw Headman standing, holding high the microphone. He said a couple of words into it, put it down, and turned off the set. I didn't need Owani to translate this for me: "Headman and his *shabono* signing off until next time."

Second Son put the radio away. He was dressed like a Yanomama for the evening. As my thoughts were slipping back to the unconnected dots, he came over and rocked my hammock. "I'm inviting you to my hearth to talk with some young people who want to know about life outside the forest."

"Okay," I said, lazily.

Second Son yelled out an announcement to the whole *shabono*. I could guess what he was saying: "Now hear this: We're going to have fun and games with Ben Candidi."

His announcement drew quite a crowd. He had me stand in the clearing in front of his hearth and people sat around me in a semicircle. Second Son was not as fearsome as his older brother, but he had enough command presence to make everyone sit down and shut up. "Now, they will ask you their questions," he said to me.

One of the teenage archers said something fast and sassy. A lot of people laughed. Second Son shook his fist in the kid's face, making him flinch.

"What did he ask?" I hollered, as loud and formidable as I could.

"He asks if you fall off the trail."

"Tell him, yes, I sometimes fall off the trail. But tell him that I have also strapped large, broad bows onto special shoes and have run down the snowy slopes of steep mountains faster than a jaguar."

Second Son used many words and gestures to describe the sport of skiing. And our answer seemed to put an end to sassy questions from the teenagers.

Next came a question from an adult clansman who sat with his wife and two children: "How many neighbors do you have?"

I answered, "About twelve that I can see from the front of my house."

"Tell me about them."

"The one who lives next to me used to fly an airplane. The woman who lives across from me works with books in a library. The ones next to her are two men. I do not know what they do. I do not know the ones on the other side of the book woman. And the rest of my neighbors? I do not know very well at all."

The man shook his head and beat his knee with his fist. Second Son interpreted. "He says he cannot understand how a man cannot know his neighbors. Do you sit before your house with your eyes shut?"

"No, I work inside my house. The others go to far places every day to work."

"What things do you make in your house?"

"I work with information on drugs like your *mamucori*." The man seemed to understand this as it was translated, so I continued. "When I give this information to other people, they give me money. Money is like trade goods — like machetes and beads. When I do work to get money, I use it to get my food, to pay for my house, my books and for the airplane that takes me where I can ski down the side of the mountain."

I answered questions about money and told them how it lets you trade things with people you do not know.

An old man asked a very interesting question: "When I was a young boy, the priest at the Mission told us that money was bad. He said that it made us do evil things. Is this true?"

"That is sometimes true. People must never forget that money is what you earn from doing honest work. It is easy to forget that fact. It is easy to tell lies to trick people out of their money. And some people will attack others to take away their money. Yes, the trouble with money is that it makes it easier to do bad things."

"The priest said that love of money can be bad like love of ebene."

"That can be true. There are some people who spend all their time finding ways to get more money faster and faster. For those people, money is like ebene. They are like people who shoot more animals than they can eat and do not share meat with their neighbors."

A young boy asked the last question: "How did you learn to turn so fast and fight crazy? How did you learn to kick so high without falling down?"

"When I was a little older than you, some bad boys in my neighborhood chased me and beat me. I paid money to a man — an old warrior from Korea — to teach me how to fight like this. After I learned my crazy fighting, the bad boys left me alone."

"Did you use your crazy fighting to attack the bad boys and hurt them?"

"No."

"Why not? They attacked you."

"I didn't hurt the bad boys because the priest taught me about a man called Jesus." I thought of my parish priest and of the Italian priest lying in the Mission. "Jesus taught that it is bad to keep on fighting and remembering the bad things people have done. Remembering bad things just makes more fighting."

The young boy asked if I could teach the *shabono* my crazy fighting. I said I'd have to ask Headman for permission. The boy asked about Korea, the place that the old warrior came from.

I turned to Second Son. "Did the Great Shaman Project give the people maps of the world?"

"No," he replied.

I turned back to my audience and wound myself up for a hand-waving explanation. "If you walk north from here as fast as you can . . . If you do this for every day and do this for a whole year, you will come to a place where it is very cold. The air is cold and the ground is frozen solid in the summer and is covered with snow in the winter. And if you make a boat with animal skins and row westward for weeks and weeks over a big river that we call an ocean, you will come to more frozen land."

I slowed my pace to let Second Son catch up. His words were triggering questions from some and nods of affirmation from others.

"And if you will walk south for six moons, you will come to the land of Korea. And that is where this fighting man was from."

"Did the man have to come over the frozen land to get to you?"

"No, he came on an airplane that took one day. But a long, long, long time ago, before there were any people living here, your ancestors did come from that distant land — Korea or China or Russia. That was thirteen thousand years ago, in the time of your grandfather's grandfather's grandfather — I'll have to keep saying "grandfather" until the fires die out, because that's how long ago it was. In this long time ago, your people came from that faraway land to the land of the Yanomama. We know that because your people dropped tools along the way. We also know that because it is a part of the teachings of your elders, like Headman."

I left it at that. The *shabono* remained silent. I thanked them for their questions. I made a short karate bow in the direction of Headman who had been listening carefully the whole time. I bowed to Second Son. Then I said I was tired and wanted to return to my hammock.

Rebecca was beaming. "Ben, you were magnificent! You surprised me. You have such an expansive mind."

First Son's Wife was enthusiastic, too, but her husband was asleep in his hammock. Rebecca said he wasn't insulting me. He needed sleep because he was going out on a dawn patrol. I climbed into the hammock. Rebecca climbed in after me, putting us side by side but head to foot. That was a good choice because I had a few things to discuss with her, face to face.

"Rebecca, I'd feel a lot more comfortable here if I knew more about this Great Shaman."

Her brow wrinkled. "Okay."

"I really need to know whether he comes from Brazil or from the United States, or from somewhere else."

"Okay, I'll find out."

"And what does he look like? And does he travel to other countries like the United States?"

"I'll try to find out from Owani. But she's been very secretive about this when I asked her before."

"Good. My most important question is what this person looks like. It may seem silly, but it could be very important. And if Owani won't tell you, ask the children. Ask if the Great Shaman is an Indian. If not, try to find out the skin color. Could it be white? And ask about hair color. Dark, blond or red? Could it be a woman rather than a man?"

"Aye aye, sir."

I caressed her leg and gazed across the *shabono*. Some more questions needed answers. "What can you tell me about Second Son?"

"He isn't very talkative, even when we bring back good results. He's a whiz with the equipment and the electronics."

"He talks like a California surfer boy. Could you find out if he went to college there?" I figured that the organization which paid for his education would also be the one running the show around here.

"Why do you need to know where he went to college?" Rebecca asked.

"I'm trying to get a grip on who composed the nasty e-mail about 'controlling our relationship.'"

"I agree. That was mean. We need to know who did that."

I was glad to hear her saying that. To whom, actually, had she made the promise of secrecy and allegiance? If the party remained unidentified, we could probably void the promise.

Thinking about the nasty e-mail made me irritated. I repeated it to her, word for word. "The language was pure California psychobabble," I said.

"I don't think that Second Son is into psychobabble, as you call it. And I don't see why you would think that's just California where they talk about one partner trying to control another in a relationship. That's a problem all over the country."

"Sure, you're right," I said quickly, with irritation. "Just as likely that it was a PC surfer girl in Baltimore as a surfer boy in California."

There might be some insight in that sarcastic thought. When I went back to Connecting The Dots, I'd have to remember that some dots were more mean spirited than others.

Rebecca fell silent, too. She hadn't asked what I meant by PC but I could see the wheels turning. "I see where you're going with this and I agree. It's not fair of him — them — to make me keep their secrets and then forge my e-mails. If they aren't playing fair with us, that could change everything. I'll see what I can find out."

Then it occurred to me what had seemed familiar about the format of the latitude/longitude numbers I'd seen yesterday on their hand-held computer.

"And if you can find out the name of the corporation that donated the equipment, could you tell me? You might find the answer inside your hand-held computer."

"Ben, you promised not to pry into their science."

"All I need is a name. You know that I have certain duties to my client back in Miami. It would help me to draw the line."

"I'll see what I can learn."

We fell silent again. I thought about telling Rebecca about my frustrations with the mysterious Michael Malencik: his Dr. Jekyll and Mr. Hyde companies and his sudden interest in the Xantha Corporation of Mountain View, California, the company with a trove of strangely formatted "spectroscopy" data. But then I'd have to tell her about the break-in, the surveillance van and the DEA visit, too. And, while I was at it, I would have to tell her about the curious visits from Nica and the calls from the phony Palo Alto journalist played by a true detective from Mountain View. And while on that subject, I'd have to tell Rebecca that an equally phony Dr. James Woodruff was doing detective work on her by calling from the cafeteria at the National Institutes of Health in Bethesda, Maryland. And my stories from home would not be complete without a full report on my heroics at the Knight Center and the elusive behavior of an ungrateful swine named Edith Pratt — from Baltimore, Maryland. No, it was too late in the evening to discuss everything.

The *shabono* was quiet except for random pronouncements from different tribesmen. They were never very long. And they always started with the same words like, "Now listen to me." Sometimes a tribesman would respond, but just as often there was no echo at all. It was so pleasantly informal. I looked across the steamer trunks at sleeping Headman and then over to First Son sleeping near us. "I notice that First Son and Second Son aren't very close."

"True. Headman is proud of them both, but they say Second Son is the bringer of the new ways and that First Son is the keeper of the old ways."

"Yeah, he never got to go to college." That wasn't a nice comment but my chest still hurt. Another thought crossed my mind. "If you wake up tomorrow morning before I do, could you tell First Son that I want to talk to him before he leaves."

"Sure, Ben."

She yawned and closed her eyes. The next time I looked at her, she was asleep. I didn't fall asleep for a long time. I went back to Connecting The Dots. I'd made good progress today, drawing solid connections between several of them: the biological samples, the off-limits Technical Center, the canvas bag and barnstorming pilot named Klaus-Dietrich. I replayed the details of my charter flight over the Mission. He didn't mind making a little extra money as long as he didn't have to fly me over this *shabono*. Did he know that Rebecca was here? Was he part of the organization's control structure or just working for them? I couldn't imagine the blustering German flyboy forging Rebecca's e-mails. Writing wasn't his forte and he wasn't mean-spirited. Heavy-handed, yes, but not mean-spirited.

I thought more about Klaus. I replayed our conversation when I'd met him in the bar at Santa Isabel, six weeks ago. Early in that conversation, he'd presented his cover story — that he was paid to fly Texas oil millionaires to their fish camps and by bureaucrats to count Indians so they wouldn't have to risk the precious tail rotors on their helicopters landing in the jungle. But later, when alcohol had loosened his tongue, he'd delivered a braying complaint about having to sit in that "shit hole" waiting for orders from "that pink swine" so he can go "hanging his tail in the jungle and hooking sausages." And now I knew that his tail was the grappling anchor and the sausages were the canvas bags full of biological samples. And I was ready to make a wild-assed guess as to the identity of "that pink swine" who gave him orders. I would go to work on that one tomorrow.

I grew tired. I looked up at the stars, thinking about constellations and how they were shifted in the sky 25 degrees from what we see in Miami. Yes, I could probably connect the dots and draw lines between two continents, spanning 25 degrees of latitude. I would soon be able to connect my equatorial experiences with what had happened 25 degrees to the north.

I descended into the forest dweller's sleep to which I was becoming accustomed — that mystical state where thoughts blended with dreams which strengthened and dampened with the flow and ebb of forest sounds and breezes. To this was added the breathing, coughing, muttering and occasional pronouncements — sometimes sleepy but often lucid — of the one hundred brethren sleeping around me. With half open eyes I slept, gazing at the stars, connecting dots and pondering a wandering star that had followed me on my equatorial journey: Jos van der Hoek, photojournalist from Amsterdam.

28   Paying the Piper

Unfortunately, First Son was gone when I awoke. So was Rebecca. With sign language, First Son's Wife told me that Rebecca had gone with Owani to help pull weeds in the garden. That was good. Maybe she could pluck some answers from Owani while she was at it.

I used the unobserved time to retrieve my pack from the steamer trunk and to take stock. I turned on the GPS, marked our position, and wrote it down. My satellite telephone was still there. Owani had not confiscated it. My big knife was there. So were my loaded .45 and two boxes of ammo. I practiced chambering rounds and reloading the magazine. I returned the equipment to my pack — high, near the zipper where I could get to it easily.

Last night's fireside chat had increased my popularity around the *shabono*; I attracted a lot of breakfast guests. Since Second Son was back at the Technical Center, I didn't have anyone to translate the questions and answers. I used sketches in the dirt to depict the North and South American continents and the Pacific Rim. I learned the Yanomama word for "day." I planted rows of sticks in the ground to illustrate generations going back in time and I paced off 13,000 years. And I answered questions about jet planes, ships, cities and countries. Maybe we could get the external organizers to download some educational television. That would really get the educational program into high gear. Hell, if everything turned out harmless, maybe I would figure on being the village schoolteacher for the next two months.

After awhile, I hooked up with the teenagers who were practicing archery in the clearing. They welcomed me into their midst and we had a great time practicing our quick draws and stationary shots. I used the opportunity to build up my vocabulary. I remembered from the ebene powder session with Owani that the Yanomama word for shaman is *shabori*. I figured that when we came to a lull in the contest, these guys could give me a physical description of the Great Shaman. I knew the Yanomama words for man and woman and I could use sign language for the rest of my question. Then Rebecca and Owani came back to the hearth and I started looking for an excuse to break off. But a few minutes later, our athletic session came to an end by itself — an abrupt end.

One boy said *shabori* without my asking him. The others stopped and shouldered their bows. Across the clearing came the Great Shaman with an entourage of one — a solitary warrior carrying a heavy pack. Headman climbed out of his hammock to render a greeting and received a loud greeting in his native language. The boys fell into tight formation and walked toward the Great Shaman to pay their respects. And I stayed put. It was better to be only an observer, right now; I would become an active participant all too soon.

All the dots were connected, now. The main question was whether Rebecca and I would fall inside or outside the constellation.

Great Shaman was a woman. The Great Woman Shaman did not seem lovable. I don't think they really loved her, either. She embraced Headman formally, then stepped back. Her gestures of acknowledgement of her adopted people reminded me of a city alderman visiting his ward. No children would hang about her legs. And no teenage boys would make fun of her, either. She asked the questions. And she received answers — gestures in the direction of the stream, gestures in the direction of the garden and Technical Center, and finally, gestures toward me. And when she did turn her heavy, khaki-clad body in my direction, I was ready for her. I knew her well. And according to my book, she owed me: I had saved her life.

Edith Pratt didn't greet me. She turned and walked up to Rebecca. Too bad we hadn't known the Great Shaman's sex or hair color last night. I would have told Rebecca about what happened at the Knight Center. It was too late for that, now. I didn't move a foot to intervene. The fundamentals were unfolding themselves now; the wrinkles could be ironed out later.

From a distance, it seemed like Rebecca was giving Pratt the deferential treatment, looking at her intently, nodding her head to apparent instructions, and occasionally looking over to Owani for approval which was not forthcoming. It really angered me to see my Rebecca Levis, M.D., reduced to the level of a ward-inexperienced third year medical student being torn apart for the sake of example by a tyrannical chief of service.

I didn't like it, but I didn't move a step. Let Edith Pratt show her true colors. And if that ungrateful reverse snob did manage to reduce Rebecca to tears, I would step in and announce that all promises were off. I would drag Rebecca off with one hand and my sardine-and-cracker laden duffel bags with the other. We would trek back to the Mission, guided by my compass and GPS. That was exactly what I was thinking when that pith-helmeted mound of khaki turned to me and issued a traffic signal to cross the *piazze*, posthaste.

I took my time walking up to Edith Pratt. Rebecca followed me with her eyes but without saying a thing. She looked at me like I was the next classmate called up to receive a tongue-lashing. I extruded my lips and tossed my head to show her that I was above it all.

Edith Pratt scowled as I closed the last couple of yards. "So, what do you have to say for yourself?" After I came to a halt, she just stared.

"Well, if all you're going to do is glare at me, maybe I should be asking *you* what you have to say for yourself. You owe me load of thanks, you know. I'm the one who stopped the bullet in Miami."

"What bullet?" Rebecca exclaimed.

"Rebecca, just chill out!" I said.

"What *were* you doing at that meeting, anyway?" Pratt asked.

"Covering it for Rebecca while she was visiting the Mission on the *Rio Marauiá*. She was one of your fans — on paper at least."

Pratt's lips parted to show both rows of teeth. They were small, short and perfectly spaced. "And now you are both here, compromising my most important project."

"Rebecca wouldn't have gotten into it if it weren't for her idealism, and for her concern for Owani's diabetes — which doesn't seem to concern you at all, even though she's Headman's sister and —"

"Shut up."

"And I wouldn't have come here if you hadn't falsified

Rebecca's e-mails. Do you think your mission is so important that you can cause people weeks of emotional anguish for their family and loved ones —"

"Oh, shush!"

"Well, well, well! One bucolic expression takes care of it all! Is that how you handle your ethics board at Johns Hopkins University?"

Her stubby toes dug deeply into the foam of her rafting sandals. She clenched her fists.

"I did it because I had to. Do you think I liked it, writing letters to you? — you moon calf! Do you understand what is at stake here? The future of the Yanomama People."

"Yeah, I guess that justifies anything — like your sending around Nica, your Brazilian stewardess to mess with my head."

Rebecca gasped. Headman was watching us carefully and Owani was speaking in his ear, obviously interpreting for him.

"And you couldn't leave her alone, could you? Couldn't keep your hands off her."

"Bullshit! She took my picture at the gate at the Manaus airport. She plunked down next to me on the flight and sounded me out with a line of idealistic crap about antibiotics in bee's wax. She wheedled my address out of me. And she showed up at my house the day after I rescued your porcine hide. And after I started getting concerned about what was happening to Rebecca, she started showing up again to give me a lot of phony assurances that everything was going to be just fine."

"And you wouldn't listen to her, would you? You had to harass her after work. You almost destroyed an important material transfer."

"Bullshit! I was cross-examining her on false information pertinent to Rebecca. And her pock-faced gumshoe drove me off with a gun. How the hell was I to know that she was carrying contraband? And who the hell gave you the right to make it okay just because you say so?"

Pratt took a step back, but she wasn't beaten. "And I'm supposed to believe that it was just a coincidence that Rebecca showed up here at the same time you started sniffing around the Xantha Corporation's website."

"Yes, it was a coincidence. Rebecca's interested in doing good in the Third World. That's one thing. And I was being paid to survey methods of drug discovery for a client. That's a separate thing."

"Drug discovery! You *are* working on drug discovery, just like Dr. Griffin suspected. You are our nemesis."

I remembered the photo in Xantha's website, the upwards-facing shot of four men standing on at the top of a cascade of stairs in front of the two-storey building. I remembered the semi-bald guy smiling down through his moustache. That was Dr. George Griffin, Vice-President for Research. And I remembered Baldie who watched over Dr. Pratt at the anthropology conference at the Knight Center. Then it clicked: Dr. Griffin and Baldie were one and the same.

It checked out, just like the numbers I'd found in the Xantha files matched the latitude and longitude that popped up on Rebecca's computer when she analyzed the plant extract. It checked out, just like the phony journalist was from the same town as the Xantha Corporation — Mountain View, California. And I wondered if the Xantha Corporation had ordered the bugging and break-in of my house after I'd stumbled into their archive of bioprospecting data. However, the situation wasn't very conducive to thinking with Edith Pratt standing in front of me like a boxer waiting for the bell.

The fight was postponed by the arrival of three tribesmen. They approached from the far edge of the clearing. First Son led the way, carrying a backpack. The second tribesman was faint and stumbling. The third was holding his comrade's bleeding arm and supporting his feeble walk. Rebecca rushed out and directed them to our hearth. They loaded the wounded man into our hammock. She dug into the steamer trunk at our hearth, looking for first aid supplies.

First Son threw down the backpack at the feet of his father who was standing close to Edith Pratt. First Son talked loudly and proudly like he was making a speech. I sidled to Owani and asked her to interpret.

"He says he found our tribesmen after it happened. Another tribesman is still out there. He helped bring these two back. The men said they were patrolling. When they were getting ready to settle down last night, they smelled smoke from a campfire. It was

already dark when they got to it. A man was standing by it — a
white man. He looked like *garimpeiro* boss. They knew he would
be danger. They crept up on him closely, in the darkness, but one
of them broke a twig and he heard it. He was crafty and evil. He
pretended not to hear them. He reached into his pack. He put on a
mask that looked like frog-eyes. He pulled out a long gun and
walked around with his back to campfire, looking through frog mask.
They ran back into the forest so he would not see them. But the frog
mask had magic. He could see in the dark and shoot at them."

"He had night vision goggles," I yelled out to anyone who
would listen.

Now the other tribesman was telling the story. Owani
interpreted:

"He could not hit us. He could not aim well. He could not look
through the telescope on the gun with his frog mask. We ran away
and he chased us. He was very good in forest at night — like a
jaguar. He was evil, like a *poré*. We went in separate directions so
he could not chase us all. I circled back and took the pack that he
left by the fire. I could not find the other pack. Maybe he was
wearing it. We used bird calls to find each other and get back
together. And we spent the night looking out.

"When the morning came we tracked him down. Ipo shot two
mamucori arrows into him. Then the *garimpeiro* shot Ipo in the
arm. The *garimpeiro* went down slowly, like a monkey. He dropped
his rifle and lay down in rocks. But Ipo was bleeding bad. I had to
get him back to the *shabono* for Little Shaman Woman to fix his
wound. I left Tachico to watch and make sure the *garimpeiro* dies
and to take his gun. I helped Ipo walk to the *shabono*. On the way
back, we met First Son."

The backpack had looked familiar and I looked through it while
the warrior was telling his story. Tucked in between 20 pounds of
provisions was a bulging envelope filled with photographs. The
first one made me shudder: a picture of me downloaded from my
website. The other photos were of Edith Pratt at the anthropology
meeting at the Knight Center wearing her "dress khaki" outfit and
surrounded by a lot of admiring people. In the background of
several Pratt photos stood Dr. George "Baldic" Griffin, smiling
through his moustache and looking very much like a panelist in an
opera quiz.

I tossed the envelope at Edith Pratt's feet and said, "You're a lucky girl. Your warriors have just foiled a *second* attempt on your life."

She grabbed up the envelope and shuffled through the pictures. And I thought about my Dutch "friend." With what I knew now, it all made sense: his laconic style; his quiet, understated air of superiority; his unstated derision for the people on the riverboat and at Santa Isabel; and his sense of ease in all situations. The only thing that made him nervous was a personal question from me. And that was because he was a mercenary — a paid killer. I wanted to kick myself for drinking his rum and believing that he would make a magazine story out of my search for Rebecca.

Edith Pratt kept staring at the photos in disbelief, saying, "No . . . no . . . it can't be."

I turned to Owani. "Ask the warrior if the *garimpeiro* is one head taller than me and has white hair."

Suddenly, Edith Pratt turned nasty. "You know him?"

"Yes. He told me he was a Dutch photojournalist for *Elsevier* magazine. He offered me his help to find Rebecca."

Owani made the inquiry and reported: "He was tall and his hair was white."

Pratt screamed at me. "We were trying to keep this quiet."

I answered, "What are you worrying about? He's dead now."

"But you led him right here."

"I had no way of knowing this was sacred ground."

"You lead him right to my doorstep."

"*Your* doorstep? Hey, I thought this was supposed to be one big, happy communal effort."

She balled her fist and took a step towards me. "You sassy little brat."

I fell back into a karate stance, arms raised. "I wouldn't have gone through hell to get here if you hadn't censored Rebecca's message."

Pratt's upper lip slid up, exposing her teeth and half an inch of gum. "You should have had more faith in your finacée, if you think yourself worthy of her."

"Well, that says it all. You can manipulate people's letters and decide who is worthy of whom. And you still haven't thanked me for saving your life. Is it too hard for you to thank a man?"

Pratt started weaving like a boxer trying to force an opening.

Rebecca abandoned her patient and ran up to us, placing herself between us. "Stop it, both of you," she commanded.

And we did stop: Several tribesmen were yelling and pointing to the sky. Then I heard it too: helicopter blades in the distance.

Pratt threw up her hands in the air and screamed. "Oh, no! The enemy is coming We are ruined. They will descend on us and destroy us."

Owani translated Pratt's words for the tribesmen.

"How do you know the helicopter isn't yours?" I asked.

"We've never had a helicopter," she snarled at me. She seemed to be vacillating between hate and the histrionics of martyrdom.

The word "enemy" had transformed the *shabono*. Men were rushing around, pulling their bows and arrows out of the roof thatch. Women were grabbing up their children.

"How do you know it isn't the Brazilian Army?"

"They have never helped us, not even during the *garimpeiro* invasion."

"Okay, suppose they *are* killers. They can't land in the clearing because of your poles and vines."

"But they can land in the garden. They can destroy the Technical Center. And they can march over here and destroy us all."

"Bullshit. You won't stay here to be slaughtered. Your people are Yanomama. They are experts close-range fighting from behind trees. Tell them to flee to the forest. Tell the warriors to ambush them on the path. They can pick them off, one by one."

The blades sounded nearer by the minute. The *shabono* was full of confusion.

"No it's hopeless. We can only stand here and die. It's all your fault. You led them to us."

I grabbed Owani's arm and dragged her to Edith Pratt. "Owani, this is your tribe. Aren't you the one who invited Edith Pratt into the tribe?"

Owani said, "Yes. She was invited by my brother and me."

I spoke to Owani, but focused on Pratt. "Now, with you as my witness, I'm going to tell this holier-than-thou, reverse-snob and self-styled candidate for martyrdom that she's got it all wrong. She should be thinking how we can defend ourselves against the people in that helicopter. Or does she think that we all have to pay with our lives because forty years ago nobody would dance with her at the high school record hop?"

This provoked a stronger reaction than I expected. Pratt made a fist and went after me. It all happened in a split second. She came in with an uppercut. Rebecca tried to throw herself between us. I deflected Pratt's punch with a twist of my arm at the elbow. And a blast of air hit me in the face. A post behind us exploded and cracked. I hit the dirt and dragged Rebecca down with me. Owani went down, too, in shock. Pratt was still standing, teetering when the second supersonic bullet came in. All in an instant, the shock blasted over our heads, and the bullet crashed through the sloping thatch roof behind us and disappeared into the forest.

I grabbed two big handfuls of Edith Pratt and dragged her down to the dirt floor.

The *shabono* was in pandemonium. Warriors crouched with bows and arrows. Women dragged their children towards the back of the *shabono*. Others were already far back, ducking under the low roof and running into the forest.

I groped in my backpack for my .45.

Pratt cried. "What can I do? I've used nothing but peaceful methods all my life. But it is only arrows against rifle bullets. It's so hopeless. And our secret is lost."

I watched in the direction the bullet came from. "Your secret was lost already. Somehow, they know about your U.S. patent applications. That's why they are coming after you. Now is the time to tell it to the world."

I saw the outline of a khaki-clad figure at the edge of the forest. I fired at him but missed. He melted into the forest.

The wounded warrior rolled out of the hammock, screaming at the top of his lungs. From the next hearth, Owani yelled me a translation. "He says it is the same white warrior that they killed. He has come back from the dead! Curare will not kill him."

"But your barbed arrows will," I answered. "Get two warriors to sneak out and flank him on both sides. Just keep him there. Kill him when you see him move."

Pratt didn't issue the order, Owani did. She spoke rapidly to First Son. With walkie-talkie, bow and a quiver full of arrows, he crawled to the back of the *shabono* and disappeared into the forest.

The helicopter blades were almost on top of us, now. I grabbed
a walkie-talkie and turned it on. "Calling Second Son and Ken
Lee at the Technical Station. Calling Technical Station."
"Second Son, here. Identify yourself."
"This is Ben Candidi. The *shabono* is under attack."
The *shabono* was mostly empty now. The helicopter appeared
over the treetops on the other side of the clearing. It was a Vietnam-
era olive-green chopper with no military markings. Through it's
open side door I could see several men armed with submachine
guns. One fired a burst at us. Someone grunted and Owani cried in
alarm. I spoke into the walkie-talkie.
"We are under attack by a helicopter full of mercenaries and
by one mercenary on the ground. They cannot land here because
of the vines strung on the center pole. They will land in the garden.
They have come to assassinate Edith Pratt and everyone else, too.
Send e-mail messages to everyone on your list saying that we are
under attack. Tell them about discovering new drugs in the rain
forest and that the mercenaries are hired by big pharmaceutical
interests that want to stop you."
"No," screamed Pratt. "We have to keep it secret."
"No," I answered. "If the world knows our story, the
mercenaries will have to stop."
I spoke into the radio again. "This is an order from Edith Pratt.
Set up automatic data streaming to Xantha. Tell them to put it on
their website. Get the digital cameras going. Photograph the attack.
Take pictures of the helicopter and mercenaries. Don't try to
attack them. Tell the warriors to attack the mercenaries when
they go into the forest. Keep broadcasting. Information will
save us. When you are through, send a shortwave message to
the *Funai* people. Tell Klaus-Dietrich to fly over here for air
surveillance."
I couldn't hear an answer from Second Son. The air was full
of exclamations in Yanomami. Thank God the men took their
walkie-talkies when they fled the *shabono*.
A helicopter rose and flew in the direction of the garden. Close
to me, I heard a man screaming in pain. Rebecca was holding him.
Owani was talking to him in Yanomami, trying to comfort him.
Rebecca tugged my elbow. "Headman is hit in the abdomen. He's
bleeding badly."

"Keep your head down," I said. "That mercenary is still out there gunning for us."

Edith Pratt was in shock, yelling that all was lost because of me.

I crawled over and grabbed her by both ears. Stared into her face. I made my argument, concluding with, "In this dense forest, a gun is no better than a bow and arrow."

Pratt finally listened. Owani listened, too. I told them how to make the mercenaries engage their warriors in the forest. Pratt would go to the garden, collecting warriors on the way. Then she would stand at the edge of the forest, cursing the mercenaries. When they pursued her, she would run into the forest where her warriors would ambush them and kill them, one by one. They could coordinate their movements with walkie-talkie.

I handed Owani my radio. She squeezed down and started giving instructions in Yanomami. Edith Pratt crawled to the back of the *shabono* and slipped into the forest. She was resolute. She would do it.

I kept looking into the forest, trying to figure out where Jos could be. I couldn't fire wildly because First Son was out there stalking him. Rebecca kept saying she was having trouble controlling Headman's bleeding. Owani kept talking into the radio. Slowly, the chaos resolved into an orderly rhythm of transmissions. I sensed martial discipline taking over. It was time for stealth warfare in the forest.

The helicopter grew softer and its blade-beat slowed. It was landing in the garden. Gradually, it grew still. The only constant noise was Headman's moaning. A shot fired in the distance, before us. It had to be Jos, fighting off First Son.

Owani interpreted the radio transmissions. "Second Son and Ken are out with cameras. The helicopter has landed in the center of the clearing." There was a long pause when we heard nothing but forest sounds and two more shots in the distance. Jos was still alive and First Son was still hunting him. "Seven men are getting out . . . Great Shaman is on the edge of the garden." I heard several shots from that direction, behind us. "They are shooting at her. She is running away. Four mercenaries are running after her . . . Three mercenaries are going in the other direction — coming to the *shabono*, coming to us."

I pulled out my magazine and replaced the expended rounds. I dug into the duffel bag and loaded the box of ammo into the pockets of my cargo pants.

Distant shots from two directions told the story: Sporadic shots from behind us told me the four mercenaries were chasing Edith Pratt through the forest. Occasional single shots in front of us told me that Jos was still fending off First Son.

Our walkie-talkie sounded and Owani interpreted. "They killed one mercenary following Great Shaman. Three mercenaries are still coming this way."

I crawled to the next hearth where Rebecca was treating Headman. "Rebecca, the bad guys are coming here. When they come, take Owani into the forest. I'll stay here and protect Headman."

"I will. Do what you have to do." She was professional and resolute, like on that night on South Beach when she'd jumped in to control that guy's bleeding. But this time it was a shot in the gut — a lot more serious.

I crawled toward the other side of the *shabono*, closer to where the mercenaries would arrive.

Owani called out the next radio transmission: "One more mercenary killed. Two are still pursuing Shaman Woman. Three are still coming toward us."

I called out to Owani, "Tell the warriors I'll start shooting bad guys where the path meets our clearing. Tell them to be careful of my bullets."

I crawled to the left crescent edge of the *shabono*. Found a good spot to cover the path, a spot that was almost in line with the path's last 25 yards. I dragged two steamer trunks to the spot and crouched behind them and practiced my aim.

Owani kept on reporting: "One more down. Only one left against Shaman Woman. He is . . . turning around. The other three are almost here!"

"Stay quiet and stay low," I yelled back.

Gunfire from the direction of the garden came in rapid bursts, now. Warriors were closing in on the last man. And I could imagine his panic. My own hands were shaking as I tried to sight the .45 down the path. Off in the distance, Jos's rifle gave off two more shots.

Before me, they came into view. Three of them. Jungle camouflage and droopy hats. Latin American faces — not Indian but not European either. Crude faces of men civilized enough to fly in helicopters and savage enough to destroy their own species. Alert faces, powerful bodies and semi-automatic rifles. If I couldn't drop all three before reloading, I probably wouldn't survive.

Lying on my stomach, my .45 pointed between the two steamer trunks, with the three men almost in a row and coming up to 30 yards, I figured my pattern. Then I did it. I aimed for the center of the first man's chest, slowly squeezing off. It kicked hard but I was able to get a piece of the second one as he raised his semi-automatic and sprayed in my direction. My third shot must have gone wild. When I tried to sight the next shot, all three were down. When I rose on a knee, a burst came in, splintering the steamer trunk on the right. I rolled to the left and came up cautiously and fired three rounds into the bushes where I thought the burst came from. I ducked before he returned fire — a burst of four that kicked dirt over me.

The rhythm of the shots told me I was probably dealing with only one man. I still had five rounds in my clip. I rolled over to the right and popped up to fire another round and almost did until I saw that my target was naked. It was a warrior, high-stepping in my direction with a raised club, treading carefully towards the spot I had been firing into. I took careful aim at the ground five yards in front of his feet, squeezed off a round, then hit the dirt.

A hail of bullets came in. I hugged the ground. And just as suddenly, the firing stopped. It took several seconds for my ears to adjust to the relative silence. There were no shots from afar and no forest noises from nearby. I heard nothing but . . . a tennis game? No, it was the sound of tennis serves — the whish of the racquet traveling through the air, the implosive thunk of the rubber ball flattening against it and the diaphragm grunt of the player delivering the serve.

My hands shook as I switched out the magazine in the .45. It took a long time to come to my senses and rise to my knees. Holding the gun before me, I looked around, cautiously. Nobody fired at me. Cautiously, I stood up and approached the source of the noise. The hardwood club rose high in the air and then swished down. Even from a distance it was plain to see that it came down with fraction-of-an-inch precision. As I drew near, its target became clear: the head of the third mercenary. The shock waves traveled mechanically from his skull all the way down to his splayed legs. But his pulped brain was incapable of generating even the most basic defensive reflexes in those limp arms lying beside the bloody body. My shot had disabled his right arm and the warrior had disabled the rest.

I went back to the other two mercenaries. The first one was lying in a pool of blood. The other had no wounds on his body except on the head. It looked like cauliflower served up in the shell of a shattered coconut and covered with catsup.

I crossed myself. The warrior ran over, let out a whoop and slapped me on the shoulder. I took a good look at him before returning the slap. He was coming down from adrenaline frenzy. It had to be frenzy to stalk three armed men with nothing but a hardwood club. I pocketed my .45, remembering to put it on safety. I walked through the splatter and I collected up the automatic rifles from the mercenaries. And I gestured to the warrior to come with me.

Rebecca had set up a little armory by the time I returned to our hearth. Next to Headman she had two bows, several quivers and a couple of blow guns and a handful of darts. "They still have one fighting near the garden, Ben."

"We got all three of them here," I replied. I turned to Owani who was crouched in the dirt next to Headman. He must have lost a quart of blood and it looked like he was slipping in and out of consciousness. "Owani, tell this warrior to go out that way and help First Son track down the white-haired mercenary. Tell him to take a bow and as many arrows as he can carry."

Owani told him and pointed the direction. The guy was still flying high on adrenaline. He ran across the clearing and disappeared into the forest.

I turned to Owani again. "And get on the radio and tell Great Shaman that we have killed the three who came to attack the *shabono*. We have their weapons. If she can spare any warriors, we need them here to secure the *shabono*. And bring any wounded here."

She started to send out the message.

We were relatively safe, now. But Rebecca was more distressed than ever. "Headman is dying from loss of blood. I don't know what to do."

"Can we find something here to stanch the bleeding?"

"The wound is too deep."

"Then you'll have to go in and tie it off."

She ran to our steamer trunk which was several steps away and started rummaging through it. "We don't have any surgical equipment. No supplies. I used up all the sterile bandages on the man with the arm wound."

"Then we'll boil my shirt. We'll rip it up for bandages and tampons. In my pack, I've got scissors, dental floss and fishing line. Got a couple of needles in my shaving kit. We can use fish hooks to hold open the incision."

She had stopped rummaging and stood up to face me. The more I said, the more hopeless she looked. "But we don't have any anesthetic. And we don't have IV fluids."

"We can get them. We can make them." I turned away from Rebecca and spoke to Owani. "Get Second Son or Ken Lee on the radio. Tell them to bring the following supplies for surgery — a spray can for cleaning circuit boards, a bunch of syringes, Millipore filters, and as much distilled water as they can carry."

"But Ben — "

I half turned, nodding to Rebecca, who was standing three arm's lengths behind me. I returned to Owani and said, "And bring sodium chloride solution if they have it."

I thrust my hands deep into my pockets and said, "If they don't have it, I have salt tablets and Gatorade." To make the point, I turned my head and threw Rebecca a brief glance.

My neck straightened my head faster than my brain could comprehend what I'd just seen over my shoulder: a big white-haired Dutchman's head atop a khaki-clad body, a couple dozen steps behind Rebecca and closing quickly in stealth movement.

No time to think.

Trying to not give myself away, I slid my hand into my cargo pocket and undid the .45's safety. Rebecca gasped. I turned clockwise to face her and stepped forward, bringing up the gun in one smooth movement ready to fire past her and hit the target. But Jos had already closed the distance and was standing behind Rebecca with a cocked .38 revolver stuck in her right ear. His left hand was holding her by the hair. Most of his face was shielded by her head.

But my gun did come up nicely at arm's length. My aim settled on his right eye. But that eye was peeking between the right side of Rebecca's head and the chamber of his revolver. I had only one square inch of target at 10 feet. And if I *did* hit the target, would his death spasm set off the gun?

"Lower your gun slowly, Ben, or your precious Rebecca will explode. And tell the old woman to put down the radio."

"Owani, put it down," I said. "And don't move." She was standing behind me, next to the supine and dying body of Headman.

Rebecca was frozen in fear, as stiff as a mannequin but emitting a little, high-pitched screech. It would be easier for me if she would faint. I tried not to look at her. I tried to focus on only two things: Watching Jos's gun hand and holding aim on his eye which was hovering under his gun's barrel. One twitch of that finger and I would pull the trigger.

"Ben, I said lower your gun slowly or Rebecca will die." He spoke so coolly.

How do you deal with a sociopath? Do they fear death? Can you reason with them? It was hard work to keep my voice steady. "I can't do that, Jos. Can't lay down my gun and still call myself a man. Can't turn a stalemate into a checkmate."

"Then she will die." His words came out in a nasty snarl, but his right hand was amazingly still. So was Rebecca. If she would only faint, her dead weight might distract him long enough to give me a good shot.

"If you kill her, Jos, I'll kill you a millisecond later. Faster than you can aim at me."

"Then that is how it must be." He sounded resigned. His eye regarded me with reptilian patience. He didn't blink. That would be my signal to shoot. He would *have* to shut his eye before squeezing the trigger or he'd be blinded from the blast of his own gun. Yes, the movement of his eyelids would be my split second's warning.

I could hear the helicopter now. It sounded like it was still on the ground but the pilot was increasing the revs. Occasional bursts of gunfire told me that the last mercenary was defending himself while making his way back to the helicopter.

"No, that isn't the only way to do it, Jos. All three of us could disengage carefully. That would leave you free to join up with your forces and assassinate Edith Pratt. Then you can ride home in the helicopter."

"No, you will call Edith Pratt here on the radio. Bring her here. This is where I will take care of her."

Behind me, to the left, Headman groaned. I sensed that Owani was still behind me, frozen.

"Too many problems with that, Jos." I expressed my disagreement in a Southwestern rhythm. It seemed to make earthy good sense. "Can't take my sights off you. What happens if a warrior makes it back here faster than Edith Pratt? They won't stand around like me, watching you hold a gun on Rebecca. They worship Rebecca." I reverted to my normal voice. "You don't want to put your fate in the hands of a *colored*, do you?"

The light blue iris dilated. His forearm tensed. "Then she will die now."

I tried to stay calm and slacken the trigger. Fell back into B-grade movie lingo. "If she dies, you die — as sure a clockwork. Now you're too smart for that, Jos. Now listen to me. None of us whites has to die — just Edith Pratt. Now here's what I say. You slowly start pointing the gun away from Rebecca and towards me. At the same time, she does a deep knee bend until she's out of the way. Then it's just you and me."

"And how is that supposed to help anything?" He stumbled through those words. He was obviously trying to think it through.

"It will help because it saves the three of us from an impossible situation. Rebecca can get me the walkie-talkie. I'll call Edith Pratt and tell her to come here but hold back the warriors."

"And then?"

"And then we get you freed up so you can get away and kill Pratt. Here's how it'll work — we will both inch our way backwards until we're farther away — far enough that we don't have a good chance of killing each other with one shot. And then we both aim our guns at the ground and I throw you the walkie-talkie. And you pick it up and back off into the forest and go after Pratt."

"I don't like it. I say the old woman must give you the walkie-talkie and you call Pratt."

"Can't do it that way, Jos," I twanged. "Too much of a distraction — like talking on the cellphone while driving. Too dangerous. And I couldn't say my part convincingly." Through my sights, I saw confusion in his eye. How to persuade him without seeming to persuade? I went back to my normal voice. "You're a tough man to survive two curare-tipped arrows. Pretty gutsy, to lie down and play dead while you're full of curare. Must have been tough, waiting for that Indian to come close so you could kill him. How'd you do it?"

"I sucked the poison out. And I always carry an auto-injector for Amazon operations. Neostigmine and atropine."

Rebecca was making a soft, high-pitched screech, but I couldn't afford to look at her.

"Good thinking, Jos. And good thinking with the night vision goggles, too. You're a real capable guy, Jos. But so am I. And I think we both understand that we're not doing ourselves any good waiting here for a hot-headed Indian to come along and — ."

The dart seemed to pop out of Jos's right eye. At the same instant his gun hand jerked upwards. The gun barrel went for the top of Rebecca's skull and she went limp and sank. I small stepped towards Jos. The instant Rebecca's head was clear, I squeezed the trigger. Jos's head jerked back with the blast. Then his gun went off in response. Jos and Rebecca fell together. With my pistol trained on his head, I followed Jos down to the ground. He fell like a sack of grain, coming to rest on his back. His right eye was stuck with the dart. His left eye was bulging. And his forehead was rouged like a Hindu caste mark. He was dead. And next to him on the ground was Rebecca — convulsing, half-dead.

As in a bad dream, I knelt down and put my hands around Rebecca's flailing head. Her eyes were open but lifeless. Please, God, tell me it didn't happen! I tried to gentle her — to ease her pain as she gasped for life. My fingers probed her face and skull for a bullet hole. Please, Lord, let her be deaf in one ear but don't let there be a bullet in her skull. Where is it? I can't find it. Please, someone tell me it went harmlessly past her. Tell me she is just convulsing in terror. Tell me that the grip of her arms means she's okay. Tell me she couldn't be pulling herself up to me with a bullet in her spine. No, the bullet couldn't have gone below the shoulders. I shot only once, didn't I? Tell me that her frantic breathing and her pitiful whimper couldn't mean —

"Ben, Ben, Ben! Oh, Ben!"

"It's all right, baby. He's dead. Can't hurt us. It's all right, now."

"Oh, Ben," she moaned. "Oh, Ben. Oh, Ben."

"Breathe slowly and deeply, darling." I held her in my arms and soothed her until her breathing normalized, until I could look into her eyes. "I love you. I loved you every minute. There was no other way to do it."

Owani came over.

"Owani, I didn't mean the things I said to him. I had to say them." My words sounded so hollow.

"I know," she said.

I turned to look at Jos again. His right eye was punctured by the thin, finger-long hardwood dart whose shaft was wrapped with spun cotton. The eye looked like a skewered olive on a buffet. His other eye bulged, lifelessly. The red hole in his forehead was about the size of a quarter; the back of his head was blown away. My aim had been true.

And someone else's aim had been true.

"Did you shoot the dart?" I asked Owani who was now kneeling beside Headman.

"No, my brother did it. He shot it past me."

Next to Headman's supine and dying body lay the blowgun. How had he done it? He must have aimed the blowgun with his feet. Where did he find the breath for that 25-foot shot? I raced to him and felt for a pulse in his neck. Present but weak.

"Get back on the radio and tell them to bring everything — distilled water, syringes, and saline solution if they have it. And I want some of those Millipore filters assemblies they have been using in their field surveys."

I placed a basket under Headman's legs to get more blood into his central circulation.

Owani turned on the radio. It was alive with excited conversation. We heard more shots from the direction of the garden. That animated my search for the things we needed: scissors, knife and needles. I pulled an unused shirt from my duffel bag and searched the hearths for a pot with boiling water. Owani put out her message and got an answer: Supplies were already on the way. The other radio transmissions in the background were in excited Yanomami. It sounded like a four-man team coordinating a pincher action against the remaining marauder. The radio went silent whenever there were bursts of gunfire. Then it got lively again. I dunked the shirt in a simmering pot at a distant hearth and fanned the flames.

Field Medicine and   29
Disinformation

I returned to Rebecca. Her hysterics were subsiding quickly. Too quickly. She was lapsing into catatonia. I would have, too, if she'd fired a gun in my face. I knelt and pulled her up in my arms.

"Rebecca, you've got to snap out of it. Headman will die if you don't stop the bleeding."

I'd never seen her in such a stupor. I half-walked her and half-carried her to Headman. She put her head on his chest. "What do you hear, Rebecca?"

"I can't operate." She sounded like a ghost and looked as pale. "His circulation is unstable. He's already in shock. An incision will kill him. He could never take the strain. He needs blood. I don't know his type, or anyone's type. Can't do a cross-match." She was making sense, but she was so despondent.

"We'll have sterile saline solution in a few minutes."

"It has to be exactly zero point nine percent or it will kill him."

Great! She was coming around. "I can make it exact," I said. "And I'll get you fishing line, dental floss, needles . . . everything. Owani! My shirt's boiling in the far hearth. Rip it up for a bandage."

Owani went to do it. I cleared off a steamer trunk. Rebecca and I picked up Headman and laid him on it. With water from my canteen, I washed around his abdomen. A tribesman came running up with a canvas bag with supplies from the Technical Center. I took it and gestured for him to stay. We might need him for another trip. I took quick stock: We had what we needed.

I took out the circuit board spray and looked at the product description. The principal ingredient was an ozone-friendly flurohydrocarbon with a molecular weight close enough to isoflurane that it should work as an inhalation anesthetic. I sprayed some around my face and inhaled the gas deeply. It even smelled a bit like isoflurane. After three breaths, I felt light-headed and had to sink to my knees.

Rebecca had been watching me. "You've made your point, Ben." Thank God she was herself again. "We'll use it. You're my anesthesiologist. Administer it under a cloth cone over his face. But administer it only as necessary to control pain."

I was sorry I'd breathed so much of the stuff because it slowed down my calculations on the saline solution. The guy hadn't brought any saline solution. He'd brought one-liter bottles of distilled water — four of them. I remembered that my salt tablets were 200 milligrams each. I made a mental calculation: If I put 50 of them in the bottle, that would make 10 grams per liter. That would be a one-percent saline solution. So I would need 45 to make a 0.9 percent solution. I counted them into the bottle and shook it like a fiend.

"Ben, you shouldn't be using your hands. You have to keep it sterile."

"Going to sterilize it by filtration — zero point two two micrometers."

Owani came back. "Do you want me to boil the dental floss and fishing line?"

"Yes," Rebecca answered. "And the fish hooks, too."

I gave Owani my scissors and knife. Owani took the stuff to the kettle where she had been boiling my shirt. She knew what she was doing — didn't need instructions from me.

I reached into the sack and pulled out a Millipore filter assembly, the type with the 0.22 micrometer pore size, and asked Rebecca to put a needle on the end of it and find a good vein. I went back to shaking my solutions. Rebecca found a vein. With the needle sitting on the one-inch-diameter filter, she needed both hands to keep it inside the vein. The largest syringe in the bag was 10 milliliters. I drew it full of solution, fitted it to the filter assembly and pushed it in, all at once.

"Don't inject so quickly, Ben. We don't know that it isn't doing harm."

That was her Hippocratic Oath in action.

"Okay." I reloaded the syringe quickly, and injected slowly. We repeated the cycle countless times. It took a quarter of an hour to get half of a liter of fluid into him. Rebecca put her ear to his chest and said that his heart sounds were improving. But we still needed to put in the remaining one-half liter before she could operate.

The distant gunfire was less frequent now. And the mercenary fired only single shots, like he was worried about running out of ammunition. Owani interpreted what we were hearing on the radio: "He is trying to get to the helicopter but our warriors are hiding among the fallen trees and are blocking his way."

"Tell them they can disable the helicopter by jamming its tail rotor with a tree branch."

"They know that. That is what they are trying to do."

We still had a quarter of a liter of solution to go when Headman regained consciousness. Rebecca told me to have Owani bring the pot. She was giving orders like a surgeon, now. When we returned, Rebecca appointed Owani nurse anesthetist. As she applied the anesthesia, Owani said comforting words to her brother in their native language. I kept infusing. Rebecca washed her hands with a rag soaked with boiling water. It hurt me to watch her do that. Headman's arm flinched as Rebecca made the first incision.

In the distance, the helicopter blades accelerated. It sounded like a lift-off. But it was a weird liftoff with strange sounds of turning and course-changing. The crash came a few seconds later, then the explosion. Then the radio exploded with cheers. As the cheers subsided, the smell of a gasoline fire drifted through the *shabono*.

But Rebecca was paying no attention to the battle. "Ben, I can't find my way in here. The cavity is full of blood."

"Owani, take a syringe and slurp it out," I said.

"And I can't move around in there. I need to relax the abdominal wall."

"Owani, tell the tribesman that we need some curare-tipped arrows. Right now."

Owani grunted several words of instruction to the clansman who was standing by. He looked through the gourds hanging from the *shabono* ceiling. It didn't take him long to find several curare-tipped arrow heads.

Rebecca was bloody, halfway up to her elbows. Figuring out how to inject the curare was up to me. "Owani, will one of these arrow tips kill a big monkey or just a middle-sized one?"

"Only a middle-sized monkey."

"Rebecca, I think that one would be a safe dose for abdominal muscle relaxation. Should I sprinkle it in the cavity or inject it into his buttock?"

"Buttock. Sprinkling the abdominal cavity might not get it into his system. Might cause infection because it's not sterile."

"Agreed." I stabbed the arrow tip into Headman's buttock and twisted it one turn. While waiting for the drug to take effect, Rebecca set some fish hooks on both sides of the incision and instructed me on how she wanted them pulled. Muscle relaxation came in about five minutes. I withdrew the arrow tip and watched Headman's breathing. I washed my hands in the water and held aside intestines so that Rebecca could sew up the damaged vein. She told me later that it was the inferior epigastric vein. Under her instructions, I blotted areas dry so she could look for more bleeding. Luckily, the intestines were not perforated. From Rebecca's face, I read the news that the operation was a success.

Rebecca was sewing Headman back together when the first members of the war party returned to the *shabono*. Second Son came running up and nearly lost control of himself when he saw his father. I told him that his father had killed the head mercenary. Told him that Rebecca had just saved his father. His eyes filled with tears.

I put my arm around him. "He should recover just fine." I had to say it many times before he would believe me. "Did you get all of the bad guys?"

"Yes. The last one gave us a hard time. The boys kept him pinned down, but nobody could get an arrow into him. I finally shot him with one of his buddy's rifles."

"What happened with the helicopter?"

"We jammed its tail rotor with a small tree we cut down. He tried to take off anyway. Climbed high enough for a good crash. Went spinning out of control. Total wipeout. And no casualties on our side."

I pointed to the remains of Jos. "Here's the guy your dad killed. Your brother, First Son had been hunting him. But this killer circled back and got the jump on Rebecca and me. I think you should head up a three-man scouting party and go looking for your brother." I pointed in the direction where I had heard the last gunshots.

"Ben, I need you again." It was Rebecca. "I need another bottle of saline solution. The other patient lost a lot of blood, too."

It was the warrior who had fled into the forest when the helicopter attacked us. He had just dragged himself back. And he looked awfully weak. I had enough tablets for another bottle. I prepared it and helped Rebecca administer it, too. It was amazing, how fast the man's lean, jungle-adapted body recovered after we restored the lost fluid volume. The severed vein in his arm was relatively easy for Rebecca to tie off without anesthesia. Soon Rebecca was treating flesh wounds on the returning warriors and organizing the village maidens into a nursing squad. Luckily, there were no other serious injuries.

With no pressing demands on me, now, I took another look at Jos's body. It was lying on top of his backpack and slung rifle. His pistol was lying next to him. I tucked it under his body and stood over him awhile, thinking. Then I went over to speak with Owani who was nursing her brother. "I am afraid that when Second Son finds his brother, he will find him dead. He will be stricken with grief. Edith Pratt is still in the forest. She may be too shocked to lead. So it may be up to you to lead."

"Yes, I fear that you may be right."

"I think your warriors should take all the mercenaries' bodies and weapons and throw them near the crashed helicopter while it is still burning. And I think that Ken Lee should e-mail Xantha that the attack has been repulsed."

Owani settled her eyes on mine and looked in deeply. "I was wrong about your *hekura*. It is a jaguar." She turned away and roused the *shabono*, issuing commands.

I shooed a couple of curious boys away from Jos's corpse. I unloaded his .38 and his rifle and gave it to a tribesman to take away. Then I went through his pockets. Found a lot of interesting documents, including a South African passport to him in the name of Jan de Weert, a corresponding driver's license, and a thick pocket address book with a lot of the names and addresses in code. I consolidated this stuff with his two backpacks, the one the warrior had stolen and the one that he was wearing when I killed him. I carried the backpacks into the forest, far away from the noise of the village, and set up shop on a fallen tree trunk.

Jos's second backpack contained a satellite phone. I inspected it and studied the telephone number taped onto its side. The number contained a country code — 41 — which I recognized as Switzerland. I ran back to the *shabono* and retrieved my hand-held tape recorder. Thought for a long, long time, mentally scripting a conversation before dialing the number and holding the tape recorder to the earpiece. Worked myself into a rough-and-ready attitude.

"*Pharma Sankt Gallen, Paul Schmidt hier,*" answered a businesslike voice on the other end. Pharma St. Gallen was one of the world's largest pharmaceutical companies.

To answer Herr Schmidt, I used a twangy nasal to create a nondescript Southern accent. "This is Randy calling for Jos. He's lost his voice but he wants me to pass on some information to you."

"*Ja?*"

"Guess that's supposed to mean yes. Anyway, Jos wants you to know that his mission is accomplished. And he's slaughtered one fat pig."

"That is an interesting message. Could I know what you are having to do with it."

Memories of barroom repartee with Sam and Lou at Captain Walley's gave me inspiration. "Boy, you Germans talk funny," I replied, turning a little querulous. "You're German, aren't you."

"Swiss."

"Swiss, like Swiss cheese? Right! So you want to know *what I am having to do with it.* Well, I've just *had at it,* I guess you could say! You might say I'm some hired talent he picked up along the way."

"What happened to Jos?"

"Got his voice box smashed. One of them Indians smashed him in the throat with a club before he could kill him. Real painful. He's using sign language and writin' stuff down to tell me what to say."

"Were there any other casualties?"

"Hell, yes! — The whole damn squad. The chopper caught its tail rotor on a vine or somethin' and crashed mighty awful. Everybody else is dead. Burnt up to a crisp. Had to do the whole job all by ourselves."

"Are you saying that the operation was unsuccessful?" Herr Schmidt asked, with concern.

"Hell no, I ain't saying that. Once we got our sights on her, Pratt went splat!"

"*Ja*, good. But you do not have to be so explicit in your descriptions. Did you catch any other forest animals?"

"Okay, I won't be so 'ex-pliss-EAT.' You want to know about the forest animals? Well ain't that a funny way of saying it! Well, we didn't have to hurt too many of them forest *coons*, if that's what you're asking about. But we bagged us every damn bird that flew down here from North America. They won't be nestin' here again — ever! I'm gonna repeat that for yer German ears — sorry, I meant Swiss ears. Now I'll make this very 'ex-pliss-EAT.' *Mission accomplished*. We did a good job and expect to get paid."

"Yes, as arranged."

"Actually, I think we earned ourselves a ten thousand dollar bonus. That Candidi pigeon was awful hard to track after he snuck away from the Mission."

"Ignoring the name of any person, we will take your request under consideration. We have talked enough. May I speak to the gentleman who is with you?"

"Yeah, but you gotta remember that Jos cain't talk back. An' don't make it long. We ain't got much life left in this battery. Might hafta use this phone again. And I've got to get Ole Jos outa here before them Indians start going on the war path again. Here he is."

I grunted into the receiver and Herr Schmidt started talking. I didn't know much German, but I knew enough to grunt in the right places. I understood Herr Schmidt's congratulations, his assurance that the second half of the payment would be deposited, and his instructions to kill Randy as soon as he got close enough to civilization to make it back by himself.

Finally, I held the phone away from myself and shouted, "Hey, they're coming again." I hung up.

Making that phone call had taken more out of me than the standoff with Jos. I'd made a rut pacing back and forth, kicking dirt and trying to hold onto that mercenary attitude. Lucky that Schmidt had a tin ear and spoke English with such a heavy accent. I couldn't have sustained the performance against a native English speaker. My heart was racing. I was still pacing. It was time to sit down and take some deep breaths.

It was time to connect more dots.

I had just talked to Herr Paul Schmidt at Pharma St. Gallen, a Swiss pharmaceutical company with an enormous international market share and a century-old reputation for discovering new drugs. Herr Schmidt was happy to hear that Jos and Randy had assassinated Edith Pratt and all the North Americans she'd brought with her. Obviously, Pharma St. Gallen had learned that Edith Pratt was bioprospecting somewhere in Brazil. Maybe they had an informant in Washington, D.C., who tipped them off when Pratt filed a bundle of patent applications. Obviously, they couldn't tolerate her patenting all the good drugs for the next several decades. They didn't want to lose market share and they were too greedy to pay royalties. It was a lot cheaper for them to hire a couple of Latin American hit men to do the job on Pratt when she was in Miami. But Ben Candidi's swinging briefcase got in the way and Edith Pratt learned someone was after her.

Yes, it all checked out. At that time, Schmidt and Pharma St. Gallen probably didn't know that Pratt was working with Xantha. They probably didn't make any connection between her and Dr. George "Baldie" Griffin. But their spy at the conference photographed them together. And eventually, they made the connection. And that was why Jos was carrying Baldie's photograph, too. Yes, that all checked out.

Could I connect some more dots? What about the break-in, the surveillance? And how did Jos know to follow Ben Candidi to find Edith Pratt and her bioprospecting operation? Okay, assume that they had drawn a connection between Pratt and me after I saved her at the Knight Center. And assume that they focused on me to find her. What did they do? No, they didn't send Nica. She belonged to Edith Pratt. She was Pratt's courier and oh-so-soft-style private investigator of Ben Candidi in Miami. Pratt's angry outburst had confirmed all that, today.

Did Herr Schmidt send the surveillance van? Maybe. Did he order my house bugged? I wondered. If he had heard my conversations, then he would have known that I had no access to Pratt. Same for the break-in. I remembered that the surveillance didn't happen right after the first assassination attempt. It happened shortly after I discovered the wormhole in Xantha's website. I would need more information to figure that one out.

I thought about a more important question: How did Jos know to pick me up at the *Estadista* Hotel in Manaus? Nobody could have known about that hotel beforehand because I picked it out from the cab window. That meant that someone latched onto me at the airport. Who knew to look for me at the airport? I had gotten rid of the bug on my phone line before making the travel reservation to Manaus. Only a few people knew that I was going back to Manaus, and except for Michael Malencik, they were close friends. And except for my travel agent, there was only one person who knew which airline I was using. And that was Michael.

Michael Malencik had to be linked to Jos or Herr Schmidt.

I got up and walked around in a circle, thinking about Michael. I had been doing a project for him dealing with increasing the efficiency of drug discovery. His first client company was a hard sell: Mr. Hyde, who didn't understand drug discovery. But then Michael got a second client company: Dr. Jekyll who couldn't get enough of my drug discovery information. Hell, they had even thrown money at me to investigate Xantha. That was it: They wanted to know everything about bioprospecting patent applications. And when I had played hard to get, that just increased their interest.

Yes, Michael's second company had to be Pharma St. Gallen. That fit with Michael's sudden interest in the fact that my fiancée was on a medical anthropology expedition. He was especially interested in the fact that I was going down there to bring her back. He told that to Herr Schmidt who had someone shadow me to the Miami International Airport and who arranged for Jos to shadow me at the Manaus airport. Jos had probably followed my cab to the *Estadista* Hotel, then checked in himself as soon as I was up in my room. Pratt was right. I *had* brought trouble to the doorstep of her bioprospecting preserve. After Jos found us, he got on the satellite phone and called in his helicopter-borne goon squad.

I'd connected enough dots for one day. I returned to the *shabono* where I found that our hearth area had been sanitized of all remnants of Jos. The tribesmen had added his body, together with the bodies of the other mercenaries, to the helicopter's gasoline fire. I conferred with a very shaken and contrite Edith Pratt. She agreed that our best defense was an information offensive. She had already ordered Ken Lee to send out an announcement, to be promulgated by Xantha, that we had survived a mercenary attack which was intended to destroy us and remove us from competition with the pharmaceutical establishment.

I gave Rebecca a kiss of congratulations and encouragement, unpacked my own satellite phone and went back to my office in the forest. I had a whole lot of important phone calls to make. I started with the U.S. State Department to whom I dictated a short statement. I followed that up with a call to the branch of the United Nations responsible for indigenous people. I phoned the Brazilian consulate in Miami to tell them I was okay but had just survived an attack by mercenaries. I gave them the latitude and longitude of the crashed helicopter, and requested that they forward this information to the appropriate branch of their government.

My next call went out to Alice McRae. I told her the whole story — everything except that Nica was smuggling natural products and live plant materials out of Brazil and into America. If word got out on that, the bureaucrats on both sides would put a serious kink in the Pratt/Xantha drug discovery pipeline. I also asked Alice to be vague about the fate of the mercenaries, and to not use my name in her stories. She agreed. My last call was to Rebecca's mom. I spoke with her for a long time — as long as the battery permitted.

It was dark when I headed back to the *shabono*. A chorus of moans guided me back. In the center of the clearing was a 12-foot stack of wood. I recognized it as a funeral pyre but wondered how they had managed to find so much dry wood in such a short time. I could almost make out the body of First Son nested in the indentation in the middle. Second Son was gathering mourners around the pyre. First Son's wife and eldest son were carrying his possessions to the top of the pyre — his bow and arrows, his beads, his hand-made tools, and finally his hammock. Women moaned and tribesmen chanted insistently. I made a deep karate bow to the pyre.

Later, they told me that the blood trail left by First Son showed that he had stalked Jos relentlessly, even after receiving mortal wounds.

The next morning they would search for the body of the other warrior, the one who had been ordered to wait for Jos to die from the curare arrows after their first encounter at the edge of the territory. Tomorrow, there would be a second funeral.

First Son's wife and children stood in front of the pyre, forlorn. Second Son embraced them, one by one, to show that they were his family, now. He picked up a palm-frond torch, lit it from his brother's hearth, and touched it to the tinder at the bottom of the pyre. Warriors knelt and blew on it. He lit another torch from another hearth, and lit another section of the pyre. He repeated this until all hearths had contributed fire. Kneeling warriors continued blowing until the flames were self-sustaining. Women cried and clutched their children. The flames grew. Thick, gray smoke rose over the shobono. For hours, the fire released the flesh from First Son's body. Oxidized and combined with wood smoke, it rose and drifted over the tops of the trees. And during those hours, the mourning matched the intensity of the fire. What I had read in the books, I was now witnessing: the wailed grief that must be finished with the last flame.

I didn't have the strength to stand waiting for the flames to flicker and die. I didn't have the strength of Rebecca, who spent the whole night taking care of Headman and the wounded warrior. I did have enough strength to stagger back to our hearth and climb into our hammock.

From the hammock, I watched the cremation through heavy eyelids, thinking about what I knew from the books. After the flames burnt out, leaving nothing of First Son's lean body but the ashes of his bones, there would be another ceremony. It would come one week after his death was announced to all the neighboring tribes. Rebecca and I would stand together with his kinsmen and watch while his bone ashes were ground up, and mixed in a banana soup which would be passed as a communion cup. The good that First Son had done would not die with his bones. No, Dr. Westley, it would not be sacrilegious to drink from that cup. With my adoptive brethren, I would take calcium from First Son's bones into my body. His calcium would trigger my muscles for the next few days and would eventually be absorbed into my bones where it would stay for many years, cementing a fleeting human relationship that had spanned geography, culture and time.

Amidst these thoughts, He-Who-Falls-Off-The-Trail became drowsy and fell asleep.

30 Press Conference

The master of ceremonies finished his introduction, the audience clapped, and Edith Pratt stepped up to the microphone in the Miami Knight Center's auditorium. Four sets of TV cameras trained on her, one for each of the major networks plus CNN. Channel Eight was not there. I guess that Sanch Riquez wasn't very keen on revisiting his mistakes. Rebecca gave my hand a squeeze.

Edith Pratt adjusted the microphone and gazed across rows and rows of academicians, students and retirees. "It is a great pleasure to be here today to read from the most recent chapter in the history of the Yanomama people. As an anthropologist, I was often asked, 'What is the value of your work?' I used to answer that the Yanomama people have a unique value — the ability to show us how people once lived as hunter-gatherers. A study of their language may reveal how men and women spoke thirteen thousand years ago. I used to answer that their ancient wisdom was the source of our muscle relaxants and local anesthetics, without which surgery would be unthinkable. I had also said that they are the natural stewards of biological diversity of the Brazilian rain forest — that we should consider them park rangers assigned to keep out the gold miners and to protect the Amazon's undiscovered riches of biodiversity for the next generation.

"But today, I answer that the Yanomama people are mining *Amazon gold*! They are busy discovering pharmaceutical riches — the true gold of the Amazon.

"In this hall, less than two months ago, I surprised a number of people by stating that we can bring such people from the Stone Age to the Information Age in one jump. Now I have returned to demonstrate it. To use the words of a great male chauvinist, General Douglas MacArthur, 'I have returned.'"

She stuck out her jaw and looked defiantly into the audience which responded with laughter and sustained applause. Some things never change, I thought.

"We have shown that Yanomama women and men are competent prospectors of the treasures of biodiversity in the rain forest. We have developed a herbal encyclopedia, with pictures of plants and insects, and tables of their pharmacological activities. It is a living, dynamic encyclopedia because it gives the location of the plant found and the date. As visiting scientist Dr. Benjamin Candidi exclaimed when he saw our system, 'This is a hell of a lot better than returning with dried-out, oxidized leaf samples pressed between sheets of newspaper.'"

Pratt used a high-pitched voice to quote me and the audience laughed.

"Using biochip technology, we assay for a thousand different pharmacological activities in thousands of different plants. And we uplink this information to our partner, the Xantha Corporation, by satellite and we make available to them actual samples of the most promising finds. They analyze the samples for molecular structure using state-of-the-art methods such as HPLC and GC mass spectroscopy. From our first months of screening, we have found fifty-seven compounds which are unique and possibly superior to existing drugs which work on nerves or control inflammation. These are being patented by the people of the *shabono* and the scientists from Xantha. These compounds will be developed as drugs by Xantha and pharmaceutical companies which it licenses. The people of the *shabono* are stockholders in Xantha. Modernization of their *shabono*, their further education in Western knowledge et cetera, will be paid by Xantha, in exchange for their service in the field. We believe that this will serve as a paradigm for the so-called development of the Amazonian basin."

I agreed. This could restore Manaus to the glory it had known with the rubber trade.

"Over the next several months, the Xantha Corporation will be readying itself for a public stock offering."

And there would be a second wave of industrial growth in Silicon Valley, making drug discovery biochips and working up a lot of small sturdy molecules to be tested as candidate drugs.

"As more North Americans become stakeholders in our efforts, we will be less vulnerable to attempts to assassinate me and to attempts at sabotage of Xantha's operations."

She was right. Our cry for help on the Internet got a lot of people behind us very quickly. Within hours, scores of conservation and anthropological organizations and tens of thousands of their members knew our story. A day later, several national news organizations ran the story of our bioprospecting and how we had repulsed the mercenary attack. The day after that, we decided that the mercenaries' charred remains must be buried "for sanitary reasons" and that we would not send out any additional information on the attack. News interest quickly shifted to the Xantha Corporation. They began receiving thousands of e-mails per week from people inquiring about how they could buy the stock.

"Hopefully, Brazilian universities will also become involved in our research. Hopefully, the medical community of Brazil can help with the clinical testing of our drug products. This country has so many sick and poor that it seems senseless to apply strict standards of rich urban countries to the testing of new medications against serious diseases."

Yes, clinical testing and new drug development could be Brazil's new growth industry.

"With Dr. Rebecca Levis, we are investigating how medical care for indigenous peoples can be upgraded and updated."

I gave Rebecca's hand a squeeze.

"The field of anthropology must also be updated. It must cast off the vestiges of the Victorian male mind-set which considers indigenous people only as objects of curiosity and never considers them to be people, unto themselves. For too long, anthropologists have been abnormally fascinated with the so-called 'primitive state.' And for too long, many have harbored a hidden desire to keep certain groups of people in that state. But believe me, dear audience, the Yanomama People have the same abilities understand the world as we do. My own blind spot was made clear to me in a heated argument by Dr. Benjamin Candidi after he attached himself to our expedition. He called me a reverse snob. He said I had taught them to do pharmaceutical surveys using high-tech tools, but that I had denied them the opportunity to see the rest of the world — through the eyes of educational television."

Rebecca gave my hand a squeeze. I had been wrong: Some things do change, Edith and Ben included.

"Just as it was wrong to preserve those people under glass, it is also wrong to try to *cultivate* them under glass. They have every right to explore the world beyond their own frontiers. And I must now concede one point to General Sosa-Pereira. There really is no way to avoid contact, because both sides are embracing each other."

I was starting to like the old girl.

She made a promise to help the Yanomami codify their laws and ethical systems.

"Customs which no longer serve any purpose can be replaced with those which do. Customs for which there will no longer be any necessity, such as infanticide, can be actively suppressed. Others, such as rape of unattached women and female children will fall to our Western standards of women's rights."

The audience applauded that statement.

"In this way, I believe that the Yanomama will be able to leap over centuries of so-called civilization and enter directly into the post-industrial Information Age."

She went on to say that the Yanomami are a self-reliant, resilient people who have been shaped and hardened by just as many centuries of Darwinian selection as we. She said it was now time for them to step forward and take their place among the great peoples of the world.

She ended with a quote from *Savages: The Life and Killing of the Yanomami* by Dennison Berwick, saying that the Yanomami have much to teach us. Then she bowed her head and the hall filled with enthusiastic applause.

The reporters had many questions. The TV news reporters made the biggest show. Each asked a couple of questions, hamming it up before the cameras. After a quarter of an hour, they left, taking with them much of the audience.

Up front, a large contingent of print journalists was still asking questions. Alice McRae was among them. She had done a bang-up job of writing our story. The *Miami Standard* serialized it over a whole week and now she is condensing it for *Time Magazine*. Xantha was moving up its target date for the stock offering to take advantage of the publicity.

It really was an ingenious method that Pratt and her people

had devised for getting the materials to Xantha. At the Technical Center, they had spotted the plant extracts onto 35-millimeter film which they rolled into film canisters. They had also freeze-dried and vacuum packed living plant samples in foil to make them look like in-flight peanut snacks. Those were the goodies they loaded into those elongated canvas bags for Klaus-Dietrich to grab with his tail-hook. After regaining altitude, he would put the plane on autopilot, crawl to the back of the plane and reel in his catch, bringing the bag and collapsible grappling anchor into the plane through the small door in the tail. Oh, what dangerous things bush pilots will do! After returning to the controls, he would head the plane for Manaus, where he turned the stuff over to Nica.

Nica's photography hobby made a good cover for the several dozen film canisters that she brought out with each trip. And to improve her chances, she always took back twice as many canisters of film with real photographs. But when she photographed me, it was not just a whim. She routinely photographed everyone on the flight as a precaution against being followed. She was also on the lookout for anyone who might be bioprospecting in Brazil.

After Rebecca and I took the dugout canoe down the *Rio Marauiá* to Santa Isabel, Klaus-Dietrich flew us to Manaus. Edith Pratt did not travel with us. She was very secretive about her routes in and out of Yanomama territory. I was a little secretive, too. I asked Klaus to fly over the confluence of the black *Rio Negro* and the red Amazon so we could finally see it. As we flew over that sharp divide, I pushed my .45 caliber pistol through the air vent and let go.

There was more to let go of. When Rebecca and I flew from Manaus to Miami, Nica was one of our flight attendants. Luckily, she wasn't serving our section of the plane. Of course, I didn't introduce her to Rebecca. I didn't want to risk blowing Nica's cover. And I didn't want to risk blowing my engagement with Rebecca, either. But as Rebecca and I said our goodbyes to the assembled flight crew by the cockpit door, I did give Nica a smile. And she smiled back at me, just like when I first met her.

Hopefully, the Xantha Corporation and the Brazilian government will come to an understanding so that materials can flow more freely. Maybe then we could invite Nica and her fiancé to come sailing with us when he visits Miami. But, then again, maybe that wouldn't be such a good idea. Foursomes don't work out as well when the organizers are one guy and one gal from each pair. Maybe that's a law of Nature, like gravity and the speed of light.

Luckily, Michael had completed the report during my absence. He gave Zeekie the second $20,000, picked up the diskettes and apparently slipped out of his European suit coat long enough to insert the hypertext links for indexing. Or maybe he had just paid a graduate student to do the work. No telling! In any case, he had handed the Mr. Hyde company the final report and they had paid for it. I never did find out the name of that company. But the second $20,000 sure helped Rebecca and me with living expenses.

I had a long talk with Michael upon returning to Miami. As I suspected, he had also been peddling much of the same information to a second company, the Dr. Jekyll company. But he told me they were no longer interested in the information. I said if that was the case, he shouldn't mind telling me the company's name. He said it was a large Swiss company. And somehow, that didn't surprise me a bit. He refused to tell me the company's name, but did admit to telling them that I was going down to Manaus to bring back my fiancée from a medical anthropology expedition. And that was enough to satisfy me that I had connected the dots correctly after my satellite phone call to Herr Schmidt at Pharma St. Gallen.

Slowly, my wandering mind returned to my body, still seated at the Knight Center. Edith Pratt invited to the platform George "Baldie" Griffin, Ph.D., Xantha's Vice-President for Research. He was answering the reporters' scientific questions with the charm of a fund-raiser at a charity ball. I still haven't figured out exactly what it was about him that was getting to me. Maybe he was just a regular guy suffering from a physical mishap. Maybe when the top of your head goes bald, you really do need to grow a moustache to divert attention. And if you grow a moustache, maybe you really do need to wear a bow tie to look less intimidating.

Anyway, George Griffin had been cordial enough with to me when Rebecca and I met him on our second day in Miami. First, I showed him how I had stumbled into his secret data archive. Then he apologized to me for sending the surveillance van that loitered outside my house. Then I apologized to him for getting his van hauled off. Then he apologized to me for sending people to bug my house and steal my computer. Then I apologized for stomping his detective's back when I jumped after him into his getaway boat. I hoped the guy's back wasn't broken. Dr. Griffin assured me that a chiropractor had been able to put the guy back together. Then I apologized for interfering with his attractive courier that night at the airport.

The next day, Dr. Griffin showed up at our doorstep unannounced. He wanted to talk about the confidentiality agreement that I had sealed with a kiss on the lips of my bioprospecting, naked, blue-tinted Little Shaman Woman. The blue dye still hadn't completely faded from her skin. We invited Dr. Griffin in. Rebecca was completely honest in retelling the details of our agreement, and so was I. Dr. Griffin laid on all his martini-party, opera-quiz charm and acted like I had given away all of my rights with that agreement. But I had some things to point out to the moustachioed baldie. And after I made him listen for a few minutes, he seemed less like a charming guest and more like an army major. He took offense when I said that the confidentiality agreement didn't cover information I already had before signing. He got mad when I said that information in publicly available scientific literature wasn't covered, either.

Our discussion quickly devolved to a chest-thumping contest, with him threatening to go to court to get an injunction and with me threatening to sue him for interference with my business relationship with Michael and one of his clients.

Then I told Dr. Griffin about my patent application and that my filing predated my rescue operation in Brazil. At that point, Dr. Griffin turned red — bald scalp and all. Seconds later, Rebecca politely suggested that we both take a walk along the Miami River. We did, and I kept the pace brisk. I'm not sure if it was the force of my arguments or the force of the Miami sun that wore him down, but after two hours we came to a tentative agreement: The confidentiality agreement would be converted into a long-term consulting contract for me. And we agreed on a monthly payment that I would be very comfortable with. Griffin promised to formalize the agreement after gaining approval of his board of directors.

Back at home that evening I reviewed all the materials that defined my business relationship with Michael. No problem there. I could sever the relationship with seven day's notice.

Dr. George Griffin apparently received approval from his board of directors that same evening, because the next morning he was on our porch, making my door buzzer bleat. I welcomed him in for a cup of freeze-dried coffee and he gave me the a sheet detailing what we had agreed to. To that he added an offer of a block of stock worth $300,000 in exchange for the rights to my patent applications. I guessed that he saw their value as "defensive patents" against interlopers.

I counter-offered, asking for an additional 30 hours a month compensation while they were pursuing the patents. He accepted that without batting an eye. We quickly hand-wrote the additional terms on his sheet and wrote the words "Headnotes to a Binding Contract" on the top. We used my photocopy machine to produce a duplicate, and we signed both copies. It was the fastest negotiation to ever occur in my office.

After we had shaken hands, Dr. Griffin delivered an important piece of information: "Don't worry about our performance. We have just entered into a partnership which guarantees us fifty million dollars."

"Great," I said. "Who's the lucky partner?"

"Pharma St. Gallen corporation of Zürich, Switzerland."

For some reason, it didn't surprise me. And I wasn't indignant either. Somehow, the $300,000 had helped me to see things . . . clearly and . . . objectively. That's par for the course in industry.

But now was the time to share some more information with Dr. Griffin. I asked, "Have you been in negotiations with them for a long time?"

"They made some general inquiries several months ago, then pulled back."

"Of course you didn't tell them where you were getting your compounds from."

"No, we kept that secret."

"But your secret wasn't keeping very good when Edith gave her first lecture at the Knight Center. They had a hit squad waiting for her there."

"Yes, they apparently knew of her U.S. patent applications on the medicinal plants. But they didn't know she was associated with us. Thank you again for saving her life. After the Knight Center incident, we took extreme precautions."

" — Which precluded even a thank-you card?"

"I'm sorry. We thought long and hard on that decision. At first we thought you were with the assassins. We didn't know who they were. And later, it seemed like any communication with you would compromise the secrecy of our project."

"Except that after I saved Edith's hide, the bad guys deduced a connection between her and me."

"Yes. That's what they eventually did."

Dr. Griffin agreed with me that when I went down to get Rebecca, the bad guys figured she was connected with Edith Pratt and followed me to the heart of her operation.

"That is true, unfortunately or you could say —" He cut himself short before saying that it could have been fortunate, depending how you looked at it.

"Yeah, I agree. In a certain way, it was fortunate for you. The shoot-out in the jungle got you a lot of free publicity. It saved you a hard sell to the executives of the big drug companies you were trying to get to partner with you. Hell, the shoot-out proved to the world that your technology was a serious threat to the pharmaceutical establishment — a threat serious enough to kill for. Of course they won't try it again now that you are allied with the establishment."

"That is correct," he said with a smile. His cocktail charm was back in full force.

"I'll bet you thought a lot about who ordered that hit squad," I said. "What interest group do you think tried to kill Edith?"

"We don't know," he said, looking away.

I let a few seconds go by to make sure that was all he had to say. "Well, I know."

"Who is it?"

"Pharma St. Gallen."

He took that without batting an eye. I laid in a long pause and he said nothing. I went over to my desk and pulled out Jos's satellite phone with the Swiss telephone number. "I hope that you've structured your 'strategic partnership' so that it's still iron-clad, even if some of your key personnel die."

I asked him to write down the telephone number taped to the side on this phone. Then I told him about how I'd pretended to be "Randy" and had talked to Herr Paul Schmidt of Pharma St.

Gallen. A trace of worry showed on Dr. Griffin's face — just a trace.

"You will have to do something about this," I said.

"We will. In fact, it is already being done." This guy really did keep his cards close to his chest.

"Good. I'm keeping this phone as evidence, along with the tape I made of the conversation with Herr Schmidt. If you decide to go the legal route, I will help you. But whatever way you handle it, you need to know that I've made multiple copies of the tape and have made arrangements for its promulgation in the event of my death."

"I assure you that it will be taken care of."

"Sure," I said, feeling world-weary at that moment. "You'll take care of it by burying it, just like we buried those mercenaries."

And that was where we left it.

My wandering mind returned to my body in the Knight Center. Edith Pratt was standing up and announcing that the press conference was over. And while sitting there watching a crowd form around her, I thought about how they took care of things in the land of Heidi, hot chocolate, pure mountain air and political neutrality. I thought of Nazi gold, of Holocaust victims' deposited fortunes, and of secret bank accounts containing dictators' flight money and profits from the arms trade.

Then a little voice told me to stop thinking. Forget about it, Ben. Don't try to move mountains. Just count your blessings. You made a lot of money on the deal. Nobody is going to bother you again. And DEA Agent Phil Henderson isn't going to make any more house calls and the demoted members of the Miami P.D. know better than to give any more hot tips on Dr. Ben Candidi.

I got up, walked up to the stage and joined Rebecca in the crowd. She was radiant and I was so glad for her. The good news had followed so rapidly on the heels of the trauma that she hadn't had a chance to process it. She was living in a dream, now. But underneath, she was still the same old Rebecca. She glanced at me and sensed my restless mood. She said goodbye to Edith Pratt and to Dr. Griffin, and we were off.

We walked down a cascade of steps to a glass tunnel. The glass tunnel was nicely landscaped — the shrubs and trees were on the outside — and I hardly noticed that we were walking under an expressway down ramp. It took us directly into the ground floor lobby of the Bank of America Tower. Silently, we rode up the two long escalators that delivered us to the MetroMover platform carved out of the side of the building. Eight floors above us was a shrub-lined roof garden where I'd once met with a high-priced lawyer. And off to the side of the roof garden towered another 30 or 40 storeys of business and high finance. Maybe Mankind *will* succeed in integrating nature and enterprise.

A MetroMover car rolled in and opened its door. The robotic car drove us along the elevated concrete guideway, snaking us through downtown, along the Miami River. Rebecca and I spoke very little; we seemed to be reading each other's thoughts.

"It looks so small compared with the Amazon, doesn't it Ben?"

"Yes."

We passed the Miami-Dade Cultural Center that houses the art and historical museums plus the main library, all in a city-block-sized building that resembles a Spanish fortress. Rebecca looked down on its courtyard and said, "That's where you used to go to search patents."

Now I download them through the Internet. "Yes, things are changing quickly," I answered.

After a couple of minutes of silence Rebecca said, "Maybe Dr. Westley would like to meet Dr. Pratt."

"No, I'm afraid she would find him too Victorian."

We both laughed and said nothing more.

We exited the robot car and took the shiny escalators to the Metrorail platform some 30 feet above. There we stood, looking out across downtown Miami. Between the buildings we could make out patches of Biscayne Bay.

I put my arm around Rebecca. "Are you going to write a research paper?"

"I don't know, Ben. I went down there with some ideas, but they all seemed so small after I got involved in the bioprospecting."

"I know how you feel. I feel the same way. I just feel lucky to be able to chip off a little piece of it for us."

Rebecca kissed me. "It was marvelous how you worked it out with the money."

I kissed her and smiled: That morning I had thought of a way to measure drug binding *without* using fluorescence. It might be useful if Xantha had trouble going from 1,000 to 10,000 glowing spots. And it would be useful to me if Dr. Griffin ever decided to drop me as a consultant.

A northbound six-car Metrorail train glided to a halt in front of us and we got in.

The first stop came after only a couple of hundred yards. The second stop, Culmer Station, took only a little bit longer. We got off there and walked silently past the old houses on the way to Northwest North River Drive. Pops' house came into view.

"Where *is* that man, anyway?" Rebecca asked.

"Visiting a lady friend in San Diego. He wrote me that he won't be back for a few weeks more."

"How many 'lady friends' does he have, anyway?"

"It seems to be an infinite supply. But don't begrudge him. He's worked hard and made his contribution to society. Now he's enjoying life."

Rebecca shrugged. We walked up to our house and I opened the door.

"You did a great job down there, Rebecca."

"Thanks. We pulled them both through," she sighed. "But Headman wouldn't have made it if I hadn't made Klaus fly to Manaus to get the antibiotics. Those tribes really do need an itinerant physician. The government should set it up. They could take her around by helicopter. Maybe that's what I'll write the paper on."

Rebecca went upstairs "to get into something more comfortable." I wandered around downstairs with nothing to do. At four in the afternoon, it was too late to start work on a new project. I had one: a pharmacological consultation for a lawyer who'd phoned the day before. I went to the kitchen and poked around under the sink until I found what I was looking for — a can of bug spray.

Rebecca called down to me from the top of the stairs. "Ben, what are you doing?"

"Yesterday, I discovered a colony of wasps on the *Alabama Tiger*. Thought I'd do Pops a favor and get rid of them."

Rebecca came down the stairs, smiling. "And I thought I might do a little work on a garden."

I looked up at her. "Not like that, you won't!"

She was wearing nothing but her loincloth and a couple of twists of beads. You couldn't count as clothing the gourd that hung on a leather strap under her arm. Rays of the low sun shown on her through the window over the stairway. Her skin still had a blueish cast.

I put down the spray can.

"I've just thought of something better for us to do — upstairs."

Epilogue

The DNA chip is in use today to measure gene activity. The drug-discovery biochip has yet to be invented.

About the Author

Dirk Wyle is the pen name of Duncan H. Haynes, Ph.D., a 30-year veteran of biomedical science with a lifelong interest in literature. He studied at the University of Pennsylvania and in Germany and served as a medical school professor, conducting research in abnormal blood coagulation and drug delivery. He invented a drug microencapsulation technology which led to the founding of three companies employing approximately 65 people. He retired as a professor in early 2001.

Dirk Wyle has a passion for fleshing out the skeleton of the mystery-thriller with the muscle and sinew of biomedical science. His critically acclaimed Ben Candidi Series (*Pharmacology Is Murder*, 1998; *Biotechnology Is Murder*, 2000; and *Medical School Is Murder*, 2001) takes place in authentically rendered medical centers and drug companies. *Amazon Gold*, the fourth novel in the Series, spans continents and cultures.

Dirk invites your visit to www.dirk-wyle.com. He is hard at work on the fifth and sixth books in the Series.